E 37/10

KT-454-040

EVERYMAN, I will go with thee,

and be thy guide,

In thy most need to go by thy side

ELIZABETH GLEGHORN GASKELL
(*née* Stevenson)

Born in 1810 at Chelsea. Spent her youth at Knutsford, Cheshire, and married in 1832 a Unitarian minister of Manchester. Died suddenly in 1865.

MRS GASKELL

Cousin Phillis

My Lady Ludlow · Half a Life-time Ago
Right at Last · The Sexton's Hero

INTRODUCTION BY
MARGARET LANE

CHESTER COLLEGE

ACC. No. | DEPT.
70/1428 |

CLASS No. 823.8
GAS ✓

LIBRARY

DENT: LONDON
EVERYMAN'S LIBRARY
DUTTON: NEW YORK

© Introduction, 1970, J. M. Dent & Sons Ltd
All rights reserved
Made in Great Britain
at the
Aldine Press · Letchworth · Herts
for
J. M. DENT & SONS LTD
Aldine House · Bedford Street · London
First included in Everyman's Library 1912
Last reprinted 1970

NO. 615

ISBN: 0 460 00615 0

INTRODUCTION

WHEN Mrs Gaskell began to write *Cousin Phillis* she was setting out to please herself in more ways than one. Dickens, for whose *Household Words* and *All the Year Round* she had written the bulk of her fiction for the past ten years, was pressing her for another novel, and she was resisting him. The strain of writing for those hugely popular magazines, together with the irritation of Dickens's highly professional and stringent editorial control, had become distasteful, and she determined that this rural tale, in which her personal as much as her professional feelings were involved, should not be fed into Dickens's serial mill. Instead she would write it in complete freedom for the new rival concern, *The Cornhill*, which George Smith, Charlotte Brontë's publisher and friend (and now Mrs Gaskell's since the completion of her *Life of Charlotte Brontë*), had recently launched with Thackeray as editor.

Dickens, she knew, would not be pleased, but she was prepared for a polite coolness, having several times crossed swords with him in the course of a professional association which had undoubtedly been founded on mutual admiration. 'I do honestly know,' he had written to her in 1850, 'that there is no living English writer whose aid I would desire to enlist in preference to the author of *Mary Barton* (a book that most profoundly affected and impressed me) . . . I should set a value on your help which your modesty can hardly imagine; and I am perfectly sure that the least result of your reflection or observation in respect of the life around you would attract attention and do good.'

Dickens was right as usual: acutely sensitive where popular taste was concerned, he had seen Mrs Gaskell's leap into fame with her first novel, and knew that in enlisting this intelligent, romantic and yet morally balanced new writer among his contributors he would be making no mistake. *Cranford* had been the enchanting (and best-selling) result, followed by *North and South*, her second industrial-social novel, and a long succession of sketches and short stories. In no time at all Mrs Gaskell had become one of the mainstays of *Household Words*, and was writing continuously for Dickens for the next decade.

They were not, however, temperamentally wholly congenial. In Dickens the professional journalist went hand in hand with the novelist of genius; the strain and hurry of serial publication was to him a stimulus rather than the reverse, though there is no doubt that the quality of his novels occasionally suffered. As an editor he was creative, dynamic and authoritarian, being more alert to the technical requirements of serial publication —length, drama, the weekly or monthly ration of suspense— than most of his contributors. Certainly his professionalism on this point was far greater than Mrs Gaskell's, and it is equally certain that the control which he tried to exercise over her work had the uncomfortable effect of inhibiting her as a writer. From time to time, as she gained self-assurance and reputation, she refused to cut her work as Dickens demanded, and rejected his suggestions for details of plot or ending. In spite of the exemplary courtesy of their letters, they succeeded in thoroughly exasperating one another, Dickens complaining to his subeditor, W. H. Wills, that Mrs Gaskell was 'conceited and heavy', and a little later, during arguments over the cutting of *North and South*, 'Mrs Gaskell fearful—fearful. If I were Mr G., oh Heaven how I would beat her!' Mrs Gaskell meanwhile, receiving admonishments more politely worded, decided to offer her best work in future to *The Cornhill*, and to consider shorter pieces which fell below this standard as—so she wrote impatiently to friends—'good enough for Dickens'.

So *Cousin Phillis* was her first story to be published under Thackeray's editorship, and whether or not Dickens regretted losing it we shall never know. It is an unusual length, which he would certainly have objected to; too short for a full-length novel, too long for a short story. It is of a length which is usually described as a *novella*, and Thackeray published it in four long instalments, from November 1863 to February 1864.

Mrs Gaskell at this time was at the height of her powers, with nothing (save occasional spells of exhaustion) to suggest that in less than two years she would be dead, leaving her finest novel, *Wives and Daughters*, unfinished. She was in her early fifties, famous and successful enough to be able to indulge herself with a simple romantic idyll, harking back to the rural England of her youth. She had no wish to write another novel of the Industrial Revolution, since she had already made her mark with *Mary Barton* and *North and South*, two aspects of the same theme. Nor was she tempted to repeat the success of *Cranford*, which had been written as a series of papers for Dickens, and only by chance, as it were, turned into a delicate masterpiece of fiction. For the beginning of her new freedom as a writer she would go back to the unspoiled Cheshire countryside of her youth, to the country town and village, the fields and farms that she remembered as a child, in the halcyon days before the railways came. And she would not concern herself with economic or social questions, but would please her imagination with a country love story of the simplest and tenderest kind.

By the 1860s, when Mrs Gaskell began to write *Cousin Phillis*, the railway had spread its tentacles pretty well all over England, but twenty years or so before that, in the period chosen for her story, there were still rural communities living in the old style from birth to death, absorbed in their farmlands and sustained by their religion, with almost no communication with the outside world. Mrs Gaskell well remembered this secluded pre-industrial life in agricultural Cheshire, for she had grown up in the quiet town of Knutsford, which had not yet seen the railway and was then much the same as it had always been, despite its near proximity to Manchester. Her mother had died when she was only a year old, and her father, William Stevenson, at that time Keeper of the Treasury Records and therefore professionally tied to London, had put her in care of his dead wife's sister, Mrs Hannah Lumb, who had lived all her life in this quiet and traditional northern country town. The setting and characters have therefore a close connection with Mrs Gaskell's own girlhood, for the Heathbridge of the tale is Sandlebridge in Cheshire, not very far from Knutsford, and the Hope Farm, where the quiet action of Phillis's love story takes place, is based on her grandfather's farm, which had been her mother's home before marriage and of which every domestic detail was a fond memory.

Mrs Gaskell was in love—as who would not be who could remember it?—with the unspoiled pre-Victorian countryside, and with the way of life that she remembered. Quiet though it was, it was rarely dull, for she had been born into a well-educated Unitarian family, and the Unitarians were always the intellectuals among Dissenters. Her father himself had originally been a Unitarian minister, and had left the ministry after being troubled by doubts as to the ethics of receiving a stipend. He had then turned farmer, bringing his active mind to bear on the problems of the land and on every intellectual interest within reach as well, always balanced by strict concern for the demands of his religion. It is not difficult to see that in Ebenezer Holman, the earnest minister-farmer of *Cousin Phillis*, Mrs Gaskell was drawing on the material of her father's early life, in the years before he migrated to London and entered Government service. He is an acutely drawn character, of a type it would be hard to find in the England of today. Serious, hard-working, dedicated, compassionate, he labours in the fields with his men for five days of the week, and on Saturday and the Sabbath 'makes himself Reverend' to attend to the spiritual welfare of his flock. The essence of the man is expressed in that scene during evening prayers in the farmhouse, when the minister, on his knees with his family and the farm servants, interrupts himself to remind the cowman that the ailing cow's warm mash must not be forgotten.

But such a man, however noble and large minded, can make mistakes. His only surviving child, Phillis, has necessarily led a secluded life, and the minister and his wife have unconsciously tried to keep her a child too long. At seventeen, charming to look at, with her father's eager mind and intellectual curiosity, she is a prodigy in their rustic circle, the pride of his heart. But she is still in pinafores, coolly unaware of the impression she might easily make on a susceptible heart. 'They've called her "the child" so long,' says Betty the servant, '. . . that she's grown up to be a woman under their very eyes, and they look on her still as if she were in her long-clothes.' The narrator of the story, Phillis's nineteen-year-old cousin Paul Manning, is not the one to awaken her instinctive nature. He arrives on the scene with the coming of the railway, an earnest young engineer paying a visit of civility to his mother's relations, and is both attracted and intimidated by Phillis. She is taller than he, studies Latin and abstruse matters with her father and looks on him as a youth, which no young man of nineteen finds ingratiating. The suddenly dangerous element is Holdsworth, the managing engineer; no villain, but an ambitious, intelligent, sophisticated man who drops like a being from another planet into Phillis's element. They are mutually attracted, the atmosphere is suddenly alive with the beginnings of love, before Holdsworth is summoned away to Canada, where he forgets her.

So far everything in the tale has shown Mrs Gaskell's feminine talent at its best. Her unforced prose, her loving response to farm and country life, her delicate humour and perception in dealing with unexpected human entanglements, are deployed to as fine an effect as in any of her work, with the grand exception, perhaps, of *Wives and Daughters*. The minister, in his trouble over this precious daughter, is beautifully understood, even to the ineptitude of his final appeal: '"Phillis! did we not make you happy here? Have we not loved you enough?" She did not seem to understand the drift of this question . . . "And yet you would have left us, left your home, left your father and your mother, and gone away with this stranger, wandering over the world!"' As if such considerations could ever weigh with a daughter in the exaltation of first love!

From this point it is on Phillis herself that our attention is concentrated, as one by one the other characters fade into the background and Mrs Gaskell tenderly beckons to us and demands our sympathy. Can we give it as wholeheartedly as her Victorian readers undoubtedly did, seeing Phillis struck down with 'brain fever' as the result of Holdsworth's defection, and lying at death's door? Alas, no; we have changed too much, perhaps; in the face of Mrs Gaskell's tenderest and most sacred feelings we find ourselves regarding Phillis with a touch of impatience. This sudden illness is certainly a part of the trouble. (Had Holdsworth, we wonder, carried the virus from the city, as well as love?) Mrs Gaskell was over-fond of deathbeds, and of long, delirious illnesses brought on by grief; she herself had been ill for weeks after the death of her baby son and, like Cousin Phillis, 'would never be what she had been before . . . in some ways', and this undoubtedly left its mark on her mind and work. The tendency, at all events, was sufficiently pronounced to worry Dickens, who had these sudden dramatic illnesses and deaths to deal with when editing her stories for *Household Words*. 'I wish to Heaven,' he wrote irritably to his subeditor, 'her people would keep a little firmer on their legs!'

But it is not only the inexplicable 'brain fever' that disturbs us. It is something in Phillis herself, a blind egotism, a determination to drown in her own sufferings—one hardly knows what to call it—which makes us hesitate to sympathize as we are meant to do. Instead we rally to the words of the plain-spoken house servant Betty, who, alarmed by the introvert apathy of Phillis's convalescence, leaves off laying the table to speak her mind. '"Now, Phillis!" said she, coming up to the sofa, "we ha' done a' we can for you, and th' doctors has done a' they can for you, and I think th' Lord has done a' He can for you, and more than you deserve, too, if you don't do something for yourself."' Which brings us to an unexpected turning point, and the end of the story. It has been an insidiously moving tale, and with Phillis's last words—'We will go back to the peace of the old days. I know we shall; I can, and I will!'—we are left wondering whether, after all, our feelings have not been stirred exactly as Mrs Gaskell intended to stir them. Phillis is not, for us, quite the heroine that she envisaged; but we still react; we go from sympathy to impatience and then, unexpectedly, are reconciled. Mrs Gaskell, it seems, has worked on a subtler level than we imagined.

Of the four stories published here with *Cousin Phillis*, 'The Sexton's Hero' is the only one that was not commissioned by Dickens for *Household Words*. It has a special interest as one of the first stories that Mrs Gaskell ever wrote, hiding her identity (as so many Victorian ladies did when they put pen to paper) under a somewhat forbidding pseudonym, Cotton Mather Mills. Before 1847 she had published nothing but a set of 'improving' and very indifferent verses in *Blackwood's Magazine*, in collaboration with her husband, the Rev. William Gaskell. She was not a poet, as she soon discovered, but she was already celebrated in her own circle as a vivid, lively and amusing letter-writer, and from letters it was a natural step (suggested by Mr Gaskell to distract her from the loss of her little son) to a serious attempt at prose fiction. 'The Sexton's Hero', published in *Howitt's Magazine* in 1847, is a descriptively powerful tale of escape and death in the fast-running tides of Lancaster Sands, a part of the Lancashire coast that Mrs Gaskell knew well. As a first attempt it is impressive, and the fact that it was written in the same months as *Mary Barton*, the novel that was to make her famous, gives one a startling idea of the speed of her literary development.

'Half a Life-time Ago' was written for *Household Words* in 1855, and one cannot help remembering with amusement that it was the story which caused Dickens to explode with 'Mrs Gaskell, fearful—fearful', for it is certainly a gloomy tale and one, moreover, in which she refused to accept his directions as to the length of instalments. It is interesting still, in spite of the five deaths, four illnesses and one madness compressed into its small compass, chiefly because of its ring of truth, which is unmistakeable. Such a clash between love and duty could occur today, but not with the harshness that was a part of life in the Cumberland hills not so very long ago. Such a story as Susan Dixon's, the hard-faced spinster-farmer with the half-witted brother, was a part of the annals of every remote fell-farming community in the early nineteenth century.

'Right at Last' is a short, neat, well-told crime story—one of the tales that Mrs Gaskell considered 'good enough for Dickens', a pot-boiler written to defray the expenses of a holiday, and none the worse for that. It appeared in *Household Words* in 1858, two months after the final instalment of *My Lady Ludlow*, a much more ambitious undertaking, a *novella* which is almost a novel, more than twice the length of *Cousin Phillis*. For the modern reader *My Lady Ludlow* has one serious flaw in construction which would probably not have disturbed her Victorian readers. The 'story within a story' was a popular device of the period (even Dickens was addicted to it in his youth, and so spoiled Chapter VI of *Nicholas Nickleby*), and the violent tale of the French Revolution, with which Lady Ludlow breaks the placid flow of her story, can be seen today as nothing but an insufferable interruption. The remedy is simple: it can be skipped, to be read on another occasion as a separate story. Taken in this divided fashion *My Lady Ludlow* has quiet charm and interest: the confrontation of the old aristocratic way of life with the new, the undermining of class distinctions, the invasion of the territory of the hunting-and-drinking parson of the eighteenth century by the sober, plebeian Evangelical clergyman, with his belief in the human rights and education of the 'lower orders'. It is quietly and beautifully done, and—the 'story within a story' set aside—can be enjoyed in almost the same spirit as *Cranford*.

MARGARET LANE.

1970.

SELECT BIBLIOGRAPHY

COLLECTED WORKS. *The Works of Mrs Gaskell*, ed. Sir A. W. Ward, 8 vols. (Knutsford edition), 1906; *The Novels and Tales of Mrs Gaskell*, ed. C. K. Shorter, 11 vols. (World's Classics), 1906–19.

NOVELS AND TALES. *Life in Manchester. By Cotton Mather Mills, Esq.*, 1848; *Mary Barton*, 2 vols., 1848; *The Moorland Cottage*, 1850; *Ruth*, 3 vols., 1853; *Cranford*, 1853; *Lizzie Leigh and Other Tales*, 1854; *Hand and Heart and Bessy's Troubles at Home*, 1855; *North and South*, 2 vols., 1855; *My Lady Ludlow*, 1858; *Round the Sofa*, 2 vols., 1859; *Right at Last, and Other Tales*, 1860; *Lois the Witch and Other Tales*, 1861; *A Dark Night's Work*, 1863; *Sylvia's Lovers*, 3 vols., 1863; *The Cage at Cranford*, first pub. in *All the Year Round*, November 1863; only reprint in World's Classics edn., 1907; *Cousin Phillis and Other Tales*, 1865; ed. T. Seccombe (Everyman's Library), 1908; *The Grey Woman and Other Tales*, 1865; *Wives and Daughters*, 2 vols., 1866; *Two Fragments of Ghost Stories*, first pub. in the Knutsford edition of the Collected Works, vol. vii, 1906.

OTHER WRITINGS. 'Account of Clopton Hall, Warwickshire' (in W. Howitt's *Visits to Remarkable Places*), 1840; 'Bran' (a poem, in *Household Words*, 22nd October 1853); 'A Christmas Carol' (in *Household Words*, 27th December 1856); *The Life of Charlotte Brontë*, 2 vols., 1857; ed. M. Sinclair (Everyman's Library), 1908; '*My Diary*,' the *Early Years of my Daughter Marianne* (written 10th March 1835–28th October 1838), privately printed, 1923; *Letters of Mrs Gaskell and Charles Eliot Norton (1855–1865)*, ed. J. Whitehill, 1932; *The Letters of Mrs Gaskell*, edited by J. A. V. Chapple and Arthur Pollard, 1966.

BIOGRAPHY AND CRITICISM. A. S. Whitfield. *Mrs Gaskell; her Life and Work*, 1929; E. S. Haldane, *Mrs Gaskell and her Friends*, 1930; Yvonne Finch, *Mrs Gaskell*, 1949; Annette B. Hopkins, *Elizabeth Gaskell, Her Life and Work*, 1952; Miriam Allott, *Mrs Gaskell* (Writers and their Work Series, 1960); Aina Rubenius, *The Woman Question in Mrs Gaskell's Life and Work*, 1960; Arthur Pollard, *Mrs Gaskell; Novelist and Biographer*, 1965.

David Cecil, *Early Victorian Novelists*, 1934; Kathleen Tillotson, *Novels of the Eighteen-Forties*, 1954.

CONTENTS

COUSIN PHILLIS

PART I

IT is a great thing for a lad, when he is first turned into the independence of lodgings. I do not think I ever was so satisfied and proud in my life as when, at seventeen, I sate down in a little three-cornered room above a pastry-cook's shop in the county-town of Eltham. My father had left me that afternoon, after delivering himself of a few plain precepts, strongly expressed, for my guidance in the new course of life on which I was entering. I was to be a clerk under the engineer who had undertaken to make the little branch line from Eltham to Hornby. My father had got me this situation, which was in a position rather above his own in life; or perhaps I should say, above the station in which he was born and bred; for he was raising himself every year in men's consideration and respect. He was a mechanic by trade; but he had some inventive genius, and a great deal of perseverance, and had devised several valuable improvements in railway machinery. He did not do this for profit, though, as was reasonable, what came in the natural course of things was acceptable; he worked out his ideas, because, as he said, "until he could put them into shape, they plagued him by night and by day." But this is enough about my dear father; it is a good thing for a country where there are many like him. He was a sturdy Independent by descent and conviction; and this it was, I believe, which made him place me in the lodgings at the pastry-cook's. The shop was kept by the two sisters of our minister at home; and this was considered as a sort of safeguard to my morals, when I was turned loose upon the temptations of the county-town, with a salary of thirty pounds a year.

My father had given up two precious days, and put on his Sunday clothes, in order to bring me to Eltham, and accompany me, first to the office, to introduce me to my new master (who was under some obligations to my father for a suggestion), and next to take me to call on the Independent minister of the little congregation at Eltham. And then he left me; and, though sorry to part with him, I now began to taste with relish the pleasure of being my own master. I unpacked the hamper that my mother had provided me with, and smelt the pots of preserve with all the delight of a possessor who might break into their contents at any time he pleased. I handled, and weighed in my fancy, the home-cured ham, which seemed to promise me interminable feasts; and, above all, there was the fine savour of knowing that I might eat of these dainties when I liked, at my sole will, not dependent on the pleasure of any one else, however indulgent. I stowed my eatables away in the little corner cupboard—that room was all corners, and everything was placed in a corner, the fireplace, the window, the cupboard; I myself seemed to be the only thing in the middle, and there was hardly room for me. The table was made of a folding leaf under the window, and the window looked out upon the market-place; so the studies for the prosecution of which my father had brought himself to pay extra for a sitting-room for me ran a considerable chance of being diverted from books to men and women. I was to have my meals with the two elderly Miss Dawsons in the little parlour behind the three-cornered shop downstairs—my breakfasts and dinners at least; for, as my hours in an evening were likely to be uncertain, my tea or supper was to be an independent meal.

Then, after this pride and satisfaction, came a sense of desolation. I had never been from home before, and I was an only child; and, though my father's spoken maxim had been, "Spare the rod, and spoil the child," yet, unconsciously, his heart had yearned after me, and his ways towards me were more tender than he knew, or would have approved of in himself, could he have known. My mother, who never professed sternness, was far more severe than my father; perhaps my boyish faults annoyed her more; for I remember, now that I have written the above words, how she pleaded for me once in my riper years, when I had really offended against my father's sense of right.

But I have nothing to do with that now. It is about cousin Phillis that I am going to write, and as yet I am far enough from even saying who cousin Phillis was.

For some months after I was settled in Eltham, the new employment in which I was engaged—the new independence of my life—occupied all my thoughts. I was at my desk by eight o'clock, home to dinner at one, back at the office by two.

The afternoon work was more uncertain than the morning's; it might be the same, or it might be that I had to accompany Mr. Holdsworth, the managing engineer, to some point on the line between Eltham and Hornby. This I always enjoyed, because of the variety, and because of the country we traversed (which was very wild and pretty), and because I was thrown into companionship with Mr. Holdsworth, who held the position of hero in my boyish mind. He was a young man of five-and-twenty or so, and was in a station above mine, both by birth and education; and he had travelled on the Continent, and wore mustachios and whiskers of a somewhat foreign fashion. I was proud of being seen with him. He was really a fine fellow, in a good number of ways, and I might have fallen into much worse hands.

Every Saturday I wrote home, telling of my weekly doings— my father had insisted upon this; but there was so little variety in my life that I often found it hard work to fill a letter. On Sundays I went twice to chapel, up a dark narrow entry, to hear droning hymns, and long prayers, and a still longer sermon, preached to a small congregation, of which I was, by nearly a score of years, the youngest member. Occasionally, Mr. Peters, the minister, would ask me home to tea after the second service. I dreaded the honour; for I usually sate on the edge of my chair all the evening, and answered solemn questions, put in a deep bass voice, until household prayer-time came, at eight o'clock, when Mrs. Peters came in, smoothing down her apron, and the maid-of-all-work followed, and first a sermon, and then a chapter, was read, and a long impromptu prayer followed, till some instinct told Mr. Peters that supper-time had come, and we rose from our knees with hunger for our predominant feeling. Over supper, the minister did unbend a little into one or two ponderous jokes, as if to show me that ministers were men, after all. And then, at ten o'clock, I went home, and enjoyed my long-repressed yawns in the three-cornered room before going to bed.

Dinah and Hannah Dawson, so their names were put on the board above the shop-door—I always called them Miss Dawson and Miss Hannah—considered these visits of mine to Mr. Peters as the greatest honour a young man could have; and evidently thought that if, after such privileges, I did not work out my salvation, I was a sort of modern Judas Iscariot. On the contrary, they shook their heads over my intercourse with Mr. Holdsworth. He had been so kind to me in many ways, that when I cut into my ham, I hovered over the thought of asking him to tea in my room; more especially as the annual fair was being held in Eltham market-place, and the sight of the booths, the merry-go-rounds, the wild-beast shows, and such country pomps, was (as I thought at seventeen) very attractive. But, when I ventured to allude to my wish in even distant terms, Miss Hannah caught me up, and spoke of the sinfulness of such sights, and something about wallowing in the mire, and then vaulted into France, and spoke evil of the nation, and all who had ever set foot therein; till, seeing that her anger was concentrating itself into a point, and that that point was Mr. Holdsworth, I thought it would be better to finish my breakfast, and make what haste I could out of the sound of her voice. I rather wondered afterwards to hear her and Miss Dawson counting up their weekly profits with glee, and saying that a pastry-cook's shop in the corner of the market-place, in Eltham-fair week, was no such bad thing. However, I never ventured to ask Mr. Holdsworth to my lodgings.

There is not much to tell about this first year of mine at Eltham. But when I was nearly nineteen, and beginning to think of whiskers on my own account, I came to know cousin Phillis, whose very existence had been unknown to me till then. Mr. Holdsworth and I had been out to Heathbridge for a day, working hard. Heathbridge was near Hornby, for our line of railway was above half finished. Of course a day's outing was a great thing to tell about in my weekly letters; and I fell to describing the country—a fault I was not often guilty of. I told my father of the bogs, all over wild myrtle and soft moss, and shaking ground, over which we had to carry our line; and how Mr. Holdsworth and I had gone for our mid-day meals—for we had to stay here for two days and a night—to a pretty village hard-by, Heathbridge proper; and how I hoped we should often have to go there, for the shaking, uncertain ground was puzzling our engineers—one end of the line going up as soon as the other was weighted down. (I had no thought for the shareholders' interests, as may be seen; we had to make a new line on firmer ground, before the junction railway was completed.) I told all this at great length, thankful to fill up my paper. By return-letter, I heard that a second cousin of my mother's was married to the Independent minister of Hornby, Ebenezer Holman by name, and lived at Heathbridge proper: the very Heathbridge I had described—or so my mother believed; for she had never seen her cousin Phillis Green, who was something of an heiress (my father believed), being her father's only child; and old Thomas Green had owned an estate of near upon fifty acres, which must have come to his daughter. My mother's feeling of kinship seemed to have been strongly stirred by the mention of Heathbridge; for my father said that she desired me, if ever I went thither again, to make inquiry for the Reverend Ebenezer Holman; and, if indeed he lived there, I was further to ask if he had not married one Phillis Green, and, if both these questions were answered in the affirmative, I was to go and introduce myself as the only child of Margaret Manning, born Moneypenny. I was enraged at myself for having named Heathbridge at all, when I found what it was drawing down upon me. One Independent minister, as I said to myself, was enough for any man; and here I knew (that is to say, I had been catechised on Sabbath-mornings by) Mr. Hunter, our minister at home; and I had had to be civil to old Peters at Eltham, and behave myself for five hours running, whenever he asked me to tea at his house; and now, just as I felt the free air blowing about me up at Heathbridge, I was to ferret out another minister, and I should perhaps have to be catechised by him, or else asked to tea at his house. Besides, I did not like pushing myself upon strangers, who perhaps had never heard of my mother's name, and, such an odd name as it was—Money-penny; and, if they had, had never cared more for her than she had for them, apparently, until this unlucky mention of Heathbridge.

Still, I would not disobey my parents in such a trifle, however irksome it might be. So, the next time our business took me to Heathbridge, and we were dining in the little sanded inn-parlour, I took the opportunity of Mr. Holdsworth's being out of the room, and asked the questions, which I was bidden to ask, of the rosy-cheeked maid. I was either unintelligible or she was stupid; for she said she did not know, but would ask master; and, of course, the landlord came in to understand what it was I wanted to know; and I had to bring out all my stammering inquiries before Mr. Holdsworth, who would never have attended to them, I dare say, if I had not blushed and blundered, and made such a fool of myself.

"Yes," the landlord said, "the Hope Farm was in Heath-bridge proper, and the owner's name was Holman, and he was an Independent minister, and, as far as the landlord could tell, his wife's Christian name was Phillis; anyhow, her maiden name was Green."

"Relations of yours?" asked Mr. Holdsworth.

"No, sir—only my mother's second cousins. Yes, I suppose they are relations. But I never saw them in my life."

"The Hope Farm is not a stone's throw from here," said the officious landlord, going to the window. "If you carry your eye over yon bed of hollyhocks, over the damson-trees in the orchard yonder, you may see a stack of queer-like stone chimneys. Them is the Hope Farm chimneys; it's an old place, though Holman keeps it in good order."

Mr. Holdsworth had risen from the table with more promptitude than I had, and was standing by the window, looking. At the landlord's last words, he turned round, smiling—"It is not often that parsons know how to keep land in order, is it?"

"Beg pardon, sir, but I must speak as I find; and minister Holman—we call the Church clergyman here 'parson,' sir; he would be a bit jealous, if he heard a Dissenter called parson—minister Holman knows what he's about, as well as e'er a farmer in the neighbourhood. He gives up five days a week to his own work, and two to the Lord's; and it is difficult to say which he works hardest at. He spends Saturday and Sunday a-writing sermons and a-visiting his flock at Hornby; and at five o'clock on Monday morning he'll be guiding his plough, in the Hope Farm yonder, just as well as if he could neither read nor write. But your dinner will be getting cold, gentlemen."

So we went back to table. After a while, Mr. Holdsworth broke the silence—"If I were you, Manning, I'd look up these relations of yours. You can go and see what they're like, while we're waiting for Dobson's estimates; and I'll smoke a cigar in the garden meanwhile."

"Thank you, sir. But I don't know them, and I don't think I want to know them."

"What did you ask all those questions for, then?" said he, looking quickly up at me. He had no notion of doing or saying things without a purpose. I did not answer; so he continued—"Make up your mind, and go off and see what this farmer-minister is like, and come back and tell me—I should like to hear."

I was so in the habit of yielding to his authority, or influence, that I never thought of resisting, but went on my errand; though I remember feeling as if I would rather have had my head cut off. The landlord, who had evidently taken an interest in the event of our discussion, in a way that country landlords have, accompanied me to the house-door and gave me repeated directions, as if I was likely to miss my way in two hundred yards. But I listened to him, for I was glad of the delay, to screw up my courage for the effort of facing unknown people and introducing myself. I went along the lane, I recollect, switching at all the taller roadside weeds; till, after a turn or two, I found myself close in front of the Hope Farm. There was a garden between the house and the shady, grassy lane; I afterwards found that this garden was called the court: perhaps because there was a low wall round it, with an iron railing on the top of the wall, and two great gates, between pillars crowned with stone balls, for a state entrance to the flagged path leading up to the front door. It was not the habit of the place to go in either by these great gates or by the front door; the gates, indeed, were locked, as I found, though the door stood wide open. I had to go round by a side-path, slightly worn, on a broad, grassy way, which led past the court-wall, past a horse-mount, half covered with stone-crop and a little wild yellow fumitory, to another door—"the curate," as I found it was termed by the master of the house, while the front door, "handsome and all for show," was termed "the rector." I knocked with my hand upon the "curate" door; a tall girl, about my own age, as I thought, came and opened it, and stood there silent, waiting to know my errand. I see her now—cousin Phillis. The westering sun shone full upon her, and made a slanting stream of light into the room within. She was dressed in dark blue cotton of some kind, up to her throat, down to her wrists, with a little frill of the same, wherever it touched her white skin. And such a white skin as it was! I have never seen the like. She had light hair, nearer yellow than any other colour. She looked me steadily in the face with large, quiet eyes, wondering, but untroubled by the sight of a stranger. I thought it odd that so old, so full-grown as she was, she should wear a pinafore over her gown.

Before I had quite made up my mind what to say in reply to her mute inquiry of what I wanted there, a woman's voice called out, "Who is it, Phillis? If it is any one for butter-milk, send them round to the back door."

I thought I would rather speak to the owner of that voice than to the girl before me; so I passed her, and stood at the entrance of a room, hat in hand; for this side-door opened straight into the hall or house-place, where the family sate when work was done. There was a brisk little woman, of forty or so, ironing some huge muslin cravats under the light of a long vine-shaded casement window. She looked at me distrustfully till I began to speak. "My name is Paul Manning," said I; but I saw she did not know the name. "My mother's name was Moneypenny," said I—"Margaret Moneypenny."

"And she married one John Manning, of Birmingham," said Mrs. Holman eagerly. "And you'll be her son. Sit down! I am right glad to see you. To think of your being Margaret's son! Why, she was almost a child not so long ago. Well, to be sure, it is five-and-twenty years ago. And what brings you into these parts?"

She sate down herself, as if oppressed by her curiosity as to all the five-and-twenty years that had passed by since she had seen my mother. Her daughter Phillis took up her knitting—a long grey worsted man's-stocking, I remember—and knitted away without looking at her work. I felt that the steady gaze of those deep grey eyes was upon me, though once, when I stealthily raised mine to hers, she was examining something on the wall above my head.

When I had answered all my cousin Holman's questions, she heaved a long breath, and said, "To think of Margaret Moneypenny's boy being in our house! I wish the minister was here. Phillis, in what field is thy father to-day?"

"In the five-acre; they are beginning to cut the corn."

"He'll not like being sent for, then; else I should have liked you to have seen the minister. But the five-acre is a good step off. You shall have a glass of wine and a bit of cake, before you stir from this house, though. You're bound to go, you say; or else the minister comes in mostly when the men have their four o'clock."

"I must go—I ought to have been off before now."

"Here, then, Phillis, take the keys." She gave her daughter some whispered directions, and Phillis left the room.

"She is my cousin, is she not?" I asked. I knew she was; but somehow I wanted to talk of her, and did not know how to begin.

"Yes—Phillis Holman. She is our only child—now."

Either from that "now," or from a strange momentary wistfulness in her eyes, I knew that there had been more children, who were now dead.

"How old is cousin Phillis?" said I, scarcely venturing on the new name, it seemed too prettily familiar for me to call her by it; but cousin Holman took no notice of it, answering straight to the purpose.

" Seventeen last May-day; but the minister does not like to hear me calling it ' May-day,' " said she, checking herself with a little awe. " Phillis was seventeen on the first day of May last," she repeated in an emended edition.

" And I am nineteen in another month," thought I to myself; I don't know why.

Then Phillis came in, carrying a tray with wine and cake upon it.

" We keep a house-servant," said cousin Holman; " but it is churning-day, and she is busy." It was meant as a little proud apology for her daughter's being the handmaiden.

" I like doing it, mother," said Phillis, in her grave, full voice.

I felt as if I were somebody in the Old Testament—who, I could not recollect — being served and waited upon by the daughter of the host. Was I like Abraham's steward, when Rebekah gave him to drink at the well? I thought Isaac had not gone the pleasantest way to work in winning him a wife. But Phillis never thought about such things. She was a stately, gracious young woman, in the dress, and with the simplicity, of a child.

As I had been taught, I drank to the health of my new-found cousin and her husband; and then I ventured to name my cousin Phillis with a little bow of my head towards her; but I was too awkward to look and see how she took my compliment. " I must go, now," said I, rising.

Neither of the women had thought of sharing in the wine; cousin Holman had broken a bit of cake for form's sake.

" I wish the minister had been within," said his wife, rising too. Secretly I was very glad he was not. I did not take kindly to ministers in those days; and I thought he must be a particular kind of man, by his objecting to the term " May-day." But, before I went, cousin Holman made me promise that I would come back on the Saturday following and spend Sunday with them: when I should see something of " the minister."

" Come on Friday, if you can," were her last words as she stood at the curate-door, shading her eyes from the sinking sun with her hand.

Inside the house sate cousin Phillis, her golden hair, her dazzling complexion, lighting up the corner of the vine-shadowed room. She had not risen, when I bade her good-bye; she had looked at me straight, as she said her tranquil words of farewell.

I found Mr. Holdsworth down at the line, hard at work superintending. As soon as he had a pause, he said, " Well,

Manning, what are the new cousins like? How do preaching and farming seem to get on together? If the minister turns out to be practical as well as reverend, I shall begin to respect him."

But he hardly attended to my answer, he was so much more occupied with directing his workpeople. Indeed, my answer did not come very readily; and the most distinct part of it was the mention of the invitation that had been given me.

"Oh! of course you can go—and on Friday, too, if you like; there is no reason why not this week; and you've done a long spell of work this time, old fellow."

I thought that I d d not want to go on Friday; but, when the day came, I found that I should prefer going to staying away; so I availed myself of Mr. Holdsworth's permission, and went over to Hope Farm some time in the afternoon, a little later than my last visit. I found the "curate" open, to admit the soft September air, so tempered by the warmth of the sun that it was warmer out of doors than in, although the wooden log lay smouldering in front of a heap of hot ashes on the hearth. The vine-leaves over the window had a tinge more yellow, their edges were here and there scorched and browned; there was no ironing about, and cousin Holman sate just outside the house, mending a shirt. Phillis was at her knitting indoors: it seemed as if she had been at it all the week. The many-speckled fowls were pecking about in the farmyard beyond, and the milk-cans glittered with brightness, hung out to sweeten. The court was so full of flowers that they crept out upon the low-covered wall and horse-mount, and were even to be found self-sown upon the turf that bordered the path to the back of the house. I fancied that my Sunday coat was scented for days afterwards by the bushes of sweetbriar and the fraxinella that perfumed the air. From time to time, cousin Holman put her hand into a covered basket at her feet, and threw handfuls of corn down for the pigeons that cooed and fluttered in the air around, in expectation of this treat.

I had a thorough welcome, as soon as she saw me. "Now, this is kind—this is right-down friendly," shaking my hand warmly. "Phillis, your cousin Manning is come!"

"Call me Paul, will you?" said I; "they call me so at home, and Manning in the office."

"Well; Paul, then. Your room is all ready for you, Paul; for, as I said to the minister, 'I'll have it ready, whether he comes o' Friday or not.' And the minister said he must go up to the Ash-field, whether you were to come or not; but he would come home betimes, to see if you were here. I'll show you to your room; and you can wash the dust off a bit."

After I came down, I think she did not quite know what to do with me; or she might think that I was dull; or she might have work to do in which I hindered her; for she called Phillis, and bade her put on her bonnet, and go with me to the Ash-field, and find father. So we set off, I in a little flutter of a desire to make myself agreeable, but wishing that my companion were not quite so tall; for she was above me in height. While I was wondering how to begin our conversation, she took up the words.

" I suppose, cousin Paul, you have to be very busy at your work all day long, in general? "

" Yes, we have to be in the office at half-past eight; and we have an hour for dinner, and then we go at it again till eight or nine."

" Then you have not much time for reading? "

" No," said I, with a sudden consciousness that I did not make the most of what leisure I had.

" No more have I. Father always gets an hour before going a-field in the mornings; but mother does not like me to get up so early."

" My mother is always wanting me to get up earlier, when I am at home."

" What time do you get up? "

" Oh!—ah!—sometimes half-past six; not often, though; " for I remembered only twice that I had done so during the past summer.

She turned her head, and looked at me.

" Father is up at three; and so was mother till she was ill. I should like to be up at four."

" Your father up at three! Why, what has he to do at that hour? "

" What has he not to do? He has his private exercise in his own room; he always rings the great bell which calls the men to milking; he rouses up Betty, our maid; as often as not, he gives the horses their feed before the man is up—for Jem, who takes care of the horses, is an old man; and father is always loth to disturb him; he looks at the calves, and the shoulders, heels, traces, chaff, and corn, before the horses go a-field; he has often to whip-cord the plough-whips; he sees the hogs fed; he looks into the swill-tubs, and writes his orders for what is wanted for food for man and beast; yes, and for fuel, too. And then, if he has a **bit of time** to spare, he comes in and reads with me—but only English; we keep Latin for the evenings, that we may have time to enjoy it; and then he calls in the man to breakfast, and cuts the boys' bread and cheese, and sees their wooden bottles filled, and sends them off to their work;—and by this time it is half-past six, and we have our breakfast. There is father!" she exclaimed, pointing out to me a man in his shirt-sleeves, taller by the head than the other two with whom he was working. We only saw him through the leaves of the ash-trees growing in the hedge, and I thought I must be confusing the figures, or mistaken: that man still looked like a very powerful labourer, and had none of the precise demureness of appearance which I had always imagined was the characteristic of a minister. It was the Reverend Ebenezer Holman, however. He gave us a nod as we entered the stubble-field; and I think he would have come to meet us, but that he was in the middle of giving some directions to his men. I could see that Phillis was built more after his type than her mother's. He, like his daughter, was largely made, and of a fair, ruddy complexion, whereas hers was brilliant and delicate. His hair had been yellow or sandy, but now was grizzled. Yet his grey hairs betokened no failure in strength. I never saw a more powerful man—deep chest, lean flanks, well-planted head. By this time we were nearly up to him; and he interrupted himself and stepped forwards, holding out his hand to me, but addressing Phillis.

"Well, my lass, this is cousin Manning, I suppose. Wait a minute, young man, and I'll put on my coat, and give you a decorous and formal welcome. But—— Ned Hall, there ought to be a water-furrow across this land: it's a nasty, stiff, clayey, dauby bit of ground, and thou and I must fall to, come next Monday—I beg your pardon, cousin Manning—and there's old Jem's cottage wants a bit of thatch; you can do that job to-morrow, while I am busy." Then, suddenly changing the tone of his deep bass voice to an odd suggestion of chapels and preachers, he added, " Now I will give out the psalm: ' Come all harmonious tongues,' to be sung to ' Mount Ephraim ' tune."

He lifted his spade in his hand, and began to beat time with it; the two labourers seemed to know both words and music, though I did not; and so did Phillis: her rich voice followed her father's, as he set the tune; and the men came in with more uncertainty, but still harmoniously. Phillis looked at me once or twice, with a little surprise at my silence; but I did not know the words. There we five stood, bareheaded, excepting Phillis, in the tawny stubble-field, from which all the shocks of corn had not yet been carried—a dark wood on one side, where the wood-pigeons were cooing; blue distance, seen through the ash-trees, on the other. Somehow, I think that, if I had known the words, and could have sung, my throat would have been choked up by the feeling of the unaccustomed scene.

The hymn was ended, and the men had drawn off, before I could stir. I saw the minister beginning to put on his coat, and looking at me with friendly inspection in his gaze, before I could rouse myself.

"I daresay you railway gentlemen don't wind up the day with singing a psalm together," said he; "but it is not a bad practice—not a bad practice. We have had it a bit earlier to-day for hospitality's sake—that's all."

I had nothing particular to say to this, though I was thinking a great deal. From time to time, I stole a look at my companion. His coat was black, and so was his waistcoat; neck-cloth he had none, his strong full throat being bare above the snow-white shirt. He wore drab-coloured knee-breeches, grey worsted stockings (I thought I knew the maker), and strong-nailed shoes. He carried his hat in his hand, as if he liked to feel the coming breeze lifting his hair. After a while, I saw that the father took hold of the daughter's hand; and so they, holding each other, went along towards home. We had to cross a lane. In it there were two little children—one lying prone on the grass in a passion of crying; the other standing stock still, with its finger in its mouth, the large tears slowly rolling down its cheeks for sympathy. The cause of their distress was evident; there was a broken brown pitcher, and a little pool of spilt milk on the road.

"Hollo! hollo! What's all this?" said the minister. "Why, what have you been about, Tommy?" lifting the little petti-coated lad, who was lying sobbing, with one vigorous arm. Tommy looked at him with surprise in his round eyes, but no affright—they were evidently old acquaintances.

"Mammy's jug!" said he at last, beginning to cry afresh.

"Well! and will crying piece mammy's jug, or pick up spilt milk? How did you manage it, Tommy?"

"He" (jerking his head at the other) "and me was running races."

"Tommy said he could beat me," put in the other.

"Now, I wonder what will make you two silly lads mind, and not run races again, with a pitcher of milk between you," said the minister, as if musing. " I might flog you, and so save mammy the trouble; for I daresay she'll do it, if I don't." The fresh burst of whimpering from both showed the probability of this. " Or I might take you to the Hope Farm, and give you some more milk; but then you'd be running races again, and my milk would follow that to the ground, and make another white pool. I think the flogging would be best—don't you? "

" We would never run races no more," said the elder of the two.

" Then you'd not be boys; you'd be angels."

" No, we shouldn't."

" Why not? "

They looked into each other's eyes for an answer to this puzzling question. At length, one said, " Angels is dead folk."

" Come; we'll not get too deep into theology. What do you think of my lending you a tin can with a lid, to carry the milk home in? That would not break, at any rate; though I would not answer for the milk not spilling, if you ran races. That's it! "

He had dropped his daughter's hand, and now held out each of his to the little fellows. Phillis and I followed, and listened to the prattle which the minister's companions now poured out to him, and which he was evidently enjoying. At a certain point, there was a sudden burst of the tawny, ruddy evening landscape. The minister turned round, and quoted a line or two of Latin.

" It's wonderful," said he, " how exactly Virgil has hit the enduring epithets, nearly two thousand years ago, and in Italy; and yet how it describes to a T what is now lying before us in the parish of Heathbridge, county——, England."

" I daresay it does," said I, all aglow with shame; for I had forgotten the little Latin I ever knew.

The minister shifted his eyes to Phillis's face; it mutely gave him back the sympathetic appreciation that I, in my ignorance, could not bestow.

" Oh! this is worse than the catechism," thought I; " that was only remembering words."

" Phillis, lass, thou must go home with these lads, and tell their mother all about the race and the milk. Mammy must always know the truth," now speaking to the children. " And tell her, too, from me that I have got the best birch-rod in the parish; and that, if she ever thinks her children want a flogging, she must bring them to me, and, if I think they deserve it, I'll give it them better than she can." So Phillis led the children towards the dairy, somewhere in the back-yard; and I followed the minister in through the " curate " into the house-place.

"Their mother," said he, " is a bit of a vixen, and apt to punish her children without rhyme or reason. I try to keep the parish-rod as well as the parish-bull."

He sate down in the three-cornered chair by the fireside, and looked around the empty room.

"Where's the missus? " said he to himself. But she was there in a minute; it was her regular plan to give him his welcome home—by a look, by a touch, nothing more—as soon as she could after his return, and he had missed her now. Regardless of my presence, he went over the day's doings to her; and then, getting up, he said he must go and make himself " reverend," and that then we would have a cup of tea in the parlour. The parlour was a large room, with two casemented windows on the other side of the broad flagged passage leading from the rector-door to the wide staircase, with its shallow, polished oaken steps, on which no carpet was ever laid. The parlour-floor was covered in the middle by a home-made carpeting of needlework and list. One or two quaint family pictures of the Holman family hung round the walls; the fire-grate and irons were much ornamented with brass; and on a table against the wall between the windows, a great beau-pot of flowers was placed upon the folio volumes of Matthew Henry's Bible. It was a compliment to me to use this room, and I tried to be grateful for it; but we never had our meals there after that first day, and I was glad of it; for the large house-place, living-room, dining-room, whichever you might like to call it, was twice as comfortable and cheerful. There was a rug in front of the great large fireplace, and an oven by the grate, and a crook, with the kettle hanging from it, over the bright wood-fire; everything that ought to be black and polished in that room was black and polished; and the flags, and window-curtains, and such things as were to be white and clean, were just spotless in their purity. Opposite to the fireplace, extending the whole length of the room, was an oaken shovel-board, with the right incline for a skilful player to send the weights into the prescribed space. There were baskets of white work about, and a small shelf of books hung against the wall—books used for reading, and not for propping up a beau-pot of flowers. I took down one or two of those books once when I was left alone in the house-place on the first evening—Virgil, Cæsar, a Greek grammar

—oh, dear! ah, me! and Phillis Holman's name in each of them! I shut them up, and put them back in their places, and walked as far away from the book-shelf as I could. Yes, and I gave my cousin Phillis a wide berth, although she was sitting at her work quietly enough, and her hair was looking more golden, her dark eyelashes longer, her round pillar of a throat whiter, than ever. We had done tea, and we had returned into the house-place, that the minister might smoke his pipe without fear of contaminating the drab damask window-curtains of the parlour. He had made himself " reverend " by putting on one of the voluminous white muslin neckcloths that I had seen cousin Holman ironing, that first visit I had paid to the Hope Farm, and by making one or two other unimportant changes in his dress. He sate looking steadily at me; but whether he saw me or not I cannot tell. At the time, I fancied that he did, and was gauging me in some unknown fashion in his secret mind. Every now and then, he took his pipe out of his mouth, knocked out the ashes, and asked me some fresh question. As long as these related to my acquirements or my reading, I shuffled uneasily and did not know what to answer. By-and-by, he got round to the more practical subject of rail-roads, and on this I was more at home. I really had taken an interest in my work; nor would Mr. Holdsworth, indeed, have kept me in his employment, if I had not given my mind as well as my time to it; and I was, besides, full of the difficulties which beset us just then, owing to our not being able to find a steady bottom on the Heathbridge moss, over which we wished to carry our line. In the midst of all my eagerness in speaking about this, I could not help being struck with the extreme pertinence of his questions. I do not mean that he did not show ignorance of many of the details of engineering: that was to have been expected; but on the premises he had got hold of he thought clearly and reasoned logically. Phillis—so like him as she was both in body and mind—kept stopping at her work and looking at me, trying to fully understand all that I said. I felt she did; and perhaps it made me take more pains in using clear expressions and arranging my words, than I otherwise should.

" She shall see I know something worth knowing, though it mayn't be her dead-and-gone languages," thought I.

" I see," said the minister at length. " I understand it all. You've a clear, good head of your own, my lad—choose how you came by it."

"From my father," said I proudly. "Have you not heard of his discovery of a new method of shunting? It was in the *Gazette*. It was patented. I thought every one had heard of Manning's patent winch."

"We don't know who invented the alphabet," said he, half-smiling, and taking up his pipe.

"No, I dare say not, sir," replied I, half-offended; "that's so long ago."

Puff—puff—puff.

"But your father must be a notable man. I heard of him once before; and it is not many a one fifty miles away whose fame reaches Heathbridge."

"My father is a notable man, sir. It is not me that says so; it is Mr. Holdsworth, and—and everybody."

"He is right to stand up for his father," said Cousin Holman, as if she were pleading for me.

I chafed inwardly, thinking that my father needed no one to stand up for him. He was man sufficient for himself.

"Yes—he is right," said the minister placidly. "Right, because it comes from his heart—right, too, as I believe, in point of fact. Else, there is many a young cockerel that will stand upon a dunghill and crow about his father, by way of making his own plumage to shine. I should like to know thy father," he went on, turning straight to me, with a kindly, frank look in his eyes.

But I was vexed, and would take no notice. Presently, having finished his pipe, he got up and left the room. Phillis put her work hastily down, and went after him. In a minute or two she returned, and sate down again. Not long after, and before I had quite recovered my good temper, he opened the door out of which he had passed, and called to me to come to him. I went across a narrow stone passage into a strange, many-cornered room, not ten feet in area, part study, part counting-house, looking into the farmyard; with a desk to sit at, a desk to stand at, a spittoon, a set of shelves with old divinity books upon them; another, smaller, filled with books on farriery, farming, manures, and such subjects, with pieces of paper containing memoranda stuck against the whitewashed walls with wafers, nails, pins, anything that came readiest to hand; a box of carpenter's tools on the floor, and some manuscripts in shorthand on the desk.

He turned round, half-laughing. "That foolish girl of mine thinks I have vexed you"—putting his large, powerful hand on my shoulder. "'Nay,' says I; 'kindly meant is kindly taken'—is it not so?'"

"It was not quite, sir," replied I, vanquished by his manner; "but it shall be in future."

"Come, that's right. You and I shall be friends. Indeed, it's not many a one I would bring in here. But I was reading a book this morning, and I could not make it out; it is a book that was left here by mistake one day; I had subscribed to Brother Robinson's sermons; and I was glad to see this instead of them, for, sermons though they be, they're . . . well, never mind! I took 'em both, and made my old coat do a bit longer; but all's fish that comes to my net. I have fewer books than leisure to read them, and I have a prodigious big appetite. Here it is."

It was a volume of stiff mechanics, involving many technical terms, and some rather deep mathematics. These last, which would have puzzled me, seemed easy enough to him; all that he wanted was the explanation of the technical words, which I could easily give.

While he was looking through the book, to find the places where he had been puzzled, my wandering eye caught on some of the papers on the wall, and I could not help reading one, which has stuck by me ever since. At first, it seemed a kind of weekly diary; but then I saw that the seven days were portioned out for special prayers and intercessions: Monday for his family, Tuesday for enemies, Wednesday for the Independent churches, Thursday for all other churches, Friday for persons afflicted, Saturday for his own soul, Sunday for all wanderers and sinners, that they might be brought home to the fold.

We were called back into the house-place to have supper. A door opening into the kitchen was opened; and all stood up in both rooms, while the minister, tall, large, one hand resting on the spread table, the other lifted up, said, in the deep voice that would have been loud, had it not been so full and rich, but with the peculiar accent or twang that I believe is considered devout by some people, "Whether we eat or drink, or whatsoever we do, let us do all to the glory of God."

The supper was an immense meat-pie. We of the house-place were helped first; then the minister hit the handle of his buck-horn carving-knife on the table once, and said—

"Now or never;" which meant, did any of us want any more; and, when we had all declined, either by silence or by words, he knocked twice with his knife on the table, and Betty came in through the open door, and carried off the great dish to the kitchen, where an old man and a young one, and a help-girl, were awaiting their meal.

"Shut the door, if you will," said the minister to Betty.

"That's in honour of you," said cousin Holman, in a tone of satisfaction, as the door was shut. "When we've no stranger with us, the minister is so fond of keeping the door open, and talking to the men and maids, just as much as to Phillis and me."

"It brings us all together, like a household, just before we meet as a household in prayer," said he in explanation. "But to go back to what we were talking about—can you tell me of any simple book on dynamics that I could put in my pocket, and study a little at leisure times in the day?"

"'Leisure times,' father?" said Phillis, with a nearer approach to a smile than I had yet seen on her face.

"Yes; leisure times, daughter. There is many an odd minute lost in waiting for other folk; and, now that railroads are coming so near us, it behoves us to know something about them."

I thought of his own description of his "prodigious big appetite" for learning. And he had a good appetite of his own for the more material victual before him. But I saw, or fancied I saw, that he had some rule for himself in the matter both of food and drink.

As soon as supper was done, the household assembled for prayer. It was a long impromptu evening prayer; and it would have seemed desultory enough, had I not had a glimpse of the kind of day that preceded it, and so been able to find a clue to the thoughts that preceded the disjointed utterances; for he kept there, kneeling down in the centre of a circle, his eyes shut, his outstretched hands pressed palm to palm—sometimes with a long pause of silence, as if waiting to see if there was anything else he wished to "lay before the Lord" (to use his own expression)—before he concluded with the blessing. He prayed for the cattle and live creatures, rather to my surprise; for my attention had begun to wander, till it was recalled by the familiar words.

And here I must not forget to name an odd incident at the conclusion of the prayer, and before we had risen from our knees (indeed, before Betty was well awake, for she made a nightly practice of having a sound nap, her weary head lying on her stalwart arms); the minister, still kneeling in our midst, but with his eyes wide open, and his arms dropped by his sides, spoke to the elder man, who turned round on his knees to attend. "John, didst see that Daisy had her warm mash to-night? for we must not neglect the means, John—two quarts of gruel, a spoonful of ginger, and a gill of beer—the poor beast needs it, and I fear it slipped out of my mind to tell thee; and here was I asking a blessing and neglecting the means, which is a mockery," said he, dropping his voice.

Before we went to bed, he told me he should see little or nothing more of me during my visit, which was to end on Sunday evening, as he always gave up both Saturday and Sabbath to his work in the ministry. I remembered that the landlord at the inn had told me this, on the day when I first inquired about these new relations of mine; and I did not dislike the opportunity which I saw would be afforded me of becoming more acquainted with cousin Holman and Phillis, though I earnestly hoped that the latter would not attack me on the subject of the dead languages.

I went to bed, and dreamed that I was as tall as cousin Phillis, and had a sudden and miraculous growth of whisker, and a still more miraculous acquaintance with Latin and Greek. Alas! I wakened up still a short, beardless lad, with "*tempus fugit*" for my sole remembrance of the little Latin I had once learnt. While I was dressing, a bright thought came over me: I could question cousin Phillis, instead of her questioning me, and so manage to keep the choice of the subjects of conversation in my own power.

Early as it was, every one had breakfasted, and my basin of bread and milk was put on the oven-top to await my coming down. Every one was gone about their work. The first to come into the house-place was Phillis, with a basket of eggs. Faithful to my resolution, I asked—

"What are those?"

She looked at me for a moment, and then said gravely—

"Potatoes."

"No! they are not," said I. "They are eggs. What do you mean by saying they are potatoes?"

"What did you mean by asking me what they were, when they were plain to be seen?" retorted she.

We were both getting a little angry with each other.

"I don't know. I wanted to begin to talk to you; and I was afraid you would talk to me about books as you did yesterday. I have not read much; and you and the minister have read so much."

"I have not," said she. "But you are our guest; and mother says I must make it pleasant to you. We won't talk of books. What must we talk about?"

"I don't know. How old are you?"

"Seventeen last May. How old are you?"

"I am nineteen. Older than you by nearly two years," said I, drawing myself up to my full height.

"I should not have thought you were above sixteen," she replied, as quietly as if she were not saying the most provoking thing she possibly could. Then came a pause.

"What are you going to do now?" asked I.

"I should be dusting the bed-chambers; but mother said I had better stay and make it pleasant to you," said she, a little plaintively, as if dusting rooms was far the easier task.

"Will you take me to see the live-stock? I like animals, though I don't know much about them."

"Oh, do you? I am so glad. I was afraid you would not like animals, as you did not like books."

I wondered why she said this. I think it was because she had begun to fancy all our tastes must be dissimilar. We went together all through the farmyard; we fed the poultry, she kneeling down with her pinafore full of corn and meal, and tempting the little timid downy chickens upon it, much to the anxiety of the fussy ruffled hen, their mother. She called to the pigeons, who fluttered down at the sound of her voice. She and I examined the great sleek cart-horses; sympathised in our dislike of pigs; fed the calves; coaxed the sick cow, Daisy; and admired the others out at pasture; and came back tired and hungry and dirty at dinner-time, having quite forgotten that there were such things as dead languages, and consequently capital friends.

PART II

COUSIN HOLMAN gave me the weekly county-newspaper to read aloud to her, while she mended stockings out of a high piled-up basket, Phillis helping her mother. I read and read, unregardful of the words I was uttering, thinking of all manner of other things; of the bright colour of Phillis's hair, as the afternoon sun fell on her bending head; of the silence of the house, which enabled me to hear the double tick of the old clock which stood half-way up the stairs; of the variety of inarticulate noises which cousin Holman made while I read, to show her sympathy, wonder, or horror at the newspaper intelligence. The tranquil monotony of that hour made me feel as if I had lived for ever, and should live for ever, droning out paragraphs in that warm sunny room, with my two quiet hearers, and the curled-up pussy-cat sleeping on the hearthrug, and the clock on the house-stairs perpetually clicking out the passage of the moments. By-and-by, Betty the servant came to the door into the kitchen, and made a sign to Phillis, who put her half-mended stocking down, and went away to the kitchen without a word. Looking at cousin Holman a minute or two afterwards, I saw that she had dropped her chin upon her breast, and had fallen fast asleep. I put the newspaper down, and was nearly following her example, when a waft of air from some unseen source slightly opened the door of communication with the kitchen, that Phillis must have left unfastened; and I saw part of her figure as she sate by the dresser, peeling apples with quick dexterity of finger, but with repeated turnings of her head towards some book lying on the dresser by her. I softly rose, and as softly went into the kitchen, and looked over her shoulder; before she was aware of my neighbourhood, I had seen that the book was in a language unknown to me, and the running title was " L'Inferno." Just as I was making out the relationship of this word to " infernal," she started and turned round, and, as if continuing her thought as she spoke, she sighed out—

" Oh! it is so difficult! Can you help me? " putting her finger below a line.

" Me! I! Not I! I don't even know what language it is in! "

" Don't you see it is Dante? " she replied, almost petulantly; she did so want help.

" Italian, then? " said I dubiously; for I was not quite sure.

" Yes. And I do so want to make it out. Father can help me a little, for he knows Latin; but then he has so little time."

" You have not much, I should think, if you have often to try and do two things at once, as you are doing now."

" Oh! that's nothing! Father bought a heap of old books cheap. And I knew something about Dante before; and I have always liked Virgil so much. Paring apples is nothing, if I could only make out this old Italian. I wish you knew it."

" I wish I did," said I, moved by her impetuosity of tone.

" If, now, only Mr. Holdsworth were here! he can speak Italian like anything, I believe."

" Who is Mr. Holdsworth? " said Phillis, looking up.

" Oh, he's our head-engineer. He's a regular first-rate fellow! He can do anything; " my hero-worship and my pride in my chief all coming into play. Besides, if I was not clever and book-learned myself, it was something to belong to some one who was.

" How is it that he speaks Italian? " asked Phillis.

" He had to make a railway through Piedmont, which is in Italy, I believe; and he had to talk to all the workmen in Italian; and I have heard him say that, for nearly two years, he had only Italian books to read in the queer outlandish places he was in."

" Oh dear!" said Phillis; " I wish "—and then she stopped. I was not quite sure whether to say the next thing that came into my mind; but I said it.

"Could I ask him anything about your book, or your difficulties? "

She was silent for a minute or so, and then she made reply—

" No! I think not. Thank you very much, though. I can generally puzzle a thing out in time. And then, perhaps, I remember it better than if some one had helped me. I'll put it away now, and you must move off, for I've got to make the paste for the pies; we always have a cold dinner on Sabbaths."

" But I may stay and help you, mayn't I? "

" Oh, yes; not that you can help at all, but I like to have you with me."

I was both flattered and annoyed at this straightforward avowal. I was pleased that she liked me; but I was young coxcomb enough to have wished to play the lover, and I was quite wise enough to perceive that, if she had any idea of the kind in her head, she would never have spoken out so frankly. I comforted myself immediately, however, by finding out the grapes were sour. A great, tall girl in a pinafore, half-a-head taller than I was, reading books that I had never heard of, and talking about them too, as of far more interest than any mere personal subjects—that was the last day on which I ever thought of my dear cousin Phillis as the possible mistress of my heart and life. But we were all the greater friends for this idea being utterly put away and buried out of sight.

Late in the evening the minister came home from Hornby. He had been calling on the different members of his flock; and unsatisfactory work it had proved to him, it seemed, from the fragments that dropped out of his thoughts into his talk.

"I don't see the men; they are all at their business, their shops, or their warehouses; they ought to be there. I have no fault to find with them; only, if a pastor's teaching or words of admonition are good for anything, they are needed by the men as much as by the women."

"Cannot you go and see them in their places of business, and remind them of their Christian privileges and duties, minister?" asked cousin Holman, who evidently thought that her husband's words could never be out of place.

"No!" said he, shaking his head. "I judge them by myself. If there are clouds in the sky, and I am getting in the hay just ready for loading, and rain sure to come in the night, I should look ill upon Brother Robinson if he came into the field to speak about serious things."

"But, at any rate, father, you do good to the women, and perhaps they repeat what you have said to them to their husbands and children?"

"It is to be hoped they do, for I cannot reach the men directly; but the women are apt to tarry before coming to me, to put on ribbons and gauds; as if they could hear the message I bear to them best in their smart clothes. Mrs. Dobson to-day—Phillis, I am thankful thou dost not care for the vanities of dress!"

Phillis reddened a little as she said, in a low humble voice—

"But I do, father, I'm afraid. I often wish I could wear pretty-coloured ribbons round my throat, like the squire's daughters."

"It's but natural, minister!" said his wife; "I'm not above liking a silk gown better than a cotton one myself!"

"The love of dress is a temptation and a snare," said he, gravely. "The true adornment is a meek and quiet spirit. And, wife," said he, as a sudden thought crossed his mind, "in that matter I, too, have sinned. I wanted to ask you, could we not sleep in the grey room, instead of our own?"

"Sleep in the grey room?—change our room at this time o' day!" cousin Holman asked, in dismay.

"Yes," said he. "It would save me from a daily temptation to anger. Look at my chin!" he continued; "I cut it this morning—I cut it on Wednesday, when I was shaving; I do not know how many times I have cut it of late, and all from impatience at seeing Timothy Cooper at his work in the yard."

"He's a downright lazy tyke!" said cousin Holman. "He's

not worth his wage. There's but little he can do; and what he can do, he does badly."

"True," said the minister. "But he is but, so to speak, a half-wit; and yet he has got a wife and children."

"More shame for him!"

"But that is past change. And, if I turn him off, no one else would take him on. Yet I cannot help watching him of a morning as he goes sauntering about his work in the yard; and I watch, and I watch, till the old Adam rises strong within me at his lazy ways; and some day, I am afraid, I shall go down and send him about his business—let alone the way in which he makes me cut myself while I am shaving—and then his wife and children will starve. I wish we could move to the grey room."

I do not remember much more of my first visit to the Hope Farm. We went to chapel in Heathbridge, slowly and decorously walking along the lanes, ruddy and tawny with the colouring of the coming autumn. The minister walked a little before us, his hands behind his back, his head bent down, thinking about the discourse to be delivered to his people, cousin Holman said; and we spoke low and quietly, in order not to interrupt his thoughts. But I could not help noticing the respectful greetings which he received from both rich and poor as we went along: greetings which he acknowledged with a kindly wave of his hand, but with no words of reply. As we drew near the town, I could see some of the young fellows we met casting admiring looks on Phillis; and that made me look too. She had on a white gown, and a short black silk cloak, according to the fashion of the day. A straw bonnet, with brown ribbon strings; that was all. But what her dress wanted in colour, her sweet bonny face had. The walk made her cheeks bloom like the rose; the very whites of her eyes had a blue tinge in them, and her dark eyelashes brought out the depth of the blue eyes themselves. Her yellow hair was put away as straight as its natural curliness would allow. If she did not perceive the admiration she excited, I am sure cousin Holman did; for she looked as fierce and as proud as ever her quiet face could look, guarding her treasure, and yet glad to perceive that others could see that it was a treasure. This afternoon I had to return to Eltham, to be ready for the next day's work. I found out afterwards that the minister and his family were all " exercised in spirit," as to whether they did well in asking me to repeat my visits at the Hope Farm, seeing that of necessity I must return to Eltham on the Sabbath-day.

However, they did go on asking me, and I went on visiting them, whenever my other engagements permitted me; Mr. Holdsworth being in this case, as in all, a kind and indulgent friend. Nor did my new acquaintances oust him from my strong regard and admiration. I had room in my heart for all, I am happy to say; and, as far as I can remember, I kept praising each to the other in a manner which, if I had been an older man, living more amongst people of the world, I should have thought unwise, as well as a little ridiculous. It was unwise, certainly, as it was almost sure to cause disappointment, if ever they did become acquainted; and perhaps it was ridiculous, though I do not think we any of us thought it so at the time. The minister used to listen to my accounts of Mr. Holdsworth's many accomplishments and various adventures in travel with the truest interest, and most kindly good faith; and Mr. Holdsworth, in return, liked to hear about my visits to the farm, and description of my cousins' life there—liked it, I mean, as much as he liked anything that was merely narrative, without leading to action.

So I went to the farm certainly, on an average, once a month during that autumn; the course of life there was so peaceful and quiet, that I can only remember one small event, and that was one that I think I took more notice of than any one else: Phillis left off wearing the pinafores that had always been so obnoxious to me: I do not know why they were banished, but on one of my visits I found them replaced by pretty linen aprons in the morning, and a black silk one in the afternoon. And the blue cotton gown became a brown stuff one as winter drew on; this sounds like some book I once read, in which migration from the blue bed to the brown was spoken of as a great family event.

Towards Christmas, my dear father came to see me, and to consult Mr. Holdsworth about the improvement which has since been known as " Manning's driving-wheel." Mr. Holdsworth, as I think I have before said, had a very great regard for my father, who had been employed in the same great machine-shop in which Mr. Holdsworth had served his apprenticeship; and he and my father had many mutual jokes about one of these gentlemen-apprentices who used to set about his smith's work in white wash-leather gloves, for fear of spoiling his hands. Mr. Holdsworth often spoke to me about my father as having the same kind of genius for mechanical invention as that of George Stephenson; and my father had come over now to consult him about several improvements, as well as an offer of partnership.

It was a great pleasure to me to see the mutual regard of these two men: Mr. Holdsworth, young, handsome, keen, well-dressed, an object of admiration to all the youth of Eltham; my father, in his decent but unfashionable Sunday clothes, his plain, sensible face full of hard lines, the marks of toil and thought,—his hands blackened, beyond the power of soap and water, by years of labour in the foundry; speaking a strong Northern dialect, while Mr. Holdsworth had a long, soft drawl in his voice, as many of the Southerners have, and was reckoned in Eltham to give himself airs.

Although most of my father's leisure-time was occupied with conversations about the business I have mentioned, he felt that he ought not to leave Eltham without going to pay his respects to the relations who had been so kind to his son. So he and I ran up on an engine along the incomplete line as far as Heath-bridge, and went, by invitation, to spend a day at the farm.

It was odd and yet pleasant to me to perceive how these two men, each having led up to this point such totally dissimilar lives, seemed to come together by instinct, after one quiet straight look into each other's faces. My father was a thin, wiry man of five foot seven; the minister was a broad-shouldered, fresh-coloured man of six foot one; they were neither of them great talkers in general—perhaps the minister the most so— but they spoke much to each other. My father went into the fields with the minister; I think I see him now, with his hands behind his back, listening intently to all explanations of tillage, and the different processes of farming; occasionally taking up an implement, as if unconsciously, and examining it with a critical eye, and now and then asking a question, which I could see was considered as pertinent by his companion. Then we returned to look at the cattle, housed and bedded in expectation of the snowstorm, hanging black on the western horizon, and my father learned the points of a cow with as much attention as if he meant to turn farmer. He had his little book that he used for mechanical memoranda and measurements in his pocket, and he took it out to write down " straight back," " small muzzle," " deep barrel," and I know not what else, under the head " cow." He was very critical on a turnip-cutting machine, the clumsiness of which first incited him to talk; and, when we went into the house, he sat thinking and quiet for a bit, while Phillis and her mother made the last preparations for tea, with a little unheeded apology from cousin Holman, because we were not sitting in the best parlour, which

she thought might be chilly on so cold a night. I wanted
nothing better than the blazing, crackling fire that sent a glow
over all the house-place, and warmed the snowy flags under our
feet, till they seemed to have more heat than the crimson rug,
right in front of the fire. After tea, as Phillis and I were talking
together very happily, I heard an irrepressible exclamation
from cousin Holman—

"Whatever is the man about!"

And, on looking round, I saw my father taking a straight
burning stick out of the fire; and, after waiting for a minute,
and examining the charred end, to see if it was fitted for his
purpose, he went to the hard-wood dresser, scoured to the last
pitch of whiteness and cleanliness, and began drawing with the
stick; the best substitute for chalk or charcoal within his reach,
for his pocket-book pencil was not strong or bold enough for his
purpose. When he had done, he began to explain his new model
of a turnip-cutting machine to the minister, who had been
watching him in silence all the time. Cousin Holman had, in
the meantime, taken a duster out of a drawer, and, under
pretence of being as much interested as her husband in the
drawing, was secretly trying on an outside mark how easily it
would come off, and whether it would leave her dresser as white
as before. Then Phillis was sent for the book of dynamics,
about which I had been consulted during my first visit; and
my father had to explain many difficulties, which he did in
language as clear as his mind, making drawings with his stick
wherever they were needed as illustrations; the minister sitting
with his massive head resting on his hands, his elbows on the
table, almost unconscious of Phillis, leaning over and listening
greedily, with her hand on his shoulder, sucking in information,
like her father's own daughter. I was rather sorry for cousin
Holman; I had been so once or twice before; for do what she
would, she was completely unable even to understand the
pleasure her husband and daughter took in intellectual pursuits,
much less to care in the least herself for the pursuits themselves,
and was thus unavoidably thrown out of some of their interests.
I had once or twice thought she was a little jealous of her own
child, as a fitter companion for her husband than she was herself;
and I fancied the minister himself was aware of this feeling, for
I had noticed an occasional sudden change of subject, and a
tenderness of appeal in his voice as he spoke to her, which always
made her look contented and peaceful again. I do not think
that Phillis ever perceived these little shadows; in the first place,

she had such complete reverence for her parents that she listened to them both as if they had been St. Peter and St. Paul; and, besides, she was always too much engrossed with any matter in hand to think about other people's manners and looks.

This night I could see, though she did not, how much she was winning on my father. She asked a few questions which showed that she had followed his explanations up to that point; possibly, too, her unusual beauty might have something to do with his favourable impression of her; but he made no scruple of expressing his admiration of her to her father and mother in her absence from the room; and from that evening I date a project of his which came out to me, a day or two afterwards, as we sate in my little three-cornered room in Eltham.

"Paul," he began, "I never thought to be a rich man; but I think it's coming upon me. Some folk are making a deal of my new machine" (calling it by its technical name); "and Ellison, of the Borough Green Works, has gone so far as to ask me to be his partner."

"Mr. Ellison, the justice—who lives in King Street? why, he drives his carriage!" said I, doubting, yet exultant.

"Ay, lad, John Ellison. But that's no sign that I shall drive my carriage. Though I should like to save thy mother walking, for she's not so young as she was. But that's a long way off, anyhow. I reckon I should start with a third profit. It might be seven hundred, or it might be more. I should like to have the power to work out some fancies o' mine. I care for that much more than for th' brass. And Ellison has no lads; and by nature the business would come to thee in course o' time. Ellison's lassies are but bits o' things, and are not like to come by husbands just yet; and, when they do, maybe they'll not be in the mechanical line. It will be an opening for thee, lad, if thou art steady. Thou'rt not great shakes, I know, in th' inventing line; but many a one gets on better without having fancies for something he does not see and never has seen. I'm right down glad to see that mother's cousins are such uncommon folk for sense and goodness. I have taken the minister to my heart like a brother, and she is a womanly, quiet sort of a body. And I'll tell you frank, Paul, it will be a happy day for me, if ever you can come and tell me that Phillis Holman is like to be my daughter. I think, if that lass had not a penny, she would be the making of a man; and she'll have yon house and lands, and you may be her match yet in fortune, if all goes well."

I was growing as red as fire; I did not know what to say, and yet I wanted to say something; but the idea of having a wife of my own at some future day, though it had often floated about in my own head, sounded so strange, when it was thus first spoken about by my father. He saw my confusion, and half-smiling said—

"Well, lad, what dost say to the old father's plans? Thou art but young, to be sure; but when I was thy age, I would ha' given my right hand, if I might ha' thought of the chance of wedding the lass I cared for "——

"My mother?" asked I, a little struck by the change of his tone of voice.

"No! not thy mother. Thy mother is a very good woman —none better. No! the lass I cared for at nineteen ne'er knew how I loved her, and a year or two after and she was dead, and ne'er knew. I think she would ha' been glad to ha' known it, poor Molly; but I had to leave the place where we lived, for to try to earn my bread—and I meant to come back—but, before ever I did, she was dead and gone: I ha' never gone there since. But, if you fancy Phillis Holman, and can get her to fancy you, my lad, it shall go different with you, Paul, to what it did with your father."

I took counsel with myself very rapidly, and I came to a clear conclusion.

"Father," said I, "if I fancied Phillis ever so much, she would never fancy me. I like her as much as I could like a sister; and she likes me as if I were her brother—her younger brother."

I could see my father's countenance fall a little.

"You see she's so clever—she's more like a man than a woman—she knows Latin and Greek."

"She'd forget 'em, if she'd a houseful of children," was my father's comment on this.

"But she knows many a thing besides, and is wise as well as learned: she has been so much with her father. She would never think much of me, and I should like my wife to think a deal of her husband."

"It is not just book-learning, or the want of it, as makes a wife think much or little of her husband," replied my father, evidently unwilling to give up a project which had taken deep root in his mind. "It's a something—I don't rightly know how to call it—if he's manly, and sensible, and straightforward; and I reckon you're that, my boy."

"I don't think I should like to have a wife taller than I am, father," said I, smiling; he smiled too, but not heartily.

"Well," said he, after a pause. "It's but a few days I've been thinking of it; but I'd got as fond of my notion as if it had been a new engine as I'd been planning out. Here's our Paul, thinks I to myself, a good sensible breed o' lad, as has never vexed or troubled his mother or me; with a good business opening out before him; age nineteen; not so bad-looking, though perhaps not to call handsome; and here's his cousin, not too near a cousin, but just nice, as one may say; aged seventeen; good and true, and well brought up to work with her hands as well as her head; a scholar—but that can't be helped, and is more her misfortune than her fault, seeing she is the only child of a scholar—and as I said afore, once she's a wife and a mother, she'll forget it all, I'll be bound—with a good fortune in land and house, when it shall please the Lord to take her parents to himself; with eyes like poor Molly's for beauty, a colour that comes and goes on a milk-white skin, and as pretty a mouth "——

"Why, Mr. Manning, what fair lady are you describing?" asked Mr. Holdsworth, who had come quickly and suddenly upon our *tête-à-tête*, and had caught my father's last words as he entered the room.

Both my father and I felt rather abashed; it was such an odd subject for us to be talking about; but my father, like a straight-forward, simple man as he was, spoke out the truth.

"I've been telling Paul of Ellison's offer, and saying how good an opening it made for him "——

"I wish I'd as good," said Mr. Holdsworth. "But has the business a 'pretty mouth'?"

"You're always so full of your joking, Mr. Holdsworth," said my father. "I was going to say that if he and his cousin Phillis Holman liked to make it up between them, I would put no spoke in the wheel."

"Phillis Holman!" said Mr. Holdsworth. "Is she the daughter of the minister-farmer out at Heathbridge? Have I been helping on the course of true love, by letting you go there so often? I knew nothing of it."

"There is nothing to know," said I, more annoyed than I chose to show. "There is no more true love in the case than may be between the first brother and sister you may choose to meet. I have been telling father she would never think of me; she's a great deal taller and cleverer; and I'd rather be taller and more learned than my wife when I have one."

"And it is she, then, that has the pretty mouth your father

spoke about? I should think that would be an antidote to the cleverness and learning. But I ought to apologise for breaking in upon your last night; I came upon business to your father."

And then he and my father began to talk about many things that had no interest for me just then, and I began to go over again my conversation with my father. The more I thought about it, the more I felt that I had spoken truly about my feelings towards Phillis Holman. I loved her dearly as a sister, but I could never fancy her as my wife. Still less could I think of her ever—yes, *condescending*, that is the word—condescending to marry me. I was roused from a reverie on what I should like my possible wife to be, by hearing my father's warm praise of the minister, as a most unusual character; how they had got back from the diameter of driving-wheels to the subject of the Holmans, I could never tell; but I saw that my father's weighty praises were exciting some curiosity in Mr. Holdsworth's mind; indeed, he said, almost in a voice of reproach—

"Why, Paul, you never told me what kind of a fellow this minister-cousin of yours was?"

"I don't know that I found out, sir," said I. "But if I had, I don't think you'd have listened to me, as you have done to my father."

"No! most likely not, old fellow," replied Mr. Holdsworth, laughing. And, again and afresh, I saw what a handsome pleasant clear face his was; and, though this evening I had been a bit put out with him—through his sudden coming, and his having heard my father's open-hearted confidence—my hero resumed all his empire over me by his bright merry laugh.

And, if he had not resumed his old place that night, he would have done so the next day: when, after my father's departure, Mr. Holdsworth spoke about him with such just respect for his character, such ungrudging admiration of his great mechanical genius, that I was compelled to say, almost unawares—

"Thank you, sir. I am very much obliged to you."

"Oh, you're not at all. I am only speaking the truth. Here's a Birmingham workman, self-educated, one may say—having never associated with stimulating minds, or had what advantages travel and contact with the world may be supposed to afford—working out his own thoughts into steel and iron, making a scientific name for himself—a fortune, if it pleases him to work for money—and keeping his singleness of heart, his perfect simplicity of manner; it puts me out of patience to think of my expensive schooling, my travels hither and thither, my heaps of scientific books—and I have done nothing to speak of! But it's evidently good blood; there's that Mr. Holman, that cousin of yours, made of the same stuff."

"But he's only cousin because he married my mother's second cousin," said I.

"That knocks a pretty theory on the head, and twice over, too. I should like to make Holman's acquaintance."

"I am sure they would be so glad to see you at Hope Farm," said I eagerly. "In fact, they've asked me to bring you several times; only I thought you would find it dull."

"Not at all. I can't go yet though, even if you do get me an invitation; for the —— —— Company want me to go to the —— Valley, and look over the ground a bit for them, to see if it would do for a branch line; it's a job which may take me away for some time; but I shall be backwards and forwards, and you're quite up to doing what is needed in my absence; the only work that may be beyond you is keeping old Jevons from drinking."

He went on giving me directions about the management of the men employed on the line; and no more was said then, or for several months, about his going to Hope Farm. He went off into —— Valley, a dark overshadowed dale, where the sun seemed to set behind the hills before four o'clock on midsummer afternoon.

Perhaps it was this that brought on the attack of low fever, which he had soon after the beginning of the new year; he was very ill for many weeks, almost many months; a married sister —his own relation, I think—came down from London to nurse him, and I went over to him when I could, to see him, and give him, "masculine news," as he called it; reports of the progress of the line, which, I am glad to say, I was able to carry on in his absence, in the slow gradual way which suited the company best, while trade was in a languid state and money dear in the market. Of course, with this occupation for my scanty leisure, I did not often go over to Hope Farm. Whenever I did go, I met with a thorough welcome; and many inquiries were made as to Holdsworth's illness, and the progress of his recovery.

At length, in June I think it was, he was sufficiently recovered to come back to his lodgings at Eltham, and resume part at least of his work. His sister, Mrs. Robinson, had been obliged to leave him some weeks before, owing to some epidemic amongst her own children. As long as I had seen Mr. Holdsworth in the rooms at the little inn at Hensleydale, where I had been accustomed to look upon him as an invalid, I had not been aware of the visible shake his fever had given to his health. But, once back in the old lodgings, where I had always seen him so buoyant, eloquent, decided, and vigorous in former days, my spirits sank at the change in one whom I had always regarded with a strong feeling of admiring affection. He sank into silence and despondency after the least exertion; he seemed as if he could not make up his mind to any action, or else, as if, when it was made up, he lacked strength to carry out his purpose. Of course, it was but the natural state of slow convalescence, after so sharp an illness; but, at the time, I did not know this, and perhaps I represented his state as more serious than it was, to my kind relations at Hope Farm; who, in their grave, simple, eager way, immediately thought of the only help they could give.

"Bring him out here," said the minister. "Our air here is good, to a proverb; the June days are fine; he may loiter away his time in the hay-field, and the sweet smells will be a balm in themselves—better than physic."

"And," said cousin Holman, scarcely waiting for her husband to finish his sentence, "tell him there is new milk and fresh eggs to be had for the asking; it's lucky Daisy has just calved, for her milk is always as good as other cows' cream; and there is the plaid-room, with the morning-sun all streaming in."

Phillis said nothing, but looked as much interested in the project as any one. I took it up myself. I wanted them to see him and him to know them. I proposed it to him, when I got home. He was too languid, after the day's fatigue, to be willing to make the little exertion of going amongst strangers; and disappointed me by almost declining to accept the invitation I brought. The next morning it was different; he apologised for his ungraciousness of the night before; and told me that he would get all things in train, so as to be ready to go out with me to Hope Farm on the following Saturday.

"For you must go with me, Manning," said he; "I used to be as impudent a fellow as need be, and rather liked going amongst strangers and making my way; but since my illness I am almost like a girl, and turn hot and cold with shyness; as they do, I fancy."

So it was fixed. We were to go out to Hope Farm on Saturday afternoon; and it was also understood that, if the air and the life suited Mr. Holdsworth, he was to remain there for a week or ten days, doing what work he could at that end of the line, while I took his place at Eltham to the best of my ability. I grew a little nervous, as the time drew near, and wondered how the brilliant Holdsworth would agree with the quiet quaint family of the minister; how they would like him and many of his half-foreign ways. I tried to prepare him, by telling him, from time to time, little things about the goings-on at Hope Farm.

"Manning," said he, "I see you don't think I am half good enough for your friends. Out with it, man!"

"No," I replied boldly. "I think you are good; but I don't know if you are quite of their kind of goodness."

"And you've found out already that there is greater chance of disagreement between two 'kinds of goodness,' each having its own idea of right, than between a given goodness and a moderate degree of naughtiness—which last often arises from an indifference to right?"

"I don't know. I think you're talking metaphysics; and I am sure that is bad for you."

"'When a man talks to you in a way that you don't understand about a thing which he does not understand, them's metaphysics.' You remember the clown's definition, don't you, Manning?"

"No, I don't," said I. "But what I do understand is, that you must go to bed, and tell me at what time we must start to-morrow; that I may go to Hepworth, and get those letters written we were talking about this morning."

"Wait till to-morrow, and let us see what the day is like," he answered, with such languid indecision as showed me he was over-fatigued. So I went my way.

The morrow was blue and sunny and beautiful; the very perfection of an early summer's day. Mr. Holdsworth was all impatience to be off into the country; morning had brought back his freshness and strength, and consequent eagerness to be going. I was afraid we were going to my cousin's farm rather too early, before they would expect us; but what could I do with such a restless vehement man as Holdsworth was that morning? We came down upon the Hope Farm, before the dew was off the grass on the shady side of the lane; the great house-dog was loose, basking in the sun, near the closed side door. I was surprised at this door being shut, for all summer long it was open from morning to night; but it was only on latch. I opened it; Rover watching me with half-suspicious, half-trustful eyes. The room was empty.

"I don't know where they can be," said I. "But come in and sit down, while I go and look for them! You must be tired."

"Not I. This sweet balmy air is like a thousand tonics. Besides, this room is hot, and smells of those pungent wood-ashes. What are we to do?"

"Go round to the kitchen. Betty will tell us where they are."

So we went round into the farm-yard, Rover accompanying us out of a grave sense of duty. Betty was washing out her milk-pans, in the cold bubbling spring water that constantly trickled in and out of a stone trough. In such weather as this, most of her kitchen-work was done out of doors.

"Eh, dear!" said she, "the minister and missus is away at Hornby! They ne'er thought of your coming so betimes! The missus had some errands to do; and she thought as she'd walk with the minister and be back by dinner-time."

"Did not they expect us to dinner?" said I.

"Well they did, and they did not, as I may say. Missus said to me, the cold lamb would do well enough, if you did not come; and, if you did, I was to put on a chicken and some bacon to boil; and I'll go do it now, for it is hard to boil bacon enough."

"And is Phillis gone, too?" Mr. Holdsworth was making friends with Rover.

"No! She's just somewhere about. I reckon you'll find her in the kitchen-garden, getting peas."

"Let us go there," said Holdsworth, suddenly leaving off his play with the dog.

So I led the way into the kitchen-garden. It was in the first promise of a summer profuse in vegetables and fruits. Perhaps it was not so much cared for as other parts of the property; but it was more attended to than most kitchen-gardens belonging to farm-houses. There were borders of flowers along each side of the gravel-walks; and there was an old sheltering wall on the north side, covered with tolerably choice fruit-trees; there was a slope down to the fish-pond at the end, where there were great strawberry-beds; and raspberry-bushes and rose-bushes grew wherever there was a space; it seemed a chance which had been planted. Long rows of peas stretched at right angles from the main walk; and I saw Phillis stooping down among them, before she saw us. As soon as she heard our cranching steps on the gravel, she stood up, and,

shading her eyes from the sun, recognised us. She was quite
still for a moment, and then came slowly towards us, blushing
a little, from evident shyness. I had never seen Phillis shy
before.

" This is Mr. Holdsworth, Phillis," said I, as soon as I had
shaken hands with her. She glanced up at him, and then looked
down, more flushed than ever at his grand formality of taking
his hat off and bowing; such manners had never been seen at
Hope Farm before.

" Father and mother are out. They will be so sorry! you
did not write, Paul, as you said you would."

" It was my fault," said Holdsworth, understanding what
she meant, as well as if she had put it more fully into words.
" I have not yet given up all the privileges of an invalid; one
of which is indecision. Last night, when your cousin asked
me at what time we were to start, I really could not make up
my mind."

Phillis seemed as if she could not make up her mind as to
what to do with us. I tried to help her—

" Have you finished getting peas? " taking hold of the half-
filled basket she was unconsciously holding in her hand; " or
may we stay and help you? "

" If you would. But perhaps it will tire you, sir? " added
she, speaking now to Holdsworth.

" Not a bit," said he. " It will carry me back twenty years
in my life, when I used to gather peas in my grandfather's
garden. I suppose I may eat a few, as I go along? "

" Certainly, sir. But, if you went to the strawberry-beds,
you would find some strawberries ripe; and Paul can show you
where they are."

" I am afraid you distrust me. I can assure you, I know
the exact fulness at which peas should be gathered. I take
great care not to pluck them when they are unripe. I will
not be turned off, as unfit for my work."

This was a style of half-joking talk that Phillis was not
accustomed to. She looked for a moment as if she would have
liked to defend herself from the playful charge of distrust made
against her; but she ended by not saying a word. We all
plucked our peas in busy silence for the next five minutes.
Then Holdsworth lifted himself up from between the rows, and
said, a little wearily—

" I am afraid I must strike work. I am not as strong as I
fancied myself."

Phillis was full of penitence immediately. He did, indeed, look pale; and she blamed herself for having allowed him to help her.

"It was very thoughtless of me. I did not know—I thought, perhaps, you really liked it. I ought to have offered you something to eat, sir! Oh, Paul, we have gathered quite enough; how stupid I was to forget that Mr. Holdsworth had been ill!" And in a blushing hurry she led the way towards the house. We went in, and she moved a heavy-cushioned chair forwards, into which Holdsworth was only too glad to sink. Then, with deft and quiet speed, she brought in a little tray—wine, water, cake, home made bread, and newly-churned butter. She stood by in some anxiety till, after bite and sup, the colour returned to Mr. Holdsworth's face, and he would fain have made us some laughing apologies for the fright he had given us. But then Phillis drew back from her innocent show of care and interest, and relapsed into the cold shyness habitual to her when she was first thrown into the company of strangers. She brought out the last week's county-paper (which Mr. Holdsworth had read five days ago), and then quietly withdrew; and then he subsided into languor, leaning back and shutting his eyes, as if he would go to sleep. I stole into the kitchen after Phillis; but she had made the round of the corner of the house outside, and I found her sitting on the horse-mount, with her basket of peas, and a basin into which she was shelling them. Rover lay at her feet, snapping now and then at the flies. I went to her, and tried to help her; but somehow the sweet, crisp young peas found their way more frequently into my mouth than into the basket, while we talked together in a low tone, fearful of being overheard through the open casements of the house-place, in which Holdsworth was resting.

"Don't you think him handsome?" asked I.

"Perhaps—yes—I have hardly looked at him," she replied. "But is not he very like a foreigner?"

"Yes, he cuts his hair foreign fashion," said I.

"I like an Englishman to look like an Englishman."

"I don't think he thinks about it. He says he began that way when he was in Italy, because everybody wore it so, and it is natural to keep it on in England."

"Not if he began it in Italy, because everybody there wore it so. Everybody here wears it differently."

I was a little offended with Phillis's logical fault-finding with my friend; and I determined to change the subject.

"When is your mother coming home?"

"I should think she might come any time now; but she had to go and see Mrs. Morton, who was ill; and she might be kept, and not be home till dinner. Don't you think you ought to go and see how Mr. Holdsworth is going on, Paul? He may be faint again."

I went at her bidding; but there was no need for it. Mr. Holdsworth was up, standing by the window, his hands in his pockets; he had evidently been watching us. He turned away as I entered.

"So that is the girl I found your good father planning for your wife, Paul, that evening when I interrupted you! Are you of the same coy mind still? It did not look like it a minute ago."

"Phillis and I understand each other," I replied sturdily. "We are like brother and sister. She would not have me as a husband, if there was not another man in the world; and it would take a deal to make me think of her—as my father wishes" (somehow I did not like to say "as a wife"); "but we love each other dearly."

"Well, I am rather surprised at it—not at your loving each other in a brother-and-sister kind of way—but at your finding it so impossible to fall in love with such a beautiful woman."

Woman! beautiful woman! I had thought of Phillis as a comely, but awkward, girl; and I could not banish the pinafore from my mind's eye when I tried to picture her to myself. Now I turned, as Mr. Holdsworth had done, to look at her again out of the window: she had just finished her task, and was standing up, her back to us, holding the basket and the basin in it, high in air, out of Rover's reach, who was giving vent to his delight at the probability of a change of place by glad leaps and barks, and snatches at what he imagined to be a withheld prize. At length she grew tired of their mutual play, and, with a feint of striking him, and a "Down, Rover! do hush!" she looked towards the window where we were standing, as if to reassure herself that no one had been disturbed by the noise; and seeing us, she coloured all over, and hurried away, with Rover still curving in sinuous lines about her as she walked.

"I should like to have sketched her," said Mr. Holdsworth, as he turned away. He went back to his chair, and rested in silence for a minute or two. Then he was up again.

"I would give a good deal for a book," said he. "It would keep me quiet." He began to look round; there were a few volumes at one end of the shovel-board.

" Fifth volume of Matthew Henry's *Commentary*," said he, reading their titles aloud. " *Housewife's Complete Manual; Berridge on Prayer; L'Inferno*—Dante!" in great surprise. " Why, who reads this? "

" I told you Phillis read it. Don't you remember? She knows Latin and Greek, too."

" To be sure! I remember! But somehow I never put two and two together. That quiet girl, full of household work, is the wonderful scholar, then, that put you to rout with her questions, when you first began to come here! To be sure, ' Cousin Phillis! ' What's here—a paper with the hard obsolete words written out. I wonder what sort of a dictionary she has got. Baretti won't tell her all these words. Stay! I have got a pencil here. I'll write down the most accepted meanings, and save her a little trouble."

So he took her book and the paper back to the little round table, and employed himself in writing explanations and definitions of the words which had troubled her. I was not sure if he was not taking a liberty; it did not quite please me, and yet I did not know why. He had only just done, and replaced the paper in the book, and put the latter back in its place, when I heard the sound of wheels stopping in the lane; and, looking out, I saw cousin Holman getting out of a neighbour's gig, making her little curtsey of acknowledgment, and then coming towards the house. I went out to meet her.

" Oh, Paul! " said she, " I am so sorry I was kept; and then Thomas Dobson said, if I would wait a quarter of an hour, he would—— But where's your friend Mr. Holdsworth? I hope he is come? "

Just then he came out and, with his pleasant cordial manner, took her hand, and thanked her for asking him to come out here to get strong.

" I'm sure I am very glad to see you, sir. It was the minister's thought. I took it into my head you would be dull in our quiet house, for Paul says you've been such a great traveller; but the minister said that dulness would perhaps suit you while you were but ailing, and that I was to ask Paul to be here as much as he could. I hope you'll find yourself happy with us, I'm sure, sir. Has Phillis given you something to eat and drink, I wonder? there's a deal in eating a little often, if one has to get strong after an illness." And then she began to question him as to the details of his indisposition, in her simple, motherly way. He seemed at once to understand her, and to enter into friendly relations with her. It was not quite the same in the evening, when the minister came home. Men have always a little natural antipathy to get over when they first meet as strangers. But, in this case, each was disposed to make an effort to like the other; only, each was to each a specimen of an unknown class. I had to leave the Hope Farm on Sunday afternoon, as I had Mr. Holdsworth's work as well as my own to look to in Eltham; and I was not at all sure how things would go on during the week that Holdsworth was to remain on his visit; I had been once or twice in hot water already, at the near clash of opinions between the minister and my much-vaunted friend. On the Wednesday I received a short note from Holdsworth; he was going to stay on, and return with me on the following Sunday, and he wanted me to send him a certain list of books, his theodolite, and other surveying instruments, all of which could easily be conveyed down the line to Heathbridge. I went to his lodgings and picked out the books. Italian, Latin, trigonometry; a pretty considerable parcel they made, besides the implements. I began to be curious as to the general progress of affairs at Hope Farm; but I could not go over till the Saturday. At Heathbridge I found Holdsworth, come to meet me. He was looking quite a different man to what I had left him: embrowned; sparkles in his eyes, so languid before. I told him how much stronger he looked.

"Yes!" said he. "I am fidging-fain to be at work again. Last week, I dreaded the thoughts of my employment; now I am full of desire to begin. This week in the country has done wonders for me."

"You have enjoyed yourself, then?"

"Oh! it has been perfect in its way. Such a thorough country-life! and yet removed from the dulness which I always used to fancy accompanied country-life, by the extraordinary intelligence of the minister. I have fallen into calling him 'the minister,' like every one else."

"You get on with him, then?" said I. "I was a little afraid."

"I was on the verge of displeasing him once or twice, I fear, with random assertions and exaggerated expressions, such as one always uses with other people, and thinks nothing of; but I tried to check myself when I saw how it shocked the good man; and really it is very wholesome exercise, this trying to make one's words represent one's thoughts, instead of merely looking to their effect on others."

" Then you are quite friends now? " I asked.

" Yes, thoroughly; at any rate as far as I go. I never met a man with such a desire for knowledge. In information, as far as it can be gained from books, he far exceeds me on most subjects; but then I have travelled and seen—— Were not you surprised at the list of things I sent for? "

" Yes; I thought it did not promise much rest."

" Oh, some of the books were for the minister, and some for his daughter. (I call her ' Phillis ' to myself, but I use a round-about way of speaking of her to others. I don't like to seem familiar, and yet ' Miss Holman ' is a term I have never heard used.")

" I thought the Italian books were for her."

" Yes! Fancy her trying at Dante for her first book in Italian! I had a capital novel by Manzoni, *I Promessi Sposi*, just the thing for a beginner! and, if she must still puzzle out Dante, my dictionary is far better than hers."

" Then she found out you had written those definitions on her list of words? "

" Oh! yes "—with a smile of amusement and pleasure. He was going to tell me what had taken place, but checked himself.

" But I don't think the minister will like your having given her a novel to read? "

" Pooh! What can be more harmless? Why make a bugbear of a word! It is as pretty and innocent a tale as can be met with. You don't suppose they take Virgil for gospel? "

By this time we were at the farm. I think Phillis gave me a warmer welcome than usual, and cousin Holman was kindness itself. Yet somehow I felt as if I had lost my place, and that Holdsworth had taken it. He knew all the ways of the house; he was full of little filial attentions to cousin Holman; he treated Phillis with the affectionate condescension of an elder brother; not a bit more; not in any way different. He questioned me about the progress of affairs in Eltham with eager interest.

" Ah! " said cousin Holman, " you'll be spending a different kind of time next week to what you have done this! I can see how busy you'll make yourself! But, if you don't take care, you'll be ill again, and have to come back to our quiet ways of going on."

" Do you suppose I shall need to be ill to wish to come back here? " he answered warmly. " I am only afraid you have treated me so kindly that I shall always be turning up on your hands."

"That's right," she replied. "Only don't go and make yourself ill by over-work. I hope you'll go on with a cup of new milk every morning, for I am sure that is the best medicine; and put a teaspoonful of rum in it, if you like; many a one speaks highly of that, only we had no rum in the house."

I brought with me an atmosphere of active life which I think he had begun to miss; and it was natural that he should seek my company, after his week of retirement. Once, I saw Phillis looking at us, as we talked together, with a kind of wistful curiosity; but, as soon as she caught my eye, she turned away, blushing deeply.

That evening I had a little talk with the minister. I strolled along the Hornby road to meet him; for Holdsworth was giving Phillis an Italian lesson, and cousin Holman had fallen asleep over her work.

Somehow, and not unwillingly on my part, our talk fell on the friend whom I had introduced to the Hope Farm.

"Yes! I like him!" said the minister, weighing his words a little as he spoke. "I like him. I hope I am justified in doing it; but he takes hold of me, as it were, and I have almost been afraid lest he carries me away, in spite of my judgment."

"He is a good fellow; indeed he is," said I. "My father thinks well of him; and I have seen a deal of him. I would not have had him come here if I did not know that you would approve of him."

"Yes" (once more hesitating), "I like him, and I think he is an upright man; there is a want of seriousness in his talk at times, but, at the same time, it is wonderful to listen to him! He makes Horace and Virgil living, instead of dead, by the stories he tells me of his sojourn in the very countries where they lived, and where to this day, he says—— But it is like dram-drinking. I listen to him till I forget my duties and am carried off my feet. Last Sabbath-evening he led us away into talk on profane subjects ill-befitting the day."

By this time we were at the house, and our conversation stopped. But before the day was out, I saw the unconscious hold that my friend had got over all the family. And no wonder: he had seen so much and done so much, as compared to them, and he told about it all so easily and naturally, and yet as I never heard any one else do; and his ready pencil was out in an instant to draw on scraps of paper all sorts of illustrations— modes of drawing up water in Northern Italy, wine-carts, buffaloes, stone-pines, I know not what. After we had all looked at these drawings, Phillis gathered them together, and took them.

It is many years since I have seen thee, Edward Holdsworth, but thou wast a delightful fellow! Ay, and a good one too; though much sorrow was caused by thee!

PART III

JUST after this I went home for a week's holiday. Everything was prospering there; my father's new partnership gave evident satisfaction to both parties. There was no display of increased wealth in our modest household; but my mother had a few extra comforts provided for her by her husband. I made acquaintance with Mr. and Mrs. Ellison, and first saw pretty Margaret Ellison, who is now my wife. When I returned to Eltham I found that a step was decided upon which had been in contemplation for some time: that Holdsworth and I should remove our quarters to Hornby; our daily presence, and as much of our time as possible, being required for the completion of the line at that end.

Of course this led to greater facility of intercourse with the Hope Farm people. We could easily walk out there, after our day's work was done, and spend a balmy evening hour or two, and yet return before the summer's twilight had quite faded away. Many a time, indeed, we would fain have stayed longer —the open air, the fresh and pleasant country, made so agreeable a contrast to the close, hot town lodgings which I shared with Mr. Holdsworth; but early hours, both at eve and morn, were an imperative necessity with the minister, and he made no scruple at turning either or both of us out of the house directly after evening prayer, or " exercise," as he called it. The remembrance of many a happy day, and of several little scenes, comes back upon me as I think of that summer. They rise like pictures to my memory, and in this way I can date their succession; for I know that corn-harvest must have come after hay-making, apple-gathering after corn-harvest.

The removal to Hornby took up some time, during which we had neither of us any leisure to go out to the Hope Farm. Mr. Holdsworth had been out there once during my absence at home. One sultry evening, when work was done, he proposed our walking out and paying the Holmans a visit. It so happened that I had omitted to write my usual weekly letter home in our press of business, and I wished to finish that before going out. Then he said that he would go, and that I could follow him if I liked. This I did in about an hour; the weather was so oppressive, I remember, that I took off my coat as I walked and hung it over my arm. All the doors and windows at the farm were open, when I arrived there, and every tiny leaf on the trees was still. The silence of the place was profound; at first I thought it was entirely deserted; but just as I drew near the door I heard a weak, sweet voice begin to sing; it was cousin Holman, all by herself in the house-place, piping up a hymn, as she knitted away in the clouded light. She gave me a kindly welcome, and poured out all the small domestic news of the fortnight past upon me; and, in return, I told her about my own people and my visit at home.

"Where were the rest?" at length I asked.

Betty and the men were in the field helping with the last load of hay, for the minister said there would be rain before the morning. Yes, and the minister himself, and Phillis, and Mr. Holdsworth, were all there helping. She thought that she herself could have done something; but perhaps she was the least fit for hay-making of any one; and somebody must stay at home and take care of the house, there were so many tramps about; if I had not had something to do with the railroad, she would have called them navvies. I asked her if she minded being left alone, as I should like to go and help; and, having her full and glad permission to leave her alone, I went off, following her directions: through the farm-yard, past the cattle-pond, into the ash-field, beyond into the higher field, with two holly-bushes in the middle. I arrived there: there was Betty with all the farming men, and a cleared field, and a heavily-laden cart; one man at the top of the great pile ready to catch the fragrant hay which the others threw up to him with their pitchforks; a little heap of cast-off clothes in a corner of the field (for the heat, even at seven o'clock, was insufferable), a few cans and baskets, and Rover lying by them, panting, and keeping watch. Plenty of loud, hearty, cheerful talking; but no minister, no Phillis, no Mr. Holdsworth. Betty saw me first, and understanding who it was that I was in search of, she came towards me.

"They're out yonder—a-gait wi' them things o' Measter Holdsworth's."

So "out yonder" I went; out on to a broad upland common,

full of red sand-banks, and sweeps and hollows; bordered by dark firs, purple in the coming shadows, but near at hand all ablaze with flowering gorse, or, as we call it in the south, furze-bushes, which, seen against the belt of distant trees, appeared brilliantly golden. On this heath, a little way from the field-gate, I saw the three. I counted their heads, joined together in an eager group over Holdsworth's theodolite. He was teaching the minister the practical art of surveying and taking a level. I was wanted to assist, and was quickly set to work to hold the chain. Phillis was as intent as her father; she had hardly time to greet me, so desirous was she to hear some answer to her father's question.

So we went on, the dark clouds still gathering, for perhaps five minutes after my arrival. Then came the blinding lightning and the rumble and quick-following rattling peal of thunder, right over our heads. It came sooner than I expected, sooner than they had looked for: the rain delayed not; it came pouring down; and what were we to do for shelter? Phillis had nothing on but her indoor things—no bonnet, no shawl. Quick as the darting lightning around us, Holdsworth took off his coat and wrapped it round her neck and shoulders, and almost without a word hurried us all into such poor shelter as one of the over-hanging sand-banks could give. There we were, cowered down, close together, Phillis innermost, almost too tight-packed to free her arms enough to divest herself of the coat, which she, in her turn, tried to put lightly over Holdsworth's shoulders. In doing so she touched his shirt.

"Oh, how wet you are!" she cried, in pitying dismay; "and you've hardly got over your fever! Oh, Mr. Holdsworth, I am so sorry!" He turned his head a little, smiling at her.

"If I do catch cold it is all my fault for having deluded you into staying out here!" But she only murmured again, "I am so sorry."

The minister spoke now. "It is a regular down-pour. Please God that the hay is saved! But there is no likelihood of its ceasing, and I had better go home at once, and send you all some wraps; umbrellas will not be safe with yonder thunder and lightning."

Both Holdsworth and I offered to go instead of him; but he was resolved, although perhaps it would have been wiser if Holdsworth, wet as he already was, had kept himself in exercise. As he moved off, Phillis crept out, and could see on to the storm-swept heath. Part of Holdsworth's apparatus still remained exposed to all the rain. Before we could have any warning, she had rushed out of the shelter and collected the various things, and brought them back in triumph to where we crouched. Holdsworth had stood up, uncertain whether to go to her assistance or not. She came running back, her long lovely hair floating and dripping, her eyes glad and bright, and her colour freshened to a glow of health by the exercise and the rain.

" Now, Miss Holman, that's what I call wilful," said Holdsworth, as she gave them to him. " No, I won't thank you " (his looks were thanking her all the time). " My little bit of dampness annoyed you, because you thought I had got wet in your service; so you were determined to make me as uncomfortable as you were yourself. It was an unchristian piece of revenge ! "

His tone of badinage (as the French call it) would have been palpable enough to any one accustomed to the world; but Phillis was not, and it distressed or rather bewildered her. " Unchristian " had to her a very serious meaning; it was not a word to be used lightly; and though she did not exactly understand what wrong it was that she was accused of doing, she was evidently desirous to throw off the imputation. At first her earnestness to disclaim unkind motives amused Holdsworth; while his light continuance of the joke perplexed her still more; but at last he said something gravely, and in too low a tone for me to hear, which made her all at once become silent, and called out her blushes. After a while the minister came back, a moving mass of shawls, cloaks, and umbrellas. Phillis kept very close to her father's side on our return to the farm. She appeared to me to be shrinking away from Holdsworth, while he had not the slightest variation in his manner from what it usually was in his graver moods; kind, protecting, and thoughtful towards her. Of course, there was a great commotion about our wet clothes; but I name the little events of that evening now, because I wondered at the time what he had said in that low voice to silence Phillis so effectually, and because, in thinking of their intercourse by the light of future events, that evening stands out with some prominence.

I have said that, after our removal to Hornby, our communications with the farm became almost of daily occurrence. Cousin Holman and I were the two who had least to do with this intimacy. After Mr. Holdsworth regained his health, he too often talked above her head in intellectual matters, and too often in his light bantering tone for her to feel quite at her ease with him. I really believe that he adopted this latter tone in speaking to her because he did not know what to talk about to a purely motherly woman, whose intellect had never been cultivated, and whose loving heart was entirely occupied with her husband, her child, her household affairs, and, perhaps, a little with the concerns of the members of her husband's congregation, because they, in a way, belonged to her husband. I had noticed before that she had fleeting shadows of jealousy even of Phillis, when her daughter and her husband appeared to have strong interests and sympathies in things which were quite beyond her comprehension. I had noticed it in my first acquaintance with them, I say, and had admired the delicate tact which made the minister, on such occasions, bring the conversation back to such subjects as those on which his wife, with her practical experience of everyday life, was an authority; while Phillis, devoted to her father, unconsciously followed his lead, totally unaware, in her filial reverence, of his motive for doing so.

To return to Holdsworth. The minister had at more than one time spoken of him to me with slight distrust, principally occasioned by the suspicion that his careless words were not always those of soberness and truth. But it was more as a protest against the fascination which the younger man evidently exercised over the elder one—more, as it were, to strengthen himself against yielding to this fascination—that the minister spoke out to me about this failing of Holdsworth's, as it appeared to him. In return, Holdsworth was subdued by the minister's uprightness and goodness, and delighted with his clear intellect —his strong healthy craving after further knowledge. I never met two men who took more thorough pleasure and relish in each other's society. To Phillis his relation continued that of an elder brother: he directed her studies into new paths; he patiently drew out the expression of many of her thoughts, and perplexities, and unformed theories, scarcely ever now falling into the vein of banter which she was so slow to understand.

One day—harvest-time—he had been drawing on a loose piece of paper—sketching ears of corn, sketching carts drawn by bullocks and laden with grapes—all the time talking with Phillis and me, cousin Holman putting in her not pertinent remarks, when suddenly he said to Phillis—

"Keep your head still; I see a sketch! I have often tried to draw your head from memory, and failed; but I think I can do it now. If I succeed, I will give it to your mother. You would like a portrait of your daughter as Ceres, would you not, ma'am?"

"I should like a picture of her; yes, very much, thank you, Mr. Holdsworth; but if you put that straw in her hair" (he was holding some wheat ears above her passive head, looking at the effect with an artistic eye), "you'll ruffle her hair. Phillis, my dear, if you're to have your picture taken, go upstairs, and brush your hair smooth."

"Not on any account. I beg your pardon; but I want hair loosely-flowing."

He began to draw, looking intently at Phillis; I could see this stare of his discomposed her—her colour came and went, her breath quickened with the consciousness of his regard; at last, when he said, "Please look at me for a minute or two, I want to get in the eyes," she looked up at him, quivered, and suddenly got up and left the room. He did not say a word, but went on with some other part of the drawing; his silence was unnatural, and his dark cheek blanched a little. Cousin Holman looked up from her work, and put her spectacles down.

"What's the matter? Where is she gone?"

Holdsworth never uttered a word, but went on drawing. I felt obliged to say something; it was stupid enough, but stupidity was better than silence just then.

"I'll go and call her," said I. So I went into the hall, and to the bottom of the stairs; but just as I was going to call Phillis, she came down swiftly with her bonnet on, and saying, "I'm going to father in the five-acre," passed out by the open "rector," right in front of the house-place windows, and out at the little white side-gate. She had been seen by her mother and Holdsworth as she passed; so there was no need for explanation; only, cousin Holman and I had a long discussion as to whether she could have found the room too hot, or what had occasioned her sudden departure. Holdsworth was very quiet during all the rest of that day; nor did he resume the portrait-taking by his own desire, only, at my cousin Holman's request, the next time that he came; and then he said he should not require any more formal sittings for only such a slight sketch as he felt himself capable of making. Phillis was just the same as ever, the next time I saw her after her abrupt passing me in the hall. She never gave any explanation of her rush out of the room.

So all things went on, at least as far as my observation

reached at the time, or memory can recall now, till the great apple-gathering of the year. The nights were frosty, the mornings and evenings were misty, but at mid-day all was sunny and bright; and it was one mid-day that, both of us being on the line near Heathbridge, and knowing that they were gathering apples at the farm, we resolved to spend the men's dinner-hour in going over there. We found the great clothes-baskets full of apples, scenting the house and stopping up the way, and an universal air of merry contentment with this the final produce of the year. The yellow leaves hung on the trees, ready to flutter down at the slightest puff of air; the great bushes of Michaelmas daisies in the kitchen-garden were making their last show of flowers. We must needs taste the fruit off the different trees, and pass our judgment as to their flavour; and we went away with our pockets stuffed with those that we liked best. As we had passed to the orchard, Holdsworth had admired and spoken about some flower which we saw; it so happened he had never seen this old-fashioned kind since the days of his boyhood. I do not know whether he had thought anything more about this chance speech of his, but I know I had not—when Phillis, who had been missing just at the last moment of our hurried visit, re-appeared with a little nosegay of this same flower, which she was tying up with a blade of grass. She offered it to Holdsworth as he stood with her father on the point of departure. I saw their faces. I saw for the first time an unmistakable look of love in his black eyes; it was more than gratitude for the little attention; it was tender and beseeching—passionate. She shrank from it in confusion, her glance fell on me; and, partly to hide her emotion, partly out of real kindness at what might appear ungracious neglect of an older friend, she flew off to gather me a few late-blooming China roses. But it was the first time she had ever done anything of the kind for me.

We had to walk fast to be back on the line before the men's return; so we spoke but little to each other, and of course the afternoon was too much occupied for us to have any talk. In the evening we went back to our joint lodgings in Hornby. There, on the table, lay a letter for Holdsworth, which had been forwarded to him from Eltham. As our tea was ready, and I had had nothing to eat since morning, I fell to directly, without paying much attention to my companion as he opened and read his letter. He was very silent for a few minutes; at length he said—

" Old fellow! I'm going to leave you."

" Leave me!" said I.   " How?   When?"

" This letter ought to have come to hand sooner.   It is from Greathed the engineer " (Greathed was well known in those days; he is dead now, and his name half-forgotten); " he wants to see me about some business; in fact, I may as well tell you, Paul, this letter contains a very advantageous proposal for me to go out to Canada, and superintend the making of a line there."

I was in utter dismay.

" But what will our Company say to that? "

" Oh, Greathed has the superintendence of this line, you know, and he is going to be engineer-in-chief to this Canadian line: many of the shareholders in this Company are going in for the other; so I fancy they will make no difficulty in following Greathed's lead.   He says he has a young man ready to put in my place."

" I hate him," said I.

" Thank you," said Holdsworth, laughing.

" But you must not," he resumed; " for this is a very good thing for me; and, of course, if no one can be found to take my inferior work, I can't be spared to take the superior.   I only wish I had received this letter a day sooner.   Every hour is of consequence, for Greathed says they are threatening a rival line.   Do you know, Paul, I almost fancy I must go up to-night?   I can take an engine back to Eltham, and catch the night train.   I should not like Greathed to think me lukewarm."

" But you'll come back? " I asked, distressed at the thought of this sudden parting.

" Oh, yes!   At least I hope so.   They may want me to go out by the next steamer; that will be on Saturday."   He began to eat and drink standing, but I think he was quite unconscious of the nature of either his food or his drink.

" I will go to-night.   Activity and readiness go a long way in our profession.   Remember that, my boy!   I hope I shall come back; but, if I don't, be sure and recollect all the words of wisdom that have fallen from my lips.   Now, where's the portmanteau?   If I can gain half-an-hour for a gathering up of my things in Eltham, so much the better.   I'm clear of debt, anyhow; and what I owe for my lodgings you can pay for me out of my quarter's salary, due November 4th."

" Then you don't think you will come back? " I said despondingly.

" I will come back some time, never fear," said he kindly.

"I may be back in a couple of days, having been found incompetent for the Canadian work; or I may not be wanted to go out so soon as I now anticipate. Anyhow, you don't suppose I am going to forget you, Paul—this work out there ought not to take me above two years, and, perhaps, after that, we may be employed together again."

Perhaps! I had very little hope. The same kind of happy days never return. However, I did all I could in helping him: clothes, papers, books, instruments; how we pushed and struggled—how I stuffed! All was done in a much shorter time than we had calculated upon, when I had run down to the sheds to order the engine. I was going to drive him to Eltham. We sat ready for a summons. Holdsworth took up the little nosegay he had brought away from the Hope Farm, and had laid on the mantelpiece on first coming into the room. He smelt at it, and caressed it with his lips.

"What grieves me is that I did not know—that I have not said good-bye to—to them."

He spoke in a grave tone, the shadow of the coming separation falling upon him at last.

"I will tell them," said I. "I am sure they will be very sorry." Then we were silent.

"I never liked any family so much."

"I knew you would like them."

"How one's thoughts change—this morning I was full of a hope, Paul." He paused, and then he said—

"You put that sketch in carefully?"

"That outline of a head?" asked I. But I knew he meant an abortive sketch of Phillis, which had not been successful enough for him to complete it with shading or colouring.

"Yes. What a sweet innocent face it is! and yet so— Oh, dear!"

He sighed and got up, his hands in his pockets, to walk up and down the room in evident disturbance of mind. He suddenly stopped opposite to me.

"You'll tell them how it all was. Be sure and tell the good minister that I was so sorry not to wish him good-bye, and to thank him and his wife for all their kindness. As for Phillis—please God, in two years I'll be back and tell her myself all in my heart."

"You love Phillis, then?" said I.

"Love her!—Yes, that I do. Who could help it, seeing her as I have done? Her character as unusual and rare as her beauty! God bless her! God keep her in her high tranquillity, her pure innocence!—Two years! It is a long time. But she lives in such seclusion, almost like the sleeping beauty, Paul,—" (he was smiling now, though a minute before I had thought him on the verge of tears) "—but I shall come back like a prince from Canada, and waken her to my love. I can't help hoping that it won't be difficult; eh, Paul?"

This touch of coxcombry displeased me a little, and I made no answer. He went on, half apologetically—

"You see, the salary they offer me is large; and, besides that, this experience will give me a name which will entitle me to expect a still larger in any future undertaking."

"That won't influence Phillis."

"No! but it will make me more eligible in the eyes of her father and mother."

I made no answer.

"You give me your best wishes, Paul," said he, almost pleading. "You would like me for a cousin?"

I heard the scream and whistle of the engine, ready down at the sheds.

"Ay, that I should," I replied, suddenly softened towards my friend, now that he was going away. "I wish you were to be married to-morrow, and I were to be best man."

"Thank you, lad. Now for this cursed portmanteau (how the minister would be shocked!)—but it is heavy!" and off we sped into the darkness.

He only just caught the night train at Eltham; and I slept, desolately enough, at my old lodgings at Miss Dawson's, for that night. Of course, the next few days I was busier than ever, doing both his work and my own. Then came a letter from him, very short and affectionate. He was going out in the Saturday steamer, as he had more than half expected; and by the following Monday the man who was to succeed him would be down at Eltham. There was a P.S., with only these words:—

"My nosegay goes with me to Canada; but I do not need it to remind me of Hope Farm."

Saturday came; but it was very late before I could go out to the farm. It was a frosty night; the stars shone clear above me, and the road was crisping beneath my feet. They must have heard my footsteps, before I got up to the house. They were sitting at their usual employments in the house-place, when I went in. Phillis's eyes went beyond me in their look of welcome, and then fell in quiet disappointment on her work.

" And where's Mr. Holdsworth? " asked cousin Holman, in a minute or two. " I hope his cold is not worse—I did not like his short cough."

I laughed awkwardly; for I felt that I was the bearer of unpleasant news.

" His cold had need be better—for he's gone—gone away to Canada! "

I purposely looked away from Phillis, as I thus abruptly told my news.

" To Canada! " said the minister.

" Gone away! " said his wife.

But no word from Phillis.

" Yes! " said I. " He found a letter at Hornby, when we got home the other night—when we got home from here; he ought to have got it sooner; he was ordered to go up to London directly, and to see some people about a new line in Canada; and he's gone to lay it down; he has sailed to-day. He was sadly grieved not to have time to come out and wish you all good-bye; but he started for London within two hours after he got that letter. He bade me thank you most gratefully for all your kindnesses; he was very sorry not to come here once again."

Phillis got up and left the room with noiseless steps.

" I am very sorry," said the minister.

" I am sure so am I! " said cousin Holman. " I was real fond of that lad, ever since I nursed him last June after that bad fever."

The minister went on asking me questions respecting Holdsworth's future plans, and brought out a large old-fashioned atlas, that he might find out the exact places between which the new railroad was to run. Then supper was ready; it was always on the table as soon as the clock on the stairs struck eight, and down came Phillis—her face white and set, her dry eyes looking defiance at me; for I am afraid I hurt her maidenly pride by my glance of sympathetic interest as she entered the room. Never a word did she say—never a question did she ask about the absent friend; yet she forced herself to talk.

And so it was all the next day. She was as pale as could be, like one who has received some shock; but she would not let me talk to her, and she tried hard to behave as usual. Two or three times I repeated, in public, the various affectionate messages to the family with which I was charged by Holdsworth; but she took no more notice of them than if my words had been empty air. And in this mood I left her on the Sabbath evening.

My new master was not half so indulgent as my old one. He kept up strict discipline as to hours; so that it was some time before I could again go out, even to pay a call at the Hope Farm.

It was a cold, misty evening in November. The air, even indoors, seemed full of haze; yet there was a great log burning on the hearth, which ought to have made the room cheerful. Cousin Holman and Phillis were sitting at the little round table before the fire, working away in silence. The minister had his books out on the dresser, seemingly deep in study, by the light of his solitary candle; perhaps the fear of disturbing him made the unusual stillness of the room. But a welcome was ready for me from all; not noisy, not demonstrative—that it never was; my damp wrappers were taken off, the next meal was hastened, and a chair placed for me on one side the fire, so that I pretty much commanded a view of the room. My eye caught on Phillis, looking so pale and weary, and with a sort of aching tone (if I may call it so) in her voice. She was doing all the accustomed things—fulfilling small household duties, but somehow differently—I can't tell you how, for she was just as deft and quick in her movements, only the light spring was gone out of them. Cousin Holman began to question me; even the minister put aside his books, and came and stood on the opposite side of the fireplace, to hear what waft of intelligence I brought. I had first to tell them why I had not been to see them for so long — more than five weeks. The answer was simple enough: business and the necessity of attending strictly to the orders of a new superintendent, who had not yet learned trust, much less indulgence. The minister nodded his approval of my conduct, and said—

"Right, Paul! 'Servants, obey in all things your masters according to the flesh.' I have had my fears lest you had too much licence under Edward Holdsworth."

"Ah," said cousin Holman, "poor Mr. Holdsworth! he'll be on the salt seas by this time!"

"No, indeed," said I; "he's landed. I have had a letter from him from Halifax."

Immediately a shower of questions fell thick upon me. "When?" "How?" "What was he doing?" "How did he like it?" "What sort of a voyage?" etc.

"Many is the time we thought of him when the wind was

blowing so hard; the old quince-tree is blown down, Paul, that on the right hand of the great pear-tree; it was blown down last Monday week, and it was that night that I asked the minister to pray in an especial manner for all them that went down in ships upon the great deep; and he said then, that Mr. Holdsworth might be already landed; but I said, even if the prayer did not fit him, it was sure to be fitting somebody out at sea, who would need the Lord's care. Both Phillis and I thought he would be a month on the seas."

Phillis began to speak; but her voice did not come rightly at first. It was a little higher pitched than usual, when she said—

"We thought he would be a month, if he went in a sailing-vessel, or perhaps longer. I suppose he went in a steamer?"

"Old Obadiah Grimshaw was more than six weeks in getting to America," observed cousin Holman.

"I presume he cannot as yet tell how he likes his new work?" asked the minister.

"No! he is but just landed; it is but one page long. I'll read it to you, shall I?—

"DEAR PAUL,—We are safe on shore, after a rough passage. Thought you would like to hear this; but homeward-bound steamer is making signals for letters. Will write again soon. It seems a year since I left Hornby. Longer, since I was at the farm. I have got my nosegay safe. Remember me to the Holmans.—Yours, E. H."

"That's not much, certainly," said the minister. "But it's a comfort to know he's on land these blowy nights."

Phillis said nothing. She kept her head bent down over her work; but I don't think she put a stitch in, while I was reading the letter. I wondered if she understood what nosegay was meant; but I could not tell. When next she lifted up her face, there were two spots of brilliant colour on the cheeks that had been so pale before. After I had spent an hour or two there, I was bound to return back to Hornby. I told them, I did not know when I could come again, as we—by which I meant the company—had undertaken the Hensleydale line; that branch for which poor Holdsworth was surveying, when he caught his fever.

"But you'll have a holiday at Christmas," said my cousin. "Surely, they'll not be such heathens as to work you then?"

"Perhaps the lad will be going home," said the minister, as

if to mitigate his wife's urgency; but, for all that, I believe he wanted me to come. Phillis fixed her eyes on me with a wistful expression, hard to resist. But, indeed, I had no thought of resisting. Under my new master I had no hope of a holiday long enough to enable me to go to Birmingham and see my parents with any comfort; and nothing could be pleasanter to me than to find myself at home at my cousin's for a day or two, then. So it was fixed that we were to meet in Hornby Chapel on Christmas-Day, and that I was to accompany them home after service, and, if possible, to stay over the next day.

I was not able to get to chapel till late on the appointed day; and so I took a seat near the door in considerable shame, although it really was not my fault. When the service was ended, I went and stood in the porch, to await the coming-out of my cousins. Some worthy people belonging to the congregation clustered into a group, just where I stood, and exchanged the good wishes of the season. It had just begun to snow; and this occasioned a little delay, and they fell into further conversation. I was not attending to what was not meant for me to hear, till I caught the name of Phillis Holman. And then I listened; where was the harm?

" I never saw any one so changed! "

" I asked Mrs. Holman," quoth another, " ' Is Phillis well? ' and she just said she had been having a cold which had pulled her down; she did not seem to think anything of it."

" They had best take care of her," said one of the oldest of the good ladies; " Phillis comes of a family as is not long-lived. Her mother's sister, Lydia Green, her own aunt as was, died of a decline just when she was about this lass's age."

This ill-omened talk was broken in upon by the coming-out of the minister, his wife and daughter, and the consequent interchange of Christmas compliments. I had had a shock, and felt heavy-hearted and anxious, and hardly up to making the appropriate replies to the kind greetings of my relations. I looked askance at Phillis. She had certainly grown taller and slighter, and was thinner; but there was a flush of colour on her face which deceived me for a time, and made me think she was looking as well as ever. I only saw her paleness after we had returned to the farm, and she had subsided into silence and quiet. Her grey eyes looked hollow and sad; her complexion was of a dead white. But she went about just as usual; at least, just as she had done the last time I was there, and seemed to have no ailment; and I was inclined to think that my cousin was right, when she had answered the inquiries of the good-natured gossips, and told them that Phillis was suffering from the consequences of a bad cold, nothing more.

I have said that I was to stay over the next day; a great deal of snow had come down, but not all, they said, though the ground was covered deep with the white fall. The minister was anxiously housing his cattle, and preparing all things for a long continuance of the same kind of weather. The men were chopping wood, sending wheat to the mill to be ground before the road should become impassable for a cart and horse. My cousin and Phillis had gone upstairs to the apple-room, to cover up the fruit from the frost. I had been out the greater part of the morning, and came in about an hour before dinner. To my surprise, knowing how she had planned to be engaged, I found Phillis sitting at the dresser, resting her head on her two hands and reading, or seeming to read. She did not look up when I came in, but murmured something about her mother having sent her down out of the cold. It flashed across me that she was crying, but I put it down to some little spurt of temper; I might have known better than to suspect the gentle, serene Phillis of crossness, poor girl; I stooped down, and began to stir and build up the fire, which appeared to have been neglected. While my head was down I heard a noise which made me pause and listen—a sob, an unmistakable, irrepressible sob. I started up.

"Phillis!" I cried, going towards her, with my hand out, to take hers for sympathy with her sorrow, whatever it was. But she was too quick for me; she held her hand out of my grasp, for fear of my detaining her; as she quickly passed out of the house, she said—

"Don't, Paul! I cannot bear it!" and passed me, still sobbing, and went out into the keen, open air.

I stood still and wondered. What could have come to Phillis? The most perfect harmony prevailed in the family; and Phillis especially, good and gentle as she was, was so beloved that, if they had found out that her finger ached, it would have cast a shadow over their hearts. Had I done anything to vex her? No: she was crying before I came in. I went to look at her book—one of those unintelligible Italian books. I could make neither head nor tail of it. I saw some pencil-notes on the margin, in Holdsworth's handwriting.

Could that be it? Could that be the cause of her white looks, her weary eyes, her wasted figure, her struggling sobs? This idea came upon me like a flash of lightning on a dark night, making all things so clear we cannot forget them afterwards, when the gloomy obscurity returns. I was still standing with the book in my hand, when I heard cousin Holman's footsteps on the stairs; and, as I did not wish to speak to her just then, I followed Phillis's example, and rushed out of the house. The snow was lying on the ground; I could track her feet by the marks they had made; I could see where Rover had joined her. I followed on, till I came to a great stack of wood in the orchard —it was built up against the back-wall of the outbuildings— and I recollected then how Phillis had told me, that first day when we strolled about together, that underneath this stack had been her hermitage, her sanctuary, when she was a child; how she used to bring her book to study there, or her work, when she was not wanted in the house; and she had now evidently gone back to this quiet retreat of her childhood, forgetful of the clue given me by her footmarks on the new-fallen snow. The stack was built up very high; but through the interstices of the sticks I could see her figure, although I did not all at once perceive how I could get to her. She was sitting on a log of wood, Rover by her. She had laid her cheek on Rover's head, and had her arm round his neck, partly for a pillow, partly from an instinctive craving for warmth on that bitter cold day. She was making a low moan, like an animal in pain, or perhaps more like the sobbing of the wind. Rover, highly flattered by her caress, and also, perhaps, touched by sympathy, was flapping his heavy tail against the ground, but not otherwise moving a hair, until he heard my approach with his quick erect ears. Then, with a short, abrupt bark of distrust, he sprang up, as if to leave his mistress. Both he and I were immovably still for a moment. I was not sure if what I longed to do was wise; and yet I could not bear to see the sweet serenity of my dear cousin's life so disturbed by a suffering which I thought I could assuage. But Rover's ears were sharper than my breathing was noiseless: he heard me, and sprang out from under Phillis's restraining hand.

" Oh, Rover, don't you leave me too! " she plained out.

" Phillis! " said I, seeing by Rover's exit that the entrance to where she sat was to be found on the other side of the stack. " Phillis, come out! You have got a cold already; and it is not fit for you to sit there on such a day as this. You know how displeased and anxious it would make them all."

She sighed, but obeyed; stooping a little, she came out, and stood upright, opposite to me in the lonely, leafless orchard. Her face looked so meek and so sad that I felt as if I ought to beg her pardon for my necessarily authoritative words.

"Sometimes I feel the house so close," she said; "and I used to sit under the wood-stack when I was a child. It was very kind of you; but there was no need to come after me. I don't catch cold easily."

"Come with me into this cow-house, Phillis! I have got something to say to you; and I can't stand this cold, if you can."

I think she would have fain run away again; but her fit of energy was all spent. She followed me unwillingly enough—that I could see. The place to which I took her was full of the fragrant breath of the cows, and was a little warmer than the outer air. I put her inside, and stood myself in the doorway, thinking how I could best begin. At last I plunged into it.

"I must see that you don't get cold for more reasons than one; if you are ill, Holdsworth will be so anxious and miserable out there " (by which I meant Canada)—

She shot one penetrating look at me, and then turned her face away, with a slightly impatient movement. If she could have run away then, she would; but I held the means of exit in my own power. "In for a penny, in for a pound," thought I; and I went on rapidly, anyhow.

"He talked so much about you, just before he left—that night after he had been here, you know—and you had given him those flowers." She put her hands up to hide her face, but she was listening now—listening with all her ears.

"He had never spoken much about you before; but the sudden going-away unlocked his heart, and he told me how he loved you, and how he hoped on his return that you might be his wife."

"Don't," said she, almost gasping out the word, which she had tried once or twice before to speak; but her voice had been choked. Now, she put her hand backwards; she had quite turned away from me, and felt for mine. She gave it a soft lingering pressure; and then she put her arms down on the wooden division, and laid her head on it, and cried quiet tears. I did not understand her at once, and feared lest I had mistaken the whole case, and only annoyed her. I went up to her. "Oh, Phillis! I am so sorry—I thought you would, perhaps, have cared to hear it; he did talk so feelingly, as if he did love you so much, and somehow I thought it would give you pleasure."

She lifted up her head and looked at me. Such a look! Her eyes, glittering with tears as they were, expressed an almost heavenly happiness; her tender mouth was curved with rapture —her colour vivid and blushing; but, as if she was afraid her face expressed too much—more than the thankfulness to me she was essaying to speak—she hid it again almost immediately. So it was all right then, and my conjecture was well-founded. I tried to remember something more to tell her of what he had said; but again she stopped me.

" Don't," she said. She still kept her face covered and hidden. In half a minute she added, in a very low voice, " Please, Paul, I think I would rather not hear any more—I don't mean but what I have—but what I am very much obliged —— Only—only, I think I would rather hear the rest from himself when he comes back."

And then she cried a little more, in quite a different way. I did not say any more; I waited for her. By-and-by, she turned towards me—not meeting my eyes, however; and, putting her hand in mine, just as if we were two children, she said—

" We had best go back now—I don't look as if I had been crying, do I? "

" You look as if you had a bad cold," was all the answer I made.

" Oh! but I am—I am quite well, only cold; and a good run will warm me. Come along, Paul."

So we ran, hand in hand, till, just as we were on the threshold of the house, she stopped—

" Paul, please, we won't speak about *that* again."

PART IV

WHEN I went over on Easter-Day, I heard the chapel-gossips complimenting cousin Holman on her daughter's blooming looks, quite forgetful of their sinister prophecies three months before. And I looked at Phillis, and did not wonder at their words. I had not seen her since the day after Christmas-Day. I had left the Hope Farm only a few hours after I had told her the news which had quickened her heart into renewed life and vigour. The remembrance of our conversation in the cowhouse was vividly in my mind, as I looked at her when her bright healthy appearance was remarked upon. As her eyes met mine, our mutual recollections flashed intelligence from one to the other. She turned away, her colour heightening as she did so. She seemed to be shy of me for the first few hours after our meeting, and I felt rather vexed with her for her conscious avoidance of me after my long absence. I had stepped a little out of my usual line in telling her what I did; not that I had received any charge of secrecy, or given even the slightest promise to Holdsworth that I would not repeat his words. But I had an uneasy feeling sometimes, when I thought of what I had done in the excitement of seeing Phillis so ill and in so much trouble. I meant to have told Holdsworth when I wrote next to him; but, when I had my half-finished letter before me, I sate with my pen in my hand, hesitating. I had more scruple in revealing what I had found out or guessed at of Phillis's secret than in repeating to her his spoken words. I did not think I had any right to say out to him what I believed—namely, that she loved him dearly, and had felt his absence even to the injury of her health. Yet, to explain what I had done in telling her how he had spoken about her that last night, it would be necessary to give my reasons, so I had settled within myself to leave it alone. As she had told me she should like to hear all the details and fuller particulars and more explicit declarations first from him, so he should have the pleasure of extracting the delicious tender secret from her maidenly lips. I would not betray my guesses, my surmises, my all but certain knowledge of the state of her heart. I had received two letters from him after he had settled to his business; they were full of life and energy; but in each there had been a message to the family at the Hope Farm of more than common regard, and a slight but distinct mention of Phillis herself, showing that she stood single and alone in his memory. These letters I had sent on to the minister; for he was sure to care for them, even supposing he had been unacquainted with their writer, because they were so clever and so picturesquely-worded that they brought, as it were, a whiff of foreign atmosphere into his circumscribed life. I used to wonder what was the trade or business in which the minister would not have thriven, mentally I mean, if it had so happened that he had been called into that state. He would have made a capital engineer, that I know; and he had a fancy for the sea, like many other land-locked men to whom the great deep is a mystery and a fascination. He read law-books with relish; and once, happening to borrow *De Lolme on the British Constitution* (or some such title), he talked about jurisprudence till he was far beyond my depth. But to return to Holdsworth's letters. When the minister sent them back, he also wrote out a list of questions suggested by their perusal, which I was to pass on in my answers to Holdsworth, until I thought of suggesting a direct correspondence between the two.

That was the state of things as regarded the absent one when I went to the farm for my Easter visit, and when I found Phillis in that state of shy reserve towards me which I have named before. I thought she was ungrateful; for I was not quite sure if I had done wisely in having told her what I did. I had committed a fault, or a folly, perhaps, and all for her sake; and here was she, less friends with me than she had ever been before. This little estrangement only lasted a few hours. I think that, as soon as she felt pretty sure of there being no recurrence, either by word, look, or allusion, to the one subject that was predominant in her mind, she came back to her old sisterly ways with me. She had much to tell me of her own familiar interests: how Rover had been ill, and how anxious they had all of them been, and how, after some little discussion between her father and her, both equally grieved by the sufferings of the old dog, he had been " remembered in the household prayers," and how he had begun to get better only the very next day; and then she would have led me into a conversation on the right ends of prayer, and on special providences, and I know not what; only I " jibbed " like their old carthorse, and refused to stir a step in that direction. Then we talked about the different broods of chickens, and she showed me the hens that were good mothers, and told me the characters of all the poultry with the utmost good-faith; and in all good-faith I listened, for I believe there was a great deal of truth in all she said. And then we strolled on into the wood beyond the ash-meadow, and both of us sought for early primroses and the fresh green crinkled leaves. She was not afraid of being alone with me after the first day. I never saw her so lovely, or so happy. I think she hardly knew why she was so happy all the time. I can see her now, standing under the budding branches of the grey trees, over which a tinge of green seemed to be deepening day after day, her sun-bonnet fallen back on her neck, her hands full of delicate wood-flowers, quite unconscious of my gaze, but intent on sweet mockery of some bird in neighbouring bush or tree. She had the art of warbling, and replying to the notes of different birds, and knew their song, their habits and ways, more accurately than any one else I ever knew. She had often done it at my request the spring before; but this year she really gurgled, and whistled, and warbled, just as they did, out of the very fulness and joy of her heart. She was more than ever the very apple of her father's eye; her mother gave her both her own share of love and that of the dead child who had died in infancy. I have heard cousin Holman murmur, after a long dreamy look at Phillis, and tell herself how like she was growing to Johnnie, and soothe herself with plaintive inarticulate sounds, and many gentle shakes of the head, for the aching sense of loss she would never get over in this world. The old servants about the place had the dumb loyal attachment to the child of the land, common to most agricultural labourers; not often stirred into activity or expression. My cousin Phillis was like a rose that had come to full bloom on the sunny side of a lonely house, sheltered from storms. I have read in some book of poetry—

> A maid whom there were none to praise,
> And very few to love.

And somehow those lines always reminded me of Phillis; yet they were not true of her either. I never heard her praised; and out of her own household there were very few to love her; but, though no one spoke out their approbation, she always did right in her parents' eyes, out of her natural simple goodness and wisdom. Holdsworth's name was never mentioned between us when we were alone; but I had sent on his letters to the minister, as I have said; and more than once he began to talk about our absent friend, when he was smoking his pipe after the day's work was done. Then Phillis hung her head a little over her work, and listened in silence.

"I miss him more that I thought for; no offence to you, Paul! I said once, his company was like dram-drinking; that was before I knew him; and perhaps I spoke in a spirit of judgment. To some men's minds everything presents itself strongly, and they speak accordingly; and so did he. And I thought, in my vanity of censorship, that his were not true and sober words; they would not have been if I had used them, but they were so to a man of his class of perceptions. I thought of the measure which I had been meting out to him, when Brother

Robinson was here last Thursday, and told me that a poor little quotation I was making from the *Georgics* savoured of vain babbling and profane heathenism. He went so far as to say that, by learning other languages than our own, we were flying in the face of the Lord's purpose when He had said, at the building of the Tower of Babel, that He would confound their languages so that they should not understand each other's speech. As Brother Robinson was to me, so was I to the quick wits, bright senses, and ready words of Holdsworth."

The first little cloud upon my peace came in the shape of a letter from Canada, in which there were two or three sentences that troubled me more than they ought to have done, to judge merely from the words employed. It was this:—" I should feel dreary enough in this out-of-the-way place, if it were not for a friendship I have formed with a French Canadian of the name of Ventadour. He and his family are a great resource to me in the long evenings. I never heard such delicious vocal music as the voices of these Ventadour boys and girls in their part-songs; and the foreign element retained in their characters and manner of living reminds me of some of the happiest days of my life. Lucille, the second daughter, is curiously like Phillis Holman." In vain I said to myself, that it was probably this likeness that made him take pleasure in the society of the Ventadour family. In vain I told my anxious fancy, that nothing could be more natural than this intimacy, and that there was no sign of its leading to any consequence that ought to disturb me. I had a presentiment, and I was disturbed; and I could not reason it away. I dare say my presentiment was rendered more persistent and keen by the doubts which would force themselves into my mind, as to whether I had done well in repeating Holdsworth's words to Phillis. Her state of vivid happiness this summer was markedly different to the peaceful serenity of former days. If, in my thoughtfulness at noticing this, I caught her eye, she blushed and sparkled all over, guessing that I was remembering our joint secret. Her eyes fell before mine, as if she could hardly bear me to see the revelation of their bright glances. And yet I considered again, and comforted myself by the reflection that, if this change had been anything more than my silly fancy, her father or her mother would have perceived it. But they went on in tranquil unconsciousness and undisturbed peace.

A change in my own life was quickly approaching. In the July of this year my occupation on the —— railway and its branches came to an end. The lines were completed; and I was to leave ——shire, to return to Birmingham, where there was a niche already provided for me in my father's prosperous business. But, before I left the north, it was an understood thing amongst us all that I was to go and pay a visit of some weeks at the Hope Farm. My father was as much pleased at this plan as I was; and the dear family of cousins often spoke of things to be done, and sights to be shown me, during this visit. My want of wisdom in having told " that thing " (under such ambiguous words I concealed the injudicious confidence I had made to Phillis) was the only drawback to my anticipations of pleasure.

The ways of life were too simple at the Hope Farm for my coming to them to make the slightest disturbance. I knew my room, like a son of the house. I knew the regular course of their days, and that I was expected to fall into it, like one of the family. Deep summer peace brooded over the place; the warm golden air was filled with the murmur of insects near at hand, the more distant sound of voices out in the fields, the clear far-away rumble of carts over the stone-paved lanes miles away. The heat was too great for the birds to be singing; only now and then one might hear the wood-pigeons in the trees beyond the ash-field. The cattle stood knee-deep in the pond, flicking their tails about to keep off the flies. The minister stood in the hay-field, without hat or cravat, coat or waistcoat, panting and smiling. Phillis had been leading the row of farm-servants, turning the swathes of fragrant hay with measured movement. She went to the end—to the hedge, and then, throwing down her rake, she came to me with her free sisterly welcome. " Go, Paul! " said the minister. " We need all hands to make use of the sunshine to-day. ' Whatsoever thine hand findeth to do, do it with all thy might.' ·It will be a healthy change of work for thee, lad; and I find my best rest in change of work." So off I went, a willing labourer, following Phillis's lead; it was the primitive distinction of rank; the boy who frightened the sparrows off the fruit was the last in our rear. We did not leave off till the red sun was gone down behind the fir-trees bordering the common. Then we went home to supper—prayers—to bed; some bird singing far into the night, as I heard it through my open window, and the poultry beginning their clatter and cackle in the earliest morning. I had carried what luggage I immediately needed with me from my lodgings, and the rest was to be sent by the carrier. He brought it to the farm betimes that morning; and along with it he brought a letter or two that had arrived since I had left. I was talking to cousin Holman—about my mother's ways of making bread, I remember; cousin Holman was questioning me, and had got me far beyond my depth—in the house-place, when the letters were brought in by one of the men, and I had to pay the carrier for his trouble before I could look at them. A bill—a Canadian letter! What instinct made me so thankful that I was alone with my dear unobservant cousin? What made me hurry them away into my coat-pocket? I do not know. I felt strange and sick, and made irrelevant answers, I am afraid. Then I went to my room, ostensibly to carry up my boxes. I sate on the side of my bed and opened my letter from Holdsworth. It seemed to me as if I had read its contents before, and knew exactly what he had got to say. I knew he was going to be married to Lucille Ventadour—nay, that he *was* married; for this was the 5th of July, and he wrote word that his marriage was fixed to take place on the 29th of June. I knew all the reasons he gave, all the raptures he went into. I held the letter loosely in my hands, and looked into vacancy; yet I saw a chaffinch's nest on the lichen-covered trunk of an old apple-tree opposite my window, and saw the mother-bird come fluttering in to feed her brood—and yet I did not see it, although it seemed to me afterwards as if I could have drawn every fibre, every feather. I was stirred up to action by the merry sound of voices and the clamp of rustic feet coming home for the mid-day meal. I knew I must go down to dinner; I knew, too, I must tell Phillis; for in his happy egotism, his new-fangled foppery, Holdsworth had put in a P.S., saying that he should send wedding-cards to me and some other Hornby and Eltham acquaintance, and "to his kind friends at Hope Farm." Phillis had faded away to one among several "kind friends." I don't know how I got through dinner that day. I remember forcing myself to eat, and talking hard; but I also recollect the wondering look in the minister's eyes. He was not one to think evil without cause; but many a one would have taken me for drunk. As soon as I decently could, I left the table, saying I would go out for a walk. At first, I must have tried to stun reflection by rapid walking, for I had lost myself on the high moorlands far beyond the familiar gorse-covered common, before I was obliged for very weariness to slacken my pace. I kept wishing—oh! how fervently wishing—I had never committed that blunder; that the one little half-hour's indiscretion could be blotted out.

Alternating with this was anger against Holdsworth; unjust
enough, I dare say. I suppose I stayed in that solitary place
for a good hour or more; and then I turned homewards, resolv-
ing to get over the telling Phillis at the first opportunity, but
shrinking from the fulfilment of my resolution so much that,
when I came into the house (doors and windows open wide in
the sultry weather) and saw Phillis alone in the kitchen, I became quite sick with apprehension. She was standing by the
dresser, cutting up a great household loaf into hunches of bread
for the hungry labourers who might come in any minute, for
the heavy thunderclouds were over-spreading the sky. She
looked round as she heard my step.

"You should have been in the field, helping with the hay,"
said she, in her calm, pleasant voice. I had heard her, as I
came near the house, softly chanting some hymn-tune; and
the peacefulness of that seemed to be brooding over her now.

"Perhaps I should. It looks as if it was going to rain."

"Yes, there is thunder about. Mother has had to go to bed
with one of her bad headaches. Now you are come in "——

"Phillis," said I, rushing at my subject and interrupting
her, " I went a long walk to think over a letter I had this morning
—a letter from Canada. You don't know how it has grieved
me." I held it out to her as I spoke. Her colour changed a
little; but it was more the reflection of my face, I think, than
because she formed any definite idea from my words. Still
she did not take the letter. I had to bid her read it, before she
quite understood what I wished. She sate down rather suddenly
as she received it into her hands; and, spreading it on the dresser
before her, she rested her forehead on the palms of her hands,
her arms supported on the table, her figure a little averted, and
her countenance thus shaded. I looked out of the open window;
my heart was very heavy. How peaceful it all seemed in the
farmyard! Peace and plenty. How still and deep was the
silence of the house! Tick-tick went the unseen clock on the
wide staircase. I had heard the rustle once, when she turned
over the page of thin paper. She must have read to the end.
Yet she did not move, or say a word, or even sigh. I kept on
looking out of the window, my hands in my pockets. I wonder
how long that time really was? It seemed to me interminable
—unbearable. At length I looked round at her. She must
have felt my look, for she changed her attitude with a quick
sharp movement, and caught my eyes.

"Don't look so sorry, Paul," she said. "Don't, please. I

can't bear it. There is nothing to be sorry for. I think not, at least. You have not done wrong, at any rate." I felt that I groaned, but I don't think she heard me. " And he—there's no wrong in his marrying, is there? I'm sure I hope he'll be happy. Oh! how I hope it!" These last words were like a wail; but I believe she was afraid of breaking down, for she changed the key in which she spoke, and hurried on. " Lucille —that's our English Lucy, I suppose? Lucille Holdsworth! It's a pretty name; and I hope——I forget what I was going to say. Oh! it was this. Paul, I think we need never speak about this again; only, remember, you are not to be sorry. You have not done wrong; you have been very, *very* kind; and, if I see you looking grieved, I don't know what I might do;— I might break down, you know."

I think she was on the point of doing so then; but the dark storm came dashing down, and the thundercloud broke right above the house, as it seemed. Her mother, roused from sleep, called out for Phillis; the men and women from the hayfield came running into shelter, drenched through. The minister followed, smiling, and not unpleasantly excited by the war of elements; for, by dint of hard work through the long summer's day, the greater part of the hay was safely housed in the barn in the field. Once or twice in the succeeding bustle I came across Phillis, always busy, and, as it seemed to me, always doing the right thing. When I was alone in my own room at night, I allowed myself to feel relieved: and to believe that the worst was over, and was not so very bad after all. But the succeeding days were very miserable. Sometimes I thought it must be my fancy that falsely represented Phillis to me as strangely changed; for surely, if this idea of mine was well-founded, her parents—her father and mother—her own flesh and blood—would have been the first to perceive it. Yet they went on in their household peace and content; if anything, a little more cheerfully than usual, for the " harvest of the first fruits," as the minister called it, had been more bounteous than usual, and there was plenty all around, in which the humblest labourer was made to share. After the one thunderstorm, came one or two lovely serene summer days, during which the hay was all carried; and then succeeded long soft rains, filling the ears of corn and causing the mown grass to spring afresh. The minister allowed himself a few more hours of relaxation and home enjoyment than usual during this wet spell: hard earth-bound frost was his winter holiday; these wet days, after the hay harvest, his summer holiday. We sate with open windows, the fragrance and the freshness called out by the soft-falling rain filling the house-place; while the quiet ceaseless patter among the leaves outside ought to have had the same lulling effect as all other gentle perpetual sounds, such as mill-wheels and bubbling springs, have on the nerves of happy people. But two of us were not happy. I was sure enough of myself, for one. I was worse than sure—I was wretchedly anxious about Phillis. Ever since that day of the thunderstorm there had been a new, sharp, discordant sound to me in her voice, a sort of jangle in her tone; and her restless eyes had no quietness in them; and her colour came and went, without a cause that I could find out. The minister, happy in ignorance of what most concerned him, brought out his books; his learned volumes and classics. Whether he read and talked to Phillis, or to me, I do not know; but, feeling by instinct that she was not, could not be, attending to the peaceful details, so strange and foreign to the turmoil in her heart, I forced myself to listen, and if possible to understand.

" Look here!" said the minister, tapping the old vellum-bound book he held; " in the first ' Georgic ' he speaks of rolling and irrigation; a little further on, he insists on choice of the best seed, and advises us to keep the drains clear. Again, no Scotch farmer could give shrewder advice than to cut light meadows while the dew is on, even though it involve night-work. It is all living truth in these days." He began beating time with a ruler upon his knee, to some Latin lines he read aloud just then. I suppose the monotonous chant irritated Phillis to some irregular energy, for I remember the quick knotting and breaking of the thread with which she was sewing. I never hear that snap repeated now, without suspecting some sting or stab troubling the heart of the worker. Cousin Holman, at her peaceful knitting, noticed the reason why Phillis had so constantly to interrupt the progress of her seam.

" It is bad thread, I'm afraid," she said, in a gentle, sympathetic voice. But it was too much for Phillis.

" The thread is bad—everything is bad—I am so tired of it all!" And she put down her work, and hastily left the room. I do not suppose that in all her life Phillis had ever shown so much temper before. In many a family the tone, the manner, would not have been noticed; but here it fell with a sharp surprise upon the sweet, calm atmosphere of home. The minister put down ruler and book, and pushed his spectacles up to his forehead. The mother looked distressed for a moment, and then smoothed her features and said in an explanatory tone —" It's the weather, I think. Some people feel it different to others. It always brings on a headache with me." She got up to follow her daughter, but half-way to the door she thought better of it, and came back to her seat. Good mother! she hoped the better to conceal the unusual spirit of temper, by pretending not to take much notice of it. " Go on, minister," she said; " it is very interesting what you are reading about; and, when I don't quite understand it, I like the sound of your voice." So he went on, but languidly and irregularly, and beat no more time with his ruler to any Latin lines. When the dusk came on, early that July night because of the cloudy sky, Phillis came softly back, making as though nothing had happened. She took up her work, but it was too dark to do many stitches; and she dropped it soon. Then I saw her hand steal into her mother's, and how this latter fondled it with quiet little caresses, while the minister, as fully aware as I was of this tender pantomime, went on talking in a happier tone of voice about things as uninteresting to him, at the time, I verily believe, as they were to me; and that is saying a good deal, and shows how much more real what was passing before him was, even to a farmer, than the agricultural customs of the ancients.

I remember one thing more—an attack which Betty the servant made upon me one day, as I came in through the kitchen where she was churning, and stopped to ask her for a drink of butter-milk.

" I say, cousin Paul " (she had adopted the family habit of addressing me generally as cousin Paul, and always speaking of me in that form), " something's amiss with our Phillis, and I reckon you've a good guess what it is. She's not one to take up wi' such as you " (not complimentary, but that Betty never was, even to those for whom she felt the highest respect); " but I'd as lief yon Holdsworth had never come near us. So there you've a bit o' my mind."

And a very unsatisfactory bit it was. I did not know what to answer to the glimpse at the real state of the case implied in the shrewd woman's speech; · so I tried to put her off by assuming surprise at her first assertion.

" Amiss with Phillis! I should like to know why you think anything is wrong with her. She looks as blooming as any one can do."

" Poor lad! you're but a big child, after all; and you've

likely never heared of a fever-flush. But you know better nor
that, my fine fellow! so don't think for to put me off wi' blooms
and blossoms and such-like talk. What makes her walk about
for hours and hours o' nights, when she used to be abed and
asleep? I sleep next room to her, and hear her plain as can be.
What makes her come in panting and ready to drop into that
chair"—nodding to one close to the door—"and it's 'Oh!
Betty, some water, please'? That's the way she comes in now,
when she used to come back as fresh and bright as she went out.
If yon friend o' yours has played her false, he's a deal for t'
answer for: she's a lass who's as sweet and as sound as a nut,
and the very apple of her father's eye, and of her mother's too,
only wi' her she ranks second to th' minister. You'll have to
look after yon chap; for I, for one, will stand no wrong to our
Phillis."

What was I to do, or to say? I wanted to justify Holdsworth,
to keep Phillis's secret, and to pacify the woman all in the same
breath. I did not take the best course, I'm afraid.

"I don't believe Holdsworth ever spoke a word of—of love
to her in all his life. I am sure he didn't."

"Ay, ay! but there's eyes, and there's hands, as well as
tongues; and a man has two o' th' one and but one o' t'other."

"And she's so young; do you suppose her parents would
not have seen it?"

"Well! if you ax me that, I'll say out boldly, 'No.' They've
called her 'the child' so long—'the child' is always their name
for her when they talk on her between themselves, as if never
anybody else had a ewe-lamb before them—that she's grown
up to be a woman under their very eyes, and they look on her
still as if she were in her long-clothes. And you ne'er heard on
a man falling in love wi' a babby in long-clothes!"

"No!" said I, half-laughing. But she went on as grave as
a judge.

"Ay! you see you'll laugh at the bare thought on it—and I'll
be bound th' minister, though he's not a laughing man, would
ha' sniggled at th' notion of falling in love wi' the child. Where's
Holdsworth off to?"

"Canada," said I shortly.

"Canada here, Canada there," she replied testily. "Tell
me how far he's off, instead of giving me your gibberish. Is he
a two days' journey away? or a three? or a week?"

"He's ever so far off—three weeks at the least," cried I in
despair. "And he's either married, or just going to be. So

there!" I expected a fresh burst of anger. But no; the matter was too serious. Betty sate down, and kept silence for a minute or two. She looked so miserable and downcast, that I could not help going on, and taking her a little into my confidence.

"It is quite true what I said. I know he never spoke a word to her. I think he liked her; but it's all over now. The best thing we can do—the best and kindest for her—and I know you love her, Betty "——

"I nursed her in my arms; I gave her little brother his last taste o' earthly food," said Betty, putting her apron up to her eyes.

"Well! don't let us show her we guess that she is grieving; she'll get over it the sooner. Her father and mother don't even guess at it, and we must make as if we didn't. It's too late now to do anything else."

"I'll never let on; I know nought. I've known true love mysel', in my day. But I wish he'd been farred before he ever came near this house, with his ' Please Betty ' this, and ' Please Betty ' that, and drinking up our new milk as if he'd been a cat. I hate such beguiling ways."

I thought it was as well to let her exhaust herself in abusing the absent Holdsworth; if it was shabby and treacherous in me, I came in for my punishment directly.

"It's a caution to a man how he goes about beguiling. Some men do it as easy and innocent as cooing doves. Don't you be none of 'em, my lad. Not that you've got the gifts to do it, either; you're no great shakes to look at, neither for figure nor yet for face; and it would need be a deaf adder to be taken in wi' your words, though there may be no great harm in 'em." A lad of nineteen or twenty is not flattered by such an outspoken opinion even from the oldest and ugliest of her sex; and I was only too glad to change the subject by my repeated injunctions to keep Phillis's secret. The end of our conversation was this speech of hers—

"You great gaupus, for all you're called cousin o' th' minister —many a one is cursed wi' fools for cousins—d'ye think I can't see sense except through your spectacles? I give you leave to cut out my tongue, and nail it up on th' barn-door for a caution to magpies, if I let out on that poor wench, either to herself, or any one that is hers, as the Bible says. Now you've heard me speak Scripture language, perhaps you'll be content, and leave me my kitchen to myself."

During all these days, from the 5th of July to the 17th, I must have forgotten what Holdsworth had said about sending cards. And yet I think I could not have quite forgotten; but, once having told Phillis about his marriage, I must have looked upon the after-consequence of cards as of no importance. At any rate, they came upon me as a surprise at last. The penny-post reform, as people call it, had come into operation a short time before; but the never-ending stream of notes and letters which seems now to flow in upon most households had not yet begun its course; at least in those remote parts. There was a post-office at Hornby; and an old fellow, who stowed away the few letters in any or all his pockets, as it best suited him, was the letter-carrier to Heathbridge and the neighbourhood. I have often met him in the lanes thereabouts, and asked him for letters. Sometimes I have come upon him, sitting on the hedge-bank resting; and he has begged me to read him an address, too illegible for his spectacled eyes to decipher. When I used to inquire if he had anything for me, or for Holdsworth (he was not particular to whom he gave up the letters, so that he got rid of them somehow, and could set off homewards), he would say he thought that he had, for such was his invariable safe form of answer; and would fumble in breast-pockets, waistcoat-pockets, breeches-pockets, and, as a last resource, in coat-tail pockets; and at length try to comfort me, if I looked disappointed, by telling me, " Hoo had missed this toime, but was sure to write to-morrow; " " hoo " representing an imaginary sweetheart.

Sometimes I had seen the minister bring home a letter which he had found lying for him at the little shop that was the post-office at Heathbridge, or from the grander establishment at Hornby. Once or twice Josiah, the carter, remembered that the old letter-carrier had trusted him with an epistle to " Measter," as they had met in the lanes. I think it must have been about ten days after my arrival at the farm, and my talk to Phillis cutting bread-and-butter at the kitchen dresser, before the day on which the minister suddenly spoke at the dinner-table, and said—

" By-the-bye, I've got a letter in my pocket. Reach me my coat here, Phillis." The weather was still sultry, and for coolness and ease the minister was sitting in his shirt-sleeves. " I went to Heathbridge about the paper they had sent me, which spoils all the pens—and I called at the post-office, and found a letter for me, unpaid—and they did not like to trust it to old

Zekiel. Ay! here it is! Now we shall hear news of Holdsworth
—I thought I'd keep it till we were all together." My heart
seemed to stop beating, and I hung my head over my plate, not
daring to look up. What would come of it now? What was
Phillis doing? How was she looking? A moment of suspense
—and then he spoke again. " Why? what's this? Here are
two visiting-tickets with his name on; no writing at all. No!
it's not his name on both. MRS. Holdsworth. The young man
has gone and got married." I lifted my head at these words;
I could not help looking just for one instant at Phillis. It
seemed to me as if she had been keeping watch over my face
and ways. Her face was brilliantly flushed; her eyes were dry
and glittering; but she did not speak; her lips were set together,
almost as if she was pinching them tight to prevent words or
sounds coming out. Cousin Holman's face expressed surprise
and interest.

" Well! " said she, " who'd ha' thought it? He's made
quick work of his wooing and wedding. I'm sure I wish him
happy. Let me see "—counting on her fingers—" October,
November, December, January, February, March, April, May,
June, July—at least we're at the 28th—it is nearly ten months
after all, and reckon a month each way off "——

" Did you know of this news before? " said the minister,
turning sharp round on me, surprised, I suppose, at my silence
—hardly suspicious, as yet.

" I knew—I had heard—something. It is to a French
Canadian young lady," I went on, forcing myself to talk. " Her
name is Ventadour."

" Lucille Ventadour! " said Phillis, in a sharp voice, out of
tune.

" Then you knew too! " exclaimed the minister.

We both spoke at once. I said, " I heard of the probability
of——, and told Phillis," She said, " He is married to Lucille
Ventadour, of French descent; one of a large family near St.
Meurice; am not I right? " I nodded. " Paul told me—that
is all we know, is not it? Did you see the Howsons, father, in
Heathbridge? " and she forced herself to talk more than she had
done for several days; asking many questions; trying, as I
could see, to keep the conversation off the one raw surface, on
which to touch was agony. I had less self-command; but I
followed her lead. I was not so much absorbed in the conversation but what I could see that the minister was puzzled and
uneasy; though he seconded Phillis's efforts to prevent her

mother from recurring to the great piece of news, and uttering continual exclamations of wonder and surprise. But, with that one exception, we were all disturbed out of our natural equanimity, more or less. Every day, every hour, I was reproaching myself more and more for my blundering officiousness. If only I had held my foolish tongue for that one half-hour; if only I had not been in such impatient haste to do something to relieve pain! I could have knocked my stupid head against the wall in my remorse. Yet all I could do now was to second the brave girl in her efforts to conceal her disappointment and keep her maidenly secret. But I thought that dinner would never, never come to an end. I suffered for her, even more than for myself. Until now, everything which I had heard spoken in that happy household were simple words of true meaning. If we had aught to say, we said it; and if any one preferred silence, nay, if all did so, there would have been no spasmodic, forced efforts to talk for the sake of talking, or to keep off intrusive thoughts or suspicions.

At length we got up from our places, and prepared to disperse; but two or three of us had lost our zest and interest in the daily labour. The minister stood looking out of the window in silence; and, when he roused himself to go out to the fields where his labourers were working, it was with a sigh; and he tried to avert his troubled face, as he passed us on his way to the door. When he had left us, I caught sight of Phillis's face, as, thinking herself unobserved, her countenance relaxed for a moment or two into sad, woeful weariness. She started into briskness again when her mother spoke, and hurried away to do some little errand at her bidding. When we two were alone, cousin Holman recurred to Holdsworth's marriage. She was one of those people who like to view an event from every side of probability, or even possibility; and she had been cut short from indulging herself in this way during dinner.

"To think of Mr. Holdsworth's being married! I can't get over it, Paul. Not but what he was a very nice young man! I don't like her name, though; it sounds foreign. Say it again, my dear. I hope she'll know how to take care of him, English fashion. He is not strong; and, if she does not see that his things are well aired, I should be afraid of the old cough."

"He always said he was stronger than he had ever been before, after that fever."

"He might think so; but I have my doubts. He was a very pleasant young man; but he did not stand nursing very well.

He got tired of being coddled, as he called it. I hope they'll soon come back to England, and then he'll have a chance for his health. I wonder, now, if she speaks English; but, to be sure, he can speak foreign tongues like anything, as I've heard the minister say."

And so we went on for some time, till she became drowsy over her knitting, on the sultry summer afternoon; and I stole away for a walk, for I wanted some solitude in which to think over things, and, alas! to blame myself with poignant stabs of remorse.

I lounged lazily as soon as I got to the wood. Here and there, the bubbling, brawling brook circled round a great stone, or a root of an old tree, and made a pool; otherwise it coursed brightly over the gravel and stones. I stood by one of these for more than half-an-hour, or, indeed, longer, throwing bits of wood or pebbles into the water, and wondering what I could do to remedy the present state of things. Of course all my meditation was of no use; and, at length, the distant sound of the horn employed to tell the men far afield to leave off work warned me that it was six o'clock, and time for me to go home. Then I caught wafts of the loud-voiced singing of the evening psalm. As I was crossing the ash-field, I saw the minister at some distance talking to a man. I could not hear what they were saying; but I saw an impatient or dissentient (I could not tell which) gesture on the part of the former, who walked quickly away, and was apparently absorbed in his thoughts; for, though he passed within twenty yards of me, as both our paths converged towards home, he took no notice of me. We passed the evening in a way which was even worse than dinner-time. The minister was silent, depressed, even irritable. Poor cousin Holman was utterly perplexed by this unusual frame of mind and temper in her husband; she was not well herself, and was suffering from the extreme and sultry heat, which made her less talkative than usual. Phillis, usually so reverently tender to her parents, so soft, so gentle, seemed now to take no notice of the unusual state of things, but talked to me—to any one—on indifferent subjects, regardless of her father's gravity, of her mother's piteous looks of bewilderment. But once my eyes fell upon her hands, concealed under the table, and I could see the passionate, convulsive manner in which she laced and interlaced her fingers perpetually, wringing them together from time to time, wringing till the compressed flesh became perfectly white. What could I do? I talked with her, as I saw she

wished; her grey eyes had dark circles round them, and a strange
kind of dark light in them; her cheeks were flushed, but her
lips were white and wan. I wondered that others did not read
these signs as clearly as I did. But perhaps they did; I think,
from what came afterwards, the minister did.

Poor cousin Holman! she worshipped her husband; and
the outward signs of his uneasiness were more patent to her
simple heart than were her daughter's. After a while, she could
bear it no longer. She got up, and, softly laying her hand on
his broad stooping shoulder, she said—

"What is the matter, minister? Has anything gone wrong?"

He started as if from a dream. Phillis hung her head, and
caught her breath in terror at the answer she feared. But he,
looking round with a sweeping glance, turned his broad, wise
face up to his anxious wife, and forced a smile, and took her
hand in a reassuring manner.

"I am blaming myself, dear. I have been overcome with
anger this afternoon. I scarcely knew what I was doing, but
I turned away Timothy Cooper. He has killed the Ribstone
pippin at the corner of the orchard; gone and piled the quick-
lime for the mortar for the new stable-wall against the trunk
of the tree — stupid fellow! killed the tree outright — and it
loaded with apples!"

"And Ribstone pippins are so scarce," said sympathetic
cousin Holman.

"Ay! But Timothy is but a half-wit; and he has a wife
and children. He had often put me to it sore, with his slothful
ways; but I had laid it before the Lord, and striven to bear
with him. But I will not stand it any longer; it's past my
patience. And he has notice to find another place. Wife, we
won't talk more about it." He took her hand gently off his
shoulder; touched it with his lips; but relapsed into a silence
as profound, if not quite so morose in appearance, as before.
I could not tell why, but this bit of talk between her father and
mother seemed to take all the factitious spirits out of Phillis.
She did not speak now, but looked out of the open casement
at the calm large moon, slowly moving through the twilight sky.
Once I thought her eyes were filling with tears; but, if so, she
shook them off, and arose with alacrity when her mother, tired
and dispirited, proposed to go to bed immediately after prayers.
We all said good-night in our separate ways to the minister, who
still sat at the table with the great Bible open before him, not
much looking up at any of our salutations, but returning them

kindly. But when I, last of all, was on the point of leaving the
room, he said, still scarcely looking up—

"Paul, you will oblige me by staying here a few minutes.
I would fain have some talk with you."

I knew what was coming, all in a moment. I carefully
shut-to the door, put out my candle, and sat down to my fate.
He seemed to find some difficulty in beginning, for, if I had not
heard that he wanted to speak to me, I should never have
guessed it, he seemed so much absorbed in reading a chapter
to the end. Suddenly he lifted his head up and said—

"It is about that friend of yours, Holdsworth! Paul, have
you any reason for thinking he has played tricks upon Phillis?"

I saw that his eyes were blazing with such a fire of anger at
the bare idea, that I lost all my presence of mind, and only
repeated—

"Played tricks on Phillis!"

"Ay! you know what I mean: made love to her, courted
her, made her think that he loved her, and then gone away and
left her. Put it as you will; only give me an answer of some
kind or another—a true answer, I mean—and don't repeat my
words, Paul."

He was shaking all over, as he said this. I did not delay
a moment in answering him—

"I do not believe that Edward Holdsworth ever played tricks
on Phillis, ever made love to her; he never, to my knowledge,
made her believe that he loved her."

I stopped; I wanted to nerve up my courage for a confession,
yet I wished to save the secret of Phillis's love for Holdsworth,
as much as I could; that secret which she had so striven to
keep sacred and safe; and I had need of some reflection, before
I went on with what I had to say.

He began again, before I had quite arranged my manner of
speech. It was almost as if to himself—"She is my only
child; my little daughter! She is hardly out of childhood;
I have thought to gather her under my wings for years to come;
her mother and I would lay down our lives to keep her from
harm and grief." Then, raising his voice, and looking at me,
he said, "Something has gone wrong with the child; and it
seems to me to date from the time she heard of that marriage.
It is hard to think that you may know more of her secret cares
and sorrows than I do—but perhaps you do, Paul, perhaps you
do—only, if it be not a sin, tell me what I can do to make her
happy again; tell me!"

"It will not do much good, I am afraid," said I; "but I will own how wrong I did; I don't mean wrong in the way of sin, but in the way of judgment. Holdsworth told me just before he went that he loved Phillis, and hoped to make her his wife; and I told her."

There! it was out; all my part in it, at least; and I set my lips tight together, and waited for the words to come. I did not see his face; I looked straight at the wall opposite; but I heard him once begin to speak, and then turn over the leaves in the book before him. How awfully still that room was! The air outside, how still it was! The open window let in no rustle of leaves, no twitter or movement of birds—no sound whatever. The clock on the stairs—the minister's hard breathing—was it to go on for ever? Impatient beyond bearing at the deep quiet, I spoke again—

"I did it for the best, as I thought."

The minister shut the book to hastily, and stood up. Then I saw how angry he was.

"For the best, do you say? It was best, was it, to go and tell a young girl what you never told a word of to her parents, who trusted you like a son of their own?"

He began walking about, up and down the room, close under the open windows, churning up his bitter thoughts of me.

"To put such thoughts into the child's head!" continued he; "to spoil her peaceful maidenhood with talk about another man's love; and such love, too!"—he spoke scornfully now— "a love that is ready for any young woman! Oh, the misery in my poor little daughter's face to-day at dinner—the misery, Paul! I thought you were one to be trusted—your father's son too, to go and put such thoughts into the child's mind; you two talking together about that man wishing to marry her!"

I could not help remembering the pinafore, the childish garment which Phillis wore so long, as if her parents were unaware of her progress towards womanhood. Just in the same way, the minister spoke and thought of her now, as a child, whose innocent peace I had spoiled by vain and foolish talk. I knew that the truth was different, though I could hardly have told it now; but, indeed, I never thought of trying to tell; it was far from my mind to add one iota to the sorrow which I had caused. The minister went on walking, occasionally stopping to move things on the table, or articles of furniture, in a sharp, impatient, meaningless way, then he began again—

"So young, so pure from the world! how could you go and

talk to such a child, raising hopes, exciting feelings—all to end thus; and best so, even though I saw her poor piteous face look as it did? I can't forgive you, Paul; it was more than wrong— it was wicked—to go and repeat that man's words."

His back was now to the door; and, in listening to his low angry tones, he did not hear it slowly open, nor did he see Phillis, standing just within the room, until he turned round; then he stood still. She must have been half undressed; but she had covered herself with a dark winter cloak, which fell in long folds to her white, naked, noiseless feet. Her face was strangely pale; her eyes heavy in the black circles round them. She came up to the table very slowly, and leant her hand upon it, saying mournfully—

"Father, you must not blame Paul. I could not help hearing a great deal of what you were saying. He did tell me, and perhaps it would have been wiser not, dear Paul!—But—oh, dear! oh, dear! I am so sick with shame! He told me out of his kind heart, because he saw—that I was so very unhappy at *his* going away."

She hung her head, and leant more heavily than before on her supporting hand.

"I don't understand," said her father; but he was beginning to understand. Phillis did not answer, till he asked her again. I could have struck him now for his cruelty; but, then, I knew all.

"I loved him, father!" she said at length, raising her eyes to the minister's face.

"Had he ever spoken of love to you? Paul says not!"

"Never." She let fall her eyes, and drooped more than ever. I almost thought she would fall.

"I could not have believed it," said he, in a hard voice, yet sighing the moment he had spoken. A dead silence for a moment. "Paul! I was unjust to you. You deserved blame, but not all that I said." Then again a silence. I thought I saw Phillis's white lips moving, but it might be the flickering of the candle-light—a moth had flown in through the open casement, and was fluttering round the flame; I might have saved it, but I did not care to do so, my heart was too full of other things. At any rate, no sound was heard for long endless minutes. Then he said—" Phillis! did we not make you happy here? Have we not loved you enough?"

She did not seem to understand the drift of this question; she looked up as if bewildered, and her beautiful eyes dilated with a painful, tortured expression. He went on, without noticing the look on her face; he did not see it, I am sure.

"And yet you would have left us, left your home, left your father and your mother, and gone away with this stranger, wandering over the world!"

He suffered, too; there were tones of pain in the voice in which he uttered this reproach. Probably, the father and daughter were never so far apart in their lives, so unsympathetic. Yet some new terror came over her, and it was to him she turned for help. A shadow came over her face, and she tottered towards her father; falling down, her arms across his knees, and moaning out—

"Father, my head! my head!" and then she slipped through his quick-enfolding arms, and lay on the ground at his feet.

I shall never forget his sudden look of agony while I live; never! We raised her up; her colour had strangely darkened; she was insensible. I ran through the back-kitchen to the yard-pump, and brought back water. The minister had her on his knees, her head against his breast, almost as though she were a sleeping child. He was trying to rise up with his poor precious burden; but the momentary terror had robbed the strong man of his strength, and he sank back in his chair with sobbing breath.

"She is not dead, Paul! is she?" he whispered, hoarse, as I came near him.

I, too, could not speak, but I pointed to the quivering of the muscles round her mouth. Just then cousin Holman, attracted by some unwonted sound, came down. I remember I was surprised at the time at her presence of mind: she seemed to know so much better what to do than the minister, in the midst of the sick affright which blanched her countenance, and made her tremble all over. I think now that it was the recollection of what had gone before; the miserable thought that possibly his words had brought on this attack, whatever it might be, that so unmanned the minister. We carried her upstairs; and, while the women were putting her to bed, still unconscious, still slightly convulsed, I slipped out, and saddled one of the horses, and rode as fast as the heavy-trotting beast could go, to Hornby, to find the doctor there, and bring him back. He was out; might be detained the whole night. I remember saying, "God help us all!" as I sate on my horse, under the window, through which the apprentice's head had appeared to answer my furious tugs at the night-bell. He was a good-natured fellow. He said—

"He may be home in half-an-hour, there's no knowing; but I dare say he will. I'll send him out to the Hope Farm directly he comes in. It's that good-looking young woman, Holman's daughter, that's ill, isn't it?"

"Yes."

"It would be a pity if she was to go. She's an only child, isn't she? I'll get up, and smoke a pipe in the surgery, ready for the governor's coming home. I might go to sleep if I went to bed again."

"Thank you, you're a good fellow!" and I rode back almost as quickly as I came.

It was a brain-fever. The doctor said so, when he came in the early summer morning. I believe we had come to know the nature of the illness in the night-watches that had gone before. As to hope of ultimate recovery, or even evil prophecy of the probable end, the cautious doctor would be entrapped into neither. He gave his directions, and promised to come again: so soon, that this one thing showed his opinion of the gravity of the case.

By God's mercy, she recovered; but it was a long, weary time first. According to previously made plans, I was to have gone home at the beginning of August. But all such ideas were put aside now, without a word being spoken. I really think that I was necessary in the house, and especially necessary to the minister at this time; my father was the last man in the world, under such circumstances, to expect me home.

I say, I think I was necessary in the house. Every person (I had almost said every creature, for all the dumb beasts seemed to know and love Phillis) about the place went grieving and sad, as though a cloud was over the sun. They did their work, each striving to steer clear of the temptation to eve-service, in fulfilment of the trust reposed in them by the minister. For, the day after Phillis had been taken ill, he had called all the men employed on the farm into the empty barn; and there he had entreated their prayers for his only child; and, then and there, he had told them of his present incapacity for thought about any other thing in this world but his little daughter, lying nigh unto death, and he had asked them to go on with their daily labours as best they could, without his direction. So, as I say, these honest men did their work to the best of their ability; but they slouched along with sad and careful faces, coming one by one in the dim mornings to ask news of the sorrow that overshadowed the house, and receiving

Betty's intelligence, always rather darkened by passing through her mind, with slow shakes of the head, and a dull wistfulness of sympathy. But, poor fellows, they were hardly fit to be trusted with hasty messages; and here my poor services came in. One time, I was to ride hard to Sir William Bentinck's, and petition for ice out of his ice-house, to put on Phillis's head. Another, it was to Eltham I must go, by train, horse, anyhow, and bid the doctor there come for a consultation; for fresh symptoms had appeared, which Mr. Brown, of Hornby, considered unfavourable. Many an hour have I sate on the window-seat, half-way up the stairs, close by the old clock, listening in the hot stillness of the house for the sounds in the sick-room. The minister and I met often, but spoke together seldom. He looked so old—so old! He shared the nursing with his wife; the strength that was needed seemed to be given to them both in that day. They required no one else about their child. Every office about her was sacred to them; even Betty only went into the room for the most necessary purposes. Once I saw Phillis through the open door; her pretty golden hair had been cut off long before; her head was covered with wet cloths, and she was moving it backwards and forwards on the pillow, with weary, never-ending motion, her poor eyes shut, trying in the old-accustomed way to croon out a hymn tune, but perpetually breaking it up into moans of pain. Her mother sate by her, tearless, changing the cloths upon her head with patient solicitude. I did not see the minister at first; but there he was, in a dark corner, down upon his knees, his hands clasped together in passionate prayer. Then the door shut, and I saw no more.

One day he was wanted; and I had to summon him. Brother Robinson and another minister, hearing of his "trial," had come to see him. I told him this upon the stair-landing in a whisper. He was strangely troubled.

"They will want me to lay bare my heart. I cannot do it. Paul, stay with me! They mean well; but as for spiritual help at such a time—it is God only, God only, who can give it."

So I went in with him. They were two ministers from the neighbourhood; both older than Ebenezer Holman, but evidently inferior to him in education and worldly position. I thought they looked at me as if I were an intruder; but, remembering the minister's words, I held my ground, and took up one of poor Phillis's books (of which I could not read a word) to have an ostensible occupation. Presently I was asked to

" engage in prayer; " and we all knelt down, Brother Robinson " leading," and quoting largely, as I remember, from the Book of Job. He seemed to take for his text, if texts are ever taken for prayers, " Behold, thou hast instructed many; but now it is come upon thee, and thou faintest; it toucheth thee, and thou art troubled." When we others rose up, the minister continued for some minutes on his knees. Then he too got up, and stood facing us, for a moment, before we all sate down in conclave. After a pause Robinson began—

" We grieve for you, Brother Holman, for your trouble is great. But we would fain have you remember you are as a light set on a hill; and the congregations are looking at you with watchful eyes. We have been talking as we came along on the two duties required of you in this strait, Brother Hodgson and me. And we have resolved to exhort you on these two points. First, God has given you the opportunity of showing forth an example of resignation." Poor Mr. Holman visibly winced at this word. I could fancy how he had tossed aside such brotherly preachings in his happier moments; but now his whole system was unstrung, and " resignation " seemed a term which presupposed that the dreaded misery of losing Phillis was inevitable. But good, stupid Mr. Robinson went on. " We hear on all sides that there are scarce any hopes of your child's recovery; and it may be well to bring you to mind of Abraham; and how he was willing to kill his only child when the Lord commanded. Take example by him, Brother Holman. Let us hear you say, ' The Lord giveth and the Lord taketh away. Blessed be the name of the Lord! ' "

There was a pause of expectancy. I verily believe the minister tried to feel it; but he could not. Heart of flesh was too strong. Heart of stone he had not.

" I will say it to my God, when He gives me strength—when the day comes," he spoke at last.

The other two looked at each other, and shook their heads. I think the reluctance to answer as they wished was not quite unexpected. The minister went on: " There are hopes yet," he said, as if to himself. " God has given me a great heart for hoping, and I will not look forward beyond the hour." Then, turning more to them, and speaking louder, he added: " Brethren, God will strengthen me when the time comes, when such resignation as you speak of is needed. Till then I cannot feel it; and what I do not feel I will not express, using words as if they were a charm." He was getting chafed, I could see.

He had rather put them out by these speeches of his; but after a short time and some more shakes of the head, Robinson began again—

"Secondly, we would have you listen to the voice of the rod, and ask yourself for what sins this trial has been laid upon you: whether you may not have been too much given up to your farm and your cattle; whether this world's learning has not puffed you up to vain conceit and neglect of the things of God; whether you have not made an idol of your daughter?"

"I cannot answer — I will not answer!" exclaimed the minister. "My sins I confess to God. But if they were scarlet—and they are so in His sight," he added humbly—"I hold with Christ that afflictions are not sent by God in wrath as penalties for sin."

"Is that orthodox, Brother Robinson?" asked the third minister, in a deferential tone of inquiry.

Despite the minister's injunction not to leave him, I thought matters were getting so serious that a little homely interruption would be more to the purpose than my continued presence, and I went round to the kitchen to ask for Betty's help.

"'Od rot 'em!" said she; "they're always a-coming at ill-convenient times; and they have such hearty appetites, they'll make nothing of what would have served master and you since our poor lass has been ill. I've but a bit of cold beef in th' house; but I'll do some ham and eggs, and that 'll rout 'em from worrying the minister. They're a deal quieter after they've had their victual. Last time as old Robinson came, he was very reprehensible upon master's learning, which he couldn't compass to save his life, so he needn't have been afeared of that temptation, and used words long enough to have knocked a body down; but after me and missus had given him his fill of victual, and he'd had some good ale and a pipe, he spoke just like any other man, and could crack a joke with me."

Their visit was the only break in the long weary days and nights. I do not mean that no other inquiries were made. I believe that all the neighbours hung about the place daily, till they could learn from some out-comer how Phillis Holman was. But they knew better than to come up to the house; for the August weather was so hot that every door and window was kept constantly open, and the least sound outside penetrated all through. I am sure the cocks and hens had a sad time of it; for Betty drove them all into an empty barn, and kept them fastened up in the dark for several days, with very little effect as regarded their crowing and clacking. At length came a sleep which was the crisis, and from which she wakened up with a new faint life. Her slumber had lasted many, many hours. We scarcely dared to breathe or move during the time; we had striven to hope so long, that we were sick at heart, and durst not trust in the favourable signs: the even breathing, the moistened skin, the slight return of delicate colour into the pale, wan lips. I recollect stealing out that evening in the dusk, and wandering down the grassy lane, under the shadow of the over-arching elms to the little bridge at the foot of the hill, where the lane to the Hope Farm joined another road to Hornby. On the low parapet of that bridge I found Timothy Cooper, the stupid, half-witted labourer, sitting, idly throwing bits of mortar into the brook below. He just looked up at me as I came near, but gave me no greeting, either by word or gesture. He had generally made some sign of recognition to me; but this time I thought he was sullen at being dismissed. Never-theless, I felt as if it would be a relief to talk a little to some one, and I sate down by him. While I was thinking how to begin, he yawned wearily.

"You are tired, Tim," said I.

"Ay," said he. "But I reckon I may go home now."

"Have you been sitting here long?"

"Welly all day long. Leastways sin' seven i' th' morning."

"Why, what in the world have you been doing?"

"Nought."

"Why have you been sitting here, then?"

"T' keep carts off." He was up now, stretching himself, and shaking his lubberly limbs.

"Carts! what carts?"

"Carts as might ha' wakened yon wench! It's Hornby market-day. I reckon yo're no better nor a half-wit yoursel'." He cocked his eye at me, as if he were gauging my intellect.

"And have you been sitting here all day to keep the lane quiet?"

"Ay. I've nought else to do. Th' minister has turned me adrift. Have yo' heard how th' lass is faring to-night?"

"They hope she'll waken better for this long sleep. Good-night to you, and God bless you, Timothy!" said I.

He scarcely took any notice of my words, as he lumbered across a stile that led to his cottage. Presently, I went home to the farm. Phillis had stirred, had spoken two or three faint

words. Her mother was with her, dropping nourishment into
her scarce conscious mouth. The rest of the household were
summoned to evening prayer, for the first time for many days.
It was a return to the daily habits of happiness and health.
But in these silent days our very lives had been an unspoken
prayer. Now, we met in the house-place, and looked at each
other with strange recognition of the thankfulness on all our
faces. We knelt down; we waited for the minister's voice.
He did not begin as usual. He could not; he was choking.
Presently we heard the strong man's sob. Then old John
turned round on his knees, and said—

"Minister, I reckon we have blessed the Lord wi' all our
souls though we've ne'er talked about it; and maybe He'll not
need spoken words this night. God bless us all, and keep our
Phillis safe from harm! Amen."

Old John's impromptu prayer was all we had that night.

"Our Phillis," as he had called her, grew better day by day
from that time. Not quickly; I sometimes grew desponding,
and feared that she would never be what she had been before;
no more she has, in some ways.

I seized an early opportunity to tell the minister about
Timothy Cooper's unsolicited watch on the bridge during the
long summer's day.

"God forgive me!" said the minister. "I have been too
proud in my own conceit. The first steps I take out of this
house shall be to Cooper's cottage."

I need hardly say Timothy was reinstated in his place on the
farm; and I have often since admired the patience with which
his master tried to teach him how to do the easy work which
was henceforward carefully adjusted to his capacity.

Phillis was carried downstairs, and lay for hour after hour
quite silent on the great sofa, drawn up under the windows of
the house-place. She seemed always the same—gentle, quiet,
and sad. Her energy did not return with her bodily strength.
It was sometimes pitiful to see her parents' vain endeavours to
rouse her to interest. One day the minister brought her a set
of blue ribbons, reminding her with a tender smile of a former
conversation, in which she had owned to a love of such feminine
vanities. She spoke gratefully to him; but, when he was gone,
she laid them on one side, and languidly shut her eyes. Another
time I saw her mother bring her the Latin and Italian books
that she had been so fond of before her illness—or, rather, before
Holdsworth had gone away. That was worst of all. She

turned her face to the wall, and cried as soon as her mother's back was turned. Betty was laying the cloth for the early dinner. Her sharp eyes saw the state of the case.

"Now, Phillis!" said she, coming up to the sofa; "we ha' done a' we can for you, and th' doctors has done a' they can for you, and I think the Lord has done a' He can for you, and more than you deserve, too, if you don't do something for yourself. If I were you, I'd rise up and snuff the moon, sooner than break your father's and your mother's hearts wi' watching and waiting, till it pleases you to fight your own way back to cheerfulness. There, I never favoured long preachings, and I've said my say."

A day or two after, Phillis asked me, when we were alone, if I thought my father and mother would allow her to go and stay with them for a couple of months. She blushed a little, as she faltered out her wish for change of thought and scene.

"Only for a short time, Paul! Then—we will go back to the peace of the old days. I know we shall; I can, and I will!"

MY LADY LUDLOW

CHAPTER I

I AM an old woman now, and things are very different to what they were in my youth. Then we, who travelled, travelled in coaches, carrying six inside, and making a two days' journey out of what people now go over in a couple of hours with a whizz and a flash, and a screaming whistle, enough to deafen one. Then letters came in but three times a week: indeed, in some places in Scotland where I have stayed when I was a girl, the post came in but once a month;—but letters were letters then; and we made great prizes of them, and read them and studied them like books. Now the post comes rattling in twice a day, bringing short jerky notes, some without beginning or end, but just a little sharp sentence, which well-bred folks would think too abrupt to be spoken. Well, well! they may all be improvements—I dare say they are; but you will never meet with a Lady Ludlow in these days.

I will try and tell you about her. It is no story: it has, as I said, neither beginning, middle, nor end.

My father was a poor clergyman with a large family. My mother was always said to have good blood in her veins; and when she wanted to maintain her position with the people she was thrown among—principally rich democratic manufacturers, all for liberty and the French Revolution—she would put on a pair of ruffles, trimmed with real old English point, very much darned to be sure—but which could not be bought new for love or money, as the art of making it was lost years before. These ruffles showed, as she said, that her ancestors had been Some-bodies, when the grandfathers of the rich folk, who now looked down upon her, had been Nobodies—if, indeed, they had any grandfathers at all. I don't know whether any one out of our own family ever noticed these ruffles—but we were all taught as children to feel rather proud when my mother put them on, and to hold up our heads as became the descendants of the lady who had first possessed the lace. Not but what my dear father often told us that pride was a great sin; we were never allowed to be proud of anything but my mother's ruffles: and she was so innocently happy when she put them on—often, poor dear creature, to a very worn and threadbare gown—that I still think, even after all my experience of life, they were a blessing to the family. You will think that I am wandering away from my Lady Ludlow. Not at all. The lady who had owned the lace, Ursula Hanbury, was a common ancestress of both my mother and my Lady Ludlow. And so it fell out, that when my poor father died, and my mother was sorely pressed to know what to do with her nine children, and looked far and wide for signs of willingness to help, Lady Ludlow sent her a letter, proffering aid and assistance. I see that letter now: a large sheet of thick yellow paper, with a straight broad margin left on the left-hand side of the delicate Italian writing—writing which contained far more in the same space of paper than all the sloping or masculine hand-writings of the present day. It was sealed with a coat of arms—a lozenge—for Lady Ludlow was a widow. My mother made us notice the motto, " Foy et Loy," and told us where to look for the quarterings of the Hanbury arms before she opened the letter. Indeed, I think she was rather afraid of what the contents might be; for, as I have said, in her anxious love for her fatherless children, she had written to many people upon whom, to tell truly, she had but little claim; and their cold, hard answers had many a time made her cry, when she thought none of us were looking. I do not even know if she had ever seen Lady Ludlow: all I knew of her was that she was a very grand lady, whose grandmother had been half-sister to my mother's great-grandmother; but of her character and circumstances I had heard nothing, and I doubt if my mother was acquainted with them.

I looked over my mother's shoulder to read the letter; it began, " Dear Cousin Margaret Dawson," and I think I felt hopeful from the moment I saw those words. She went on to say—stay, I think I can remember the very words:

" DEAR COUSIN MARGARET DAWSON,—I have been much grieved to hear of the loss you have sustained in the death of so good a husband, and so excellent a clergyman as I have always heard that my late cousin Richard was esteemed to be."

" There! " said my mother, laying her finger on the passage, " read that aloud to the little ones. Let them hear how their father's good report travelled far and wide, and how well he is spoken of by one whom he never saw. COUSIN Richard, how prettily her ladyship writes! Go on, Margaret!" She wiped her eyes as she spoke: and laid her fingers on her lips, to still my little sister, Cecily, who, not understanding anything about the important letter, was beginning to talk and make a noise.

"You say you are left with nine children. I too should have had nine, if mine had all lived. I have none left but Rudolph, the present Lord Ludlow. He is married, and lives, for the most part, in London. But I entertain six young gentlewomen at my house at Connington, who are to me as daughters—save that, perhaps, I restrict them in certain indulgences in dress and diet that might be befitting in young ladies of a higher rank, and of more probable wealth. These young persons— all of condition, though out of means—are my constant companions, and I strive to do my duty as a Christian lady towards them. One of these young gentlewomen died (at her own home, whither she had gone upon a visit) last May. Will you do me the favour to allow your eldest daughter to supply her place in my household? She is, as I make out, about sixteen years of age. She will find companions here who are but a little older than herself. I dress my young friends myself, and make each of them a small allowance for pocket-money. They have but few opportunities for matrimony, as Connington is far removed from any town. The clergyman is a deaf old widower; my agent is married; and as for the neighbouring farmers, they are, of course, below the notice of the young gentlewomen under my protection. Still, if any young woman wishes to marry, and has conducted herself to my satisfaction, I give her a wedding dinner, her clothes, and her house-linen. And such as remain with me to my death, will find a small competency provided for them in my will. I reserve to myself the option of paying their travelling expenses—disliking gadding women, on the one hand; on the other, not wishing by too long absence from the family home to weaken natural ties.

"If my proposal pleases you and your daughter—or rather, if it pleases you, for I trust your daughter has been too well brought up to have a will in opposition to yours—let me know, dear cousin Margaret Dawson, and I will make arrangements for meeting the young gentlewoman at Cavistock, which is the nearest point to which the coach will bring her."

My mother dropped the letter, and sat silent.

"I shall not know what to do without you, Margaret."

A moment before, like a young untried girl as I was, I had been pleased at the notion of seeing a new place, and leading a

new life. But now—my mother's look of sorrow, and the
children's cry of remonstrance: "Mother; I won't go," I said.

"Nay! but you had better," replied she, shaking her head.
"Lady Ludlow has much power. She can help your brothers.
It will not do to slight her offer."

So we accepted it, after much consultation. We were rewarded—or so we thought—for, afterwards, when I came to
know Lady Ludlow, I saw that she would have done her duty
by us, as helpless relations, however we might have rejected her
kindness—by a presentation to Christ's Hospital for one of my
brothers.

And this was how I came to know my Lady Ludlow.

I remember well the afternoon of my arrival at Hanbury
Court. Her ladyship had sent to meet me at the nearest post-
town at which the mail-coach stopped. There was an old groom
inquiring for me, the ostler said, if my name was Dawson—from
Hanbury Court, he believed. I felt it rather formidable; and
first began to understand what was meant by going among
strangers, when I lost sight of the guard to whom my mother
had intrusted me. I was perched up in a high gig with a hood
to it, such as in those days was called a chair, and my companion was driving deliberately through the most pastoral
country I had ever yet seen. By-and-by we ascended a long
hill, and the man got out and walked at the horse's head. I
should have liked to walk, too, very much indeed; but I did not
know how far I might do it; and, in fact, I dared not speak to
ask to be helped down the deep steps of the gig. We were at
last at the top—on a long, breezy, sweeping, unenclosed piece
of ground, called. as I afterwards learnt, a Chase. The groom
stopped, breathed, patted his horse, and then mounted again to
my side.

"Are we near Hanbury Court?" I asked.

"Near! Why, Miss! we've a matter of ten mile yet to go."

Once launched into conversation, we went on pretty glibly.
I fancy he had been afraid of beginning to speak to me, just as I
was to him; but he got over his shyness with me sooner than I
did mine with him. I let him choose the subjects of conversation, although very often I could not understand the points of
interest in them: for instance, he talked for more than a quarter
of an hour of a famous race which a certain dog-fox had given
him, above thirty years before; and spoke of all the covers and
turns just as if I knew them as well as he did; and all the time
I was wondering what kind of an animal a dog-fox might be.

After we left the Chase, the road grew worse. No one in these days, who has not seen the byroads of fifty years ago, can imagine what they were. We had to quarter, as Randal called it, nearly all the way along the deep-rutted, miry lanes; and the tremendous jolts I occasionally met with made my seat in the gig so unsteady that I could not look about me at all, I was so much occupied in holding on. The road was too muddy for me to walk without dirtying myself more than I liked to do, just before my first sight of my Lady Ludlow. But by-and-by, when we came to the fields in which the lane ended, I begged Randal to help me down, as I saw that I could pick my steps among the pasture grass without making myself unfit to be seen; and Randal, out of pity for his steaming horse, wearied with the hard struggle through the mud, thanked me kindly, and helped me down with a springing jump.

The pastures fell gradually down to the lower land, shut in on either side by rows of high elms, as if there had been a wide grand avenue here in former times. Down the grassy gorge we went, seeing the sunset sky at the end of the shadowed descent. Suddenly we came to a long flight of steps.

" If you'll run down there, Miss, I'll go round and meet you, and then you'd better mount again, for my lady will like to see you drive up to the house."

" Are we near the house? " said I, suddenly checked by the idea.

" Down there, Miss," replied he, pointing with his whip to certain stacks of twisted chimneys rising out of a group of trees, in deep shadow against the crimson light, and which lay just beyond a great square lawn at the base of the steep slope of a hundred yards, on the edge of which we stood.

I went down the steps quietly enough. I met Randal and the gig at the bottom; and, falling into a side road to the left, we drove sedately round, through the gateway, and into the great court in front of the house.

The road by which we had come lay right at the back.

Hanbury Court is a vast red-brick house—at least, it is cased in part with red bricks; and the gate-house and walls about the place are of brick—with stone facings at every corner, and door, and window, such as you see at Hampton Court. At the back are the gables, and arched doorways, and stone mullions, which show (so Lady Ludlow used to tell us) that it was once a priory. There was a prior's parlour, I know—only we called it Mrs. Medlicott's room; and there was a tithe-barn as big as a church, and rows of fish-ponds, all got ready for the monks' fasting-days in old time. But all this I did not see till afterwards. I hardly noticed, this first night, the great Virginian Creeper (said to have been the first planted in England by one of my lady's ancestors) that half covered the front of the house. As I had been unwilling to leave the guard of the coach, so did I now feel unwilling to leave Randal, a known friend of three hours. But there was no help for it; in I must go; past the grand-looking old gentleman holding the door open for me, on into the great hall on the right hand, into which the sun's last rays were sending in glorious red light—the gentleman was now walking before me—up a step on to the dais, as I afterwards learned that it was called—then again to the left, through a series of sitting-rooms, opening one out of another, and all of them look-ing into a stately garden, glowing, even in the twilight, with the bloom of flowers. We went up four steps out of the last of these rooms, and then my guide lifted up a heavy silk curtain, and I was in the presence of my Lady Ludlow.

She was very small of stature, and very upright. She wore a great lace cap, nearly half her own height, I should think, that went round her head (caps which tied under the chin, and which we called "mobs," came in later, and my lady held them in great contempt, saying people might as well come down in their night caps). In front of my lady's cap was a great bow of white satin ribbon; and a broad band of the same ribbon was tied tight round her head and served to keep the cap straight. She had a fine Indian muslin shawl folded over her shoulders and across her chest, and an apron of the same; a black silk mode gown, made with short sleeves and ruffles, and with the tail thereof pulled through the pocket-hole, so as to shorten it to a useful length: beneath it she wore, as I could plainly see, a quilted lavender satin petticoat. Her hair was snowy white, but I hardly saw it, it was so covered with her cap: her skin, even at her age, was waxen in texture and tint; her eyes were large and dark blue, and must have been her great beauty when she was young, for there was nothing particular, as far as I can re-member, either in mouth or nose. She had a great gold-headed stick by her chair; but I think it was more as a mark of state and dignity than for use; for she had as light and brisk a step when she chose as any girl of fifteen, and, in her private early walk of meditation in the mornings, would go as swiftly from garden alley to garden alley as any one of us.

She was standing up when I went in. I dropped my curtsey

at the door, which my mother had always taught me as a part of good manners, and went up instinctively to my lady. She did not put out her hand, but raised herself a little on tiptoe, and kissed me on both cheeks.

" You are cold, my child. You shall have a dish of tea with me." She rang a little hand-bell on the table by her, and her waiting-maid came in from a small anteroom; and, as if all had been prepared, and was awaiting my arrival, brought with her a small china service with tea ready made, and a plate of delicately-cut bread and butter, every morsel of which I could have eaten, and been none the better for it, so hungry was I after my long ride. The waiting-maid took off my cloak, and I sat down, sorely alarmed at the silence, the hushed foot-falls of the subdued maiden over the thick carpet, and the soft voice and clear pronunciation of my Lady Ludlow. My teaspoon fell against my cup with a sharp noise, that seemed so out of place and season that I blushed deeply. My lady caught my eye with hers—both keen and sweet were those dark-blue eyes of her ladyship's:—

" Your hands are very cold, my dear; take off those gloves " (I wore thick serviceable doeskin, and had been too shy to take them off unbidden), " and let me try and warm them—the evenings are very chilly." And she held my great red hands in hers —soft, warm, white, ring-laden. Looking at last a little wist-fully into my face, she said—" Poor child! And you're the eldest of nine! I had a daughter who would have been just your age; but I cannot fancy her the eldest of nine." Then came a pause of silence; and then she rang her bell, and desired her waiting-maid, Adams, to show me to my room.

It was so small that I think it must have been a cell. The walls were whitewashed stone; the bed was of white dimity. There was a small piece of red stair carpet on each side of the bed, and two chairs. In a closet adjoining were my washstand and toilet-table. There was a text of Scripture painted on the wall right opposite to my bed; and below hung a print, common enough in those days, of King George and Queen Charlotte, with all their numerous children, down to the little Princess Amelia in a go-cart. On each side hung a small portrait, also engraved: on the left, it was Louis the Sixteenth; on the other, Marie-Antoinette. On the chimney-piece there was a tinder-box and a Prayer-book. I do not remember anything else in the room. Indeed, in those days people did not dream of writing-tables, and inkstands, and portfolios, and easy chairs, and what not. We were taught to go into our bedrooms for the purposes of dressing, and sleeping, and praying.

Presently I was summoned to supper. I followed the young lady who had been sent to call me, down the wide shallow stairs, into the great hall, through which I had first passed on my way to my Lady Ludlow's room. There were four other young gentlewomen, all standing, and all silent, who curtsied to me when I first came in. They were dressed in a kind of uniform: muslin caps bound round their heads with blue ribbons, plain muslin handkerchiefs, lawn aprons, and drab-coloured stuff gowns. They were all gathered together at a little distance from the table, on which were placed a couple of cold chickens, a salad, and a fruit tart. On the dais there was a smaller round table, on which stood a silver jug filled with milk, and a small roll. Near that was set a carved chair, with a countess's coronet surmounting the back of it. I thought that some one might have spoken to me; but they were shy, and I was shy; or else there was some other reason; but, indeed, almost the minute after I had come into the hall by the door at the lower hand, her ladyship entered by the door opening upon the dais; whereupon we all curtsied very low; I because I saw the others do it. She stood, and looked at us for a moment.

"Young gentlewomen," said she, "make Margaret Dawson welcome among you;" and they treated me with the kind politeness due to a stranger, but still without any talking beyond what was required for the purposes of the meal. After it was over, and grace was said by one of our party, my lady rang her hand-bell, and the servants came in and cleared away the supper things: then they brought in a portable reading-desk, which was placed on the dais, and, the whole household trooping in, my lady called to one of my companions to come up and read the Psalms and Lessons for the day. I remember thinking how afraid I should have been had I been in her place. There were no prayers. My lady thought it schismatic to have any prayers excepting those in the Prayer-book; and would as soon have preached a sermon herself in the parish church, as have allowed any one not a deacon at the least to read prayers in a private dwelling-house. I am not sure that even then she would have approved of his reading them in an unconsecrated place.

She had been maid of honour to Queen Charlotte: a Hanbury of that old stock that flourished in the days of the Plantagenets, and heiress of all the land that remained to the family, of the great estates which had once stretched into four separate counties. Hanbury Court was hers by right. She had married Lord Ludlow, and had lived for many years at his various seats, and away from her ancestral home. She had lost all her children but one, and most of them had died at these houses of Lord Ludlow's; and, I dare say, that gave my lady a distaste to the places, and a longing to come back to Hanbury Court, where she had been so happy as a girl. I imagine her girlhood had been the happiest time of her life; for, now I think of it, most of her opinions, when I knew her in later life, were singular enough then, but had been universally prevalent fifty years before. For instance, while I lived at Hanbury Court, the cry for education was beginning to come up: Mr. Raikes had set up his Sunday Schools; and some clergymen were all for teaching writing and arithmetic, as well as reading. My lady would have none of this; it was levelling and revolutionary, she said. When a young woman came to be hired, my lady would have her in, and see if she liked her looks and her dress, and question her about her family. Her ladyship laid great stress upon this latter point, saying that a girl who did not warm up when any interest or curiosity was expressed about her mother, or the " baby " (if there was one), was not likely to make a good servant. Then she would make her put out her feet, to see if they were well and neatly shod. Then she would bid her say the Lord's Prayer and the Creed. Then she inquired if she could write. If she could, and she had liked all that had gone before, her face sank—it was a great disappointment, for it was an all but inviolable rule with her never to engage a servant who could write. But I have known her ladyship break through it, although in both cases in which she did so she put the girl's principles to a further and unusual test in asking her to repeat the Ten Commandments. One pert young woman—and yet I was sorry for her too, only she afterwards married a rich draper in Shrewsbury—who had got through her trials pretty tolerably, considering she could write, spoilt all, by saying glibly, at the end of the last Commandment, " An't please your ladyship, I can cast accounts."

" Go away, wench," said my lady in a hurry, " you're only fit for trade; you will not suit me for a servant." The girl went away crestfallen: in a minute, however, my lady sent me after her to see that she had something to eat before leaving the house; and, indeed, she sent for her once again, but it was only to give her a Bible, and to bid her beware of French principles, which had led the French to cut off their king's and queen's heads.

The poor, blubbering girl said, " Indeed, my lady, I wouldn't hurt a fly, much less a king, and I cannot abide the French, nor frogs neither, for that matter."

But my lady was inexorable, and took a girl who could neither read nor write, to make up for her alarm about the progress of education towards addition and subtraction; and afterwards, when the clergyman who was at Hanbury parish when I came there, had died, and the bishop had appointed another, and a younger man, in his stead, this was one of the points on which he and my lady did not agree. While good old deaf Mr. Mountford lived, it was my lady's custom, when indisposed for a sermon, to stand up at the door of her large square pew—just opposite to the reading-desk—and to say (at that part of the morning service where it is decreed that, in quires and places where they sing, here followeth the anthem): " Mr. Mountford, I will not trouble you for a discourse this morning." And we all knelt down to the Litany with great satisfaction; for Mr. Mountford, though he could not hear, had always his eyes open about this part of the service, for any of my lady's movements. But the new clergyman, Mr. Gray, was of a different stamp. He was very zealous in all his parish work; and my lady, who was just as good as she could be to the poor, was often crying him up as a godsend to the parish, and he never could send amiss to the Court when he wanted broth, or wine, or jelly, or sago for a sick person. But he needs must take up the new hobby of education; and I could see that this put my lady sadly about one Sunday, when she suspected, I know not how, that there was something to be said in his sermon about a Sunday-school which he was planning. She stood up, as she had not done since Mr. Mountford's death, two years and better before this time, and said—

" Mr. Gray, I will not trouble you for a discourse this morning."

But her voice was not well-assured and steady; and we knelt down with more of curiosity than satisfaction in our minds. Mr. Gray preached a very rousing sermon, on the necessity of establishing a Sabbath-school in the village. My lady shut her eyes, and seemed to go to sleep; but I don't believe she lost a word of it, though she said nothing about it that I heard until the next Saturday, when two of us, as was the custom, were riding out with her in her carriage, and we went to see a poor bedridden woman, who lived some miles away at the other end of the estate and of the parish: and as we came out of the cottage we met Mr. Gray walking up to it, in a great heat, and looking very tired. My lady beckoned him to her, and told him she should wait and take him home with her, adding that she wondered to see him there, so far from his home, for that it was beyond a Sabbath-day's journey, and, from what she had gathered from his sermon the last Sunday, he was all for Judaism against Christianity. He looked as if he did not understand what she meant; but the truth was that, besides the way in which he had spoken up for schools and schooling, he had kept calling Sunday the Sabbath: and, as her ladyship said, "The Sabbath is the Sabbath, and that's one thing—it is Saturday; and if I keep it, I'm a Jew, which I'm not. And Sunday is Sunday; and that's another thing; and if I keep it, I'm a Christian, which I humbly trust I am."

But when Mr. Gray got an inkling of her meaning in talking about a Sabbath-day's journey, he only took notice of a part of it: he smiled and bowed, and said no one knew better than her ladyship what were the duties that abrogated all inferior laws regarding the Sabbath; and that he must go in and read to old Betty Brown, so that he would not detain her ladyship.

"But I shall wait for you, Mr. Gray," said she. "Or I will take a drive round by Oakfield, and be back in an hour's time." For, you see, she would not have him feel hurried or troubled with a thought that he was keeping her waiting, while he ought to be comforting and praying with old Betty.

"A very pretty young man, my dears," said she, as we drove away. "But I shall have my pew glazed all the same."

We did not know what she meant at the time; but the next Sunday but one we did. She had the curtains all round the grand old Hanbury family seat taken down, and, instead of them, there was glass up to the height of six or seven feet. We entered by a door, with a window in it that drew up or down just like what you see in carriages. This window was generally down, and then we could hear perfectly; but if Mr. Gray used the word "Sabbath," or spoke in favour of schooling and education, my lady stepped out of her corner, and drew up the window with a decided clang and clash.

I must tell you something more about Mr. Gray. The presentation to the living of Hanbury was vested in two trustees, of whom Lady Ludlow was one: Lord Ludlow had exercised this right in the appointment of Mr. Mountford, who had won his lordship's favour by his excellent horsemanship. Nor was Mr. Mountford a bad clergyman, as clergymen went in those

days. He did not drink, though he liked good eating as much
as any one. And if any poor person was ill, and he heard of it,
he would send them plates from his own dinner of what he
himself liked best; sometimes of dishes which were almost as
bad as poison to sick people. He meant kindly to everybody
except dissenters, whom Lady Ludlow and he united in trying
to drive out of the parish; and among dissenters he particularly
abhorred Methodists—some one said, because John Wesley had
objected to his hunting. But that must have been long ago,
for when I knew him he was far too stout and too heavy to
hunt; besides, the bishop of the diocese disapproved of hunting,
and had intimated his disapprobation to the clergy. For my
own part, I think a good run would not have come amiss, even
in a moral point of view, to Mr. Mountford. He ate so much,
and took so little exercise, that we young women often heard
of his being in terrible passions with his servants, and the
sexton and clerk. But they none of them minded him much,
for he soon came to himself, and was sure to make them some
present or other—some said in proportion to his anger; so that
the sexton, who was a bit of a wag (as all sextons are, I think),
said that the vicar's saying, " The Devil take you," was worth a
shilling any day, whereas " The Deuce " was a shabby sixpenny
speech, only fit for a curate.

There was a great deal of good in Mr. Mountford, too. He
could not bear to see pain, or sorrow, or misery of any kind;
and, if it came under his notice, he was never easy till he had
relieved it, for the time, at any rate. But he was afraid of being
made uncomfortable; so, if he possibly could, he would avoid
seeing any one who was ill or unhappy; and he did not thank
any one for telling him about them.

" What would your ladyship have me to do? " he once said
to my Lady Ludlow, when she wished him to go and see a poor
man who had broken his leg. " I cannot piece the leg as the
doctor can; I cannot nurse him as well as his wife does; I may
talk to him, but he no more understands me than I do the
language of the alchemists. My coming puts him out; he
stiffens himself into an uncomfortable posture, out of respect
to the cloth, and dare not take the comfort of kicking, and
swearing, and scolding his wife, while I am there. I hear him,
with my figurative ears, my lady, heave a sigh of relief when
my back is turned, and the sermon that he thinks I ought to
have kept for the pulpit, and have delivered to his neighbours
(whose case, as he fancies, it would just have fitted, as it seemed

to him to be addressed to the sinful), is all ended, and done, for the day. I judge others as myself; I do to them as I would be done to. That's Christianity, at any rate. I should hate—saving your ladyship's presence—to have my Lord Ludlow coming and seeing me, if I were ill. 'Twould be a great honour, no doubt; but I should have to put on a clean nightcap for the occasion; and sham patience, in order to be polite, and not weary his lordship with my complaints. I should be twice as thankful to him if he would send me game, or a good fat haunch, to bring me up to that pitch of health and strength one ought to be in, to appreciate the honour of a visit from a nobleman. So I shall send Jerry Butler a good dinner every day till he is strong again; and spare the poor old fellow my presence and advice."

My lady would be puzzled by this, and by many other of Mr. Mountford's speeches. But he had been appointed by my lord, and she could not question her dead husband's wisdom; and she knew that the dinners were always sent, and often a guinea or two to help to pay the doctor's bills; and Mr. Mountford was true blue, as we call it, to the back-bone; hated the dissenters and the French; and could hardly drink a dish of tea without giving out the toast of "Church and King, and down with the Rump." Moreover, he had once had the honour of preaching before the king and queen, and two of the princesses, at Weymouth; and the king had applauded his sermon audibly with—"Very good; very good;" and that was a seal put upon his merit in my lady's eyes.

Besides, in the long winter Sunday evenings, he would come up to the Court, and read a sermon to us girls, and play a game of picquet with my lady afterwards; which served to shorten the tedium of the time. My lady would, on those occasions, invite him to sup with her on the dais; but as her meal was invariably bread and milk only, Mr. Mountford preferred sitting down amongst us, and made a joke about its being wicked and heterodox to eat meagre on Sunday, a festival of the Church. We smiled at this joke just as much the twentieth time we heard it as we did at the first; for we knew it was coming, because he always coughed a little nervously before he made a joke, for fear my lady should not approve: and neither she nor he seemed to remember that he had ever hit upon the idea before.

Mr. Mountford died quite suddenly at last. We were all very sorry to lose him. He left some of his property (for he had a private estate) to the poor of the parish, to furnish them with an annual Christmas dinner of roast beef and plum-pudding, for which he wrote out a very good receipt in the codicil to his will.

Moreover, he desired his executors to see that the vault, in which the vicars of Hanbury were interred, was well aired, before his coffin was taken in; for, all his life long, he had had a dread of damp, and latterly he kept his rooms to such a pitch of warmth that some thought it hastened his end.

Then the other trustee, as I have said, presented the living to Mr. Gray, Fellow of Lincoln College, Oxford. It was quite natural for us all, as belonging in some sort to the Hanbury family, to disapprove of the other trustee's choice. But when some ill-natured person circulated the report that Mr. Gray was a Moravian Methodist, I remember my lady said, " She could not believe anything so bad, without a great deal of evidence."

CHAPTER II

BEFORE I tell you about Mr. Gray, I think I ought to make you understand something more of what we did all day long at Hanbury Court. There were five of us at the time of which I am speaking, all young women of good descent, and allied (however distantly) to people of rank. When we were not with my lady, Mrs. Medlicott looked after us; a gentle little woman, who had been companion to my lady for many years, and was indeed, I have been told, some kind of relation to her. Mrs. Medlicott's parents had lived in Germany, and the consequence was, she spoke English with a very foreign accent. Another consequence was, that she excelled in all manner of needlework, such as is not known even by name in these days. She could darn either lace, table-linen, India muslin, or stockings, so that no one could tell where the hole or rent had been. Though a good Protestant, and never missing Guy Faux day at church, she was as skilful at fine work as any nun in a Papist convent. She would take a piece of French cambric, and by drawing out some threads, and working in others, it became delicate lace in a very few hours. She did the same by Hollands cloth, and made coarse strong lace, with which all my lady's napkins and table-linen were trimmed. We worked under her during a great part of the day, either in the still-room, or at our sewing in a chamber that opened out of the great hall. My lady despised every kind of work that would now be called Fancy-work. She considered that the use of coloured threads or worsted was only fit to amuse children; but that grown women ought not to be taken with mere blues and reds, but to restrict their pleasure in sewing to making small and delicate stitches. She would speak of the old tapestry in the hall as the work of her ancestresses, who lived before the Reformation, and were consequently unacquainted with pure and simple tastes in work, as well as in religion. Nor would my lady sanction the fashion of the day, which, at the beginning of this century, made all the fine ladies take to making shoes. She said that such work was a consequence of the French Revolution, which had done much to annihilate all distinctions of rank and class, and hence it was, that she saw young ladies of birth and breeding handling lasts, and awls, and dirty cobblers'-wax, like shoemakers daughters.

Very frequently one of us would be summoned to my lady to read aloud to her, as she sat in her small withdrawing-room, some improving book. It was generally Mr. Addison's *Spectator;* but one year, I remember, we had to read *Sturm's Reflections*, translated from a German book Mrs. Medlicott recommended. Mr. Sturm told us what to think about for every day in the year; and very dull it was; but I believe Queen Charlotte had liked the book very much, and the thought of her royal approbation kept my lady awake during the read-ing. *Mrs. Chapone's Letters* and *Dr. Gregory's Advice to Young Ladies* composed the rest of our library for week-day reading. I, for one, was glad to leave my fine sewing, and even my reading aloud (though this last did keep me with my dear lady) to go to the still-room and potter about among the preserves and the medicated waters. There was no doctor for many miles round, and with Mrs. Medlicott to direct us, and Dr. Buchan to go by for recipes, we sent out many a bottle of physic, which, I dare say, was as good as what comes out of the druggist's shop. At any rate, I do not think we did much harm; for if any of our physics tasted stronger than usual, Mrs. Medlicott would bid us let it down with cochineal and water, to make all safe, as she said. So our bottles of medicine had very little real physic in them at last; but we were careful in putting labels on them, which looked very mysterious to those who could not read, and helped the medicine to do its work. I have sent off many a bottle of salt and water coloured red; and whenever we had nothing else to do in the still-room, Mrs. Medlicott would set us to making bread-pills, by way of practice; and, as far as I can say, they were very efficacious, as before we gave out a box Mrs. Medlicott always told the patient what symptoms to expect; and I hardly ever inquired without hearing that they had produced their effect. There was one old man, who took six pills a-night, of any kind we liked to give him, to make him sleep; and if, by any chance, his daughter had forgetten to let us know that he was out of his medicine, he was so restless and miserable that, as he said, he thought he was like to die. I think ours was what would be called homœopathic practice now-a-days. Then we learnt to make all the cakes and dishes of the season in the still-room. We had plum-porridge and mince-pies at Christmas, fritters and pancakes on Shrove Tuesday, furmenty on Mother-ing Sunday, violet-cakes in Passion Week, tansy-pudding on Easter Sunday, three-cornered cakes on Trinity Sunday, and so on through the year: all made from good old Church receipts, handed down from one of my lady's earliest Protestant ances-tresses. Every one of us passed a portion of the day with Lady Ludlow; and now and then we rode out with her in her coach and four. She did not like to go out with a pair of horses, con-sidering this rather beneath her rank; and, indeed, four horses were very often needed to pull her heavy coach through the stiff mud. But it was rather a cumbersome equipage through the narrow Warwickshire lanes; and I used often to think it was well that countesses were not plentiful, or else we might have met another lady of quality in another coach and four, where there would have been no possibility of turning, or passing each other, and very little chance of backing. Once when the idea of this danger of meeting another countess in a narrow, deep-rutted lane was very prominent in my mind, I ventured to ask Mrs. Medlicott what would have to be done on such an occasion; and she told me that " de latest creation must back, for sure," which puzzled me a good deal at the time, although I under-stand it now. I began to find out the use of the *Peerage*, a book which had seemed to me rather dull before; but, as I was always a coward in a coach, I made myself well acquainted with the dates of creation of our three Warwickshire earls, and was happy to find that Earl Ludlow ranked second, the oldest earl being a hunting widower, and not likely to drive out in a carriage.

All this time I have wandered from Mr. Gray. Of course, we first saw him in church when he read himself in. He was very red-faced, the kind of redness which goes with light hair and a blushing complexion; he looked slight and short, and his bright light frizzy hair had hardly a dash of powder in it. I remember my lady making this observation, and sighing over it; for, though since the famine in seventeen hundred and ninety-nine and eighteen hundred there had been a tax on hair-powder, yet it was reckoned very revolutionary and Jacobin not to wear a good deal of it. My lady hardly liked the opinions of any man who wore his own hair; but this she would say was rather a prejudice: only in her youth none but the mob had gone wigless, and she could not get over the association of wigs with birth and breeding; a man's own hair with that class of people who had formed the rioters in seventeen hundred and eighty, when Lord George Gordon had been one of the bugbears of my lady's life. Her husband and his brothers, she told us, had been put into breeches, and had their heads shaved on their seventh birthday, each of them; a handsome little wig of the newest fashion forming the old Lady Ludlow's invariable birthday present to her sons as they each arrived at that age; and afterwards, to the day of their death, they never saw their own hair. To be without powder, as some underbred people were talking of being now, was in fact to insult the proprieties of life, by being undressed. It was English sans-culottism. But Mr. Gray did wear a little powder, enough to save him in my lady's good opinion; but not enough to make her approve of him decidedly.

The next time I saw him was in the great hall. Mary Mason and I were going to drive out with my lady in her coach, and when we went down stairs with our best hats and cloaks on, we found Mr. Gray awaiting my lady's coming. I believe he had paid his respects to her before, but we had never seen him; and he had declined her invitation to spend Sunday evening at the Court (as Mr. Mountford used to do pretty regularly—and play a game at picquet too—), which, Mrs. Medlicott told us, had caused my lady to be not over well pleased with him.

He blushed redder than ever at the sight of us, as we entered the hall and dropped him our curtsies. He coughed two or three times, as if he would have liked to speak to us, if he could but have found something to say: and every time he coughed he became hotter-looking than ever. I am ashamed to say, we were nearly laughing at him; half because we, too, were so shy that we understood what his awkwardness meant.

My lady came in, with her quick active step—she always walked quickly when she did not bethink herself of her cane—

as if she was sorry to have us kept waiting—and, as she entered, she gave us all round one of those graceful sweeping curtsies, of which I think the art must have died out with her,—it implied so much courtesy;—this time it said, as well as words could do, " I am sorry to have kept you all waiting,—forgive me."

She went up to the mantelpiece, near which Mr. Gray had been standing until her entrance, and curtseying afresh to him, and pretty deeply this time, because of his cloth, and her being hostess, and he, a new guest.   She asked him if he would not prefer speaking to her in her own private parlour, and looked as though she would have conducted him there.   But he burst out with his errand, of which he was full even to choking, and which sent the glistening tears into his large blue eyes, which stood farther and farther out with his excitement.

" My lady, I want to speak to you, and to persuade you to exert your kind interest with Mr. Lathom—Justice Lathom, of Hathaway Manor—"

" Harry Lathom? " inquired my lady—as Mr. Gray stopped to take the breath he had lost in his hurry—" I did not know he was in the commission."

" He is only just appointed; he took the oaths not a month ago—more's the pity! "

" I do not understand why you should regret it.   The Lathoms have held Hathaway since Edward the First, and Mr. Lathom bears a good character, although his temper is hasty—"

" My lady! he has committed Job Gregson for stealing—a fault of which he is as innocent as I—and all the evidence goes to prove it, now that the case is brought before the Bench; only the squires hang so together that they can't be brought to see justice, and are all for sending Job to gaol, out of compliment to Mr. Lathom, saying it is his first committal, and it won't be civil to tell him there is no evidence against his man.   For God's sake, my lady, speak to the gentlemen; they will attend to you, while they only tell me to mind my own business."

Now my lady was always inclined to stand by her order, and the Lathoms of Hathaway Court were cousins to the Hanburys. Besides, it was rather a point of honour in those days to encourage a young magistrate, by passing a pretty sharp sentence on his first committals; and Job Gregson was the father of a girl who had been lately turned away from her place as scullery-maid for sauciness to Mrs. Adams, her ladyship's own maid; and Mr. Gray had not said a word of the reasons why he believed

the man innocent—for he was in such a hurry, I believe he
would have had my lady drive off to the Henley Court-house
then and there;—so there seemed a good deal against the man,
a d nothing but Mr. Gray's bare word for him; and my lady
d ew herself a little up, and said—

"Mr. Gray! I do not see what reason either you or I have to
interfere. Mr. Harry Lathom is a sensible kind of young man,
well capable of ascertaining the truth without our help—"

"But more evidence has come out since," broke in Mr. Gray.
My lady went a little stiffer, and spoke a little more coldly:—

"I suppose this additional evidence is before the justices:
men of good family, and of honour and credit, well known in the
county. They naturally feel that the opinion of one of themselves must have more weight than the words of a man like
Job Gregson, who bears a very indifferent character—has been
strongly suspected of poaching, coming from no one knows
where, squatting on Hareman's Common—which, by the way,
is extra-parochial, I believe; consequently you, as a clergyman,
are not responsible for what goes on there; and, although im-
politic, there might be some truth in what the magistrates said,
in advising you to mind your own business"—said her ladyship,
smiling—"and they might be tempted to bid me mind mine, if
I interfered, Mr. Gray: might they not?"

He looked extremely uncomfortable; half angry. Once or
twice he began to speak, but checked himself, as if his words
would not have been wise or prudent. At last he said—

"It may seem presumptuous in me—a stranger of only a few
weeks' standing—to set up my judgment as to men's character
against that of residents—" Lady Ludlow gave a little bow of
acquiescence, which was, I think, involuntary on her part, and
which I don't think he perceived—"but I am convinced that
the man is innocent of this offence—and besides, the justices
themselves allege this ridiculous custom of paying a compliment to a newly-appointed magistrate as their only reason."

That unlucky word "ridiculous!" It undid all the good his
modest beginning had done him with my lady. I knew as well
as words could have told me, that she was affronted at the
expression being used by a man inferior in rank to those whose
actions he applied it to—and, truly, it was a great want of tact,
considering to whom he was speaking.

Lady Ludlow spoke very gently and slowly; she always did
so when she was annoyed; it was a certain sign, the meaning of
which we had all learnt.

"I think, Mr. Gray, we will drop the subject. It is one on which we are not likely to agree."

Mr. Gray's ruddy colour grew purple and then faded away, and his face became pale. I think both my lady and he had forgotten our presence; and we were beginning to feel too awkward to wish to remind them of it. And yet we could not help watching and listening with the greatest interest.

Mr. Gray drew himself up to his full height, with an unconscious feeling of dignity. Little as was his stature, and awkward and embarrassed as he had been only a few minutes before, I remember thinking he looked almost as grand as my lady when he spoke.

"Your ladyship must remember that it may be my duty to speak to my parishioners on many subjects on which they do not agree with me. I am not at liberty to be silent, because they differ in opinion from me."

Lady Ludlow's great blue eyes dilated with surprise, and—I do think—anger, at being thus spoken to. I am not sure whether it was very wise in Mr. Gray. He himself looked afraid of the consequences, but as if he was determined to bear them without flinching. For a minute there was silence. Then my lady replied—

"Mr. Gray, I respect your plain speaking, although I may wonder whether a young man of your age and position has any right to assume that he is a better judge than one with the experience which I have naturally gained at my time of life, and in the station I hold."

"If I, madam, as the clergyman of this parish, am not to shrink from telling what I believe to be the truth to the poor and lowly, no more am I to hold my peace in the presence of the rich and titled." Mr. Gray's face showed that he was in that state of excitement which in a child would have ended in a good fit of crying. He looked as if he had nerved himself up to doing and saying things, which he disliked above everything, and which nothing short of serious duty could have compelled him to do and say. And at such times every minute circumstance which could add to pain comes vividly before one. I saw that he became aware of our presence, and that it added to his discomfiture.

My lady flushed up. "Are you aware, sir," asked she, "that you have gone far astray from the original subject of conversation? But as you talk of your parish, allow me to remind you that Hareman's Common is beyond the bounds, and that you are really not responsible for the characters and lives of the squatters on that unlucky piece of ground."

" Madam, I see I have only done harm in speaking to you about the affair at all. I beg your pardon and take my leave."

He bowed, and looked very sad. Lady Ludlow caught the expression of his face.

" Good morning! " she cried, in rather a louder and quicker way than that in which she had been speaking. " Remember, Job Gregson is a notorious poacher and evildoer, and you really are not responsible for what goes on at Hareman's Common."

He was near the hall-door, and said something—half to himself, which we heard (being nearer to him), but my lady did not; although she saw that he spoke. " What did he say? " she asked in a somewhat hurried manner, as soon as the door was closed—" I did not hear." We looked at each other, and then I spoke:

" He said, my lady, that ' God help him! he was responsible for all the evil he did not strive to overcome.' "

My lady turned sharp round away from us, and Mary Mason said afterwards she thought her ladyship was much vexed with both of us, for having been present, and with me for having repeated what Mr. Gray had said. But it was not our fault that we were in the hall, and when my lady asked what Mr. Gray had said, I thought it right to tell her.

In a few minutes she bade us accompany her in her ride in the coach.

Lady Ludlow always sat forwards by herself, and we girls backwa ds. Somehow this was a rule, which we never thought of questioning. It was true that riding backwards made some of us feel very uncomfortable and faint; and to remedy this my lady always drove with both windows open, which occasionally gave her the rheumatism; but we always went on in the old way. This day she did not pay any great attention to the road by which we were going, and coachman took his own way. We were very silent, as my lady did not speak, and looked very serious. Or else, in general, she made these rides very pleasant (to those who were not qualmish with riding backwards), by talking to us in a very agreeable manner, and telling us of the different things which had happened to her at various places,— at Paris and Versailles, where she had been in her youth,—at Windsor and Kew and Weymouth, where she had been with the queen, when maid-of-honour—and so on. But this day she did not talk at all. All at once she put her head out of the window.

"John Footman," said she, "where are we? Surely this is Hareman's Common."

"Yes, an't please my lady," said John Footman, and waited for further speech or orders. My lady thought a while, and then said she would have the steps put down and get out.

As soon as she was gone, we looked at each other, and then without a word began to gaze after her. We saw her pick her dainty way in the little high-heeled shoes she always wore (because they had been in fashion in her youth), among the yellow pools of stagnant water that had gathered in the clayey soil. John Footman followed, stately, after; afraid too, for all his stateliness, of splashing his pure white stockings. Suddenly my lady turned round and said something to him, and he returned to the carriage with a half-pleased, half-puzzled air.

My lady went on to a cluster of rude mud houses at the higher end of the Common; cottages built, as they were occasionally at that day, of wattles and clay, and thatched with sods. As far as we could make out from dumb show, Lady Ludlow saw enough of the interiors of these places to make her hesitate before entering, or even speaking to any of the children who were playing about in the puddles. After a pause, she disappeared into one of the cottages. It seemed to us a long time before she came out; but I dare say it was not more than eight or ten minutes. She came back with her head hanging down, as if to choose her way,—but we saw it was more in thought and bewilderment than for any such purpose.

She had not made up her mind where we should ride to when she got into the carriage again. John Footman stood, bare-headed, waiting for orders.

"To Hathaway. My dears, if you are tired, or if you have anything to do for Mrs. Medlicott, I can drop you at Barford Corner, and it is but a quarter of an hour's brisk walk home."

But luckily we could safely say that Mrs. Medlicott did not want us; and as we had whispered to each other, as we sat alone in the coach, that surely my lady must have gone to Job Gregson's, we were far too anxious to know the end of it all to say that we were tired. So we all set off to Hathaway. Mr. Harry Lathom was a bachelor squire, thirty or thirty-five years of age, more at home in the field than in the drawing-room, and with sporting men than with ladies.

My lady did not alight, of course; it was Mr. Lathom's place to wait upon her, and she bade the butler,—who had a smack of the gamekeeper in him, very unlike our own powdered venerable fine gentleman at Hanbury,—tell his master, with her compliments, that she wished to speak to him. You may think how pleased we were to find that we should hear all that was said; though, I think, afterwards we were half sorry when we saw how our presence confused the squire, who would have found it bad enough to answer my lady's questions, even without two eager girls for audience.

"Pray, Mr. Lathom," began my lady, something abruptly for her,—but she was very full of her subject,—"what is this I hear about Job Gregson?"

Mr. Lathom looked annoyed and vexed, but dared not show it in his words.

"I gave out a warrant against him, my lady, for theft,—that is all. You are doubtless aware of his character; a man who sets nets and springes in long cover, and fishes wherever he takes a fancy. It is but a short step from poaching to thieving."

"That is quite true," replied Lady Ludlow (who had a horror of poaching for this very reason): "but I imagine you do not send a man to gaol on account of his bad character."

"Rogues and vagabonds," said Mr. Lathom. "A man may be sent to prison for being a vagabond; for no specific act, but for his general mode of life."

He had the better of her ladyship for one moment; but then she answered—

"But in this case, the charge on which you committed him is for theft; now his wife tells me he can prove he was some miles distant from Holmwood, where the robbery took place, all that afternoon; she says you had the evidence before you."

Mr. Lathom here interrupted my lady, by saying, in a somewhat sulky manner—

"No such evidence was brought before me when I gave the warrant. I am not answerable for the other magistrates' decision, when they had more evidence before them. It was they who committed him to gaol. I am not responsible for that."

My lady did not often show signs of impatience; but we knew she was feeling irritated, by the little perpetual tapping of her high-heeled shoe against the bottom of the carriage. About the same time we, sitting backwards, caught a glimpse of Mr. Gray through the open door, standing in the shadow of the hall. Doubtless Lady Ludlow's arrival had interrupted a conversation between Mr. Lathom and Mr. Gray. The latter must have heard every word of what she was saying; but of this she was not aware, and caught at Mr. Lathom's disclaimer of responsibility with pretty much the same argument which she had heard (through our repetition) that Mr. Gray had used not two hours before.

"And do you mean to say, Mr. Lathom, that you don't consider yourself responsible for all injustice or wrong-doing that you might have prevented, and have not? Nay, in this case the first germ of injustice was your own mistake. I wish you had been with me a little while ago, and seen the misery in that poor fellow's cottage." She spoke lower, and Mr. Gray drew near, in a sort of involuntary manner; as if to hear all she was saying. We saw him, and doubtless Mr. Lathom heard his footstep, and knew who it was that was listening behind him, and approving of every word that was said. He grew yet more sullen in manner; but still my lady was my lady, and he dared not speak out before her, as he would have done to Mr. Gray. Lady Ludlow, however, caught the look of stubbornness in his face, and it roused her as I had never seen her roused.

"I am sure you will not refuse, sir, to accept my bail. I offer to bail the fellow out, and to be responsible for his appearance at the sessions. What say you to that, Mr. Lathom?"

"The offence of theft is not bailable, my lady."

"Not in ordinary cases, I dare say. But I imagine this is an extraordinary case. The man is sent to prison out of compliment to you, and against all evidence, as far as I can learn. He will have to rot in gaol for two months, and his wife and children to starve. I, Lady Ludlow, offer to bail him out, and pledge myself for his appearance at next quarter-sessions."

"It is against the law, my lady."

"Bah! Bah! Bah! Who makes laws? Such as I, in the House of Lords—such as you, in the House of Commons. We, who make the laws in St. Stephen's, may break the mere forms of them, when we have right on our sides, on our own land, and amongst our own people."

"The lord-lieutenant may take away my commission, if he heard of it."

"And a very good thing for the country, Harry Lathom; and for you too, if he did,—if you don't go on more wisely than you have begun. A pretty set you and your brother magistrates are to administer justice through the land! I always said a good despotism was the best form of government; and I am twice as much in favour of it now I see what a quorum is! My dears!" suddenly turning round to us, "if it would n)t tire you to walk home, I would beg Mr. Lathom to take a seat in my coach, and we would drive to Henley Gaol, and have the poor man out at once."

"A walk over the fields at this time of day is hardly fitting for young ladies to take alone," said Mr. Lathom, anxious no doubt to escape from his *tête-à-tête* drive with my lady, and possibly not quite prepared to go to the illegal length of prompt measures, which she had in contemplation.

But Mr. Gray now stepped forward, too anxious for the release of the prisoner to allow any obstacle to intervene which he could do away with. To see Lady Ludlow's face when she first perceived whom she had had for auditor and spectator of her interview with Mr. Lathom, was as good as a play. She had been doing and saying the very things she had been so much annoyed at Mr. Gray's saying and proposing only an hour or two ago. She had been setting down Mr. Lathom pretty smartly, in the presence of the very man to whom she had spoken of that gentleman as so sensible, and of such a standing in the county, that it was presumption to question his doings. But before Mr. Gray had finished his offer of escorting us back to Hanbury Court, my lady had recovered herself. There was neither surprise nor displeasure in her manner, as she answered—

"I thank you, Mr. Gray. I was not aware that you were here, but I think I can understand on what errand you came. And seeing you here, recalls me to a duty I owe Mr. Lathom. Mr. Lathom, I have spoken to you pretty plainly,—forgetting, until I saw Mr. Gray, that only this very afternoon I differed from him on this very question; taking completely, at that time, the same view of the whole subject which you have done; thinking that the county would be well rid of such a man as Job Gregson, whether he had committed this theft or not. Mr. Gray and I did not part quite friends," she continued, bowing towards him; "but it so happened that I saw Job Gregson's wife and home,—I felt that Mr. Gray had been right and I had been wrong, so, with the famous inconsistency of my sex, I came hither to scold you," smiling towards Mr. Lathom, who looked half-sulky yet, and did not relax a bit of his gravity at her smile, "for holding the same opinions that I had done an hour before. Mr. Gray" (again bowing towards him), "these young ladies will be very much obliged to you for your escort, and so shall I. Mr. Lathom, may I beg of you to accompany me to Henley?"

Mr. Gray bowed very low, and went very red; Mr. Lathom said something which we none of us heard, but which was, I think, some remonstrance against the course he was, as it were, compelled to take. Lady Ludlow, however, took no notice of his murmur, but sat in an attitude of polite expectancy; and as we turned off on our walk, I saw Mr. Lathom getting into the coach with the air of a whipped hound. I must say, considering my lady's feeling, I did not envy him his ride,—though, I believe, he was quite in the right as to the object of the ride being illegal.

Our walk home was very dull. We had no fears; and would far rather have been without the awkward, blushing young man, into which Mr. Gray had sunk. At every stile he hesitated,—sometimes he half got over it, thinking that he could assist us better in that way; then he would turn back unwilling to go before ladies. He had no ease of manner, as my lady once said of him, though on any occasion of duty, he had an immense deal of dignity.

CHAPTER III

As far as I can remember, it was very soon after this that I first began to have the pain in my hip, which has ended in making me a cripple for life. I hardly recollect more than one walk after our return under Mr. Gray's escort from Mr. Lathom's. Indeed, at the time, I was not without suspicions (which I never named) that the beginning of all the mischief was a great jump I had taken from the top of one of the stiles on that very occasion.

Well, it is a long while ago, and God disposes of us all, and I am not going to tire you out with telling you how I thought and felt, and how, when I saw what my life was to be, I could hardly bring myself to be patient, but rather wished to die at once. You can every one of you think for yourselves what becoming all at once useless and unable to move, and by and by growing hopeless of cure, and feeling that one must be a burden to some one all one's life long, would be to an active, wilful, strong girl of seventeen, anxious to get on in the world, so as, if possible, to help her brothers and sisters. So I shall only say, that one among the blessings which arose out of what seemed at the time a great, black sorrow was, that Lady Ludlow for many years took me, as it were, into her own especial charge; and now, as I lie still and alone in my old age, it is such a pleasure to think of her!

Mrs. Medlicott was great as a nurse, and I am sure I can never be grateful enough to her memory for all her kindness. But she was puzzled to know how to manage me in other ways. I used to have long, hard fits of crying; and, thinking that I ought to go home—and yet what could they do with me there?—and a hundred and fifty other anxious thoughts, some of which I could tell to Mrs. Medlicott, and others I could not. Her way of comforting me was hurrying away for some kind of tempting or strengthening food—a basin of melted calves'-foot jelly was, I am sure she thought, a cure for every woe.

"There! take it, dear, take it!" she would say; "and don't go on fretting for what can't be helped."

But, I think, she got puzzled at length at the non-efficacy of good things to eat; and one day, after I had limped down to see the doctor, in Mrs. Medlicott's sitting-room—a room lined with cupboards, containing preserves and dainties of all kinds, which she perpetually made, and never touched herself—when I was returning to my bedroom to cry away the afternoon, under pretence of arranging my clothes, John Footman brought me a message from my lady (with whom the doctor had been having a conversation) to bid me go to her in that private sitting-room at the end of the suite of apartments, about which I spoke in describing the day of my first arrival at Hanbury. I had hardly been in it since; as, when we read to my lady, she generally sat in the small withdrawing-room out of which this private room of hers opened. I suppose great people do not require what we smaller people value so much,—I mean privacy. I do not think that there was a room which my lady occupied that had not two doors, and some of them had three or four. Then my lady had always Adams waiting upon her in her bed-chamber; and it was Mrs. Medlicott's duty to sit within call, as it were, in a sort of ante-room that led out of my lady's own sitting-room, on the opposite side of the drawing-room door. To fancy the house, you must take a great square, and halve it by a line; at one end of this line was the hall-door, or public entrance; at the opposite the private entrance from a terrace, which was terminated at one end by a sort of postern door in an old grey stone wall, beyond which lay the farm buildings and offices; so that people could come in this way to my lady on business, while, if she were going into the garden from her own room, she had nothing to do but to pass through Mrs. Medlicott's apartment, out into the lesser hall, and then turning to the right as she passed on to the terrace, she could go down the flight of broad, shallow steps at the corner of the house into the lovely garden, with stretching, sweeping lawns, and gay flower-beds, and beautiful, bossy laurels, and other blooming or massy shrubs, with full grown beeches, or larches feathering down to the ground a little farther off. The whole was set in a frame, as it were, by the more distant woodlands. The house had been modernised in the days of Queen Anne, I think; but the money had fallen short that was requisite to carry out all the improvements, so it was only the suite of withdrawing-rooms and the terrace-rooms, as far as the private entrance, that had the new, long, high windows put in, and these were old enough by this time to be draped with roses, and honeysuckles, and pyracanthus, winter and summer long.

Well, to go back to that day when I limped into my lady's sitting-room, trying hard to look as if I had not been crying, and not to walk as if I was in much pain. I do not know whether my lady saw how near my tears were to my eyes, but she told me she had sent for me, because she wanted some help in arranging the drawers of her bureau, and asked me—just as if it was a favour I was to do her—if I could sit down in the easy-chair near the window—(all quietly arranged before I came in, with a footstool, and a table quite near)—and assist her. You will wonder, perhaps, why I was not bidden to sit or lie on the sofa; but (although I found one there a morning or two afterwards, when I came down) the fact was, that there was none in the room at this time. I have even fancied that the easy-chair was brought in on purpose for me; for it was not the chair in which I remembered my lady sitting the first time I saw her. That chair was very much carved and gilded, with a countess' coronet at the top. I tried it one day, some time afterwards, when my lady was out of the room, and I had a fancy for seeing how I could move about, and very uncomfortable it was. Now my chair (as I learnt to call it, and to think it) was soft and luxurious, and seemed somehow to give one's body rest just in that part where one most needed it.

I was not at my ease that first day, nor indeed for many days afterwards, notwithstanding my chair was so comfortable. Yet I forgot my sad pain in silently wondering over the meaning of many of the things we turned out of those curious old drawers.

I was puzzled to know why some were kept at all; a scrap of writing may-be, with only half a dozen common-place words written on it, or a bit of broken riding-whip, and here and there a stone, of which I thought I could have picked up twenty just as good in the first walk I took. But it seems that was just my ignorance; for my lady told me they were pieces of valuable marble, used to make the floors of the great Roman emperors' palaces long ago; and that when she had been a girl, and made the grand tour long ago, her cousin Sir Horace Mann, the Ambassador or Envoy at Florence, had told her to be sure to go into the fields inside the walls of ancient Rome, when the farmers were preparing the ground for the onion-sowing, and had to make the soil fine, and pick up what bits of marble she could find. She had done so, and meant to have had them made into a table; but somehow that plan fell through, and there they were with all the dirt out of the onion-field upon them; but once when I thought of cleaning them with soap and water, at any rate, she bade me not to do so, for it was Roman dirt—earth, I think, she called it—but it was dirt all the same.

Then, in this bureau, were many other things, the value of which I could understand—locks of hair carefully ticketed, which my lady looked at very sadly; and lockets and bracelets with miniatures in them—very small pictures to what they make now-a-days, and called miniatures; some of them had even to be looked at through a microscope before you could see the individual expression of the faces, or how beautifully they were painted. I don't think that looking at these made my lady seem so melancholy, as the seeing and touching of the hair did. But, to be sure, the hair was, as it were, a part of some beloved body which she might never touch and caress again, but which lay beneath the turf, all faded and disfigured, except perhaps the very hair, from which the lock she held had been dissevered; whereas the pictures were but pictures after all—likenesses, but not the very things themselves. This is only my own conjecture, mind. My lady rarely spoke out her feelings. For, to begin with, she was of rank: and I have heard her say that people of rank do not talk about their feelings except to their equals, and even to them they conceal them, except upon rare occasions. Secondly—and this is my own reflection—she was an only child and an heiress; and as such was more apt to think than to talk, as all well-brought-up heiresses must be, I think. Thirdly, she had long been a widow, without any companion of her own age with whom it would have been natural for her to refer to old associations, past pleasures, or mutual sorrows. Mrs. Medlicott came nearest to her as a companion of this sort; and her ladyship talked more to Mrs. Medlicott, in a kind of familiar way, than she did to all the rest of the household put together. But Mrs. Medlicott was silent by nature, and did not reply at any great length. Adams, indeed, was the only one who spoke much to Lady Ludlow.

After we had worked away about an hour at the bureau, her ladyship said we had done enough for one day; and as the time was come for her afternoon ride, she left me, with a volume of engravings from Mr. Hogarth's pictures on one side of me (I don't like to write down the names of them, though my lady thought nothing of it, I am sure), and upon a stand her great prayer-book open at the evening psalms for the day, on the other. But as soon as she was gone, I troubled myself little with either, but amused myself with looking round the room at my leisure. The side on which the fire-place stood was all panelled—part of the old ornaments of the house, for there was an Indian paper with birds and beasts and insects on it, on all the other sides. There were coats of arms, of the various families with whom the Hanburys had intermarried, all over these panels, and up and down the ceiling as well. There was very little looking-glass in the room, though one of the great drawing-rooms was called the " Mirror Room," because it was lined with glass, which my lady's great-grandfather had brought from Venice when he was ambassador there. There were china jars of all shapes and sizes round and about the room, and some china monsters, or idols, of which I could never bear the sight, they were so ugly, though I think my lady valued them more than all. There was a thick carpet on the middle of the floor, which was made of small pieces of rare wood fitted into a pattern; the doors were opposite to each other, and were composed of two heavy tall wings, and opened in the middle, moving on brass grooves inserted into the floor—they would not have opened over a carpet. There were two windows reaching up nearly to the ceiling, but very narrow, and with deep window-seats in the thickness of the wall. The room was full of scent, partly from the flowers outside, and partly from the great jars of pot-pourri inside. The choice of odours was what my lady piqued herself upon, saying nothing showed birth like a keen susceptibility of smell. We never named musk in her presence, her antipathy to it was so well understood through the household: her opinion on the subject was believed to be, that no scent derived from an animal could ever be of a sufficiently pure nature to give pleasure to any person of good family, where, of course, the delicate perception of the senses had been cultivated for generations. She would instance the way in which sportsmen preserve the breed of dogs who have shown keen scent; and how such gifts descend for generations amongst animals, who cannot be supposed to have anything of ancestral pride, or hereditary fancies about them. Musk, then, was never mentioned at Hanbury Court. No more were bergamot or southern-wood, although vegetable in their nature. She considered these two latter as betraying a vulgar taste in the person who chose to gather or wear them. She was sorry to notice sprigs of them in the button-hole of any young man in whom she took an interest, either because he was engaged to a servant of hers or otherwise, as he came out of church on a Sunday afternoon. She was afraid that he liked coarse pleasures; and I am not sure if she did not think that his preference for these coarse sweetnesses did not imply a probability that he would take to drinking. But she distinguished between vulgar and common. Violets, pinks, and sweetbriar were common enough; roses and mignonette, for those who had gardens, honeysuckle for those who walked along the bowery lanes; but wearing them betrayed no vulgarity of taste: the queen upon her throne might be glad to smell at a nosegay of the flowers. A beau-pot (as we called it) of pinks and roses freshly gathered was placed every morning that they were in bloom on my lady's own particular table. For lasting vegetable odours she preferred lavender and sweet-woodroof to any extract whatever. Lavender reminded her of old customs, she said, and of homely cottage-gardens, and many a cottager made his offering to her of a bundle of lavender. Sweet-woodroof, again, grew in wild, woodland places, where the soil was fine and the air delicate: the poor children used to go and gather it for her up in the woods on the higher lands; and for this service she always rewarded them with bright new pennies, of which my lord, her son, used to send her down a bagful fresh from the Mint in London every February.

Attar of roses, again, she disliked. She said it reminded her of the city and of merchants' wives, over-rich, over-heavy in its perfume. And lilies-of-the-valley somehow fell under the same condemnation. They were most graceful and elegant to look at (my lady was quite candid about this), flower, leaf, colour—everything was refined about them but the smell. That was too strong. But the great hereditary faculty on which my lady piqued herself, and with reason, for I never met with any person who possessed it, was the power she had of perceiving the delicious odour arising from a bed of strawberries in the late autumn, when the leaves were all fading and dying. *Bacon's Essays* was one of the few books that lay about in my lady's room; and if you took it up and opened it carelessly, it was sure to fall apart at his *Essay on Gardens.* " Listen," her ladyship would say, " to what that great philosopher and statesman says. ' Next to that,'—he is speaking of violets, my dear—' is the musk-rose,'—of which you remember the great bush, at the corner of the south wall just by the Blue Drawing-room windows; that is the old musk-rose, Shakespeare's musk-rose, which is dying out through the kingdom now. But to return to my Lord Bacon: ' Then the strawberry leaves, dying with a most excellent cordial smell.' Now the Hanburys can always smell this excellent cordial odour, and very delicious and refreshing it is. You see, in Lord Bacon's time, there had not been so many intermarriages between the court and the city as there have been since the needy days of his majesty Charles the Second; and altogether in the time of Queen Elizabeth, the great, old families of England were a distinct race, just as a cart-horse is one creature and very useful in its place, and Childers or Eclipse is another creature, though both are of the same species. So the old families have gifts and powers of a different and higher class to what the other orders have. My dear, remember that you try if you can smell the scent of dying straw-berry-leaves in this next autumn. You have some of Ursula Hanbury's blood in you, and that gives you a chance."

But when October came, I sniffed and sniffed, and all to no purpose; and my lady—who had watched the little experiment rather anxiously—had to give me up as a hybrid. I was morti-fied, I confess, and thought that it was in some ostentation of her own powers that she ordered the gardener to plant a border of strawberries on that side of the terrace that lay under her windows.

I have wandered away from time and place. I tell you all the remembrances I have of those years just as they come up, and I hope that, in my old age, I am not getting too like a certain Mrs. Nickleby, whose speeches were once read out aloud to me.

I came by degrees to be all day long in this room which I have been describing; sometimes sitting in the easy-chair, doing some little piece of dainty work for my lady, or sometimes arranging flowers, or sorting letters according to their handwriting, so that she could arrange them afterwards, and destroy or keep, as she planned, looking ever onward to her death. Then, after the sofa was brought in, she would watch my face, and if she saw my colour change, she would bid me lie down and rest. And I used to try to walk upon the terrace every day for a short time: it hurt me very much, it is true, but the doctor had ordered it, and I knew her ladyship wished me to obey.

Before I had seen the background of a great lady's life, I had thought it all play and fine doings. But whatever other grand people are, my lady was never idle. For one thing, she had to superintend the agent for the large Hanbury estate. I believe it was mortgaged for a sum of money which had gone to improve the late lord's Scotch lands; but she was anxious to pay off this before her death, and so to leave her own inheritance free of incumbrance to her son, the present earl; whom, I secretly think, she considered a greater person, as being the heir of the Hanburys (though through a female line), than as being my Lord Ludlow with half a dozen other minor titles.

With this wish of releasing her property from the mortgage, skilful care was much needed in the management of it: and as far as my lady could go, she took every pains. She had a great book, in which every page was ruled into three divisions; on the first column was written the date and the name of the tenant who addressed any letter on business to her, on the second was briefly stated the subject of the letter, which generally contained a request of some kind. This request would be surrounded and enveloped in so many words, and often inserted amidst so many odd reasons and excuses, that Mr. Horner (the steward) would sometimes say it was like hunting through a bushel of chaff to find a grain of wheat. Now, in the second column of this book, the grain of meaning was placed, clean and dry, before her ladyship every morning. She sometimes would ask to see the original letter; sometimes she simply answered the request by a " Yes " or a " No; " and often she would send for leases and papers, and examine them well, with Mr. Horner at her elbow, to see if such petitions, as to be allowed to plough up pasture fields, etc., were provided for in the terms of the original agreement. On every Thursday she made herself at liberty to see her tenants, from four to six in the afternoon. Mornings would have suited my lady better, as far as convenience went, and I believe the old custom had been to have these levées (as her ladyship used to call them) held before twelve. But, as she said to Mr. Horner, when he urged returning to the former hours, it spoilt a whole day for a farmer, if he had to dress himself in his best and leave his work in the forenoon (and my lady li ed to see her tenants come in their Sunday clothes; she would not say a word, maybe, but she would take her spectacles slowly out, and put them on with silent gravity, and look at a dirty or raggedly-dressed man so solemnly and earnestly, that his nerves must have been pretty strong if he did not wince, and resolve that, however poor he might be, soap and water, and needle and thread, should be used before he again appeared in her lady-ship's ante room). The outlying tenants had always a supper provided for them in the servants'-hall on Thursdays, to which, indeed, all comers were welcome to sit down. For my lady said, though there were not many hours left of a working man's day when their business with her was ended, yet that they needed food and rest, and that she should be ashamed if they sought either at the Fighting Lion (called at this day the Hanbury Arms). They had as much beer as they could drink while they were eating; and when the food was cleared away, they had a cup a-piece of good ale, in which the oldest tenant present, stand-ing up, gave Madam's health; and after that was drunk, they were expected to set off homewards; at any rate, no more liquor was given them. The tenants one and all called her "Madam;" for they recognised in her the married heiress of the Hanburys, not the widow of a Lord Ludlow, of whom they and their fore-fathers knew nothing; and against whose memory, indeed, there rankled a dim unspoken grudge, the cause of which was accurately known to the very few who understood the nature of a mortgage, and were therefore aware that Madam's money had been taken to enrich my lord's poor land in Scotland. I am sure—for you can understand I was behind the scenes, as it were, and had many an opportunity of seeing and hearing, as I lay or sat motionless in my lady's room with the double doors open between it and the ante-room beyond, where Lady Ludlow saw her steward, and gave audience to her tenants—I am certain, I say, that Mr. Horner was silently as much annoyed at the money that was swallowed up by this mortgage as any one; and, some time or other, he had probably spoken his mind out to my lady; for there was a sort of offended reference on her part, and respect-ful submission to blame on his, while every now and then there was an implied protest—whenever the payments of the interest became due, or whenever my lady stinted herself of any personal expense, such as Mr. Horner thought was only decorous and becoming in the heiress of the Hanburys. Her carriages were old and cumbrous, wanting all the improvements which had been adopted by those of her rank throughout the county. Mr. Horner would fain have had the ordering of a new coach. The carriage-horses, too, were getting past their work; yet all the promising colts bred on the estate were so d for ready money; and so on. My lord, her son, was ambassador at some foreign place; and very proud we all were of his glory and dignity; but I fancy it cost money, and my lady would have lived on bread and water sooner than have called upon him to help her in paying off the mortgage, although he was the one who was to benefit by it in the end.

Mr. Horner was a very faithful steward, and very respectful to my lady; although sometimes I thought she was sharper to him than to any one else; perhaps because she knew that, although he never said anything, he disapproved of the Hanburys being made to pay for the Earl Ludlow's estates and state.

The late lord had been a sailor, and had been as extravagant in his habits as most sailors are, I am told—for I never saw the sea; and yet he had a long sight to his own interests; but whatever he was, my lady loved him and his memory, with about as fond and proud a love as ever wife gave husband, I should think.

For a part of his life Mr. Horner, who was born on the Hanbury property, had been a clerk to an attorney in Firmingham; and these few years had given him a kind of worldly wisdom, which, though always exerted for her benefit, was antipathetic to her ladyship, who thought that some of her steward's maxims savoured of trade and commerce. I fancy that if it had been possible, she would have preferred a return to the primitive system, of living on the produce of the land, and exchanging the surplus for such articles as were needed, without the intervention of money.

But Mr. Horner was bitten with new-fangled notions, as she would say, though his new-fangled notions were what folk at the present day would think sadly behindhand; and some of Mr. Gray's ideas fell on Mr. Horner's mind like sparks on tow, though they started from two different points. Mr. Horner wanted to make every man useful and active in this world, and to direct as much activity and usefulness as possible to the improvement of the Hanbury estates, and the aggrandisement of the Hanbury family, and therefore he fell into the new cry for education.

Mr. Gray did not care much,—Mr. Horner thought not enough,

—for this world, and where any man or family stood in their earthly position; but he would have every one prepared for the world to come, and capable of understanding and receiving certain doctrines, for which latter purpose, it stands to reason, he must have heard of these doctrines; and therefore Mr. Gray wanted education. The answer in the Catechism that Mr. Horner was most fond of calling upon a child to repeat, was that to, " What is thy duty towards thy neighbour? " The answer Mr. Gray liked best to hear repeated with unction, was that to the question, " What is the inward and spiritual grace? " The reply to which Lady Ludlow bent her head the lowest, as we said our Catechism to her on Sundays, was to, " What is thy duty towards God? " But neither Mr. Horner nor Mr. Gray had heard many answers to the Catechism as yet.

Up to this time there was no Sunday-school in Hanbury. Mr. Gray's desires were bounded by that object. Mr. Horner looked farther on: he hoped for a day-school at some future time, to train up intelligent labourers for working on the estate. My lady would hear of neither one nor the other: indeed, not the boldest man whom she ever saw would have dared to name the project of a day-school within her hearing.

So Mr. Horner contented himself with quietly teaching a sharp, clever lad to read and write, with a view to making use of him as a kind of foreman in process of time. He had his pick of the farm-lads for this purpose; and, as the brightest and sharpest, although by far the raggedest and dirtiest, singled out Job Gregson's son. But all this—as my lady never listened to gossip, or indeed, was spoken to unless she spoke first—was quite unknown to her, until the unlucky incident took place which I am going to relate.

CHAPTER IV

I think my lady was not aware of Mr. Horner's views on education (as making men into more useful members of society) or the practice to which he was putting his precepts in taking Harry Gregson as pupil and protégé; if, indeed, she were aware of Harry's distinct existence at all, until the following unfortunate occasion. The ante-room, which was a kind of business-place for my lady to receive her steward and tenants in, was surrounded by shelves. I cannot call them book-shelves, though there were many books on them; but the contents of the volumes were principally manuscript, and relating to details connected with the Hanbury property. There were also one or two dictionaries, gazetteers, works of reference on the management of property; all of a very old date (the dictionary was Bailey's, I remember; we had a great Johnson in my lady's room, but where lexicographers differed, she generally preferred Bailey).

In this ante-chamber a footman generally sat, awaiting orders from my lady: for she clung to the grand old customs, and despised any bells, except her own little hand-bell, as modern inventions; she would have her people always within summons of this silvery bell, or her scarce less silvery voice. This man had not the sinecure you might imagine. He had to reply to the private entrance; what we should call the back door in a smaller house. As none came to the front door but my lady, and those of the county whom she honoured by visiting, and her nearest acquaintance of this kind lived eight miles (of bad road) off, the majority of comers knocked at the nail-studded terrace-door; not to have it opened (for open it stood, by my lady's orders, winter and summer, so that the snow often drifted into the back hall, and lay there in heaps when the weather was severe), but to summon some one to receive their message, or carry their request to be allowed to speak to my lady. I remember it was long before Mr. Gray could be made to understand that the great door was only open on state occasions, and even to the last he would as soon come in by that as the terrace entrance. I had been received there on my first setting foot over my lady's threshold; every stranger was led in by that way the first time they came; but after that (with the exceptions I have named) they went round by the terrace, as it were by instinct. It was an assistance to this instinct to be aware that from time immemorial, the magnificent and fierce Hanbury wolf-hounds, which were extinct in every other part of the island, had been and still were kept chained in the front quadrangle, where they bayed through a great part of the day and night, and were always ready with their deep, savage growl at the sight of every person and thing, excepting the man who fed them, my lady's carriage and four, and my lady herself. It was pretty to see her small figure go up to the great, crouching b utes, thumping the flags with their heavy, wagging tails, and slobbering in an ecstasy of delight, at her light approach and

soft caress. She had no fear of them; but she was a Hanbury
born, and the tale went, that they and their kind knew all Hanburys instantly, and acknowledged their supremacy, ever since
the ancestors of the breed had been brought from the East by
the great Sir Urian Hanbury, who lay with his legs crossed on
the altar-tomb in the church. Moreover, it was reported that,
not fifty years before, one of these dogs had eaten up a child
which had inadvertently strayed within reach of its chain. So
you may imagine how most people preferred the terrace-door.
Mr. Gray did not seem to care for the dogs. It might be absence
of mind, for I have heard of his starting away from their sudden
spring when he had unwittingly walked within reach of their
chains; but it could hardly have been absence of mind, when
one day he went right up to one of them, and patted him in the
most friendly manner, the dog meanwhile looking pleased, and
affably wagging his tail, just as if Mr. Gray had been a Hanbury.
We were all very much puzzled by this, and to this day I have
not been able to account for it.

But now let us go back to the terrace-door, and the footman
sitting in the ante-chamber.

One morning we heard a parleying, which rose to such a
vehemence, and lasted for so long, that my lady had to ring her
hand-bell twice before the footman heard it.

" What is the matter, John? " asked she, when he entered.

" A little boy, my lady, who says he comes from Mr. Horner,
and must see your ladyship. Impudent little lad! " (This last
to himself.)

" What does he want? "

" That's just what I have asked him, my lady, but he won't
tell me, please your ladyship."

" It is, probably, some message from Mr. Horner," said Lady
Ludlow, with just a shade of annoyance in her manner; for it
was against all etiquette to send a message to her, and by such
a messenger too!

" No! please your ladyship, I asked him if he had any message,
and he said no, he had none; but he must see your ladyship for
all that."

" You had better show him in then, without more words," said
her ladyship, quietly, but still, as I have said, rather annoyed.

As if in mockery of the humble visitor, the footman threw
open both battants of the door, and in the opening there stood a
lithe, wiry lad, with a thick head of hair, standing out in every
direction, as if stirred by some electrical current, a short, brown

face, red now from affright and excitement, wide, resolute mouth, and bright, deep-set eyes, which glanced keenly and rapidly round the room, as if taking in everything (and all was new and strange), to be thought and puzzled over at some future time. He knew enough of manners not to speak first to one above him in rank, or else he was afraid.

"What do you want with me?" asked my lady; in so gentle a tone that it seemed to surprise and stun him.

"An't please your ladyship?" said he, as if he had been deaf.

"You come from Mr. Horner's: why do you want to see me?" again asked she, a little more loudly.

"An't please your ladyship, Mr. Horner was sent for all on a sudden to Warwick this morning."

His face began to work; but he felt it, and closed his lips into a resolute form.

"Well?"

"And he went off all on a sudden like."

"Well?"

"And he left a note for your ladyship with me, your ladyship."

"Is that all? You might have given it to the footman."

"Please your ladyship, I've clean gone and lost it."

He never took his eyes off her face. If he had not kept his look fixed, he would have burst out crying.

"That was very careless," said my lady gently. "But I am sure you are very sorry for it. You had better try and find it; it may have been of consequence."

"Please, mum—please your ladyship—I can say it off by heart."

"You! What do you mean?" I was really afraid now. My lady's blue eyes absolutely gave out light, she was so much displeased, and, moreover, perplexed. The more reason he had for affright, the more his courage rose. He must have seen,—so sharp a lad must have perceived her displeasure; but he went on quickly and steadily.

"Mr. Horner, my lady, has taught me to read, write, and cast accounts, my lady. And he was in a hurry, and he folded his paper up, but he did not seal it; and I read it, my lady; and now, my lady, it seems like as if I had got it off by heart;" and he went on with a high pitched voice, saying out very loud what, I have no doubt, were the identical words of the letter, date, signature and all: it was merely something about a deed, which required my lady's signature.

When he had done, he stood almost as if he expected commendation for his accurate memory.

My lady's eyes contracted till the pupils were as needle-points; it was a way she had when much disturbed. She looked at me, and said—

"Margaret Dawson, what will this world come to?" And then she was silent.

The lad, beginning to perceive he had given deep offence, stood stock still—as if his brave will had brought him into this presence, and impelled him to confession, and the best amends he could make, but had now deserted him, or was extinct, and left his body motionless, until some one else with word or deed made him quit the room. My lady looked again at him, and saw the frowning, dumb-foundering terror at his misdeed, and the manner in which his confession had been received.

"My poor lad!" said she, the angry look leaving her face, "into whose hands have you fallen?"

The boy's lips began to quiver.

"Don't you know what tree we read of in Genesis?—No! I hope you have not got to read so easily as that." A pause. "Who has taught you to read and write?"

"Please, my lady, I meant no harm, my lady." He was fairly blubbering, overcome by her evident feeling of dismay and regret, the soft repression of which was more frightening to him than any strong or violent words would have been.

"Who taught you, I ask?"

"It were Mr. Horner's clerk who learned me, my lady."

"And did Mr. Horner know of it?"

"Yes, my lady. And I am sure I thought for to please him."

"Well! perhaps you were not to blame for that. But I wonder at Mr. Horner. However, my boy, as you have got possession of edge-tools, you must have some rules how to use them. Did you never hear that you were not to open letters?"

"Please, my lady, it were open. Mr. Horner forgot for to seal it, in his hurry to be off."

"But you must not read letters that are not intended for you. You must never try to read any letters that are not directed to you, even if they be open before you."

"Please, my lady, I thought it were good for practice, all as one as a book."

My lady looked bewildered as to what way she could farther explain to him the laws of honour as regarded letters.

" You would not listen, I am sure," said she, " to anything you were not intended to hear? "

He hesitated for a moment, partly because he did not fully comprehend the question. My lady repeated it. The light of intelligence came into his eager eyes, and I could see that he was not certain if he could tell the truth.

" Please, my lady, I always hearken when I hear folk talking secrets; but I mean no harm."

My poor lady sighed: she was not prepared to begin a long way off in morals. Honour was, to her, second nature, and she had never tried to find out on what principle its laws were based. So, telling the lad that she wished to see Mr. Horner when he returned from Warwick, she dismissed him with a despondent look; he, meanwhile, right glad to be out of the awful gentleness of her presence.

" What is to be done? " said she, half to herself and half to me. I could not answer, for I was puzzled myself.

" It was a right word," she continued, " that I used, when I called reading and writing ' edge-tools.' If our lower orders have these edge-tools given to them, we shall have the terrible scenes of the French Revolution acted over again in England. When I was a girl, one never heard of the rights of men, one only heard of the duties. Now, here was Mr. Gray, only last night, talking of the right every child had to instruction. I could hardly keep my patience with him, and at length we fairly came to words; and I told him I would have no such thing as a Sunday-school (or a Sabbath-school, as he calls it, just like a Jew) in my village."

" And what did he say, my lady? " I asked; for the struggle that seemed now to have come to a crisis, had been going on for some time in a quiet way.

" Why, he gave way to temper, and said he was bound to remember, he was under the bishop's authority, not under mine; and implied that he should persevere in his designs, notwithstanding my expressed opinion."

" And your ladyship—" I half inquired.

" I could only rise and curtsey, and civilly dismiss him. When two persons have arrived at a certain point of expression on a subject, about which they differ as materially as I do from Mr. Gray, the wisest course, if they wish to remain friends, is to drop the conversation entirely and suddenly. It is one of the few cases where abruptness is desirable."

I was sorry for Mr. Gray. He had been to see me several

times, and had helped me to bear my illness in a better spirit than I should have done without his good advice and prayers. And I had gathered, from little things he said, how much his heart was set upon this new scheme. I liked him so much, and I loved and respected my lady so well, that I could not bear them to be on the cool terms to which they were constantly getting. Yet I could do nothing but keep silence.

I suppose my lady understood something of what was passing in my mind; for, after a minute or two, she went on:—

"If Mr. Gray knew all I know,—if he had my experience, he would not be so ready to speak of setting up his new plans in opposition to my judgment. Indeed," she continued, lashing herself up with her own recollections, "times are changed when the parson of a village comes to beard the liege lady in her own house. Why, in my grandfather's days, the parson was family chaplain too, and dined at the Hall every Sunday. He was helped last, and expected to have done first. I remember seeing him take up his plate and knife and fork, and say with his mouth full all the time he was speaking: 'If you please, Sir Urian, and my lady, I'll follow the beef into the housekeeper's room;' for, you see, unless he did so, he stood no chance of a second helping. A greedy man, that parson was, to be sure! I recollect his once eating up the whole of some little bird at dinner, and by way of diverting attention from his greediness, he told how he had heard that a rook soaked in vinegar and then dressed in a particular way, could not be distinguished from the bird he was then eating. I saw by the grim look of my grandfather's face that the parson's doing and saying displeased him; and, child as I was, I had some notion of what was coming, when, as I was riding out on my little, white pony, by my grandfather's side, the next Friday, he stopped one of the game-keepers, and bade him shoot one of the oldest rooks he could find. I knew no more about it till Sunday, when a dish was set right before the parson, and Sir Urian said: 'Now, Parson Hemming, I have had a rook shot, and soaked in vinegar, and dressed as you described last Sunday. Fall to, man, and eat it with as good an appetite as you had last Sunday. Pick the bones clean, or by ——, no more Sunday dinners shall you eat at my table!' I gave one look at poor Mr. Hemming's face, as he tried to swallow the first morsel, and make believe as though he thought it very good; but I could not look again, for shame, although my grandfather laughed, and kept asking us all round if we knew what could have become of the parson's appetite."

" And did he finish it? " I asked.

" O yes, my dear. What my grandfather said was to be done, was done always. He was a terrible man in his anger! But to think of the difference between Parson Hemming and Mr. Gray! or even of poor dear Mr. Mountford and Mr. Gray. Mr. Mountford would never have withstood me as Mr. Gray did! "

" And your ladyship really thinks that it would not be right to have a Sunday-school? " I asked, feeling very timid as I put the question.

" Certainly not. As I told Mr. Gray, I consider a knowledge of the Creed, and of the Lord's Prayer, as essential to salvation; and that any child may have, whose parents bring it regularly to church. Then there are the Ten Commandments, which teach simple duties in the plainest language. Of course, if a lad is taught to read and write (as that unfortunate boy has been who was here this morning) his duties become complicated, and his temptations much greater, while, at the same time, he has no hereditary principles and honourable training to serve as safe-guards. I might take up my old simile of the race-horse and cart-horse. I am distressed," continued she, with a break in her ideas, " about that boy. The whole thing reminds me so much of a story of what happened to a friend of mine—Clément de Créquy. Did I ever tell you about him? "

" No, your ladyship," I replied.

" Poor Clément! More than twenty years ago, Lord Ludlow and I spent a winter in Paris. He had many friends there; perhaps not very good or very wise men, but he was so kind that he liked every one, and every one liked him. We had an apartment, as they call it there, in the Rue de Lille; we had the first-floor of a grand hôtel, with the basement for our servants. On the floor above us lived the owner of the house, a Marquise de Créquy, a widow. They tell me that the Créquy coat-of-arms is still emblazoned, after all these terrible years, on a shield above the arched *porte-coc ère*, just as it was then, though the family is quite extinct. Madame de Créquy had only one son, Clément, who was just the same age as my Urian —you may see his portrait in the great hall—Urian's, I mean." I knew that Master Urian had been drowned at sea; and often had I looked at the presentment of his bonny hopeful face, in his sailor's dress, with right hand outstretched to a ship on the sea in the distance, as if he had just said, " Look at her! all her sails are set, and I'm just off." Poor Master Urian! he went down in this very ship not a year after the picture was taken! But now I will go back to my lady's story. "I can see those two boys playing now," continued she, softly, shutting her eyes, as if the better to call up the vision, "as they used to do five-and-twenty years ago in those old-fashioned French gardens behind our hôtel. Many a time have I watched them from my windows. It was, perhaps, a better play-place than an English garden would have been, for there were but few flower-beds, and no lawn at all to speak about; but, instead, terraces and balustrades and vases and flights of stone steps more in the Italian style; and there were *jets-d'eau*, and little fountains that could be set playing by turning water-cocks that were hidden here and there. How Clément delighted in turning the water on to surprise Urian, and how gracefully he did the honours, as it were, to my dear, rough, sailor lad! Urian was as dark as a gipsy boy, and cared little for his appearance, and resisted all my efforts at setting off his black eyes and tangled curls; but Clément, without ever showing that he thought about himself and his dress, was always dainty and elegant, even though his clothes were sometimes but threadbare. He used to be dressed in a kind of hunter's green suit, open at the neck and half-way down the chest to beautiful old lace frills; his long golden curls fell behind just like a girl's, and his hair in front was cut over his straight dark eyebrows in a line almost as straight. Urian learnt more of a gentleman's carefulness and propriety of appearance from that lad in two months than he had done in years from all my lectures. I recollect one day, when the two boys were in full romp—and, my window being open, I could hear them perfectly—and Urian was daring Clément to some scrambling or climbing, which Clément refused to undertake, but in a hesitating way, as though he longed to do it if some reason had not stood in the way; and at times, Urian, who was hasty and thoughtless, poor fellow, told Clément that he was afraid. 'Fear!' said the French boy, drawing himself up; 'you do not know what you say. If you will be here at six to-morrow morning, when it is only just light, I will take that starling's nest on the top of yonder chimney.' 'But why not now, Clément?' said Urian, putting his arm round Clément's neck. 'Why then, and not now, just when we are in the humour for it?' 'Because we De Créquys are poor, and my mother cannot afford me another suit of clothes this year, and yonder stone carving is all jagged, and would tear my coat and breeches. Now, to-morrow morning I could go up with nothing on but an old shirt.'

" ' But you would tear your legs.'

" ' My race do not care for pain,' said the boy, drawing himself from Urian's arm, and walking a few steps away, with a becoming pride and reserve; for he was hurt at being spoken to as if he were afraid, and annoyed at having to confess the true reason for declining the feat. But Urian was not to be thus baffled. He went up to Clément, and put his arm once more about his neck, and I could see the two lads as they walked down the terrace away from the hôtel windows: first Urian spoke eagerly, looking with imploring fondness into Clément's face, which sought the ground, till at last the French boy spoke, and by and by his arm was round Urian too, and they paced backwards and forwards in deep talk, but gravely, as became men, rather than boys.

" All at once, from the little chapel at the corner of the large garden belonging to the Missions Etrangères, I heard the tinkle of the little bell, announcing the elevation of the host. Down on his knees went Clément, hands crossed, eyes bent down: while Urian stood looking on in respectful thought.

" What a friendship that might have been! I never dream of Urian without seeing Clément too—Urian speaks to me, or does something,—but Clément only flits round Urian, and never seems to see any one else!

" But I must not forget to tell you, that the next morning, before he was out of his room, a footman of Madame de Créquy's brought Urian the starling's nest.

" Well! we came back to England, and the boys were to correspond; and Madame de Créquy and I exchanged civilities; and Urian went to sea.

" After that, all seemed to drop away. I cannot tell you all. However, to confine myself to the De Créquys. I had a letter from Clément; I knew he felt his friend's death deeply; but I should never have learnt it from the letter he sent. It was formal, and seemed like chaff to my hungering heart. Poor fellow! I dare say he had found it hard to write. What could he—or any one—say to a mother who has lost her child? The world does not think so, and, in general, one must conform to the customs of the world; but, judging from my own experience, I should say that reverent silence at such times is the tenderest balm. Madame de Créquy wrote too. But I knew she could not feel my loss so much as Clément, and therefore her letter was not such a disappointment. She and I went on being civil and polite in the way of commissions, and occasionally intro-

ducing friends to each other, for a year or two, and then we
ceased to have any intercourse. Then the terrible Revolution
came. No one who did not live at those times can imagine
the daily expectation of news,—the hourly terror of rumours
affecting the fortunes and lives of those whom most of us had
known as pleasant hosts, receiving us with peaceful welcome
in their magnificent houses. Of course, there was sin enough
and suffering enough behind the scenes; but we English visitors
to Paris had seen little or nothing of that,—and I had sometimes
thought, indeed, how even Death seemed loth to choose his
victims out of that brilliant throng whom I had known.
Madame de Créquy's one boy lived; while three out of my six
were gone since we had met! I do not think all lots are equal,
even now that I know the end of her hopes; but I do say that
whatever our individual lot is, it is our duty to accept it, without
comparing it with that of others.

" The times were thick with gloom and terror. ' What next? '
was the question we asked of every one who brought us news
from Paris. Where were these demons hidden when, so few
years ago, we danced and feasted, and enjoyed the brilliant
salons and the charming friendships of Paris?

" One evening, I was sitting alone in Saint James's Square;
my lord off at the club with Mr. Fox and others: he had left
me, thinking that I should go to one of the many places to
which I had been invited for that evening; but I had no heart
to go anywhere, for it was poor Urian's birthday, and I had
not even rung for lights, though the day was fast closing in,
but was thinking over all his pretty ways, and on his warm
affectionate nature, and how often I had been too hasty in
speaking to him, for all I loved him so dearly; and how I
seemed to have neglected and dropped his dear friend Clément,
who might even now be in need of help in that cruel, bloody
Paris. I say I was thinking reproachfully of all this, and
particularly of Clément de Créquy in connection with Urian,
when Fenwick brought me a note, sealed with a coat-of-arms
I knew well, though I could not remember at the moment
where I had seen it. I puzzled over it, as one does sometimes,
for a minute or more, before I opened the letter. In a moment
I saw it was from Clément de Créquy. ' My mother is here,'
he said: ' she is very ill, and I am bewildered in this strange
country. May I entreat you to receive me for a few minutes? '
The bearer of the note was the woman of the house where they
lodged. I had her brought up into the ante-room, and questioned

her myself, while my carriage was being brought round. They had arrived in London a fortnight or so before: she had not known their quality, judging them (according to her kind) by their dress and their luggage; poor enough, no doubt. The lady had never left her bedroom since her arrival; the young man waited upon her, did everything for her, never left her, in fact; only she (the messenger) had promised to stay within call, as soon as she returned, while he went out somewhere. She could hardly understand him, he spoke English so badly. He had never spoken it, I dare say, since he had talked to my Urian.

CHAPTER V

" In the hurry of the moment I scarce knew what I did. I bade the housekeeper put up every delicacy she had, in order to tempt the invalid, whom yet I hoped to bring back with me to our house. When the carriage was ready I took the good woman with me to show us the exact way, which my coachman professed not to know; for, indeed, they were staying at but a poor kind of place at the back of Leicester Square, of which they had heard, as Clément told me afterwards, from one of the fishermen who had carried them across from the Dutch coast in their disguises as a Friesland peasant and his mother. They had some jewels of value concealed round their persons; but their ready money was all spent before I saw them, and Clément had been unwilling to leave his mother, even for the time necessary to ascertain the best mode of disposing of the diamonds. For, overcome with distress of mind and bodily fatigue, she had reached London only to take to her bed in a sort of low, nervous fever, in which her chief and only idea seemed to be that Clément was about to be taken from her to some prison or other; and if he were out of her sight, though but for a minute, she cried like a child, and could not be pacified or comforted. The landlady was a kind, good woman, and though she but half understood the case, she was truly sorry for them, as foreigners, and the mother sick in a strange land.

" I sent her forwards to request permission for my entrance. In a moment I saw Clément—a tall, elegant young man, in a curious dress of coarse cloth, standing at the open door of a room, and evidently—even before he accosted me—striving to soothe the terrors of his mother inside. I went towards him, and would have taken his hand, but he bent down and kissed m ne.

" ' May I come in, madame? ' I asked, looking at the poor sick lady, lying in the dark, dingy bed, her head propped up on coarse and dirty pillows, and gazing with affrighted eyes at all that was going on.

" ' Clément! Clément! come to me! ' she cried; and when he went to the bedside she turned on one side, and took l is hand in both of hers, and began stroking it, and looking up in his face. I could scarce keep back my tears.

" He stood there quite still, except that from time to time he spoke to her in a low tone. At last I advanced into the room, so that I could talk to him, without renewing her alarm. I asked for the doctor's address; for I had heard that they had called in some one, at their landlady's recommendation: but l could hardly understand Clément's broken English, and mispronunciation of our proper names, and was obliged to apply to the woman herself. I could not say much to Clément, for his attention was perpetually needed by his mother, who never seemed to perceive that I was there. But I told him not to fear, however long I might be away, for that I would return before night; and, bidding the woman take charge of all the heterogeneous things the housekeeper had put up, and leaving one of my men in the house, who could understand a few words of French, with directions that he was to hold himself at Madame de Créquy's orders until I sent or gave him fresh commands, I drove off to the doctor's. What I wanted was his permission to remove Madame de Créquy to my own house, and to learn how it best could be done; for I saw that every movement in the room, every sound except Clément's voice, brought on a fresh access of trembling and nervous agitation.

" The doctor was, I should think, a clever man; but he had that kind of abrupt manner which people get who have much to do with the lower orders.

" I told him the story of his patient, the interest I had in her, and the wish I entertained of removing her to my own house.

" ' It can't be done,' said he. ' Any change will kill her.'

" ' But it must be done,' I replied. ' And it shall not kill her.'

" ' Then I have nothing more to say,' said he, turning away

from the carriage door, and making as though he would go back into the house.

" ' Stop a moment. You must help me; and, if you do, you shall have reason to be glad, for I will give you fifty pounds down with pleasure. If you won't do it, another shall.'

" He looked at me, then (furtively) at the carriage, hesitated, and then said: ' You do not mind expense, apparently. I suppose you are a rich lady of quality. Such folks will not stick at such trifles as the life or death of a sick woman to get their own way. I suppose I must e'en help you, for if I don't, another will.'

" I did not mind what he said, so that he would assist me. I was pretty sure that she was in a state to require opiates; and I had not forgotten Christopher Sly, you may be sure, so I told him what I had in my head. That in the dead of night—the quiet time in the streets—she should be carried in a hospital litter, softly and warmly covered over, from the Leicester Square lodging-house to rooms that I would have in perfect readiness for her. As I planned, so it was done. I let Clément know, by a note, of my design. I had all prepared at home, and we walked about my house as though shod with velvet, while the porter watched at the open door. At last, through the darkness, I saw the lanterns carried by my men, who were leading the little procession. The litter looked like a hearse; on one side walked the doctor, on the other Clément; they came softly and swiftly along. I could not try any farther experiment; we dared not change her clothes; she was laid in the bed in the landlady's coarse night-gear, and covered over warmly, and left in the shaded, scented room, with a nurse and the doctor watching by her, while I led Clément to the dressing-room adjoining, in which I had had a bed placed for him. Farther than that he would not go; and there I had refreshments brought. Meanwhile, he had shown his gratitude by every possible action (for we none of us dared to speak): he had kneeled at my feet, and kissed my hand, and left it wet with his tears. He had thrown up his arms to Heaven, and prayed earnestly, as I could see by the movement of his lips. I allowed him to relieve himself by these dumb expressions, if I may so call them—and then I left him, and went to my own rooms to sit up for my lord, and tell him what I had done.

" Of course, it was all right; and neither my lord nor I could sleep for wondering how Madame de Créquy would bear her awakening. I had engaged the doctor, to whose face and voice she was accustomed, to remain with her all night: the nurse was experienced, and Clément was within call. But it was with the greatest relief that I heard from my own woman, when she brought me my chocolate, that Madame de Créquy (Monsieur had said) had awakened more tranquil than she had been for many days. To be sure, the whole aspect of the bed-chamber must have been more familiar to her than the miserable place where I had found her, and she must have intuitively felt herself among friends.

"My lord was scandalised at Clément's dress, which, after the first moment of seeing him I had forgotten, in thinking of other things, and for which I had not prepared Lord Ludlow. He sent for his own tailor, and bade him bring patterns of stuffs, and engage his men to work night and day till Clément could appear as became his rank. In short, in a few days so much of the traces of their flight were removed, that we had almost forgotten the terrible causes of it, and rather felt as if they had come on a visit to us than that they had been compelled to fly their country. Their diamonds, too, were sold well by my lord's agents, though the London shops were stocked with jewellery, and such portable valuables, some of rare and curious fashion, which were sold for half their real value by emigrants who could not afford to wait. Madame de Créquy was recovering her health, although her strength was sadly gone, and she would never be equal to such another flight as the perilous one which she had gone through, and to which she could not bear the slightest reference. For some time things continued in this state;—the De Créquys still our honoured visitors—many houses besides our own, even among our own friends, open to receive the poor flying nobility of France, driven from their country by the brutal republicans, and every freshly-arrived emigrant bringing new tales of horror, as if these revolutionists were drunk with blood, and mad to devise new atrocities. One day Clément;—I should tell you he had been presented to our good King George and the sweet queen, and they had accosted him most graciously, and his beauty and elegance, and some of the circumstances attendant on his flight, made him be received in the world quite like a hero of romance: he might have been on intimate terms in many a distinguished house, had he cared to visit much; but he accompanied my lord and me with an air of indifference and languor, which I sometimes fancied made him be all the more sought after: Monkshaven (that was the title my eldest son bore) tried in vain to interest him in all young men's sports.

But no! it was the same through all. His mother took far more interest in the *on-dits* of the London world, into which she was far too great an invalid to venture, than he did in the absolute events themselves, in which he might have been an actor. One day, as I was saying, an old Frenchman of a humble class presented himself to our servants, several of whom understood French; and through Medlicott, I learnt that he was in some way connected with the De Créquys; not with their Paris life; but I fancy he had been intendant of their estates in the country; estates which were more useful as hunting-grounds than as adding to their income. However, there was the old man; and with him, wrapped round his person, he had brought the long parchment rolls, and deeds relating to their property. These he would deliver up to none but Monsieur de Créquy, the rightful owner; and Clément was out with Monkshaven, so the old man waited; and when Clément came in, I told him of the steward's arrival, and how he had been cared for by my people. Clément went directly to see him. He was a long time away, and I was waiting for him to drive out with me, for some purpose or another, I scarce know what, but I remember I was tired of waiting, and was just in the act of ringing the bell to desire that he might be reminded of his engagement with me, when he came in, his face as white as the powder in his hair, his beautiful eyes dilated with horror. I saw that he had heard something that touched him even more closely than the usual tales which every fresh emigrant brought.

" ' What is it, Clément? ' I asked.

" He clasped his hands, and looked as though he tried to speak, but could not bring out the words.

" ' They have guillotined my uncle! ' said he at last. Now, I knew that there was a Count de Créquy; but I had always understood that the elder branch held very little communication with him; in fact, that he was a vaurien of some kind, and rather a disgrace than otherwise to the family. So, perhaps, I was hard-hearted; but I was a little surprised at this excess of emotion, till I saw that peculiar look in his eyes that many people have when there is more terror in their hearts than they dare put into words. He wanted me to understand something without his saying it; but how could I? I had never heard of a Mademoiselle de Créquy.

" ' Virginie! ' at last he uttered. In an instant I understood it all, and remembered that, if Urian had lived, he too might have been in love.

" ' Your uncle's daughter? ' I inquired.

" ' My cousin,' he replied.

" I did not say, ' your betrothed,' but I had no doubt of it. I was mistaken, however.

" ' O madame! ' he continued, ' her mother died long ago—her father now—and she is in daily fear,—alone, deserted——'

" ' Is she in the Abbaye? ' asked I.

" ' No! she is in hiding with the widow of her father's old concierge. Any day they may search the house for aristocrats. They are seeking them everywhere. Then, not her life alone, but that of the old woman, her hostess, is sacrificed. The old woman knows this, and trembles with fear. Even if she is brave enough to be faithful, her fears would betray her, should the house be searched. Yet, there is no one to help Virginie to escape. She is alone in Paris.'

" I saw what was in his mind. He was fretting and chafing to go to his cousin's assistance; but the thought of his mother restrained him. I would not have kept back Urian from such an errand at such a time. How should I restrain him? And yet, perhaps, I did wrong in not urging the chances of danger more. Still, if it was danger to him, was it not the same or even greater danger to her?—for the French spared neither age nor sex in those wicked days of terror. So I rather fell in with his wish, and encouraged him to think how best and most prudently it might be fulfilled; never doubting, as I have said, that he and his cousin were troth-plighted.

" But when I went to Madame de Créquy—after he had imparted his, or rather our plan to her—I found out my mistake. She, who was in general too feeble to walk across the room save slowly, and with a stick, was going from end to end with quick, tottering steps; and, if now and then she sank upon a chair, it seemed as if she could not rest, for she was up again in a moment, pacing along, wringing her hands, and speaking rapidly to herself. When she saw me, she stopped: ' Madame,' she said, ' you have lost your own boy. You might have left me mine.'

" I was so astonished—I hardly knew what to say. I had spoken to Clément as if his mother's consent were secure (as I had felt my own would have been if Urian had been alive to ask it). Of course, both he and I knew that his mother's consent must be asked and obtained, before he could leave her to go on such an undertaking; but, somehow, my blood always rose at the sight or sound of danger; perhaps, because my life had been so peaceful. Poor Madame de Créquy! it was otherwise with her; she despaired while I hoped, and Clément trusted.

"'Dear Madame de Créquy,' said I, 'he will return safely to us; every precaution shall be taken, that either he or you, or my lord, or Monkshaven can think of; but he cannot leave a girl —his nearest relation save you—his betrothed, is she not?'

"'His betrothed!' cried she, now at the utmost pitch of her excitement. 'Virginie betrothed to Clément?—no! thank heaven, not so bad as that! Yet it might have been. But mademoiselle scorned my son! She would have nothing to do with him. Now is the time for him to have nothing to do with her!'

"Clément had entered at the door behind his mother as she thus spoke. His face was set and pale, till it looked as grey and immovable as if it had been carved in stone. He came forward and stood before his mother. She stopped her walk, threw back her haughty head, and the two looked each other steadily in the face. After a minute or two in this attitude, her proud and resolute gaze never flinching or wavering, he went down upon one knee, and, taking her hand—her hard, stony hand, which never closed on his, but remained straight and stiff:

"'Mother,' he pleaded, 'withdraw your prohibition. Let me go!'

"'What were her words?' Madame de Créquy replied, slowly, as if forcing her memory to the extreme of accuracy. '"My cousin," she said, "when I marry, I marry a man, not a petit-maître. I marry a man who, whatever his rank may be, will add dignity to the human race by his virtues, and not be content to live in an effeminate court on the traditions of past grandeur." She borrowed her words from the infamous Jean-Jacques Rousseau, the friend of her scarce less infamous father, —nay! I will say it,—if not her words, she borrowed her principles. And my son to request her to marry him!'

"'It was my father's written wish,' said Clément.

"'But did you not love her? You plead your father's words, —words written twelve years before—and as if that were your reason for being indifferent to my dislike to the alliance. But you requested her to marry you—and she refused you with insolent contempt; and now you are ready to leave me—leave me desolate in a foreign land——'

"'Desolate! my mother! and the Countess Ludlow stands there!'

"'Pardon, madame! But all the earth, though it were full

of kind hearts, is but a desolation and a desert place to a mother when her only child is absent. And you, Clément, would leave me for this Virginie—this degenerate De Créquy, tainted with the atheism of the Encyclopédistes! She is only reaping some of the fruit of the harvest whereof her friends have sown the seed. Let her alone! Doubtless she has friends—it may be lovers—among these demons, who, under the cry of liberty, commit every licence. Let her alone, Clément! She refused you with scorn: be too proud to notice her now.'

" ' Mother, I cannot think of myself; only of her.'

" ' Think of me, then! I, your mother, forbid you to go.'

" Cl ment bowed low, and went out of the room instantly, as one blinded. She saw his groping movement, and for an instant I think her heart was touched. But she turned to me, and tried to exculpate her past violence by dilating upon her wrongs, and they certainly were many. The count, her husband's younger brother, had invariably tried to make mischief between husband and wife. He had been the cleverer man of the two, and had possessed extraordinary influence over her husband. She suspected him of having instigated that clause in her husband's will, by which the marquis expressed his wish for the marriage of the cousins. The count had had some interest in the management of the De Créquy property during her son's minority. Indeed, I remembered then, that it was through Count de Créquy that Lord Ludlow had first heard of the apartment which we afterwards took in the Hôtel de Créquy; and then the recollection of a past feeling came distinctly out of the mist, as it were; and I called to mind how, when we first took up our abode in the Hôtel de Créquy, both Lord Ludlow and I imagined that the arrangement was displeasing to our hostess; and how it had taken us a considerable time before we had been able to establish relations of friendship with her. Years after our visit, she began to suspect that Clément (whom she could not forbid to visit at his uncle's house, considering the terms on which his father had been with his brother; though she herself never set foot over the Count de Créquy's threshold) was attaching himself to mademoiselle, his cousin; and she made cautious inquiries as to the appearance, character, and disposition of the young lady. Mademoiselle was not handsome, they said; but of a fine figure, and generally considered as having a very no le and attractive presence. In character she was daring and wilful (said one set); original and independent (said another). She was much indulged by her father, who had given her something

of a man's education, and selected for her intimate friend a young
lady below her in rank, one of the Bureaucracie, a Mademoiselle
Necker, daughter of the Minister of Finance. Mademoiselle
de Créquy was thus introduced into all the free-thinking salons
of Paris; among people who were always full of plans for
subverting society. 'And did Clément affect such people?'
Madame de Créquy had asked with some anxiety. No!
Monsieur de Créquy had neither eyes nor ears, nor thought for
anything but his cousin, while she was by. And she? She
hardly took notice of his devotion, so evident to every one else.
The proud creature! But perhaps that was her haughty way
of concealing what she felt. And so Madame de Créquy listened,
and questioned, and learnt nothing decided, until one day she
surprised Clément with the note in his hand, of which she remembered the stinging words so well, in which Virginie had
said, in reply to a proposal Clément had sent her through her
father, that 'When she married she married a man, not a *petit-
maitre*.'

" Clément was justly indignant at the insulting nature of the
answer Virginie had sent to a proposal, respectful in its tone, and
which was, after all, but the cool, hardened lava over a burning
heart. He acquiesced in his mother's desire, that he should not
again present himself in his uncle's salons; but he did not forget
Virginie, though he never mentioned her name.

" Madame de Créquy and her son were among the earliest
proscr ts, as they were of the strongest possible royalists, and
aristocrats, as it was the custom of the horrid Sansculottes to
term those who adhered to the habits of expression and action in
which it was their pride to have been educated. They had left
Paris some weeks before they had arrived in England, and
Clément's belief at the time of quitting the Hôtel de Créquy had
certainly been, that his uncle was not merely safe, but rather a
popular man with the party in power. And, as all communication having relation to private individuals of a reliable kind was
intercepted, Monsieur de Créquy had felt but little anxiety for
his uncle and cousin, in comparison with what he did for many
other friends of very different opinions in politics, until the day
when he was stunned by the fatal information that even his
progressive uncle was guillotined, and learnt that his cousin was
imprisoned by the licence of the mob, whose rights (as she called
them) she was always advocating.

" When I had heard all this story, I confess I lost in sympathy
for Clément what I gained for his mother. Virginie's life did

not seem to me worth the risk that Clément's would run. But
when I saw him—sad, depressed, nay, hopeless—going about
like one oppressed by a heavy dream which he cannot shake off;
caring neither to eat, drink, nor sleep, yet bearing all with silent
dignity, and even trying to force a poor, faint smile when he
caught my anxious eyes; I turned round again, and wondered
how Madame de Créquy could resist this mute pleading of her
son's altered appearance. As for my Lord Ludlow and Monkshaven, as soon as they understood the case, they were indignant
that any mother should attempt to keep a son out of honourable
danger; and it was honourable, and a clear duty (according to
them) to try to save the life of a helpless orphan girl, his next
of kin. None but a Frenchman, said my lord, would hold himself bound by an old woman's whimsies and fears, even though
she were his mother. As it was, he was chafing himself to death
under the restraint. If he went, to be sure, the —— wretches
might make an end of him, as they had done of many a fine
fellow: but my lord would take heavy odds, that, instead of
being guillotined, he would save the girl, and bring her safe to
England, just desperately in love with her preserver, and then
we would have a jolly wedding down at Monkshaven. My lord
repeated his opinion so often that it became a certain prophecy
in his mind of what was to take place; and, one day seeing
Clément look even paler and thinner than he had ever done
before, he sent a message to Madame de Créquy, requesting
permission to speak to her in private.

" ' For, by George! ' said he, ' she shall hear my opinion, and
not let that lad of hers kill himself by fretting. He's too good
for that. If he had been an English lad, he would have been off
to his sweetheart long before this, without saying with your
leave or by your leave; but being a Frenchman, he is all for
Æneas and filial piety—filial fiddle-sticks! ' (My lord had run
away to sea, when a boy, against his father's consent, I am sorry
to say; and, as all had ended well, and he had come back to find
both his parents alive, I do not think he was ever as much aware
of his fault as he might have been under other circumstances.)
' No, my lady,' he went on, ' don't come with me. A woman can
manage a man best when he has a fit of obstinacy, and a man can
persuade a woman out of her tantrums, when all her own sex, the
whole army of them, would fail. Allow me to go alone to my
tête-à-tête with madame.'

" What he said, what passed, he never could repeat; but
he came back graver than he went. However, the point was

gained; Madame de Créquy withdrew her prohibition, and had given him leave to tell Clément as much.

" ' But she is an old Cassandra,' said he. ' Don't let the lad be much with her; her talk would destroy the courage of the bravest man; she is so given over to superstition.' Something that she had said had touched a chord in my lord's nature which he inherited from his Scotch ancestors. Long afterwards, I heard what this was. Medlicott told me.

" However, my lord shook off all fancies that told against the fulfilment of Clément's wishes. All that afternoon we three sat together, planning; and Monkshaven passed in and out, executing our commissions, and preparing everything. Towards nightfall all was ready for Clément's start on his journey towards the coast.

" Madame had declined seeing any of us since my lord's stormy interview with her. She sent word that she was fatigued, and desired repose. But, of course, before Clément set off, he was bound to wish her farewell, and to ask for her blessing. In order to avoid an agitating conversation between mother and son, my lord and I resolved to be present at the interview. Clément was already in his travelling-dress, that of a Norman fisherman, which Monkshaven had, with infinite trouble, discovered in the possession of one of the *emigrés* who thronged London, and who had made his escape from the shores of France in this disguise. Clément's plan was, to go down to the coast of Sussex, and get some of the fishing or smuggling boats to take him across to the French coast near Dieppe. There again he would have to change his dress. Oh, it was so well planned! His mother was startled by his disguise (of which we had not thought to forewarn her) as he entered her apartment. And either that, or the being suddenly roused from the heavy slumber into which she was apt to fall when she was left alone, gave her manner an air of wildness that was almost like insanity.

" ' Go, go!' she said to him, almost pushing him away as he knelt to kiss her hand. ' Virginie is beckoning to you, but you don't see what kind of a bed it is——'

" ' Clément, make haste!' said my lord, in a hurried manner, as if to interrupt madame. ' The time is later than I thought, and you must not miss the morning's tide. Bid your mother good-bye at once, and let us be off.' For my lord and Monkshaven were to ride with him to an inn near the shore, from whence he was to walk to his destination. My lord almost took him by the arm to pull him away; and they were gone, and I was left alone with Madame de Créquy. When she heard the horses' feet, she seemed to find out the truth, as if for the first time. She set her teeth together. ' He has left me for her!' she almost screamed. ' Left me for her!' she kept muttering; and then, as the wild look came back into her eyes, she said, almost with exultation, ' But I did not give him my blessing!' "

CHAPTER VI

" ALL night Madame de Créquy raved in delirium. If I could, I would have sent for Clément back again. I did send off one man, but I suppose my directions were confused, or they were wrong, for he came back after my lord's return, on the following afternoon. By this time Madame de Créquy was quieter: she was, indeed, asleep from exhaustion when Lord Ludlow and Monkshaven came in. They were in high spirits, and their hopefulness brought me round to a less dispirited state. All had gone well: they had accompanied Clément on foot along the shore, until they had met with a lugger, which my lord had hailed in good nautical language. The captain had responded to these freemason terms by sending a boat to pick up his passenger, and by an invitation to breakfast sent through a speaking-trumpet. Monkshaven did not approve of either the meal or the company, and had returned to the inn, but my lord had gone with Clément, and breakfasted on board, upon grog, biscuit, fresh-caught fish—' the best breakfast he ever ate,' he said, but that was probably owing to the appetite his night's ride had given him. However, his good-fellowship had evidently won the captain's heart, and Clément had set sail under the best auspices. It was agreed that I should tell all this to Madame de Créquy, if she inquired; otherwise, it would be wiser not to renew her agitation by alluding to her son's journey.

" I sat with her constantly for many days; but she never spoke of Clément. She forced herself to talk of the little occurrences of Parisian society in former days: she tried to be conversational and agreeable, and to betray no anxiety or even interest in the object of Clément's journey; and, as far as unremitting efforts could go, she succeeded. But the tones of her voice were sharp and yet piteous, as if she were in constant pain; and the glance of her eye hurried and fearful, as if she dared not let it rest on any object.

" In a week we heard of Clément's safe arrival on the French coast. He sent a letter to this effect by the captain of the smuggler, when the latter returned. We hoped to hear again; but week after week elapsed, and there was no news of Clément. I had told Lord Ludlow, in Madame de Créquy's presence, as he and I had arranged, of the note I had received from her son, informing us of his landing in France. She heard, but she took no notice, and evidently began to wonder that we did not mention any further intelligence of him in the same manner before her; and daily I began to fear that her pride would give way, and that she would supplicate for news before I had any to give her.

" One morning, on my awakening, my maid told me that Madame de Créquy had passed a wretched night, and had bidden Medlicott (whom, as understanding French, and speaking it pretty well, though with that horrid German accent, I had put about her) request that I would go to madame's room as soon as I was dressed.

" I knew what was coming, and I trembled all the time they were doing my hair, and otherwise arranging me. I was not encouraged by my lord's speeches. He had heard the message, and kept declaring that he would rather be shot than have to tell her that there was no news of her son; and yet he said, every now and then, when I was at the lowest pitch of uneasiness, that he never expected to hear again: that some day soon we should see him walking in, and introducing Mademoiselle de Créquy to us.

" However, at last I was ready, and go I must.

" Her eyes were fixed on the door by which I entered. I went up to the bedside. She was not rouged,—she had left it off now for several days,—she no longer attempted to keep up the vain show of not feeling, and loving, and fearing.

" For a moment or two she did not speak, and I was glad of the respite.

" ' Clément? ' she said at length, covering her mouth with a handkerchief the minute she had spoken, that I might not see it quiver.

" ' There has been no news since the first letter, saying how well the voyage was performed, and how safely he had landed— near Dieppe, you know,' I replied as cheerfully as possible. ' My lord does not expect that we shall have another letter; he thinks that we shall see him soon.'

" There was no answer. As I looked, uncertain whether to

do or say more, she slowly turned herself in bed, and lay with
her face to the wall; and, as if that did not shut out the light
of day and the busy, happy world enough, she put out her trembling hands, and covered her face with her handkerchief. There
was no violence: hardly any sound.

" I told her what my lord had said about Clément's coming
in some day, and taking us all by surprise. I did not believe
it myself, but it was just possible,—and I had nothing else to
say. Pity, to one who was striving so hard to conceal her feelings, would have been impertinent. She let me talk; but she
did not reply. She knew that my words were vain and idle, and
had no root in my belief, as well as I did myself.

" I was very thankful when Medlicott came in with madame's
breakfast, and gave me an excuse for leaving.

" But I think that conversation made me feel more anxious
and impatient than ever. I felt almost pledged to Madame de
Créquy for the fulfilment of the vision I had held out. She had
taken entirely to her bed by this time: not from illness, but
because she had no hope within her to stir her up to the effort
of dressing. In the same way she hardly cared for food. She
had no appetite,—why eat to prolong a life of despair? But
she let Medlicott feed her, sooner than take the trouble of
resisting.

" And so it went on,—for weeks, months,—I could hardly
count the time, it seemed so long. Medlicott told me she noticed
a preternatural sensitiveness of ear in Madame de Créquy, induced by the habit of listening silently for the slightest unusual
sound in the house. Medlicott was always a minute watcher of
any one whom she cared about; and, one day, she made me
notice by a sign madame's acuteness of hearing, although the
quick expectation was but evinced for a moment in the turn
of the eye, the hushed breath—and then, when the unusual footstep turned into my lord's apartments, the soft quivering sigh,
and the closed eyelids.

" At length the intendant of the De Créquy estates,—the old
man, you will remember, whose information respecting Virginie
de Créquy first gave Clément the desire to return to Paris,—
came to St. James's Square, and begged to speak to me. I
made haste to go down to him in the housekeeper's room, sooner
than that he should be ushered into mine, for fear of madame
hearing any sound.

" The old man stood—I see him now—with his hat held before him in both his hands; he slowly bowed till his face touched

it when I came in. Such long excess of courtesy augured ill. He waited for me to speak.

" ' Have you any intelligence? ' I inquired. He had been often to the house before, to ask if we had received any news; and once or twice I had seen him, but this was the first time he had begged to see me.

" ' Yes, madame,' he replied, still standing with his head bent down, like a child in disgrace.

" ' And it is bad! ' I exclaimed.

" ' It is bad.' For a moment I was angry at the cold tone in which my words were echoed; but directly afterwards I saw the large, slow, heavy tears of age falling down the old man's cheeks, and on to the sleeves of his poor, threadbare coat.

" I asked him how he had heard it: it seemed as though I could not all at once bear to hear what it was. He told me that the night before, in crossing Long Acre, he had stumbled upon an old acquaintance of his; one who, like himself, had been a dependent upon the De Créquy family, but had managed their Paris affairs, while Fléchier had taken charge of their estates in the country. Both were now emigrants, and living on the proceeds of such small available talents as they possessed. Fléchier, as I knew, earned a very fair livelihood by going about to dress salads for dinner parties. His compatriot, Le Fèbvre, had begun to give a few lessons as a dancing-master. One of them took the other home to his lodgings; and there, when their most immediate personal adventures had been hastily talked over, came the inquiry from Fléchier as to Monsieur de Créquy.

" ' Clément was dead — guillotined. Virginie was dead — guillotined.'

" When Fléchier had told me thus much, he could not speak for sobbing; and I, myself, could hardly tell how to restrain my tears sufficiently, until I could go to my own room and be at liberty to give way. He asked my leave to bring in his friend Le Fèbvre, who was walking in the square, awaiting a possible summons to tell his story. I heard afterwards a good many details, which filled up the account, and made me feel—which brings me back to the point I started from—how unfit the lower orders are for being trusted indiscriminately with the dangerous powers of education. I have made a long preamble, but now I am coming to the moral of my story."

My lady was trying to shake off the emotion which she evidently felt in recurring to this sad history of Monsieur de Créquy's death. She came behind me, and arranged my pillows, and then, seeing I had been crying—for, indeed, I was weak-spirited at the time, and a little served to unloose my tears —she stooped down, and kissed my forehead, and said " Poor child ! " almost as if she thanked me for feeling that old grief of hers.

" Being once in France, it was no difficult thing for Clément to get into Paris. The difficulty in those days was to leave, not to enter. He came in dressed as a Norman peasant, in charge of a load of fruit and vegetables, with which one of the Seine barges was freighted. He worked hard with his companions in landing and arranging their produce on the quays; and then, when they dispersed to get their breakfasts at some of the *estaminets* near the old Marché aux Fleurs, he sauntered up a street which conducted him, by many an odd turn, through the Quartier Latin to a horrid back alley, leading out of the Rue l'Ecole de Médecine; some atrocious place, as I have heard, not far from the shadow of that terrible Abbaye where so many of the best blood of France awaited their deaths. But here some old man lived, on whose fidelity Clément thought that he might rely. I am not sure if he had not been gardener in those very gardens behind the Hôtel Créquy where Clément and Urian used to play together years before. But, whatever the old man's dwelling might be, Clément was only too glad to reach it, you may be sure. He had been kept in Normandy, in all sorts of disguises, for many days after landing in Dieppe, through the difficulty of entering Paris unsuspected by the many ruffians who were always on the look-out for aristocrats.

" The old gardener was, I believe, both faithful and tried, and sheltered Clément in his garret as well as might be. Before he could stir out, it was necessary to procure a fresh disguise, and one more in character with an inhabitant of Paris than that of a Norman carter was procured; and after waiting indoors for one or two days, to see if any suspicion was excited, Clément set off to discover Virginie.

" He found her at the old concierge's dwelling. Madame Babette was the name of this woman, who must have been a less faithful—or rather, perhaps, I should say, a more interested— friend to her guest than the old gardener Jaques was to Clément.

" I have seen a miniature of Virginie, which a French lady of quality happened to have in her possession at the time of her flight from Paris, and which she brought with her to England unwittingly; for it belonged to the Count de Créquy, with whom she was slightly acquainted. I should fancy from it, that Virginie was taller and of a more powerful figure for a woman than her cousin Clément was for a man. Her dark-brown hair was arranged in short curls—the way of dressing the hair announced the politics of the individual, in those days, just as patches did in my grandmother's time; and Virginie's hair was not to my taste, or according to my principles: it was too classical. Her large, black eyes looked out at you steadily. One cannot judge of the shape of a nose from a full-face miniature, but the nostrils were clearly cut and largely opened. I do not fancy her nose could have been pretty; but her mouth had a character all its own, and which would, I think, have redeemed a plainer face. It was wide, and deep set into the cheeks at the corners; the upper lip was very much arched, and hardly closed over the teeth; so that the whole face looked (from the serious, intent look in the eyes, and the sweet intelligence of the mouth) as if she were listening eagerly to something to which her answer was quite ready, and would come out of those red, opening lips as soon as ever you had done speaking, and you longed to know what she would say.

" Well: this Virginie de Créquy was living with Madame Babette in the concièrgerie of an old French inn, somewhere to the north of Paris, so, far enough from Clément's refuge. The inn had been frequented by farmers from Britanny and such kind of people, in the days when that sort of intercourse went on between Paris and the provinces which had nearly stopped now. Few Bretons came near it now, and the inn had fallen into the hands of Madame Babette's brother, as payment for a bad wine debt of the last proprietor. He put his sister and her child in, to keep it open, as it were, and sent all the people he could to occupy the half-furnished rooms of the house. They paid Babette for their lodging every morning as they went out to breakfast, and returned or not as they chose, at night. Every three days, the wine-merchant or his son came to Madame Babette, and she accounted to them for the money she had received. She and her child occupied the porter's office (in which the lad slept at nights) and a little miserable bedroom which opened out of it, and received all the light and air that was admitted through the door of communication, which was half glass. Madame Babette must have had a kind of attachment for the De Créquys—her De Créquys, you understand— Virginie's father, the count; for, at some risk to herself, she had warned both him and his daughter of the danger impending over them. But he, infatuated, would not believe that his dear Human Race could ever do him harm; and, as long as he did not fear, Virginie was not afraid. It was by some ruse, the nature of which I never heard, that Madame Babette induced Virginie to come to her abode at the very hour in which the count had been recognised in the streets, and hurried off to the Lanterne. It was after Babette had got her there, safe shut up in the little back den, that she told her what had befallen her father. From that day, Virginie had never stirred out of the gates, or crossed the threshold of the porter's lodge. I do not say that Madame Babette was tired of her continual presence, or regretted the impulse which made her rush to the De Créquys' well-known house—after being compelled to form one of the mad crowds that saw the Count de Créquy seized and hung—and hurry his daughter out, through alleys and backways, until at length she had the orphan safe in her own dark sleeping-room, and could tell her tale of horror: but Madame Babette was poorly paid for her porter's work by her avaricious brother; and it was hard enough to find food for herself and her growing boy; and, though the poor girl ate little enough, I dare say, yet there seemed no end to the burthen that Madame Babette had imposed upon herself: the De Créquys were plundered, ruined, had become an extinct race, all but a lonely friendless girl, in broken health and spirits; and, though she lent no positive encouragement to his suit, yet, at the time, when Clément reappeared in Paris, Madame Babette was beginning to think that Virginie might do worse than encourage the attentions of Monsieur Morin Fils, her nephew, and the wine merchant's son. Of course, he and his father had the entrée into the concièrgerie of the hotel that belonged to them, in right of being both proprietors and relations. The son, Morin, had seen Virginie in this manner. He was fully aware that she was far above him in rank, and guessed from her whole aspect that she had lost her natural protectors by the terrible guillotine; but he did not know her exact name or station, nor could he persuade his aunt to tell him. However, he fell head over ears in love with her, whether she were princess or peasant; and though at first there was something about her which made his passionate love conceal itself with shy, awkward reserve, and then made it only appear in the guise of deep, respectful devotion; yet, by-and-by,—by the same process of reasoning, I suppose, that his aunt had gone through even before him—Jean Morin began to let Hope oust Despair from his heart.

Sometimes, he thought—perhaps years hence—that solitary, friendless lady, pent up in squalor, might turn to him as to a friend and comforter—and then—and then——. Meanwhile Jean Morin was most attentive to his aunt, whom he had rather slighted before. He would linger over the accounts; would bring her little presents; and, above all, he made a pet and favourite of Pierre, the little cousin, who could tell him about all the ways of going on of Mam'selle Cannes, as Virginie was called. Pierre was thoroughly aware of the drift and cause of his cousin's inquiries; and was his ardent partisan, as I have heard, even before Jean Morin had exactly acknowledged his wishes to himself.

" It must have required some patience and much diplomacy, before Clément de Créquy found out the exact place where his cousin was hidden. The old gardener took the cause very much to heart; as, judging from my recollections, I imagine he would have forwarded any fancy, however wild, of Monsieur Clément's. (I will tell you afterwards how I came to know all these particulars so well.)

" After Clément's return, on two succeeding days, from his dangerous search, without meeting with any good result, Jacques entreated Monsieur de Créquy to let him take it in hand. He represented that he, as gardener for the space of twenty years and more at the Hotel de Créquy, had a right to be acquainted with all the successive concièrges at the Count's house; that he should not go among them as a stranger, but as an old friend, anxious to renew pleasant intercourse; and that if the Intendant's story, which he had told Monsieur de Créquy in England, was true, that mademoiselle was in hiding at the house of a former concièrge, why, something relating to her would surely drop out in the course of conversation. So he persuaded Clément to remain indoors, while he set off on his round, with no apparent object but to gossip.

" At night he came home,—having seen mademoiselle. He told Clément much of the story relating to Madame Babette that I have told to you. Of course, he had heard nothing of the ambitious hopes of Morin Fils,—hardly of his existence, I should think. Madame Babette had received him kindly; although, for some time, she had kept him standing in the carriage gateway outside her door. But, on his complaining of the draught and his rheumatism, she had asked him in: first looking round with some anxiety, to see who was in the room behind her. No one was there when he entered and sat down. But, in a minute or two, a tall, thin young lady, with great, sad eyes, and pale cheeks, came from the inner room, and, seeing him, retired. 'It is Mademoiselle Cannes,' said Madame Babette, rather unnecessarily; for, if he had not been on the watch for some sign of Mademoiselle de Créquy, he would hardly have noticed the entrance and withdrawal.

"Clément and the good old gardener were always rather perplexed by Madame Babette's evident avoidance of all mention of the De Créquy family. If she were so much interested in one member as to be willing to undergo the pains and penalites of a domiciliary visit, it was strange that she never inquired after the existence of her charge's friends and relations from one who might very probably have heard something of them. They settled that Madame Babette must believe that the Marquise and Clément were dead; and admired her for her reticence in never speaking of Virginie. The truth was, I suspect, that she was so desirous of her nephew's success by this time, that she did not like letting any one into the secret of Virginie's whereabouts who might interfere with their plan. However, it was arranged between Clément and his humble friend, that the former, dressed in the peasant's clothes in which he had entered Paris, but smartened up in one or two particulars, as if, although a countryman, he had money to spare, should go and engage a sleeping-room in the old Bréton Inn; where, as I told you, accommodation for the night was to be had. This was accordingly done, without exciting Madame Babette's suspicions, for she was unacquainted with the Normandy accent, and consequently did not perceive the exaggeration of it which Monsieur de Créquy adopted in order to disguise his pure Parisian. But after he had for two nights slept in a queer dark closet, at the end of one of the numerous short galleries in the Hôtel Duguesclin, and paid his money for such accommodation each morning at the little bureau under the window of the concièrgerie, he found himself no nearer to his object. He stood outside in the gateway: Madame Babette opened a pane in her window, counted out the change, gave polite thanks, and shut to the pane with a clack, before he could ever find out what to say that might be the means of opening a conversation. Once in the streets, he was in danger from the bloodthirsty mob, who were ready in those days to hunt to death every one who looked like a gentleman, as an aristocrat: and Clément, depend upon it, looked a gentleman, whatever dress he wore. Yet it was unwise to traverse Paris to his old friend the gardener's grénier, so he had to loiter about, where I hardly know. Only he did leave the Hôtel Duguesclin, and he did not go to old Jacques, and there was not another house in Paris open to him. At the end of two days, he had made out Pierre's existence; and he began to try to make friends with the lad. Pierre was too sharp and shrewd not to suspect something from the confused attempts at friendliness. It was not for nothing that the Norman farmer lounged in the court and doorway, and brought home presents of galette. Pierre accepted the galette, reciprocated the civil speeches, but kept his eyes open. Once, returning home pretty late at night, he surprised the Norman studying the shadows on the blind, which was drawn down when Madame Babette's lamp was lighted. On going in, he found Mademoiselle Cannes with his mother, sitting by the table, and helping in the family mending.

" Pierre was afraid that the Norman had some view upon the money which his mother, as concièrge, collected for her brother. But the money was all safe next evening, when his cousin, Monsieur Morin Fils, came to collect it. Madame Babette asked her nephew to sit down, and skilfully barred the passage to the inner door, so that Virginie, had she been ever so much disposed, could not have retreated. She sat silently sewing. All at once the little party were startled by a very sweet tenor voice, just close to the street window, singing one of the airs out of Beaumarchais' operas, which, a few years before, had been popular all over Paris. But after a few moments of silence, and one or two remarks, the talking went on again. Pierre, however, noticed an increased air of abstraction in Virginie, who, I suppose, was recurring to the last time that she had heard the song, and did not consider, as her cousin had hoped she would have done, what were the words set to the air, which he imagined she would remember, and which would have told her so much. For, only a few years before, Adam's opera of Richard le Roi had made the story of the minstrel Blondel and our English Cœur de Lion familiar to all the opera-going part of the Parisian public, and Clément had bethought him of establishing a communication with Virginie by some such means.

" The next night, about the same hour, the same voice was singing outside the window again. Pierre, who had been irritated by the proceeding the evening before, as it had diverted Virginie's attention from his cousin, who had been doing his utmost to make himself agreeable, rushed out to the door, just as the Norman was ringing the bell to be admitted for the night. Pierre looked up and down the street; no one else was to be seen. The next day, the Norman mollified him somewhat by knocking at the door of the concièrgerie, and begging Monsieur Pierre's acceptance of some knee-buckles, which had taken the country farmer's fancy the day before, as he had been gazing into the shops, but which, being too small for his purpose, he took the liberty of offering to Monsieur Pierre. Pierre, a French boy, inclined to foppery, was charmed, ravished by the beauty of the present and with monsieur's goodness, and he began to adjust them to his breeches immediately, as well as he cou d, at least, in his mother's absence. The Norman, whom Pierre kept carefully on the outside of the threshold, stood by, as if amused at the boy's eagerness.

" ' Take care,' said he, clearly and distinctly; ' take care, my little friend, lest you become a fop; and, in that case, some day, years hence, when your heart is devoted to some young lady, she may be inclined to say to you '—here he raised his voice—' No, thank you; when I marry, I marry a man, not a petit-maître; I marry a man, who, whatever his position may be, will add dignity to the human race by his virtues.' Farther than that in his quotation Clément dared not go. His sentiments (so much above the apparent occasion) met with applause from Pierre, who liked to contemplate himself in the light of a lover, even though it should be a rejected one, and who hailed the mention of the words ' virtues ' and ' dignity of the human race ' as belonging to the cant of a good citizen.

" But Clément was more anxious to know how the invisible lady took his speech. There was no sign at the time. But when he returned at night, he heard a voice, low singing, behind Madame Babette, as she handed him his candle, the very air he had sung without effect for two nights past. As if he had caught it up from her murmuring voice, he sang it loudly and clearly as he crossed the court.

" ' Here is our opera-singer!' exclaimed Madame Babette. ' Why, the Norman grazier sings like Boupré,' naming a favourite singer at the neighbouring theatre.

" Pierre was struck by the remark, and quietly resolved to look after the Norman; but again, I believe, it was more because of his mother's deposit of money than with any thought of Virginie.

" However, the next morning, to the wonder of both mother and son, Mademoiselle Cannes proposed, with much hesitation,

to go out and make some little purchase for herself. A month
or two ago, this was what Madame Babette had been never
weary of urging. But now she was as much surprised as if she
had expected Virginie to remain a prisoner in her rooms all the
rest of her life. I suppose she had hoped that her first time of
quitting it would be when she left it for Monsieur Morin's house
as his wife.

"A quick look from Madame Babette towards Pierre was all
that was needed to encourage the boy to follow her. He went
out cautiously. She was at the end of the street. She looked
up and down, as if waiting for some one. No one was there.
Back she came, so swiftly that she nearly caught Pierre before
he could retreat through the *porte-coc ère*. There he looked
out again. The neighbourhood was low and wild, and strange;
and some one spoke to Virginie—nay, laid his hand upon her
arm—whose dress and aspect (he had emerged out of a side-
street) Pierre did not know; but, after a start, and (Pierre could
fancy) a little scream, Virginie recognised the stranger, and the
two turned up the side street whence the man had come. Pierre
stole swiftly to the corner of this street; no one was there: they
had disappeared up some of the alleys. Pierre returned home
to excite his mother's infinite surprise. But they had hardly
done talking, when Virginie returned with a colour and a
radiance in her face which they had never seen there since her
father's death."

CHAPTER VII

"I HAVE told you that I heard much of this story from a friend
of the Intendant of the De Créquy's, whom he met with in
London. Some years afterwards—the summer before my
lord's death—I was travelling with him in Devonshire, and we
went to see the French prisoners of war on Dartmoor. We fell
into conversation with one of them, whom I found out to be the
very Pierre of whom I had heard before, as having been involved
in the fatal story of Clément and Virginie, and by him I was told
much of their last days, and thus I learnt how to have some
sympathy with all those who were concerned in those terrible
events; yes, even with the younger Morin himself, on whose behalf
Pierre spoke warmly, even after so long a time had elapsed.

"For when the younger Morin called at the porter's lodge,

on the evening of the day when Virginie had gone out for the
first time after so many months' confinement to the concièrgerie,
he was struck with the improvement in her appearance. It
seems to have hardly been that he thought her beauty greater;
for, in addition to the fact that she was not beautiful, Morin had
arrived at that point of being enamoured when it does not
signify whether the beloved one is plain or handsome—she has
enchanted one pair of eyes, which henceforward see her through
their own medium. But Morin noticed the faint increase of
colour and light in her countenance. It was as though she had
broken through her thick cloud of hopeless sorrow, and was
dawning forth into a happier life. And so, whereas during her
grief, he had revered and respected it even to a point of silent
sympathy, now that she was gladdened, his heart rose on the
wings of strengthened hopes. Even in the dreary monotony of
this existence in his Aunt Babette's concièrgerie, Time had not
failed in his work, and now, perhaps, soon he might humbly
strive to help Time. The very next day he returned—on some
pretence of business—to the Hôtel Duguesclin, and made his
aunt's room, rather than his aunt herself, a present of roses and
geraniums tied up in a bouquet with a tricolor ribbon. Virginie
was in the room, sitting at the coarse sewing she liked to do for
Madame Babette. He saw her eyes brighten at the sight of the
flowers: she asked his aunt to let her arrange them; he saw her
untie the ribbon, and with a gesture of dislike, throw it on the
ground, and give it a kick with her little foot, and even in this
girlish manner of insulting his dearest prejudices, he found
something to admire.

"As he was coming out, Pierre stopped him. The lad had
been trying to arrest his cousin's attention by futile grimaces
and signs played off behind Virginie's back; but Monsieur
Morin saw nothing but Mademoiselle Cannes. However, Pierre
was not to be baffled, and Monsieur Morin found him in waiting
just outside the threshold. With his finger on his lips, Pierre
walked on tiptoe by his companion's side till they would have
been long past sight or hearing of the concièrgerie, even had the
inhabitants devoted themselves to the purposes of spying or
listening.

"'Chut!' said Pierre, at last. 'She goes out walking.'

"'Well?' said Monsieur Morin, half curious, half annoyed at
being disturbed in the delicious reverie of the future into which
he longed to fall.

"'Well! It is not well. It is bad.'

"'Why? I do not ask who she is, but I have my ideas. She is an aristocrat. Do the people about here begin to suspect her?'

"'No, no!' said Pierre. 'But she goes out walking. She has gone these two mornings. I have watched her. She meets a man—she is friends with him, for she talks to him as eagerly as he does to her—mamma cannot tell who he is.'

"'Has my aunt seen him?'

"'No, not so much as a fly's wing of him. I myself have only seen his back. It strikes me like a familiar back, and yet I cannot think who it is. But they separate with sudden darts, like two birds who have been together to feed their young ones. One moment they are in close talk, their heads together chuckotting; the next he has turned up some bye-street, and Mademoiselle Cannes is close upon me—has almost caught me.'

"'But she did not see you?' inquired Monsieur Morin, in so altered a voice that Pierre gave him one of his quick penetrating looks. He was struck by the way in which his cousin's features—always coarse and commonplace—had become contracted and pinched; struck, too, by the livid look on his sallow complexion. But as if Morin was conscious of the manner in which his face belied his feelings, he made an effort, and smiled, and patted Pierre's head, and thanked him for his intelligence, and gave him a five-franc piece, and bade him go on with his observations of Mademoiselle Cannes' movements, and report all to him.

"Pierre returned home with a light heart, tossing up his five-franc piece as he ran. Just as he was at the concièrgerie door, a great tall man bustled past him, and snatched his money away from him, looking back with a laugh, which added insult to injury. Pierre had no redress; no one had witnessed the impudent theft, and if they had, no one to be seen in the street was strong enough to give him redress. Besides, Pierre had seen enough of the state of the streets of Paris at that time to know that friends, not enemies, were required, and the man had a bad air about him. But all these considerations did not keep Pierre from bursting out into a fit of crying when he was once more under his mother's roof; and Virginie, who was alone there (Madame Babette having gone out to make her daily purchases), might have imagined him pommeled to death by the loudness of his sobs.

"'What is the matter?' asked she. 'Speak, my child. What hast thou done?'

" ' He has robbed me! he has robbed me!' was all Pierre could gulp out.

" ' Robbed thee! and of what, my poor boy?' said Virginie, stroking his hair gently.

" ' Of my five-franc piece—of a five-franc piece,' said Pierre, correcting himself, and leaving out the word my, half fearful lest Virginie should inquire how he became possessed of such a sum, and for what services it had been given him. But, of course, no such idea came into her head, for it would have been impertinent, and she was gentle-born.

" ' Wait a moment, my lad,' and going to the one small drawer in the inner apartment, which held all her few possessions, she brought back a little ring—a ring just with one ruby in it— which she had worn in the days when she cared to wear jewels. ' Take this,' said she, ' and run with it to a jeweller's. It is but a poor, valueless thing, but it will bring you in your five francs, at any rate. Go! I desire you.'

" ' But I cannot,' said the boy, hesitating; some dim sense of honour flitting through his misty morals.

" ' Yes, you must!' she continued, urging him with her hand to the door. ' Run! if it brings in more than five francs, you shall return the surplus to me.'

" Thus tempted by her urgency, and, I suppose, reasoning with himself to the effect that he might as well have the money, and then see whether he thought it right to act as a spy upon her or not—the one action did not pledge him to the other, nor yet did she make any conditions with her gift—Pierre went off with her ring; and, after repaying himself his five francs, he was enabled to bring Virginie back two more, so well had he managed his affairs. But, although the whole transaction did not leave him bound, in any way, to discover or forward Virginie's wishes, it did leave him pledged, according to his code, to act according to her advantage, and he considered himself the judge of the best course to be pursued to this end. And, moreover, this little kindness attached him to her personally. He began to think how pleasant it would be to have so kind and generous a person for a relation; how easily his troubles might be borne if he had always such a ready helper at hand; how much he should like to make her like him, and come to him for the protection of his masculine power! First of all his duties, as her self-appointed squire, came the necessity of finding out who her strange new acquaintance was. Thus, you see, he arrived at the same end, viâ supposed duty, that he was previously pledged to viâ interest. I fancy a good number of us, when any line of action will promote our own interest, can make ourselves believe that reasons exist which compel us to it as a duty.

" In the course of a very few days, Pierre had so circumvented Virginie as to have discovered that her new friend was no other than the Norman farmer in a different dress. Th s was a great piece of knowledge to impart to Morin. But Pierre was not prepared for the immediate physical effect it had on his cousin. Morin sat suddenly down on one of the seats in the Boulevards —it was there Pierre had met with him accidentally—when he heard who it was that Virginie met. I do not suppose the man had the faintest idea of any relationship or even previous acquaintanceship between Clément and Virginie. If he thought of anything beyond the mere fact presented to him, that his idol was in communication with another, younger, handsomer man than himself, it must have been that the Norman farmer had seen her at the concièrgerie, and had been attracted by her, and, as was but natural, had tried to make her acquaintance, and had succeeded. But, from what Pierre told me, I should not think that even this much thought passed through Morin's mind. He seems to have been a man of rare and concentrated attachments; violent, though restrained and undemonstrative passions; and, above all, a capability of jealousy, of which his dark oriental comple ion must have been a type. I could fancy that if he had married Virginie, he would have coined his life-blood for luxuries to make her happy; would have watched over and petted her, at every sacrifice to himself, as long as she would have been content to live with him alone. But, as Pierre expressed it to me: ' When I saw what my cousin was, when I learned his nature too late, I perceived that he would have strangled a bird if she whom he loved was attracted by it from him.'

" When Pierre had told Morin of his discovery, Morin sat down, as I said, quite suddenly, as if he had been shot. He found out that the first meeting between the Norman and Virginie was no accidental, isolated circumstance. Pierre was torturing him with his accounts of daily rendezvous: if but for a moment, they were seeing each other every day, sometimes twice a day. And Virginie could speak to this man, though to himself she was coy and reserved as hardly to utter a sentence. Pierre caught these broken words while his cousin's comple ion grew more and more livid, and then purple, as if some great effect were produced on his circulation by the news he had just heard. Pierre was so startled by his cousin's wandering, senseless eyes, and otherwise disordered looks, that he rushed into a neighbouring cabaret for a glass of absinthe, which he paid for, as he recollected afterwards, with a portion of Virginie's five francs. By-and-by Morin recovered his natural appearance; but he was gloomy and silent; and all that Pierre could get out of him was, that the Norman farmer should not sleep another night at the Hôtel Duguesclin, giving him such opportunities of passing and repassing by the concièrgerie door. He was too much absorbed in his own thoughts to repay Pierre the half franc he had spent on the absinthe, which Pierre perceived, and seems to have noted down in the ledger of his mind as on Virginie's balance of favour.

" Altogether, he was much disappointed at his cousin's mode of receiving intelligence, which the lad thought worth another five-franc piece at least; or, if not paid for in money, to be paid for in open-mouthed confidence and expression of feeling, that he was, for a time, so far a partisan of Virginie's—unconscious Virginie—against his cousin, as to feel regret when the Norman returned no more to his night's lodging, and when Virginie's eager watch at the crevice of the closely-drawn blind ended only with a sigh of disappointment. If it had not been for his mother's presence at the time, Pierre thought he should have told her all. But how far was his mother in his cousin's confidence as regarded the dismissal of the Norman?

" In a few days, however, Pierre felt almost sure that they had established some new means of communication. Virginie went out for a short time every day; but though Pierre followed her as closely as he could without exciting her observation, he was unable to discover what kind of intercourse she held with the Norman. She went, in general, the same short round among the little shops in the neighbourhood; not entering any, but stopping at two or three. Pierre afterwards remembered that she had invariably paused at the nosegays displayed in a certain window, and studied them long; but, then, she stopped and looked at caps, hats, fashions, confectionery (all of the humble kind common in that quarter), so how should he have known that any particular attraction existed among the flowers? Morin came more regularly than ever to his aunt's; but Virginie was apparently unconscious that she was the attraction. She looked healthier and more hopeful than she had done for months, and her manners to all were gentler and not so reserved. Almost as if she wished to manifest her gratitude to Madame Babette for her long continuance of kindness, the necessity for which was nearly ended, Virginie showed an unusual alacrity in rendering the old woman any little service in her power, and evidently tried to respond to Monsieur Morin's civilities, he being Madame Babette's nephew, with a soft graciousness which must have made one of her principal charms; for all who knew her speak of the fascination of her manners, so winning and attentive to others, while yet her opinions, and often her actions, were of so decided a character. For, as I have said, her beauty was by no means great; yet every man who came near her seems to have fallen into the sphere of her influence. Monsieur Morin was deeper than ever in love with her during these last few days: he was worked up into a state capable of any sacrifice, either of himself or others, so that he might obtain her at last. He sat 'devouring her with his eyes' (to use Pierre's expression) whenever she could not see him; but, if she looked towards him, he looked to the ground—anywhere—away from her, and almost stammered in his replies if she addressed any question to him.

"He had been, I should think, ashamed of his extreme agitation on the Boulevards, for Pierre thought that he absolutely shunned him for these few succeeding days. He must have believed that he had driven the Norman (my poor Clément!) off the field, by banishing him from his inn; and thought that the intercourse between him and Virginie, which he had thus interrupted, was of so slight and transient a character as to be quenched by a little difficulty.

"But he appears to have felt that he had made but little way, and he awkwardly turned to Pierre for help—not yet confessing his love, though; he only tried to make friends again with the lad after their silent estrangement. And Pierre for some time did not choose to perceive his cousin's advances. He would reply to all the roundabout questions Morin put to him respecting household conversations when he was not present, or household occupations and tone of thought, without mentioning Virginie's name any more than his questioner did. The lad would seem to suppose that his cousin's strong interest in their domestic ways of going on was all on account of Madame Babette. At last he worked his cousin up to the point of making him a confidant; and then the boy was half frightened at the torrent of vehement words he had unloosed. The lava came down with a greater rush for having been pent up so long. Morin cried out his words in a hoarse, passionate voice, clenched his teeth, his fingers, and seemed almost convulsed, as he spoke out his terrible love for Virginie, which would lead him to kill her sooner than see her another's; and if another stepped in between him and her!—and then he smiled a fierce, triumphant smile, but did not say any more.

" Pierre was, as I said, half frightened; but also half admiring. This was really love—a ' grande passion,'—a really fine dramatic thing,—like the plays they acted at the little theatre yonder. He had a dozen times the sympathy with his cousin now that he had had before, and readily swore by the infernal gods, for they were far too enlightened to believe in one God, or Christianity, or anything of the kind,—that he would devote himself, body and soul, to forwarding his cousin's views. Then his cousin took him to a shop, and bought him a smart second-hand watch, on which they scratched the word Fidélité, and thus was the compact sealed. Pierre settled in his own mind, that if he were a woman, he should like to be beloved as Virginie was, by his cousin, and that it would be an extremely good thing for her to be the wife of so rich a citizen as Morin Fils,—and for Pierre himself, too, for doubtless their gratitude would lead them to give him rings and watches *ad infinitum*.

" A day or two afterwards, Virginie was taken ill. Madame Babette said it was because she had persevered in going out in all weathers, after confining herself to two warm rooms for so long; and very probably this was really the cause, for, from Pierre's account, she must have been suffering from a feverish cold, aggravated, no doubt, by her impatience at Madame Babette's familiar prohibitions of any more walks until she was better. Every day, in spite of her trembling, aching limbs, she would fain have arranged her dress for her walk at the usual time; but Madame Babette was fully prepared to put physical obstacles in her way, if she was not obedient in remaining tranquil on the little sofa by the side of the fire. The third day, she called Pierre to her, when his mother was not attending (having, in fact, locked up Mademoiselle Cannes' out-of-door things).

" ' See, my child,' said Virginie. ' Thou must do me a great favour. Go to the gardener's shop in the Rue des Bons-Enfans, and look at the nosegays in the window. I long for pinks; they are my favourite flower. Here are two francs. If thou seest a nosegay of pinks displayed in the window, if it be ever so faded,—nay, if thou seest two or three nosegays of pinks, remember, buy them all, and bring them to me, I have so great a desire for the smell.' She fell back weak and exhausted.

Pierre hurried out. Now was the time; here was the clue to the long inspection of the nosegay in this very shop.

" Sure enough, there was a drooping nosegay of pinks in the window. Pierre went in, and, with all his impatience, he made as good a bargain as he could, urging that the flowers were faded, and good for nothing. At last he purchased them at a very moderate price. And now you will learn the bad consequences of teaching the lower orders anything beyond what is immediately necessary to enable them to earn their daily bread! The silly Count de Créquy,—he who had been sent to his bloody rest, by the very canaille of whom he thought so much,—he who had made Virginie (indirectly, it is true) reject such a man as her cousin Clément, by inflating her mind with his bubbles of theories,—this Count de Créquy had long ago taken a fancy to Pierre, as he saw the bright sharp child playing about his court-yard. Monsieur de Créquy had even begun to educate the boy himself, to try to work out certain opinions of his into practice, —but the drudgery of the affair wearied him, and, beside, Babette had left his employment. Still the count took a kind of interest in his former pupil; and made some sort of arrangement by which Pierre was to be taught reading and writing, and accounts, and Heaven knows what besides,—Latin, I dare say. So Pierre, instead of being an innocent messenger, as he ought to have been—(as Mr. Horner's little lad Gregson ought to have been this morning)—could read writing as well as either you or I. So what does he do, on obtaining the nosegay, but examine it well. The stalks of the flowers were tied up with slips of matting in wet moss. Pierre undid the strings, unwrapped the moss, and out fell a piece of wet paper, with the writing all blurred with moisture. It was but a torn piece of writing-paper, apparently, but Pierre's wicked mischievous eyes read what was written on it,—written so as to look like a fragment,— ' Ready, every and any night at nine. All is prepared. Have no fright. Trust one who, whatever hopes he might once have had, is content now to serve you as a faithful cousin; ' and a place was named, which I forget, but which Pierre did not, as it was evidently the rendezvous. After the lad had studied every word, till he could say it off by heart, he placed the paper where he had found it, enveloped it in moss, and tied the whole up again carefully. Virginie's face coloured scarlet as she received it. She kept smelling at it, and trembling: but she did not untie it, although Pierre suggested how much fresher it would be if the stalks were immediately put into water. But

once, after his back had been turned for a minute, he saw it
untied when he looked round again, and Virginie was blushing,
and hiding something in her bosom.

" Pierre was now all impatience to set off and find his cousin.
But his mother seemed to want him for small domestic purposes
even more than usual; and he had chafed over a multitude of
errands connected with the hôtel before he could set off and
search for his cousin at his usual haunts. At last the two met;
and Pierre related all the events of the morning to Morin. He
said the note off word by word. (That lad this morning had
something of the magpie look of Pierre—it made me shudder to
see him, and hear him repeat the note by heart.) Then Morin
asked him to tell him all over again. Pierre was struck by
Morin's heavy sighs as he repeated the story. When he came
the second time to the note, Morin tried to write the words down;
but either he was not a good, ready scholar, or his fingers
trembled too much. Pierre hardly remembered, but, at any
rate, the lad had to do it, with his wicked reading and writing.
When this was done, Morin sat heavily silent. Pierre would
have preferred the expected outburst, for this impenetrable
gloom perplexed and baffled him. He had even to speak to his
cousin to rouse him; and when he replied, what he said had so
little apparent connection with the subject which Pierre had
expected to find uppermost in his mind, that he was half afraid
that his cousin had lost his wits.

" ' My Aunt Babette is out of coffee.'

" ' I am sure I do not know,' said Pierre.

" ' Yes, she is. I heard her say so. Tell her that a friend of
mine has just opened a shop in the Rue Saint Antoine, and that
if she will join me there in an hour, I will supply her with a
good stock of coffee, just to give my friend encouragement. His
name is Antoine Meyer, Number One hundred and Fifty, at the
sign of the Cap of Liberty.'

" ' I could go with you now. I can carry a few pounds of
coffee better than my mother,' said Pierre, all in good faith. He
told me he should never forget the look on his cousin's face, as
he turned round, and bade him begone, and give his mother
the message without another word. It had evidently sent him
home promptly to obey his cousin's command. Morin's message perplexed Madame Babette.

" ' How could he know I was out of coffee? ' said she. ' I am;
but I only used the last up this morning. How could Victor
know about it? '

" ' I am sure I can't tell,' said Pierre, who by this time had recovered his usual self-possession. ' All I know is, that monsieur is in a pretty temper, and that if you are not sharp to your time at this Antoine Meyer's you are likely to come in for some of his black looks.'

" ' Well, it is very kind of him to offer to give me some coffee, to be sure! But how could he know I was out? '

" Pierre hurried his mother off impatiently, for he was certain that the offer of the coffee was only a blind to some hidden purpose on his cousin's part; and he made no doubt that when his mother had been informed of what his cousin's real intention was, he, Pierre, could extract it from her by coaxing or bullying. But he was mistaken. Madame Babette returned home, grave, depressed, silent, and loaded with the best coffee. Some time afterwards he learnt why his cousin had sought for this interview. It was to extract from her, by promises and threats, the real name of Mam'selle Cannes, which would give him a clue to the true appellation of The Faithful Cousin. He concealed this second purpose from his aunt, who had been quite unaware of his jealousy of the Norman farmer, or of his identification of him with any relation of Virginie's. But Madame Babette instinctively shrank from giving him any information: she must have felt that, in the lowering mood in which she found him, his desire for greater knowledge of Virginie's antecedents boded her no good. And yet he made his aunt his confidante—told her what she had only suspected before—that he was deeply enamoured of Mam'selle Cannes, and would gladly marry her. He spoke to Madame Babette of his father's hoarded riches; and of the share which he, as partner, had in them at the present time; and of the prospect of the succession to the whole, which he had, as only child. He told his aunt of the provision for her (Madame Babette's) life, which he would make on the day when he married Mam'selle Cannes. And yet—and yet—Babette saw that in his eye and look which made her more and more reluctant to confide in him. By-and-by he tried threats. She should leave the concièrgerie, and find employment where she liked. Still silence. Then he grew angry, and swore that he would inform against her at the bureau of the Directory, for harbouring an aristocrat; an aristocrat he knew mademoiselle was, whatever her real name might be. His aunt should have a domiciliary visit, and see how she liked that. The officers of the Government were the people for finding out secrets. In vain she reminded him that, by so doing, he would expose to

imminent danger the lady whom he had professed to love. He
told her, with a sullen relapse into silence after his vehement
outpouring of passion, never to trouble herself about that. At
last he wearied out the old woman, and, frightened alike of herself, and of him, she told him all,—that Mam'selle Cannes was
Mademoiselle Virginie de Créquy, daughter of the count of that
name. Who was the count? Younger brother of the marquis.
Where was the marquis? Dead long ago, leaving a widow and
child. A son? (eagerly). Yes, a son. Where was he? Parbleu!
how should she know?—for her courage returned a little as the
talk went away from the only person of the De Créquy family
that she cared about. But, by dint of some small glasses out
of a bottle of Antoine Meyer's, she told him more about the
De Créquys than she liked afterwards to remember. For the
exhilaration of the brandy lasted but a very short time, and
she came home, as I have said, depressed, with a presentiment
of coming evil. She would not answer Pierre, but cuffed him
about in a manner to which the spoilt boy was quite unaccustomed. His cousin's short, angry words, and sudden withdrawal
of confidence,—his mother's unwonted crossness and fault-
finding, all made Virginie's kind, gentle treatment more than
ever charming to the lad. He half resolved to tell her how he
had been acting as a spy upon her actions, and at whose desire
he had done it. But he was afraid of Morin, and of the
vengeance which he was sure would fall upon him for any
breach of confidence. Towards half-past eight that evening—
Pierre, watching, saw Virginie arrange several little things—
she was in the inner room, but he sat where he could see her
through the glazed partition. His mother sat—apparently
sleeping—in the great easy-chair; Virginie moved about softly,
for fear of disturbing her. She made up one or two little parcels
of the few things she could call her own: one packet she concealed about herself,—the others she directed, and left on the
shelf. 'She is going,' thought Pierre, and (as he said in giving
me the account) his heart gave a spring, to think that he should
never see her again. If either his mother or his cousin had been
more kind to him, he might have endeavoured to intercept her;
but as it was, he held his breath, and when she came out he
pretended to read, scarcely knowing whether he wished her to
succeed in the purpose which he was almost sure she entertained,
or not. She stopped by him, and passed her hand over his hair.
He told me that his eyes filled with tears at this caress. Then
she stood for a moment, looking at the sleeping Madame Babette,

and stooped down and softly kissed her on the forehead.   Pierre
dreaded lest his m)ther should awake (for by this time the
wayward, vacillating boy must have been quite on Virginie's
side), but the brandy she had drunk made her slumber heavily.
Virginie went.   Pierre's heart beat fast.   He was sure his cousin
would try to intercept her; but how, he could not imagine.
He longed to run out and see the catastrophe,—but he had let
the moment slip; he was also afraid of reawakening his mother
to her unusual state of anger and violence."

CHAPTER VIII

" PIERRE went on pretending to read, but in reality listening
with acute tension of ear to every little sound.   His perceptions
became so sensitive in this respect that he was incapable of
measuring time, every moment had seemed so full of noises,
from the beating of his heart up to the roll of the heavy carts
in the distance.   He wondered whether Virginie would have
reached the place of rendezvous, and yet he was unable to
compute the passage of minutes.   His mother slept soundly:
that was well.   By this time Virginie must have met the
' faithful cousin: ' if, indeed, Morin had not made his appearance.

" At length, he felt as if he could no longer sit still, awaiting
the issue, but must run out and see what course events had
taken.   In vain his mother, half rousing herself, called after
him to ask whither he was going: he was already out of hearing
before she had ended her sentence, and he ran on until, stopped
by the sight of Mademoiselle Cannes walking along at so swift
a pace that it was almost a run; while at her side, resolutely
keeping by her, Morin was striding abreast.   Pierre had just
turned the corner of the street, when he came upon them.
Virginie would have passed him without recognising him, she
was in such passionate agitation, but for Morin's gesture, by
which he would fain have kept Pierre from interrupting them.
Then, when Virginie saw the lad, she caught at his arm, and
thanked God, as if in that boy of twelve or fourteen she held
a protector.   Pierre felt her tremble from head to foot, and
was afraid lest she would fall, there where she stood, in the
hard rough street.

"'Begone, Pierre!' said Morin.

"'I cannot,' replied Pierre, who indeed was held firmly by Virginie. 'Besides, I won't,' he added. 'Who has been frightening mademoiselle in this way?' asked he, very much inclined to brave his cousin at all hazards.

"'Mademoiselle is not accustomed to walk in the streets alone,' said Morin, sulkily. 'She came upon a crowd attracted by the arrest of an aristocrat, and their cries alarmed her. I offered to take charge of her home. Mademoiselle should not walk in these streets alone. We are not like the cold-blooded people of the Faubourg Saint Germain.'

"Virginie did not speak. Pierre doubted if she heard a word of what they were saying. She leant upon him more and more heavily.

"'Will mademoiselle condescend to take my arm?' said Morin, with sulky, and yet humble, uncouthness. I dare say he would have given worlds if he might have had that little hand within his arm; but, though she still kept silence, she shuddered up away from him, as you shrink from touching a toad. He had said something to her during that walk, you may be sure, which had made her loathe him. He marked and understood the gesture. He held himself aloof while Pierre gave her all the assistance he could in their slow progress homewards. But Morin accompanied her all the same. He had played too desperate a game to be baulked now. He had given information against the ci-devant Marquis de Créquy, as a returned *emigré*, to be met with at such a time, in such a place. Morin had hoped that all sign of the arrest would have been cleared away before Virginie reached the spot—so swiftly were terrible deeds done in those days. But Clément defended himself desperately: Virginie was punctual to a second; and, though the wounded man was borne off to the Abbaye, amid a crowd of the unsympathising jeerers who mingled with the armed officials of the Directory, Morin feared lest Virginie had recognised him; and he would have preferred that she should have thought that the 'faithful cousin' was faithless, than that she should have seen him in bloody danger on her account. I suppose he fancied that, if Virginie never saw or heard more of him, her imagination would not dwell on his simple disappearance, as it would do if she knew what he was suffering for her sake.

"At any rate, Pierre saw that his cousin was deeply mortified by the whole tenor of his behaviour during their walk home.

When they arrived at Madame Babette's, Virginie fell fainting on the floor; her strength had but just sufficed for this exertion of reaching the shelter of the house. Her first sign of restoring consciousness consisted in avoidance of Morin. He had been most assiduous in his efforts to bring her round; quite tender in his way, Pierre said; and this marked, instinctive repugnance to him evidently gave him extreme pain. I suppose Frenchmen are more demonstrative than we are; for Pierre declared that he saw his cousin's eyes fill with tears, as she shrank away from his touch, if he tried to arrange the shawl they had laid under her head like a pillow, or as she shut her eyes when he passed before her. Madame Babette was urgent with her to go and lie down on the bed in the inner room; but it was some time before she was strong enough to rise and do this.

"When Madame Babette returned from arranging the girl comfortably, the three relations sat down in silence; a silence which Pierre thought would never be broken. He wanted his mother to ask his cousin what had happened. But Madame Babette was afraid of her nephew, and thought it more discreet to wait for such crumbs of intelligence as he might think fit to throw to her. But, after she had twice reported Virginie to be asleep, without a word being uttered in reply to her whispers by either of her companions, Morin's powers of self-containment gave way.

" 'It is hard!' he said.

" 'What is hard?' asked Madame Babette, after she had paused for a time, to enable him to add to, or to finish, his sentence, if he pleased.

" 'It is hard for a man to love a woman as I do,' he went on. 'I did not seek to love her, it came upon me before I was aware —before I had ever thought about it at all, I loved her better than all the world beside. All my life, before I knew her, seems a dull blank. I neither know nor care for what I did before then. And now there are just two lives before me. Either I have her, or I have not. That is all: but that is everything. And what can I do to make her have me? Tell me, aunt,' and he caught at Madame Babette's arm, and gave it so sharp a shake, that she half screamed out, Pierre said, and evidently grew alarmed at her nephew's excitement.

" 'Hush, Victor!' said she. 'There are other women in the world, if this one will not have you.'

" 'None other for me,' he said, sinking back as if hopeless. 'I am plain and coarse, not one of the scented darlings of the aristocrats. Say that I am ugly, brutish; I did not make myself so, any more than I made myself love her. It is my fate. But am I to submit to the consequences of my fate without a struggle? Not I. As strong as my love is, so strong is my will. It can be no stronger,' continued he, gloomily. 'Aunt Babette, you must help me—you must make her love me.' He was so fierce here, that Pierre said he did not wonder that his mother was frightened.

"'I, Victor!' she exclaimed. 'I make her love you? How can I? Ask me to speak for you to Mademoiselle Didot, or to Mademoiselle Cauchois even, or to such as they, and I'll do it, and welcome. But to Mademoiselle de Créquy, why you don't know the difference! Those people—the old nobility I mean— why they don't know a man from a dog, out of their own rank! And no wonder, for the young gentlemen of quality are treated differently to us from their very birth. If she had you to-morrow, you would be miserable. Let me alone for knowing the aristocracy. I have not been a concièrge to a duke and three counts for nothing. I tell you, all your ways are different to her ways.'

"'I would change my "ways," as you call them.'

"'Be reasonable, Victor.'

"'No, I will not be reasonable, if by that you mean giving her up. I tell you two lives are before me; one with her, one without her. But the latter will be but a short career for both of us. You said, aunt, that the talk went in the concièrgerie of her father's hotel, that she would have nothing to do with this cousin whom I put out of the way to-day?'

"'So the servants said. How could I know? All I know is, that he left off coming to our hotel, and that at one time before then he had never been two days absent.'

"'So much the better for him. He suffers now for having come between me and my object—in trying to snatch her away out of my sight. Take you warning, Pierre! I did not like your meddling to-night.' And so he went off, leaving Madame Babette rocking herself backwards and forwards, in all the depression of spirits consequent upon the reaction after the brandy, and upon her knowledge of her nephew's threatened purpose combined.

"In telling you most of this, I have simply repeated Pierre's account, which I wrote down at the time. But here what he had to say came to a sudden break; for, the next morning, when Madame Babette rose, Virginie was missing, and it was some time before either she, or Pierre, or Morin, could get the slightest clue to the missing girl.

"And now I must take up the story as it was told to the intendant Fléchier by the old gardener Jacques, with whom Clément had been lodging on his first arrival in Paris. The old man could not, I dare say, remember half as much of what had happened as Pierre did; the former had the dulled memory of age, while Pierre had evidently thought over the whole series of events as a story—as a play, if one may call it so—during the solitary hours in his after-life, wherever they were passed, whether in lonely camp watches, or in the foreign prison, where he had to drag out many years. Clément had, as I said, returned to the gardener's garret after he had been dismissed from the Hôtel Duguesclin. There were several reasons for his thus doubling back. One was, that he put nearly the whole breadth of Paris between him and an enemy; though why Morin was an enemy, and to what extent he carried his dislike or hatred, Clément could not tell, of course. The next reason for returning to Jacques was, no doubt, the conviction that, in multiplying his residences, he multiplied the chances against his being suspected and recognised. And then, again, the old man was in his secret, and his ally, although perhaps but a feeble kind of one. It was through Jacques that the plan of communication, by means of a nosegay of pinks, had been devised; and it was Jacques who procured him the last disguise that Clément was to use in Paris —as he hoped and trusted. It was that of a respectable shop-keeper of no particular class; a dress that would have seemed perfectly suitable to the young man who would naturally have worn it; and yet, as Clément put it on, and adjusted it—giving it a sort of finish and elegance which I always noticed about his appearance, and which I believed was innate in the wearer— I have no doubt it seemed like the usual apparel of a gentleman. No coarseness of texture, nor clumsiness of cut could disguise the nobleman of thirty descents, it appeared; for immediately on arriving at the place of rendezvous, he was recognised by the men placed there on Morin's information to seize him. Jacques, following at a little distance, with a bundle under his arm containing articles of feminine disguise for Virginie, saw four men attempt Clément's arrest—saw him, quick as lightning, draw a sword hitherto concealed in a clumsy stick—saw his agile figure spring to his guard—and saw him defend himself with the rapidity and art of a man skilled in arms. But what good did it do? as Jacques piteously used to ask, Monsieur Fléchier told

me. A great blow from a heavy club on the sword-arm of
Monsieur de Créquy laid it helpless and immovable by his side.
Jacques always thought that that blow came from one of the
spectators, who by this time had collected round the scene of
the affray. The next instant, his master—his little marquis—
was down among the feet of the crowd, and though he was up
again before he had received much damage—so active and light
was my poor Clément—it was not before the old gardener had
hobbled forwards, and, with many an old-fashioned oath and
curse, proclaimed himself a partisan of the losing side—a follower
of a ci-devant aristocrat. It was quite enough. He received
one or two good blows, which were, in fact, aimed at his master;
and then, almost before he was aware, he found his arms pinioned
behind him with a woman's garter, which one of the viragos in
the crowd had made no scruple of pulling off in public, as soon
as she heard for what purpose it was wanted. Poor Jacques was
stunned and unhappy—his master was out of sight, on before;
and the old gardener scarce knew whither they were taking him.
His head ached from the blows which had fallen upon it; it
was growing dark—June day though it was—and when first he
seems to have become exactly aware of what had happened to
him, it was when he was turned into one of the larger rooms of
the Abbaye, in which all were put who had no other allotted
place wherein to sleep. One or two iron lamps hung from the
ceiling by chains, giving a dim light for a little circle. Jacques
stumbled forwards over a sleeping body lying on the ground.
The sleeper wakened up enough to complain; and the apology
of the old man in reply caught the ear of his master, who, until
this time, could hardly have been aware of the straits and difficulties of his faithful Jacques. And there they sat—against a
pillar, the livelong night, holding one another's hands, and each
restraining expressions of pain, for fear of adding to the other's
distress. That night made them intimate friends, in spite of
the difference of age and rank. The disappointed hopes, the
acute suffering of the present, the apprehensions of the future,
made them seek solace in talking of the past. Monsieur de
Créquy and the gardener found themselves disputing with
interest in which chimney of the stack the starling used to build
—the starling whose nest Clément sent to Urian, you remember
—and discussing the merits of different espalier-pears which
grew, and may grow still, in the old garden of the Hôtel de
Créquy. Towards morning both fell asleep. The old man
wakened first. His frame was deadened to suffering, I suppose,

for he felt relieved of his pain; but Clément moaned and cried in feverish slumber. His broken arm was beginning to inflame his blood. He was, besides, much injured by some kicks from the crowd as he fell. As the old man looked sadly on the white, baked lips, and the flushed cheeks, contorted with suffering even in his sleep, Clément gave a sharp cry, which disturbed his miserable neighbours, all slumbering around in uneasy attitudes. They bade him with curses be silent; and then turning round, tried again to forget their own misery in sleep. For you see, the bloodthirsty canaille had not been sated with guillotining and hanging all the nobility they could find, but were now informing, right and left, even against each other; and when Clément and Jacques were in the prison, there were few of gentle blood in the place, and fewer still of gentle manners. At the sound of the angry words and threats, Jacques thought it best to awaken his master from his feverish uncomfortable sleep, lest he should provoke more enmity; and, tenderly lifting him up, he tried to adjust his own body, so that it should serve as a rest and a pillow for the younger man. The motion aroused Clément, and he began to talk in a strange, feverish way, of Virginie, too— whose name he would not have breathed in such a place had he been quite himself. But Jacques had as much delicacy of feeling as any lady in the land, although, mind you, he knew neither how to read nor write—and bent his head low down, so that his master might tell him in a whisper what messages he was to take to Mademoiselle de Créquy, in case—Poor Clément, he knew it must come to that! No escape for him now, in Norman disguise or otherwise! Either by gathering fever or guillotine, death was sure of his prey. Well! when that happened, Jacques was to go and find Mademoiselle de Créquy, and tell her that her cousin loved her at the last as he had loved her at the first; but that she should never have heard another word of his attachment from his living lips; that he knew he was not good enough for her, his queen; and that no thought of earning her love by his devotion had prompted his return to France, only that, if possible, he might have the great privilege of serving her whom he loved. And then he went off into rambling talk about petit-maîtres, and such kind of expressions, said Jacques to Fléchier, the intendant, little knowing what a clue that one word gave to much of the poor lad's suffering.

" The summer morning came slowly on in that dark prison, and when Jacques could look round—his master was now sleeping on his shoulder, still the uneasy, starting sleep of fever—he saw that there were many women among the prisoners. (I have heard some of those who have escaped from the prisons say, that the look of despair and agony that came into the faces of the prisoners on first wakening, as the sense of their situation grew upon them, was what lasted the longest in the memory of the survivors. This look, they said, passed away from the women's faces sooner than it did from those of the men.)

" Poor old Jacques kept falling asleep, and plucking himself up again for fear lest, if he did not attend to his master, some harm might come to the swollen, helpless arm. Yet his weariness grew upon him in spite of all his efforts, and at last he felt as if he must give way to the irresistible desire, if only for five minutes. But just then there was a bustle at the door. Jacques opened his eyes wide to look.

" ' The gaoler is early with breakfast,' said some one, lazily.

" ' It is the darkness of this accursed place that makes us think it early,' said another.

" All this time a parley was going on at the door. Some one came in; not the gaoler—a woman. The door was shut to and locked behind her. She only advanced a step or two, for it was too sudden a change, out of the light into that dark shadow, for any one to see clearly for the first few minutes. Jacques had his eyes fairly open now, and was wide awake. It was Mademoiselle de Créquy, looking bright, clear, and resolute. The faithful heart of the old man read that look like an open page. Her cousin should not die there on her behalf, without at least the comfort of her sweet presence.

" ' Here he is,' he whispered as her gown would have touched him in passing, without her perceiving him, in the heavy obscurity of the place.

" ' The good God bless you, my friend!' she murmured, as she saw the attitude of the old man, propped against a pillar, and holding Clément in his arms, as if the young man had been a helpless baby, while one of the poor gardener's hands supported the broken limb in the easiest position. Virginie sat down by the old man, and held out her arms. Softly she moved Clément's head to her own shoulder; softly she transferred the task of holding the arm to herself. Clément lay on the floor, but she supported him, and Jacques was at liberty to arise and stretch and shake his stiff, weary old body. He then sat down at a little distance, and watched the pair until he fell asleep. Clément had muttered ' Virginie,' as they half-roused him by their movements out of his stupor; but Jacques thought he was only dreaming; nor did he seem fully awake when once his eyes opened, and he looked full at Virginie's face bending over him, and growing crimson under his gaze, though she never stirred, for fear of hurting him if she moved. Clément looked in silence, until his heavy eyelids came slowly down, and he fell into his oppressive slumber again. Either he did not recognise her, or she came in too completely as a part of his sleeping visions for him to be disturbed by her appearance there.

" When Jacques awoke it was full daylight—at least as full as it would ever be in that place. His breakfast—the gaol-allowance of bread and vin ordinaire—was by his side. He must have slept soundly. He looked for his master. He and Virginie had recognised each other now — hearts, as well as appearance. They were smiling into each other's faces, as if that dull, vaulted room in the grim Abbaye were the sunny gardens of Versailles, with music and festivity all abroad. Apparently they had much to say to each other; for whispered questions and answers never ceased.

" Virginie had made a sling for the poor broken arm; nay, she had obtained two splinters of wood in some way, and one of their fellow-prisoners—having, it appeared, some knowledge of surgery—had set it. Jacques felt more desponding by far than they did, for he was suffering from the night he had passed, which told upon his aged frame; while they must have heard some good news, as it seemed to him, so bright and happy did they look. Yet Clément was still in bodily pain and suffering, and Virginie, by her own act and deed, was a prisoner in that dreadful Abbaye, whence the only issue was the guillotine. But they were together: they loved: they understood each other at length.

" When Virginie saw that Jacques was awake, and languidly munching his breakfast, she rose from the wooden stool on which she was sitting, and went to him, holding out both hands, and refusing to allow him to rise, while she thanked him with pretty eagerness for all his kindness to Monsieur. Monsieur himself came towards him, following Virginie, but with tottering steps, as if his head was weak and dizzy, to thank the poor old man, who now on his feet stood between them, ready to cry while they gave him credit for faithful actions which he felt to have been almost involuntary on his part—for loyalty was like an instinct in the good old days, before your educational cant had come up. And so two days went on. The only event was the morning call for the victims, a certain number of whom

were summoned to trial every day. And to be tried was to be
condemned. Every one of the prisoners became grave, as the
hour for their summons approached. Most of the victims went
to their doom with uncomplaining resignation, and for a while
after their departure there was comparative silence in the
prison. But, by-and-by — so said Jacques — the conversation
or amusements began again. Human nature cannot stand the
perpetual pressure of such keen anxiety, without an effort to
relieve itself by thinking of something else. Jacques said that
Monsieur and Mademoiselle were for ever talking together of
the past days—it was 'Do you remember this?' or, 'Do you
remember that?' perpetually. He sometimes thought they
forgot where they were, and what was before them. But Jacques
did not, and every day he trembled more and more as the list
was called over.

"The third morning of their incarceration, the gaoler brought
in a man whom Jacques did not recognise, and therefore did not
at once observe; for he was waiting, as in duty bound, upon his
master and his sweet young lady (as he always called her in
repeating the story). He thought that the new introduction was
some friend of the gaoler, as the two seemed well acquainted,
and the latter stayed a few minutes talking with his visitor
before leaving him in prison. So Jacques was surprised when,
after a short time had elapsed, he looked round and saw the
fierce stare with which the stranger was regarding Monsieur and
Mademoiselle de Créquy, as the pair sat at breakfast—the said
breakfast being laid as well as Jacques knew how, on a bench
fastened into the prison wall—Virginie sitting on her low stool,
and Clément half lying on the ground by her side, and submitting
gladly to be fed by her pretty white fingers; for it was one of
her fancies, Jacques said, to do all she could for him, in consideration of his broken arm. And, indeed, Clément was wasting
away daily; for he had received other injuries, internal and
more serious than that to his arm, during the *mêlée* which had
ended in his capture. The stranger made Jacques conscious of
his presence by a sigh, which was almost a groan. All three
prisoners looked round at the sound. Clément's face expressed
little but scornful indifference; but Virginie's face froze into
stony hate. Jacques said he never saw such a look, and hoped
that he never should again. Yet after that first revelation of
feeling, her look was steady and fixed in another direction to
that in which the stranger stood—still motionless—still watching.
He came a step nearer at last.

" ' Mademoiselle,' he said. Not the quivering of an eyelash showed that she heard him. ' Mademoiselle!' he said again, with an intensity of beseeching that made Jacques—not knowing who he was—almost pity him, when he saw his young lady's obdurate face.

" There was perfect silence for a space of time which Jacques could not measure. Then again the voice, hesitatingly, saying, ' Monsieur!' Clément could not hold the same icy countenance as Virginie; he turned his head with an impatient gesture of disgust; but even that emboldened the man.

" ' Monsieur, do ask mademoiselle to listen to me—just two words.'

" ' Mademoiselle de Créquy only listens to whom she chooses.' Very haughtily my Clément would say that, I am sure.

" ' But, mademoiselle,'—lowering his voice, and coming a step or two nearer. Virginie must have felt his approach, though she did not see it; for she drew herself a little on one side, so as to put as much space as possible between him and her.— ' Mademoiselle, it is not too late. I can save you; but to-morrow your name is down on the list. I can save you, if you will listen.'

" Still no word or sign. Jacques did not understand the affair. Why was she so obdurate to one who might be ready to include Clément in the proposal, as far as Jacques knew?

" The man withdrew a little, but did not offer to leave the prison. He never took his eyes off Virginie; he seemed to be suffering from some acute and terrible pain as he watched her.

" Jacques cleared away the breakfast-things as well as he could. Purposely, as I suspect, he passed near the man.

" ' Hist!' said the stranger. ' You are Jacques, the gardener, arrested for assisting an aristocrat. I know the gaoler. You shall escape, if you will. Only take this message from me to mademoiselle. You heard. She will not listen to me: I did not want her to come here. I never knew she was here, and she will die to-morrow. They will put her beautiful round throat under the guillotine. Tell her, good old man, tell her how sweet life is; and how I can save her; and how I will not ask for more than just to see her from time to time. She is so young; and death is annihilation, you know. Why does she hate me so? I want to save her; I have done her no harm. Good old man, tell her how terrible death is; and that she will die to-morrow, unless she listens to me.'

" Jacques saw no harm in repeating this message. Clément

listened in silence, watching Virginie with an air of infinite tenderness.

"'Will you not try him, my cherished one?' he said. 'Towards you he may mean well' (which makes me think that Virginie had never repeated to Clément the conversation which she had overheard that last night at Madame Babette's); 'you would be in no worse a situation than you were before!'

"'No worse, Clément! and I should have known what you were, and have lost you. My Clément!' said she, reproachfully.

"'Ask him,' said she, turning to Jacques, suddenly, 'if he can save Monsieur de Créquy as well—if he can?—O Clément, we might escape to England; we are but young.' And she hid her face on his shoulder.

"Jacques returned to the stranger, and asked him Virginie's question. His eyes were fixed on the cousins; he was very pale, and the twitchings or contortions, which must have been involuntary whenever he was agitated, convulsed his whole body. "He made a long pause. 'I will save mademoiselle and monsieur, if she will go straight from prison to the mairie, and be my wife.'

"'Your wife!' Jacques could not help exclaiming, 'That she will never be—never!'

"'Ask her!' said Morin, hoarsely.

"But almost before Jacques thought he could have fairly uttered the words, Clément caught their meaning.

"'Begone!' said he; 'not one word more.' Virginie touched the old man as he was moving away. 'Tell him he does not know how he makes me welcome death.' And smiling, as if triumphant, she turned again to Clément.

"The stranger did not speak as Jacques gave him the meaning, not the words, of their replies. He was going away, but stopped. A minute or two afterwards, he beckoned to Jacques. The old gardener seems to have thought it undesirable to throw away even the chance of assistance from such a man as this, for he went forward to speak to him.

"'Listen! I have influence with the gaoler. He shall let thee pass out with the victims to-morrow. No one will notice it, or miss thee——. They will be led to trial—even at the last moment, I will save her, if she sends me word she relents. Speak to her, as the time draws on. Life is very sweet—tell her how sweet. Speak to him; he will do more with her than thou canst. Let him urge her to live. Even at the last, I will be at the Palais de Justice—at the Grève. I have followers—

I have interest. Come among the crowd that follow the victims
—I shall see thee. It will be no worse for him, if she escapes'——

" ' Save my master, and I will do all,' said Jacques.

" ' Only on my one condition,' said Morin, doggedly; and
Jacques was hopeless of that condition ever being fulfilled.
But he did not see why his own life might not be saved. By
remaining in prison until the next day, he should have rendered
every service in his power to his master and the young lady.
He, poor fellow, shrank from death; and he agreed with Morin
to escape, if he could, by the means Morin had suggested, and to
bring him word if Mademoiselle de Créquy relented. (Jacques
had no expectation that she would; but I fancy he did not think
it necessary to tell Morin of this conviction of his.) This
bargaining with so base a man for so slight a thing as life, was
the only flaw that I heard of in the old gardener's behaviour. Of
course, the mere reopening of the subject was enough to stir
Virginie to displeasure. Clément urged her, it is true; but the
light he had gained upon Morin's motions, made him rather try
to set the case before her in as fair a manner as possible than use
any persuasive arguments. And, even as it was, what he said
on the subject made Virginie shed tears—the first that had fallen
from her since she entered the prison. So, they were summoned
and went together, at the fatal call of the muster-roll of victims
the next morning. He, feeble from his wounds and his injured
health; she, calm and serene, only petitioning to be allowed to
walk next to him, in order that she might hold him up when he
turned faint and giddy from his extreme suffering.

" Together they stood at the bar; together they were condemned. As the words of judgment were pronounced, Virginie
turned to Clément, and embraced him with passionate fondness.
Then, making him lean on her, they marched out towards the
Place de la Grève.

" Jacques was free now. He had told Morin how fruitless
his efforts at persuasion had been; and scarcely caring to note
the effect of his information upon the man, he had devoted
himself to watching Monsieur and Mademoiselle de Créquy.
And now he followed them to the Place de la Grève. He saw
them mount the platform; saw them kneel down together till
plucked up by the impatient officials; could see that she was
urging some request to the executioner; the end of which
seemed to be, that Clément advanced first to the guillotine, was
executed (and just at this moment there was a stir among the
crowd, as of a man pressing forward towards the scaffold).

Then she, standing with her face to the guillotine, slowly made the sign of the cross, and knelt down.

"Jacques covered his eyes, blinded with tears. The report of a pistol made him look up. She was gone—another victim in her place—and where there had been a little stir in the crowd not five minutes before, some men were carrying off a dead body. A man had shot himself, they said. Pierre told me who that man was."

CHAPTER IX

AFTER a pause, I ventured to ask what became of Madame de Créquy, Clément's mother.

"She never made any inquiry about him," said my lady. "She must have known that he was dead; though how, we never could tell. Medlicott remembered afterwards that it was about, if not on—Medlicott to this day declares that it was on the very Monday, June the nineteenth, when her son was executed, that Madame de Créquy left off her rouge and took to her bed, as one bereaved and hopeless. It certainly was about that time; and Medlicott—who was deeply impressed by that dream of Madame de Créquy's (the relation of which I told you had had such an effect on my lord), in which she had seen the figure of Virginie — as the only light object amid much surrounding darkness as of night, smiling and beckoning Clément on—on—till at length the bright phantom stopped, motionless, and Madame de Créquy's eyes began to penetrate the murky darkness, and to see closing around her the gloomy dripping walls which she had once seen and never forgotten—the walls of the vault of the chapel of the De Créquys in Saint Germain l'Auxerrois; and there the two last of the Créquys laid them down among their forefathers, and Madame de Créquy had wakened to the sound of the great door, which led to the open air, being locked upon her—I say Medlicott, who was predisposed by this dream to look out for the supernatural, always declared that Madame de Créquy was made conscious in some mysterious way of her son's death on the very day and hour when it occurred, and that after that she had no more anxiety, but was only conscious of a kind of stupefying despair."

"And what became of her, my lady?" I again asked.

"What could become of her?" replied Lady Ludlow. "She

never could be induced to rise again, though she lived more
than a year after her son's departure. She kept her bed; her
room darkened, her face turned towards the wall, whenever any
one besides Medlicott was in the room. She hardly ever spoke,
and would have died of starvation but for Medlicott's tender
care, in putting a morsel to her lips every now and then, feeding
her, in fact, just as an old bird feeds her young ones. In the
height of summer my lord and I left London. We would fain
have taken her with us into Scotland, but the doctor (we had
the old doctor from Leicester Square) forbade her removal; and
this time he gave such good reasons against it that I acquiesced.
Medlicott and a maid were left with her. Every care was taken
of her. She survived till our return. Indeed, I thought she
was in much the same state as I had left her in, when I came
back to London. But Medlicott spoke of her as much weaker;
and one morning on awakening they told me she was dead. I
sent for Medlicott, who was in sad distress, she had become so
fond of her charge. She said that, about two o'clock, she had
been awakened by unusual restlessness on Madame de Créquy's
part; that she had gone to her bedside, and found the poor lady
feebly but perpetually moving her wasted arm up and down—
and saying to herself in a wailing voice: ' I did not bless him
when he left me—I did not bless him when he left me! ' Medlicott gave her a spoonful or two of jelly, and sat by her, stroking
her hand, and soothing her till she seemed to fall asleep. But
in the morning she was dead."

" It is a sad story, your ladyship," said I, after a while.

" Yes it is. People seldom arrive at my age without having
watched the beginning, middle, and end of many lives and many
fortunes. We do not talk about them, perhaps; for they are
often so sacred to us, from having touched into the very quick
of our own hearts, as it were, or into those of others who are
dead and gone, and veiled over from human sight, that we
cannot tell the tale as if it was a mere story. But young people
should remember that we have had this solemn experience of
life on which to base our opinions and form our judgments, so
that they are not mere untried theories. I am not alluding to
Mr. Horner just now, for he is nearly as old as I am—within
ten years, I dare say—but I am thinking of Mr. Gray, with his
endless plans for some new thing—schools, education, Sabbaths,
and what not. Now he has not seen what all this leads to."

" It is a pity he has not heard your ladyship tell the story of
poor Monsieur de Créquy."

"Not at all a pity, my dear. A young man like him, who, both by position and age, must have had his experience confined to a very narrow circle, ought not to set up his opinion against mine; he ought not to require reasons from me, nor to need such explanation of my arguments (if I condescend to argue), as going into relation of the circumstances on which my arguments are based in my own mind would be."

"But, my lady, it might convince him," I said, with perhaps injudicious perseverance.

"And why should he be convinced?" she asked, with gentle inquiry in her tone. "He has only to acquiesce. Though he is appointed by Mr. Croxton, I am the lady of the manor, as he must know. But it is with Mr. Horner that I must have to do about this unfortunate lad Gregson. I am afraid there will be no method of making him forget his unlucky knowledge. His poor brains will be intoxicated with the sense of his powers, without any counterbalancing principles to guide him. Poor fellow! I am quite afraid it will end in his being hanged!"

The next day Mr. Horner came to apologise and explain. He was evidently—as I could tell from his voice, as he spoke to my lady in the next room—extremely annoyed at her ladyship's discovery of the education he had been giving to this boy. My lady spoke with great authority, and with reasonable grounds of complaint. Mr. Horner was well acquainted with her thoughts on the subject, and had acted in defiance of her wishes. He acknowledged as much, and should on no account have done it, in any other instance, without her leave.

"Which I could never have granted you," said my lady.

But this boy had extraordinary capabilities; would, in fact, have taught himself much that was bad, if he had not been rescued, and another direction given to his powers. And in all Mr. Horner had done, he had had her ladyship's service in view. The business was getting almost beyond his power, so many letters and so much account-keeping was required by the complicated state in which things were.

Lady Ludlow felt what was coming—a reference to the mortgage for the benefit of my lord's Scottish estates, which, she was perfectly aware, Mr. Horner considered as having been a most unwise proceeding—and she hastened to observe—

"All this may be very true, Mr. Horner, and I am sure I should be the last person to wish you to overwork or distress yourself; but of that we will talk another time. What I am now anxious to remedy is, if possible, the state of this poor little Gregson's mind. Would not hard work in the fields be a wholesome and excellent way of enabling him to forget?"

"I was in hopes, my lady, that you would have permitted me to bring him up to act as a kind of clerk," said Mr. Horner, jerking out his project abruptly.

"A what?" asked my lady, in infinite surprise.

"A kind of—of assistant, in the way of copying letters and doing up accounts. He is already an excellent penman and very quick at figures."

"Mr. Horner," said my lady, with dignity, "the son of a poacher and vagabond ought never to have been able to copy letters relating to the Hanbury estates; and, at any rate, he shall not. I wonder how it is that, knowing the use he has made of his power of reading a letter, you should venture to propose such an employment for him as would require his being in your confidence, and you the trusted agent of this family. Why, every secret (and every ancient and honourable family has its secrets, as you know, Mr. Horner!) would be learnt off by heart, and repeated to the first comer!"

"I should have hoped to have trained him, my lady, to understand the rules of discretion."

"Trained! Train a barn-door fowl to be a pheasant, Mr. Horner! That would be the easier task. But you did right to speak of discretion rather than honour. Discretion looks to the consequences of actions—honour looks to the action itself, and is an instinct rather than a virtue. After all, it is possible you might have trained him to be discreet."

Mr. Horner was silent. My lady was softened by his not replying, and began, as she always did in such cases, to fear lest she had been too harsh. I could tell that by her voice and by her next speech, as well as if I had seen her face.

"But I am sorry you are feeling the pressure of the affairs; I am quite aware that I have entailed much additional trouble upon you by some of my measures: I must try and provide you with some suitable assistance. Copying letters and doing up accounts, I think you said?"

Mr. Horner had certainly had a distant idea of turning the little boy, in process of time, into a clerk; but he had rather urged this possibility of future usefulness beyond what he had at first intended, in speaking of it to my lady as a palliation of his offence, and he certainly was very much inclined to retract his statement that the letter-writing, or any other business, had increased, or that he was in the slightest want of help of any kind, when my lady after a pause of consideration, suddenly said—

" I have it. Miss Galindo will, I am sure, be glad to assist you. I will speak to her myself. The payment we should make to a clerk would be of real service to her! "

I could hardly help echoing Mr. Horner's tone of surprise as he said—

" Miss Galindo! "

For, you must be told who Miss Galindo was; at least, told as much as I know. Miss Galindo had lived in the village for many years, keeping house on the smallest possible means, yet always managing to maintain a servant. And this servant was invariably chosen because she had some infirmity that made her undesirable to every one else. I believe Miss Galindo had had lame and blind and hump-backed maids. She had even at one time taken in a girl hopelessly gone in consumption, because if not she would have had to go to the workhouse, and not have had enough to eat. Of course the poor creature could not perform a single duty usually required of a servant, and Miss Galindo herself was both servant and nurse.

Her present maid was scarcely four feet high, and bore a terrible character for ill-temper. Nobody but Miss Galindo would have kept her; but, as it was, mistress and servant squabbled perpetually, and were, at heart, the best of friends. For it was one of Miss Galindo's peculiarities to do all manner of kind and self-denying actions, and to say all manner of provoking things. Lame, blind, deformed, and dwarf, all came in for scoldings without number: it was only the consumptive girl that never had heard a sharp word. I don't think any of her servants liked her the worse for her peppery temper, and passionate odd ways, for they knew her real and beautiful kindness of heart; and, besides, she had so great a turn for humour, that very often her speeches amused as much or more than they irritated; and on the other side, a piece of witty impudence from her servant would occasionally tickle her so much and so suddenly, that she would burst out laughing in the middle of her passion.

But the talk about Miss Galindo's choice and management of her servants was confined to village gossip, and had never reached my Lady Ludlow's ears, though doubtless Mr. Horner was well acquainted with it. What my lady knew of her amounted to this. It was the custom in those days for the wealthy ladies of the county to set on foot a repository, as it was called, in the assize-town. The ostensible manager of this repository was generally a decayed gentlewoman, a clergyman's widow, or so forth. She was, however, controlled by a committee of ladies; and paid by them in proportion to the amount of goods she sold; and these goods were the small manufactures of ladies of little or no fortune, whose names, if they chose it, were only signified by initials.

Poor water-colour drawings, indigo and Indian ink; screens, ornamented with moss and dried leaves; paintings on velvet, and such faintly ornamental works were displayed on one side of the shop. It was always reckoned a mark of characteristic gentility in the repository, to have only common heavy-framed sash-windows, which admitted very little light, so I never was quite certain of the merit of these Works of Art as they were entitled. But, on the other side, where the Useful Work placard was put up, there was a great variety of articles, of whose unusual excellence every one might judge. Such fine sewing, and stitching, and button-holing! Such bundles of soft delicate knitted stockings and socks; and, above all, in Lady Ludlow's eyes, such hanks of the finest spun flaxen thread!

And the most delicate dainty work of all was done by Miss Galindo, as Lady Ludlow very well knew. Yet, for all their fine sewing, it sometimes happened that Miss Galindo's patterns were of an old-fashioned kind; and the dozen night-caps, maybe, on the materials for which she had expended *bonâ-fide* money, and on the making-up no little time and eye-sight, would lie for months in a yellow neglected heap; and at such times, it was said, Miss Galindo was more amusing than usual, more full of dry drollery and humour; just as at the times when an order came in to X. (the initial she had chosen) for a stock of well-paying things, she sat and stormed at her servant as she stitched away. She herself explained her practice in this way:—

"When everything goes wrong, one would give up breathing if one could not lighten one's heart by a joke. But when I've to sit still from morning till night, I must have something to stir my blood, or I should go off into an apoplexy; so I set to, and quarrel with Sally."

Such were Miss Galindo's means and manner of living in her own house. Out of doors, and in the village, she was not popular, although she would have been sorely missed had she left the place. But she asked too many home questions (not to say impertinent) respecting the domestic economies (for even the very poor liked to spend their bit of money their own way), and would open cupboards to find out hidden extravagances, and question closely respecting the weekly amount of butter, till one day she met with what would have been a rebuff to any other person, but which she rather enjoyed than otherwise.

She was going into a cottage, and in the doorway met the good woman chasing out a duck, and apparently unconscious of her visitor.

" Get out, Miss Galindo!" she cried, addressing the duck. " Get out! O, I ask your pardon," she continued, as if seeing the lady for the first time. " It's only that weary duck will come in. Get out, Miss Gal——" (to the duck).

" And so you call it after me, do you? " inquired her visitor.

" O, yes, ma'am; my master would have it so, for he said, sure enough the unlucky bird was always poking herself where she was not wanted."

" Ha, ha! very good! And so your master is a wit, is he? Well! tell him to come up and speak to me to-night about my parlour chimney, for there is no one like him for chimney doctoring."

And the master went up, and was so won over by Miss Galindo's merry ways, and sharp insight into the mysteries of his various kinds of business (he was a mason, chimney-sweeper, and ratcatcher), that he came home and abused his wife the next time she called the duck the name by which he himself had christened her.

But odd as Miss Galindo was in general, she could be as well-bred a lady as any one when she chose. And choose she always did when my Lady Ludlow was by. Indeed, I don't know the man, woman, or child, that did not instinctively turn out its best side to her ladyship. So she had no notion of the qualities which, I am sure, made Mr. Horner think that Miss Galindo would be most unmanageable as a clerk, and heartily wish that the idea had never come into my lady's head. But there it was; and he had annoyed her ladyship already more than he liked to-day, so he could not directly contradict her, but only urge difficulties which he hoped might prove insuperable. But every one of them Lady Ludlow knocked down. Letters to copy? Doubtless. Miss Galindo could come up to the Hall; she should have a room to herself; she wrote a beautiful hand; and writing would save her eye sight. " Capability with regard to accounts? " My lady would answer for that too; and for more than Mr. Horner seemed to think it necessary to inquire about. Miss Galindo was by birth and breeding a lady of the strictest honour, and would, if possible, forget the substance of any letters that passed through her hands; at any rate, no one would ever hear of them again from her. "Remuneration?" Oh! as for that, Lady Ludlow would herself take care that it was managed in the most delicate manner possible. She would send to invite Miss Galindo to tea at the Hall that very afternoon, if Mr. Horner would only give her ladyship the slightest idea of the average length of time that my lady was to request Miss Galindo to sacrifice to her daily. "Three hours! Very well." Mr. Horner looked very grave as he passed the windows of the room where I lay. I don't think he liked the idea of Miss Galindo as a clerk.

Lady Ludlow's invitations were like royal commands. Indeed, the village was too quiet to allow the inhabitants to have many evening engagements of any kind. Now and then, Mr. and Mrs. Horner gave a tea and supper to the principal tenants and their wives, to which the clergyman was invited, and Miss Galindo, Mrs. Medlicott, and one or two other spinsters and widows. The glory of the supper-table on these occasions was invariably furnished by her ladyship: it was a cold roasted peacock, with his tail stuck out as if in life. Mrs. Medlicott would take up the whole morning arranging the feathers in the proper semicircle, and was always pleased with the wonder and admiration it excited. It was considered a due reward and fitting compliment to her exertions that Mr. Horner always took her in to supper, and placed her opposite to the magnificent dish, at which she sweetly smiled all the time they were at table. But since Mrs. Horner had had the paralytic stroke these parties had been given up; and Miss Galindo wrote a note to Lady Ludlow in reply to her invitation, saying that she was entirely disengaged, and would have great pleasure in doing herself the honour of waiting upon her ladyship.

Whoever visited my lady took their meals with her, sitting on the dais, in the presence of all my former companions. So I did not see Miss Galindo until some time after tea; as the young gentlewomen had had to bring her their sewing and spinning, to hear the remarks of so competent a judge. At length her ladyship brought her visitor into the room where I lay,—it was one of my bad days, I remember,—in order to have her little bit of private conversation. Miss Galindo was dressed in her best gown, I am sure, but I had never seen anything like it except in a picture, it was so old-fashioned. She wore a white muslin apron, delicately embroidered, and put on a little crookedly, in order, as she told us, even Lady Ludlow, before the evening was over, to conceal a spot whence the colour had been discharged by a lemon-stain. This crookedness had an odd effect, especially when I saw that it was intentional; indeed, she was so anxious about her apron's right adjustment in the wrong place, that she told us straight out why she wore it so, and asked her ladyship if the spot was properly hidden, at the same time lifting up her apron and showing her how large it was.

"When my father was alive, I always took his right arm, so, and used to remove any spotted or discoloured breadths to the left side, if it was a walking-dress. That's the convenience of a gentleman. But widows and spinsters must do what they can. Ah, my dear (to me)! when you are reckoning up the blessings in your lot,—though you may think it a hard one in some respects,—don't forget how little your stockings want darning, as you are obliged to lie down so much! I would rather knit two pairs of stockings than darn one, any day."

"Have you been doing any of your beautiful knitting lately?" asked my lady, who had now arranged Miss Galindo in the pleasantest chair, and taken her own little wicker-work one, and, having her work in her hands, was ready to try and open the subject.

"No, and alas! your ladyship. It is partly the hot weather's fault, for people seem to forget that winter must come; and partly, I suppose, that every one is stocked who has the money to pay four-and-sixpence a pair for stockings."

"Then may I ask if you have any time in your active days at liberty?" said my lady, drawing a little nearer to her proposal, which I fancy she found it a little awkward to make.

"Why, the village keeps me busy, your ladyship, when I have neither knitting or sewing to do. You know I took X. for my letter at the repository, because it stands for Xantippe, who was a great scold in old times, as I have learnt. But I'm sure I don't know how the world would get on without scolding, your ladyship. It would go to sleep, and the sun would stand still."

"I don't think I could bear to scold, Miss Galindo," said her ladyship, smiling.

"No! because your ladyship has people to do it for you. Begging your pardon, my lady, it seems to me the generality of people may be divided into saints, scolds, and sinners. Now, your ladyship is a saint, because you have a sweet and holy nature, in the first place; and have people to do your anger and vexation for you, in the second place. And Jonathan Walker is a sinner, because he is sent to prison. But here am I, half way, having but a poor kind of disposition at best, and yet hating sin, and all that leads to it, such as wasting, and extravagance, and gossiping,—and yet all this lies right under my nose in the village, and I am not saint enough to be vexed at it; and so I scold. And though I had rather be a saint, yet I think I do good in my way."

"No doubt you do, dear Miss Galindo," said Lady Ludlow. "But I am sorry to hear that there is so much that is bad going on in the village,—very sorry."

"O, your ladyship! then I am sorry I brought it out. It was only by way of saying, that when I have no particular work to do at home, I take a turn abroad, and set my neighbours to rights, just by way of steering clear of Satan.

> For Satan finds some mischief still
> For idle hands to do,

you know, my lady."

There was no leading into the subject by delicate degrees, for Miss Galindo was evidently so fond of talking that, if asked a question, she made her answer so long, that before she came to an end of it, she had wandered far away from the original starting point. So Lady Ludlow plunged at once into what she had to say.

"Miss Galindo, I have a great favour to ask of you."

"My lady, I wish I could tell you what a pleasure it is to hear you say so," replied Miss Galindo, almost with tears in her eyes; so glad were we all to do anything for her ladyship, which could be called a free service and not merely a duty.

"It is this. Mr. Horner tells me that the business-letters, relating to the estate, are multiplying so much that he finds it impossible to copy them all himself, and I therefore require the services of some confidential and discreet person to copy these letters, and occasionally to go through certain accounts. Now, there is a very pleasant little sitting-room very near to Mr. Horner's office (you know Mr. Horner's office—on the other side of the stone hall?), and if I could prevail upon you to come here to breakfast and afterwards sit there for three hours every morning, Mr. Horner should bring or send you the papers——"

Lady Ludlow stopped. Miss Galindo's countenance had fallen. There was some great obstacle in her mind to her wish for obliging Lady Ludlow.

" What would Sally do? " she asked at length. Lady Ludlow had not a notion who Sally was. Nor if she had had a notion, would she have had a conception of the perplexities that poured into Miss Galindo's mind, at the idea of leaving her rough forgetful dwarf without the perpetual monitorship of her mistress. Lady Ludlow, accustomed to a household where everything went on noiselessly, perfectly, and by clock-work, conducted by a number of highly-paid, well-chosen, and accomplished servants, had not a conception of the nature of the rough material from which her servants came. Besides, in her establishment, so that the result was good, no one inquired if the small economies had been observed in the production. Whereas every penny— every halfpenny, was of consequence to Miss Galindo; and visions of squandered drops of milk and wasted crusts of bread filled her mind with dismay. But she swallowed all her apprehensions down, out of her regard for Lady Ludlow, and desire to be of service to her. No one knows how great a trial it was to her when she thought of Sally, unchecked and unscolded for three hours every morning. But all she said was—

" ' Sally, go to the Deuce.' I beg your pardon, my lady, if I was talking to myself; it's a habit I have got into of keeping my tongue in practice, and I am not quite aware when I do it. Three hours every morning! I shall be only too proud to do what I can for your ladyship; and I hope Mr. Horner will not be too impatient with me at first. You know, perhaps, that I was nearly being an authoress once, and that seems as if I was destined to ' employ my time in writing.' "

" No, indeed; we must return to the subject of the clerkship afterwards, if you please. An authoress, Miss Galindo! You surprise me! "

" But, indeed, I was. All was quite ready. Doctor Burney used to teach me music: not that I ever could learn, but it was a fancy of my poor father's. And his daughter wrote a book, and they said she was but a very young lady, and nothing but a music-master's daughter; so why should not I try? "

" Well? "

" Well! I got paper and half-a-hundred good pens, a bottle of ink, all ready——"

" And then——"

" O, it ended in my having nothing to say, when I sat down to write. But sometimes, when I get hold of a book, I wonder why I let such a poor reason stop me. It does not others."

" But I think it was very well it did, Miss Galindo," said her ladyship. "I am extremely against women usurping men's employments, as they are very apt to do. But perhaps, after all, the notion of writing a book improved your hand. It is one of the most legible I ever saw."

"I despise z's without tails," said Miss Galindo, with a good deal of gratified pride at my lady's praise. Presently, my lady took her to look at a curious old cabinet, which Lord Ludlow had picked up at the Hague; and while they were out of the room on this errand, I suppose the question of remuneration was settled, for I heard no more of it.

When they came back, they were talking of Mr. Gray. Miss Galindo was unsparing in her expressions of opinion about him: going much farther than my lady—in her language, at least.

"A little blushing man like him, who can't say bo to a goose without hesitating and colouring, to come to this village—which is as good a village as ever lived—and cry us down for a set of sinners, as if we had all committed murder and that other thing! —I have no patience with him, my lady. And then, how is he to help us to heaven, by teaching us our a b, ab—b a, ba? And yet, by all accounts, that's to save poor children's souls. O, I knew your ladyship would agree with me. I am sure my mother was as good a creature as ever breathed the blessed air; and if she's not gone to heaven I don't want to go there; and she could not spell a letter decently. And does Mr. Gray think God took note of that?"

"I was sure you would agree with me, Miss Galindo," said my lady. "You and I can remember how this talk about education —Rousseau, and his writings—stirred up the French people to their Reign of Terror, and all those bloody scenes."

"I'm afraid that Rousseau and Mr. Gray are birds of a feather," replied Miss Galindo, shaking her head. "And yet there is some good in the young man too. He sat up all night with Billy Davis, when his wife was fairly worn out with nursing him."

"Did he, indeed!" said my lady, her face lighting up, as it always did when she heard of any kind or generous action, no matter who performed it. "What a pity he is bitten with these new revolutionary ideas, and is so much for disturbing the established order of society!"

When Miss Galindo went, she left so favourable an impression of her visit on my lady, that she said to me with a pleased smile—

"I think I have provided Mr. Horner with a far better clerk than he would have made of that lad Gregson in twenty years.

And I will send the lad to my lord's grieve, in Scotland, that he may be kept out of harm's way."

But something happened to the lad before this purpose could be accomplished.

CHAPTER X

THE next morning, Miss Galindo made her appearance, and, by some mistake, unusual to my lady's well-trained servants, was shown into the room where I was trying to walk; for a certain amount of exercise was prescribed for me, painful although the exertion had become.

She brought a little basket along with her; and while the footman was gone to inquire my lady's wishes (for I don't think that Lady Ludlow expected Miss Galindo so soon to assume her clerkship; nor, indeed, had Mr. Horner any work of any kind ready for his new assistant to do), she launched out into conversation with me.

" It was a sudden summons, my dear! However, as I have often said to myself, ever since an occasion long ago, if Lady Ludlow ever honours me by asking for my right hand, I'll cut it off, and wrap the stump up so tidily she shall never find out it bleeds. But, if I had had a little more time, I could have mended my pens better. You see, I have had to sit up pretty late to get these sleeves made "—and she took out of her basket a pair of brown-holland over-sleeves, very much such as a grocer's apprentice wears—" and I had only time to make seven or eight pens, out of some quills Farmer Thomson gave me last autumn. As for ink, I'm thankful to say, that's always ready; an ounce of steel filings, an ounce of nut-gall, and a pint of water (tea, if you're extravagant, which, thank Heaven! I'm not), put all in a bottle, and hang it up behind the house door, so that the whole gets a good shaking every time you slam it to—and even if you are in a passion and bang it, as Sally and I often do, it is all the better for it—and there's my ink ready for use; ready to write my lady's will with, if need be."

" O, Miss Galindo!" said I, " don't talk so; my lady's will! and she not dead yet."

" And if she were, what would be the use of talking of making her will? Now, if you were Sally, I should say, ' Answer me that, you goose!' But, as you're a relation of my lady's, I must be civil and only say, ' I can't think how you can talk so like a fool!' To be sure, poor thing, you're lame!"

I do not know how long she would have gone on; but my lady came in, and I, released from my duty of entertaining Miss Galindo, made my limping way into the next room. To tell the truth, I was rather afraid of Miss Galindo's tongue, for I never knew what she would say next.

After a while my lady came, and began to look in the bureau for something: and as she looked she said—

" I think Mr. Horner must have made some mistake, when he said he had so much work that he almost required a clerk, for this morning he cannot find anything for Miss Galindo to do; and there she is, sitting with her pen behind her ear, waiting for something to write. I am come to find her my mother's letters, for I should like to have a fair copy made of them. O, here they are: don't trouble yourself, my dear child."

When my lady returned again, she sat down and began to talk of Mr. Gray.

" Miss Galindo says she saw him going to hold a prayer-meeting in a cottage. Now that really makes me unhappy, it is so like what Mr. Wesley used to do in my younger days; and since then we have had rebellion in the American colonies and the French Revolution. You may depend upon it, my dear, making religion and education common—vulgarising them, as it were— is a bad thing for a nation. A man who hears prayers read in the cottage where he has just supped on bread and bacon, forgets the respect due to a church: he begins to think that one place is as good as another, and, by-and-by, that one person is as good as another; and after that, I always find that people begin to talk of their rights, instead of thinking of their duties. I wish Mr. Gray had been more tractable, and had left well alone. What do you think I heard this morning? Why that the Home Hill estate, which niches into the Hanbury property, was bought by a Baptist baker from Birmingham!"

" A Baptist baker!" I exclaimed. I had never seen a Dissenter, to my knowledge; but, having always heard them spoken of with horror, I looked upon them almost as if they were rhinoceroses. I wanted to see a live Dissenter, I believe, and yet I wished it were over. I was almost surprised when I heard that any of them were engaged in such peaceful occupations as baking.

" Yes! so Mr. Horner tells me. A Mr. Lambe, I believe. But, at any rate, he is a Baptist, and has been in trade. What with his schismatism and Mr. Gray's methodism, I am afraid all the primitive character of this place will vanish."

From what I could hear, Mr. Gray seemed to be taking his own way, at any rate, more than he had done when he first came to the village, when his natural timidity had made him defer to my lady, and seek her consent and sanction before embarking in any new plan. But newness was a quality Lady Ludlow especially disliked. Even in the fashions of dress and furniture, she clung to the old, to the modes which had prevailed when she was young; and though she had a deep personal regard for Queen Charlotte (to whom, as I have already said, she had been maid-of-honour), yet there was a tinge of Jacobitism about her, such as made her extremely dislike to hear Prince Charles Edward called the young Pretender, as many loyal people did in those days, and made her fond of telling of the thorn-tree in my lord's park in Scotland, which had been planted by bonny Queen Mary herself, and before which every guest in the Castle of Monkshaven was expected to stand bare-headed, out of respect to the memory and misfortunes of the royal planter.

We might play at cards, if we so chose, on a Sunday; at least, I suppose we might, for my lady and Mr. Mountford used to do so often when I first went. But we must neither play cards, nor read, nor sew on the fifth of November and on the thirtieth of January, but must go to church, and meditate all the rest of the day—and very hard work meditating was. I would far rather have scoured a room. That was the reason, I suppose, why a passive life was seen to be better discipline for me than an active one.

But I am wandering away from my lady, and her dislike to all innovation. Now, it seemed to me, as far as I heard, that Mr. Gray was full of nothing but new things, and that what he first did was to attack all our established institutions, both in the village and the parish, and also in the nation. To be sure, I heard of his ways of going on principally from Miss Galindo, who was apt to speak more strongly than accurately.

" There he goes," she said, " clucking up the children just like an old hen, and trying to teach them about their salvation and their souls, and I don't know what—things that it is just blasphemy to speak about out of church. And he potters old people about reading their Bibles. I am sure I don't want to speak disrespectfully about the Holy Scriptures, but I found old Job Horton busy reading his Bible yesterday. Says I, 'What are you reading, and where did you get it, and who gave it you?'

So he made answer, 'That he was reading Susannah and the Elders, for that he had read Bel and the Dragon till he could pretty near say it off by heart, and they were two as pretty stories as ever he had read, and that it was a caution to him what bad old chaps there were in the world.' Now, as Job is bedridden, I don't think he is likely to meet with the Elders, and I say that I think repeating his Creed, the Commandments, and the Lord's Prayer, and, maybe, throwing in a verse of the Psalms, if he wanted a bit of a change, would have done him far more good than his pretty stories, as he called them. And what's the next thing our young parson does? Why he tries to make us all feel pitiful for the black slaves, and leaves little pictures of negroes about, with the question printed below, 'Am I not a man and a brother?' just as if I was to be hail-fellow-well-met with every negro footman. They do say he takes no sugar in his tea, because he thinks he sees spots of blood in it. Now I call that superstition.

The next day it was a still worse story.

"Well, my dear! and how are you? My lady sent me in to sit a bit with you, while Mr. Horner looks out some papers for me to copy. Between ourselves, Mr. Steward Horner does not like having me for a clerk. It is all very well he does not; for, if he were decently civil to me, I might want a chaperone, you know, now poor Mrs. Horner is dead." This was one of Miss Galindo's grim jokes. "As it is, I try to make him forget I'm a woman, I do everything as ship-shape as a masculine man-clerk. I see he can't find a fault—writing good, spelling correct, sums all right. And then he squints up at me with the tail of his eye, and looks glummer than ever, just because I'm a woman —as if I could help that. I have gone good lengths to set his mind at ease. I have stuck my pen behind my ear, I have made him a bow instead of a curtsey, I have whistled—not a tune, I can't pipe up that—nay, if you won't tell my lady, I don't mind telling you that I have said 'Confound it!' and 'Zounds!' I can't get any farther. For all that, Mr. Horner won't forget I am a lady, and so I am not half the use I might be, and if it were not to please my Lady Ludlow, Mr. Horner and his books might go hang (see how natural that came out!). And there is an order for a dozen nightcaps for a bride, and I am so afraid I shan't have time to do them. Worst of all, there's Mr. Gray taking advantage of my absence to seduce Sally!"

"To seduce Sally! Mr. Gray!"

"Pooh, pooh, child! There's many a kind of seduction. Mr.

Gray is seducing Sally to want to go to church. There has he
been twice at my house, while I have been away in the mornings,
talking to Sally about the state of her soul and that sort of thing.
But when I found the meat all roasted to a cinder, I said,
' Come, Sally, let's have no more praying when beef is down at
the fire. Pray at six o'clock in the morning and nine at night,
and I won't hinder you.' So she sauced me, and said something
about Martha and Mary, implying that, because she had let the
beef get so overdone that I declare I could hardly find a bit for
Nancy Pole's sick grandchild, she had chosen the better part.
I was very much put about, I own, and perhaps you'll be shocked
at what I said—indeed, I don't know if it was right myself—but
I told her I had a soul as well as she, and if it was to be saved by
my sitting still and thinking about salvation and never doing my
duty, I thought I had as good a right as she had to be Mary, and
save my soul. So, that afternoon I sat quite still, and it was
really a comfort, for I am often too busy, I know, to pray as
I ought. There is first one person wanting me, and then another,
and the house and the food and the neighbours to see after. So,
when tea-time comes, there enters my maid with her hump on
her back, and her soul to be saved. ' Please, ma'am, did you
order the pound of butter? '—' No, Sally,' I said, shaking my
head, ' this morning I did not go round by Hale's farm, and this
afternoon I have been employed in spiritual things.'

" Now, our Sally likes tea and bread-and-butter above everything, and dry bread was not to her taste.

" ' I'm thankful,' said the impudent hussy, " that you have
taken a turn towards godliness. It will be my prayers, I trust,
that's given it you.'

" I was determined not to give her an opening towards the
carnal subject of butter, so she lingered still, longing to ask
leave to run for it. But I gave her none, and munched my dry
bread myself, thinking what a famous cake I could make for
little Ben Pole with the bit of butter we were saving; and when
Sally had had her butterless tea, and was in none of the best of
tempers because Martha had not bethought herself of the butter,
I just quietly said—

" ' Now, Sally, to-morrow we'll try to hash that beef well, and
to remember the butter, and to work out our salvation all at the
same time; for I don't see why it can't all be done, as God has set
us to do it all.' But I heard her at it again about Mary and
Martha, and I have no doubt that Mr. Gray will teach her to
consider me a lost sheep."

I had heard so many little speeches about Mr. Gray from one person or another, all speaking against him, as a mischief-maker, a setter-up of new doctrines, and of a fanciful standard of life (and you may be sure that, where Lady Ludlow led, Mrs. Medlicott and Adams were certain to follow, each in their different ways showing the influence my lady had over them), that I believe I had grown to consider him as a very instrument of evil, and to expect to perceive in his face marks of his presumption, and arrogance, and impertinent interference. It was now many weeks since I had seen him, and when he was one morning shown into the blue drawing-room (into which I had been removed for a change), I was quite surprised to see how innocent and awkward a young man he appeared, confused even more than I was at our unexpected *tête-à-tête*. He looked thinner, his eyes more eager, his expression more anxious, and his colour came and went more than it had done when I had seen him last. I tried to make a little conversation, as I was, to my own surprise, more at my ease than he was; but his thoughts were evidently too much preoccupied for him to do more than answer me with monosyllables.

Presently my lady came in. Mr. Gray twitched and coloured more than ever; but plunged into the middle of his subject at once.

" My lady, I cannot answer it to my conscience, if I allow the children of this village to go on any longer the little heathens that they are. I must do something to alter their condition. I am quite aware that your ladyship disapproves of many of the plans which have suggested themselves to me; but nevertheless I must do something, and I am come now to your ladyship to ask respectfully, but firmly, what you would advise me to do."

His eyes were dilated, and I could almost have said they were full of tears with his eagerness. But I am sure it is a bad plan to remind people of decided opinions which they have once expressed, if you wish them to modify those opinions. Now, Mr. Gray had done this with my lady; and though I do not mean to say she was obstinate, yet she was not one to retract.

She was silent for a moment or two before she replied.

" You ask me to suggest a remedy for an evil of the existence of which I am not conscious," was her answer—very coldly, very gently given. " In Mr. Mountford's time I heard no such complaints: whenever I see the village children (and they are not unfrequent visitors at this house, on one pretext or another), they are well and decently behaved."

"Oh, madam, you cannot judge," he broke in. "They are trained to respect you in word and deed; you are the highest they ever look up to; they have no notion of a higher."

"Nay, Mr. Gray," said my lady, smiling, "they are as loyally disposed as any children can be. They come up here every fourth of June, and drink his Majesty's health, and have buns, and (as Margaret Dawson can testify) they take a great and respectful interest in all the pictures I can show them of the royal family."

"But, madam, I think of something higher than any earthly dignities."

My lady coloured at the mistake she had made; for she herself was truly pious. Yet when she resumed the subject, it seemed to me as if her tone was a little sharper than before.

"Such want of reverence is, I should say, the clergyman's fault. You must excuse me, Mr. Gray, if I speak plainly."

"My lady, I want plain-speaking. I myself am not accustomed to those ceremonies and forms which are, I suppose, the etiquette in your ladyship's rank of life, and which seem to hedge you in from any power of mine to touch you. Among those with whom I have passed my life hitherto, it has been the custom to speak plainly out what we have felt earnestly. So, instead of needing any apology from your ladyship for straightforward speaking, I will meet what you say at once, and admit that it is the clergyman's fault, in a great measure, when the children of his parish swear, and curse, and are brutal, and ignorant of all saving grace; nay, some of them of the very name of God. And because this guilt of mine, as the clergyman of this parish, lies heavy on my soul, and every day leads but from bad to worse, till I am utterly bewildered how to do good to children who escape from me as if I were a monster, and who are growing up to be men fit for and capable of any crime, but those requiring wit or sense, I come to you, who seem to me all-powerful, as far as material power goes—for your ladyship only knows the surface of things, and barely that, that pass in your village—to help me with advice, and such outward help as you can give."

Mr. Gray had stood up and sat down once or twice while he had been speaking, in an agitated, nervous kind of way, and now he was interrupted by a violent fit of coughing, after which he trembled all over.

My lady rang for a glass of water, and looked much distressed.

" Mr. Gray," said she, " I am sure you are not well; and that makes you exaggerate childish faults into positive evils. It is always the case with us when we are not strong in health. I hear of your exerting yourself in every direction: you overwork yourself, and the consequence is, that you imagine us all worse people than we are."

And my lady smiled very kindly and pleasantly at him, as he sat, a little panting, a little flushed, trying to recover his breath. I am sure that now they were brought face to face, she had quite forgotten all the offence she had taken at his doings when she heard of them from others; and, indeed, it was enough to soften any one's heart to see that young, almost boyish face, looking in such anxiety and distress.

" Oh, my lady, what shall I do? " he asked, as soon as he could recover breath, and with such an air of humility, that I am sure no one who had seen it could have ever thought him conceited again. " The evil of this world is too strong for me. I can do so little. It is all in vain. It was only to-day——" and again the cough and agitation returned.

" My dear Mr. Gray," said my lady (the day before I could never have believed she could have called him My dear), " you must take the advice of an old woman about yourself. You are not fit to do anything just now but attend to your own health: rest, and see a doctor (but, indeed, I will take care of that), and when you are pretty strong again, you will find that you have been magnifying evils to yourself."

" But, my lady, I cannot rest. The evils do exist, and the burden of their continuance lies on my shoulders. I have no place to gather the children together in, that I may teach them the things necessary to salvation. The rooms in my own house are too small; but I have tried them. I have money of my own; and, as your ladyship knows, I tried to get a piece of leasehold property, on which to build a school-house at my own expense. Your ladyship's lawyer comes forward, at your instructions, to enforce some old feudal right, by which no building is allowed on leasehold property without the sanction of the lady of the manor. It may be all very true; but it was a cruel thing to do, —that is, if your ladyship had known (which I am sure you do not) the real moral and spiritual state of my poor parishioners. And now I come to you to know what I am to do. Rest! I cannot rest, while children whom I could possibly save are being left in their ignorance, their blasphemy, their uncleanness, their cruelty. It is known through the village that your ladyship disapproves of my efforts, and opposes all my plans. If you think them wrong, foolish, ill-digested (I have been a student, living in a college, and eschewing all society but that of pious men, until now: I may not judge for the best, in my ignorance of this sinful human nature), tell me of better plans and wiser projects for accomplishing my end; but do not bid me rest, with Satan compassing me round, and stealing souls away."

"Mr. Gray," said my lady, " there may be some truth in what you have said. I do not deny it, though I think, in your present state of indisposition and excitement, you exaggerate it much. I believe—nay, the experience of a pretty long life has convinced me—that education is a bad thing, if given indiscriminately. It unfits the lower orders for their duties, the duties to which they are called by God; of submission to those placed in authority over them; of contentment with that state of life to which it has pleased God to call them, and of ordering themselves lowly and reverently to all their betters. I have made this conviction of mine tolerably evident to you; and have expressed distinctly my disapprobation of some of your ideas. You may imagine, then, that I was not well pleased when I found that you had taken a rood or more of Farmer Hale's land, and were laying the foundations of a school-house. You had done this without asking for my permission, which, as Farmer Hale's liege lady, ought to have been obtained legally, as well as asked for out of courtesy. I put a stop to what I believed to be calculated to do harm to a village, to a population in which, to say the least of it, I may be disposed to take as much interest as you can do. How can reading, and writing, and the multiplication-table (if you choose to go so far) prevent blasphemy, and uncleanness, and cruelty? Really, Mr. Gray, I hardly like to express myself so strongly on the subject in your present state of health, as I should do at any other time. It seems to me that books do little; character much; and character is not formed from books."

"I do not think of character: I think of souls. I must get some hold upon these children, or what will become of them in the next world? I must be found to have some power beyond what they have, and which they are rendered capable of appreciating, before they will listen to me. At present physical force is all they look up to; and I have none."

"Nay, Mr. Gray, by your own admission, they look up to me."

" They would not do anything your ladyship disliked if it was likely to come to your knowledge; but if they could conceal it from you, the knowledge of your dislike to a particular line of conduct would never make them cease from pursuing it."

" Mr. Gray "—surprise in her air, and some little indignation —" they and their fathers have lived on the Hanbury lands for generations ! "

" I cannot help it, madam. I am telling you the truth, whether you believe me or not." There was a pause; my lady looked perplexed, and somewhat ruffled; Mr. Gray as though hopeless and wearied out. " Then, my lady," said he, at last, rising as he spoke, " you can suggest nothing to ameliorate the state of things which, I do assure you, does exist on your lands, and among your tenants. Surely, you will not object to my using Farmer Hale's great barn every Sabbath? He will allow me the use of it, if your ladyship will grant your permission."

" You are not fit for any extra work at present," (and indeed he had been coughing very much all through the conversation). " Give me time to consider of it. Tell me what you wish to teach. You will be able to take care of your health, and grow stronger while I consider. It shall not be the worse for you, if you leave it in my hands for a time."

My lady spoke very kindly; but he was in too excited a state to recognise the kindness, while the idea of delay was evidently a sore irritation. I heard him say: " And I have so little time in which to do my work. Lord ! lay not this sin to my charge."

But my lady was speaking to the old butler, for whom, at her sign, I had rung the bell some little time before. Now she turned round.

" Mr. Gray, I find I have some bottles of Malmsey, of the vintage of seventeen hundred and seventy-eight, yet left. Malmsey, as perhaps you know, used to be considered a specific for coughs arising from weakness. You must permit me to send you half-a-dozen bottles, and, depend upon it, you will take a more cheerful view of life and its duties before you have finished them, especially if you will be so kind as to see Dr. Trevor, who is coming to see me in the course of the week. By the time you are strong enough to work, I will try and find some means of preventing the children from using such bad language, and otherwise annoying you."

" My lady, it is the sin, and not the annoyance. I wish I could make you understand." He spoke with some impatience.

Poor fellow! he was too weak, exhausted, and nervous. "I am perfectly well; I can set to work to-morrow; I will do anything not to be oppressed with the thought of how little I am doing. I do not want your wine. Liberty to act in the manner I think right, will do me far more good. But it is of no use. It is preordained that I am to be nothing but a cumberer of the ground. I beg you ladyship's pardon for this call."

He stood up, and then turned dizzy. My lady looked on, deeply hurt, and not a little offended. He held out his hand to her, and I could see that she had a little hesitation before she took it. He then saw me, I almost think, for the first time; and put out his hand once more, drew it back, as if undecided, put it out again, and finally took hold of mine for an instant in his damp, listless hand, and was gone.

Lady Ludlow was dissatisfied with both him and herself, I was sure. Indeed, I was dissatisfied with the result of the interview myself. But my lady was not one to speak out her feelings on the subject; nor was I one to forget myself, and begin on a topic which she did not begin. She came to me, and was very tender with me; so tender, that that, and the thoughts of Mr. Gray's sick, hopeless, disappointed look, nearly made me cry.

"You are tired, little one," said my lady. "Go and lie down in my room, and hear what Medlicott and I can decide upon in the way of strengthening dainties for that poor young man, who is killing himself with his over-sensitive conscientiousness."

"Oh, my lady!" said I, and then I stopped.

"Well. What?" asked she.

"If you would but let him have Farmer Hale's barn at once, it would do him more good than all."

"Pooh, pooh, child!" though I don't think she was displeased, "he is not fit for more work just now. I shall go and write for Dr. Trevor."

And, for the next half-hour, we did nothing but arrange physical comforts and cures for poor Mr. Gray. At the end of the time, Mrs. Medlicott said—

"Has your ladyship heard that Harry Gregson has fallen from a tree, and broken his thigh-bone, and is like to be a cripple for life?"

"Harry Gregson! That black-eyed lad who read my letter? It all comes from over-education!"

CHAPTER XI

But I don't see how my lady could think it was over-education that made Harry Gregson break his thigh, for the manner in which he met with the accident was this:—

Mr. Horner, who had fallen sadly out of health since his wife's death, had attached himself greatly to Harry Gregson. Now, Mr. Horner had a cold manner to every one, and never spoke more than was necessary, at the best of times. And, latterly, it had not been the best of times with him. I dare say, he had had some causes for anxiety (of which I knew nothing) about my lady's affairs; and he was evidently annoyed by my lady's whim (as he once inadvertently called it) of placing Miss Galindo under him in the position of a clerk. Yet he had always been friends, in his quiet way, with Miss Galindo, and she devoted herself to her new occupation with diligence and punctuality, although more than once she had moaned to me over the orders for needlework which had been sent to her, and which, owing to her occupation in the service of Lady Ludlow, she had been unable to fulfil.

The only living creature to whom the staid Mr. Horner could be said to be attached, was Harry Gregson. To my lady he was a faithful and devoted servant, looking keenly after her interests, and anxious to forward them at any cost of trouble to himself. But the more shrewd Mr. Horner was, the more probability was there of his being annoyed at certain peculiarities of opinion which my lady held with a quiet, gentle pertinacity; against which no arguments, based on mere worldly and business calculations, made any way. This frequent opposition to views which Mr. Horner entertained, although it did not interfere with the sincere respect which the lady and the steward felt for each other, yet prevented any warmer feeling of affection from coming in. It seems strange to say it, but I must repeat it—the only person for whom, since his wife's death, Mr. Horner seemed to feel any love, was the little imp Harry Gregson, with his bright, watchful eyes, his tangled hair hanging right down to his eyebrows, for all the world like a Skye terrier. This lad, half gipsy and whole poacher, as many people esteemed him, hung about the silent, respectable, staid Mr. Horner, and followed his steps with something of the affectionate fidelity of the dog which he resembled. I suspect, this demonstration of attachment to his person on Harry Gregson's part was what won Mr. Horner's regard. In the first instance, the steward had only chosen the lad out as the cleverest instrument he could find for his purpose; and I don't mean to say that, if Harry had not been almost as shrewd as Mr. Horner himself was, both by original disposition and subsequent experience, the steward would have taken to him as he did, let the lad have shown ever so much affection for him.

But even to Harry Mr. Horner was silent. Still, it was pleasant to find himself in many ways so readily understood; to perceive that the crumbs of knowledge he let fall were picked up by his little follower, and hoarded like gold; that here was one to hate the persons and things whom Mr. Horner coldly disliked, and to reverence and admire all those for whom he had any regard. Mr. Horner had never had a child, and unconsciously, I suppose, something of the paternal feeling had begun to develop itself in him towards Harry Gregson. I heard one or two things from different people, which have always made me fancy that Mr. Horner secretly and almost unconsciously hoped that Harry Gregson might be trained so as to be first his clerk, and next his assistant, and finally his successor in his steward-ship to the Hanbury estates.

Harry's disgrace with my lady, in consequence of his reading the letter, was a deeper blow to Mr. Horner than his quiet manner would ever have led any one to suppose, or than Lady Ludlow ever dreamed of inflicting, I am sure.

Probably Harry had a short, stern rebuke from Mr. Horner at the time, for his manner was always hard even to those he cared for the most. But Harry's love was not to be daunted or quelled by a few sharp words. I dare say, from what I heard of them afterwards, that Harry accompanied Mr. Horner in his walk over the farm the very day of the rebuke; his presence apparently unnoticed by the agent, by whom his absence would have been painfully felt nevertheless. That was the way of it, as I have been told. Mr. Horner never bade Harry go with him; never thanked him for going, or being at his heels ready to run on any errands, straight as the crow flies to his point, and back to heel in as short a time as possible. Yet, if Harry were away, Mr. Horner never inquired the reason from any of the men who might be supposed to know whether he was detained by his father, or otherwise engaged; he never asked Harry himself where he had been. But Miss Galindo said that those labourers who knew Mr. Horner well, told her that he was always more quick-eyed to shortcomings, more savage-like in fault-finding, on those days when the lad was absent.

Miss Galindo, indeed, was my great authority for most of the village news which I heard. She it was who gave me the particulars of poor Harry's accident.

"You see, my dear," she said, "the little poacher has taken some unaccountable fancy to my master." (This was the name by which Miss Galindo always spoke of Mr. Horner to me, ever since she had been, as she called it, appointed his clerk.)

"Now, if I had twenty hearts to lose, I never could spare a bit of one of them for that good, grey, square, severe man. But different people have different tastes, and here is that little imp of a gipsy-tinker ready to turn slave for my master; and, odd enough, my master—who, I should have said beforehand, would have made short work of imp, and imp's family, and have sent Hall, the Bang-beggar, after them in no time—my master, as they tell me, is in his way quite fond of the lad, and if he could, without vexing my lady too much, he would have made him what the folks here call a Latiner. However, last night, it seems that there was a letter of some importance forgotten (I can't tell you what it was about, my dear, though I know perfectly well, but 'service oblige,' as well as 'noblesse,' and you must take my word for it that it was important, and one that I am surprised my master could forget), till too late for the post. (The poor, good, orderly man is not what he was before his wife's death.) Well, it seems that he was sore annoyed by his forgetfulness, and well he might be. And it was all the more vexatious, as he had no one to blame but himself. As for that matter, I always scold somebody else when I'm in fault; but I suppose my master would never think of doing that, else it's a mighty relief. However, he could eat no tea, and was altogether put out and gloomy. And the little faithful imp-lad, perceiving all this, I suppose, got up like a page in an old ballad, and said he would run for his life across country to Comberford, and see if he could not get there before the bags were made up. So my master gave him the letter, and nothing more was heard of the poor fellow till this morning, for the father thought his son was sleeping in Mr. Horner's barn, as he does occasionally, it seems, and my master, as was very natural, that he had gone to his father's."

"And he had fallen down the old stone quarry, had he not?"

"Yes, sure enough. Mr. Gray had been up here fretting my lady with some of his new-fangled schemes, and because

the young man could not have it all his own way, from what
I understand, he was put out, and thought he would go home
by the back lane, instead of through the village, where the
folks would notice if the parson looked glum. But, however,
it was a mercy, and I don't mind saying so, ay, and meaning
it too, though it may be like methodism; for, as Mr. Gray
walked by the quarry, he heard a groan, and at first he thought
it was a lamb fallen down; and he stood still, and then he
heard it again; and then I suppose, he looked down and saw
Harry. So he let himself down by the boughs of the trees to
the ledge where Harry lay half-dead, and with his poor thigh
broken. There he had lain ever since the night before: he
had been returning to tell the master that he had safely posted
the letter, and the first words he said, when they recovered
him from the exhausted state he was in, were " (Miss Galindo
tried hard not to whimper, as she said it), " ' It was in time,
sir. I see'd it put in the bag with my own eyes.' "

" But where is he? " asked I. " How did Mr. Gray get him
out? "

" Ay! there it is, you see. Why the old gentleman (I daren't
say Devil in Lady Ludlow's house) is not so black as he is
painted; and Mr. Gray must have a deal of good in him, as I
say at times; and then at others, when he has gone against me,
I can't bear him, and think hanging too good for him. But he
lifted the poor lad, as if he had been a baby, I suppose, and
carried him up the great ledges that were formerly used for
steps; and laid him soft and easy on the wayside grass, and
ran home and got help and a door, and had him carried to his
house, and laid on his bed; and then somehow, for the first
time either he or any one else perceived it, he himself was all
over blood—his own blood—he had broken a blood-vessel;
and there he lies in the little dressing-room, as white and as
still as if he were dead; and the little imp in Mr. Gray's own
bed, sound asleep, now his leg is set, just as if linen sheets and
a feather bed were his native element, as one may say. Really,
now he is doing so well, I've no patience with him, lying there
where Mr. Gray ought to be. It is just what my lady always
prophesied would come to pass, if there was any confusion of
ranks."

" Poor Mr. Gray! " said I, thinking of his flushed face, and
his feverish, restless ways, when he had been calling on my
lady not an hour before his exertions on Harry's behalf. And
I told Miss Galindo how ill I had thought him.

"Yes," said she. "And that was the reason my lady had sent for Doctor Trevor. Well, it has fallen out admirably, for he looked well after that old donkey of a Prince, and saw that he made no blunders."

Now "that old donkey of a Prince" meant the village surgeon, Mr. Prince, between whom and Miss Galindo there was war to the knife, as they often met in the cottages, when there was illness, and she had her queer, odd recipes, which he, with his grand pharmacopœia, held in infinite contempt, and the consequence of their squabbling had been, not long before this very time, that he had established a kind of rule, that into whatever sick-room Miss Galindo was admitted, there he refused to visit. But Miss Galindo's prescriptions and visits cost nothing, and were often backed by kitchen-physic; so, though it was true that she never came but she scolded about something or other, she was generally preferred as medical attendant to Mr. Prince.

"Yes, the old donkey is obliged to tolerate me, and be civil to me; for, you see, I got there first, and had possession, as it were, and yet my lord the donkey likes the credit of attending the parson, and being in consultation with so grand a county-town doctor as Doctor Trevor. And Doctor Trevor is an old friend of mine" (she sighed a little, some time I may tell you why), "and treats me with infinite bowing and respect; so the donkey, not to be out of medical fashion, bows too, though it is sadly against the grain; and he pulled a face as if he had heard a slate-pencil gritting against a slate, when I told Doctor Trevor I meant to sit up with the two lads, for I call Mr. Gray little more than a lad, and a pretty conceited one, too, at times."

"But why should you sit up, Miss Galindo? It will tire you sadly."

"Not it. You see, there is Gregson's mother to keep quiet: for she sits by her lad, fretting and sobbing, so that I'm afraid of her disturbing Mr. Gray; and there's Mr. Gray to keep quiet, for Doctor Trevor says his life depends on it; and there is medicine to be given to the one, and bandages to be attended to for the other; and the wild horde of gipsy brothers and sisters to be turned out, and the father to be held in from showing too much gratitude to Mr. Gray, who can't bear it— and who is to do it all but me? The only servant is old lame Betty, who once lived with me, and *would* leave me because she said I was always bothering—(there was a good deal of truth in what she said, I grant, but she need not have said it; a good deal of truth is best let alone at the bottom of the well), and what can she do,—deaf as ever she can be, too?"

So Miss Galindo went her ways; but not the less was she at her post in the morning; a little crosser and more silent than usual; but the first was not to be wondered at, and the last was rather a blessing.

Lady Ludlow had been extremely anxious both about Mr. Gray and Harry Gregson. Kind and thoughtful in any case of illness and accident, she always was; but somehow, in this, the feeling that she was not quite—what shall I call it?—" friends " seems hardly the right word to use, as to the possible feeling between the Countess Ludlow and the little vagabond messenger, who had only once been in her presence,—that she had hardly parted from either as she could have wished to do, had death been near, made her more than usually anxious. Doctor Trevor was not to spare obtaining the best medical advice the county could afford; whatever he ordered in the way of diet, was to be prepared under Mrs. Medlicott's own eye, and sent down from the Hall to the Parsonage. As Mr. Horner had given somewhat similar directions, in the case of Harry Gregson at least, there was rather a multiplicity of counsellors and dainties, than any lack of them. And, the second night, Mr. Horner insisted on taking the superintendence of the nursing himself, and sat and snored by Harry's bedside, while the poor, exhausted mother lay by her child,—thinking that she watched him, but in reality fast asleep, as Miss Galindo told us; for, distrusting any one's powers of watching and nursing but her own, she had stolen across the quiet village street in cloak and dressing-gown, and found Mr. Gray in vain trying to reach the cup of barley-water which Mr. Horner had placed just beyond his reach.

In consequence of Mr. Gray's illness, we had to have a strange curate to do duty; a man who dropped his h's, and hurried through the service, and yet had time enough to stand in my lady's way, bowing to her as she came out of church, and so subservient in manner, that I believe that sooner than remain unnoticed by a countess, he would have preferred being scolded, or even cuffed. Now I found out, that great as was my lady's liking and approval of respect, nay, even reverence, being paid to her as a person of quality,—a sort of tribute to her Order, which she had no individual right to remit, or, indeed, not to exact,—yet she, being personally simple, sincere, and holding herself in low esteem, could not endure anything like the servility of Mr. Crosse, the temporary curate. She grew absolutely to loathe his perpetual smiling and bowing; his instant agreement with the slightest opinion she uttered; his veering round as she blew the wind. I have often said that my lady did not talk much, as she might have done had she lived among her equals. But we all loved her so much, that we had learnt to interpret all her little ways pretty truly; and I knew what particular turns of her head, and contractions of her delicate fingers meant, as well as if she had expressed herself in words. I began to suspect that my lady would be very thankful to have Mr. Gray about again, and doing his duty even with a conscientiousness that might amount to worrying himself, and fidgeting others; and although Mr. Gray might hold her opinions in as little esteem as those of any simple gentlewoman, she was too sensible not to feel how much flavour there was in his conversation, compared to that of Mr. Crosse, who was only her tasteless echo.

As for Miss Galindo, she was utterly and entirely a partisan of Mr. Gray's, almost ever since she had begun to nurse him during his illness.

"You know, I never set up for reasonableness, my lady. So I don't pretend to say, as I might do if I were a sensible woman and all that,—that I am convinced by Mr. Gray's arguments of this thing or t'other. For one thing, you see, poor fellow! he has never been able to argue, or hardly indeed to speak, for Doctor Trevor has been very peremptory. So there's been no scope for arguing! But what I mean is this:—When I see a sick man thinking always of others, and never of himself; patient, humble—a trifle too much at times, for I've caught him praying to be forgiven for having neglected his work as a parish priest," (Miss Galindo was making horrible faces, to keep back tears, squeezing up her eyes in a way which would have amused me at any other time, but when she was speaking of Mr. Gray); "when I see a downright good, religious man, I'm apt to think he's got hold of the right clue, and that I can do no better than hold on by the tails of his coat and shut my eyes, if we've got to go over doubtful places on our road to Heaven. So, my lady, you must excuse me if, when he gets about again, he is all agog about a Sunday-school, for if he is, I shall be agog too, and perhaps twice as bad as him, for, you see, I've a strong constitution compared to his, and strong ways of speaking and acting. And I tell your ladyship this now, because I think from your rank—and still more, if I may say so, for all your kindness to me long ago, down to this very day—you've a right to be first told of anything about me. Change of opinion I can't exactly call it, for I don't see the good of schools and teaching A B C, any more than I did before, only Mr. Gray does, so I'm to shut my eyes, and leap over the ditch to the side of education. I've told Sally already, that if she does not mind her work, but stands gossiping with Nelly Mather, I'll teach her her lessons; and I've never caught her with old Nelly since."

I think Miss Galindo's desertion to Mr. Gray's opinions in this matter hurt my lady just a little bit; but she only said—

"Of course, if the parishioners wish for it, Mr. Gray must have his Sunday-school. I shall, in that case, withdraw my opposition. I am sorry I cannot alter my opinions as easily as you."

My lady made herself smile as she said this. Miss Galindo saw it was an effort to do so. She thought a minute before she spoke again.

"Your ladyship has not seen Mr. Gray as intimately as I have done. That's one thing. But, as for the parishioners, they will follow your ladyship's lead in everything; so there is no chance of their wishing for a Sunday-school."

"I have never done anything to make them follow my lead, as you call it, Miss Galindo," said my lady, gravely.

"Yes, you have," replied Miss Galindo, bluntly. And then, correcting herself, she said, "Begging your ladyship's pardon, you have. Your ancestors have lived here time out of mind, and have owned the land on which their forefathers have lived ever since there were forefathers. You yourself were born amongst them, and have been like a little queen to them ever since, I might say, and they've never known your ladyship do anything but what was kind and gentle; but I'll leave fine speeches about your ladyship to Mr. Crosse. Only you, my lady, lead the thoughts of the parish; and save some of them a world of trouble, for they could never tell what was right if they had to think for themselves. It's all quite right that they should be guided by you, my lady,—if only you would agree with Mr. Gray."

"Well," said my lady, "I told him only the last day that he was here, that I would think about it. I do believe I could make up my mind on certain subjects better if I were left alone, than while being constantly talked to about them."

My lady said this in her usual soft tones; but the words had a tinge of impatience about them; indeed, she was more ruffled than I had often seen her; but, checking herself in an instant, she said—

"You don't know how Mr. Horner drags in this subject of education apropos of everything. Not that he says much about it at any time: it is not his way. But he cannot let the thing alone."

"I know why, my lady," said Miss Galindo. "That poor lad, Harry Gregson, will never be able to earn his livelihood in any active way, but will be lame for life. Now, Mr. Horner thinks more of Harry than of any one else in the world,—except, perhaps, your ladyship." Was it not a pretty companionship for my lady? "And he has schemes of his own for teaching Harry; and if Mr. Gray could but have his school, Mr. Horner and he think Harry might be schoolmaster, as your ladyship would not like to have him coming to you as steward's clerk. I wish your ladyship would fall into this plan; Mr. Gray has it so at heart."

Miss Galindo looked wistfully at my lady as she said this. But my lady only said, drily, and rising at the same time, as if to end the conversation—

"So! Mr. Horner and Mr. Gray seem to have gone a long way in advance of my consent to their plans."

"There!" exclaimed Miss Galindo, as my lady left the room, with an apology for going away; "I have gone and done mischief with my long, stupid tongue. To be sure, people plan a long way ahead of to-day; more especially when one is a sick man, lying all through the weary day on a sofa."

"My lady will soon get over her annoyance," said I, as it were apologetically. I only stopped Miss Galindo's self-reproaches to draw down her wrath upon myself.

"And has not she a right to be annoyed with me, if she likes, and to keep annoyed as long as she likes? Am I complaining of her, that you need tell me that? Let me tell you, I have known my lady these thirty years; and if she were to take me by the shoulders, and turn me out of the house, I should only love her the more. So don't you think to come between us with any little mincing, peace-making speeches. I have been a mischief-making parrot, and I like her the better for being vexed with me. So good-bye to you, Miss; and wait till you know Lady Ludlow as well as I do, before you next think of telling me she will soon get over her annoyance!" And off Miss Galindo went.

I could not exactly tell what I had done wrong; but I took care never again to come in between my lady and her by any remark about the one to the other; for I saw that some most powerful bond of grateful affection made Miss Galindo almost worship my lady.

Meanwhile, Harry Gregson was limping a little about in the village, still finding his home in Mr. Gray's house; for there he could most conveniently be kept under the doctor's eye, and receive the requisite care, and enjoy the requisite nourishment. As soon as he was a little better, he was to go to Mr. Horner's house; but, as the steward lived some distance out of the way, and was much from home, he had agreed to leave Harry at the house to which he had first been taken, until he was quite strong again; and the more willingly, I suspect, from what I heard afterwards, because Mr. Gray gave up all the little strength of speaking which he had, to teaching Harry in the very manner which Mr. Horner most desired.

As for Gregson the father—he—wild man of the woods, poacher, tinker, jack-of-all-trades—was getting tamed by this kindness to his child. Hitherto his hand had been against every man, as every man's had been against him. That affair before the justice, which I told you about, when Mr. Gray and even my lady had interested themselves to get him released from unjust imprisonment, was the first bit of justice he had ever met with; it attracted him to the people, and attached him to the spot on which he had but squatted for a time. I am not sure if any of the villagers were grateful to him for remaining in their neighbourhood, instead of decamping as he had often done before, for good reasons, doubtless, of personal safety. Harry was only one out of a brood of ten or twelve children, some of whom had earned for themselves no good character in service: one, indeed, had been actually transported, for a robbery committed in a distant part of the county; and the tale was yet told in the village of how Gregson the father came back from the trial in a state of wild rage, striding through the place, and uttering oaths of vengeance to himself, his great black eyes gleaming out of his matted hair, and his arms working by his side, and now and then tossed up in his impotent despair. As I heard the account, his wife followed him, child-laden and weeping. After this, they had vanished from the country for a time, leaving their mud hovel locked up, and the door-key, as the neighbours said, buried in a hedge bank. The Gregsons had reappeared much about the same time that Mr. Gray came to Hanbury. He had either never heard of their evil character, or considered that it gave them all the more claims upon his Christian care; and the end of it was, that this rough, untamed, strong giant of a heathen was loyal slave to the weak, hectic, nervous, self-distrustful parson. Gregson had also a kind of grumbling respect for Mr. Horner: he did not quite like the steward's monopoly of his Harry: the mother submitted to that with a better grace, swallowing down her maternal jealousy in the prospect of her child's advancement to a better and more respectable position than that in which his parents had struggled through life. But Mr. Horner, the steward, and Gregson, the poacher and squatter, had come into disagreeable contact too often in former days for them to be perfectly cordial at any future time. Even now, when there was no immediate cause for anything but gratitude for his child's sake on Gregson's part, he would skulk out of Mr. Horner's way, if he saw him coming; and it took all Mr. Horner's natural reserve and acquired self-restraint to keep him from occasionally holding up his father's life as a warning to Harry. Now Gregson had nothing of this desire for avoidance with regard to Mr. Gray. The poacher had a feeling of physical protection towards the parson; while the latter had shown the moral courage, without which Gregson would never have respected him, in coming right down upon him more than once in the exercise of unlawful pursuits, and simply and boldly telling him he was doing wrong, with such a quiet reliance upon Gregson's better feeling, at the same time, that the strong poacher could not have lifted a finger against Mr. Gray, though it had been to save himself from being apprehended and taken to the lock-ups the very next hour. He had rather listened to the parson's bold words with an approving smile, much as Mr. Gulliver might have hearkened to a lecture from a Lilliputian. But when brave words passed into kind deeds, Gregson's heart mutely acknowledged its master and keeper. And the beauty of it all was, that Mr. Gray knew nothing of the good work he had done, or recognised himself as the instrument which God had employed. He thanked God, it is true, fervently and often, that the work was done; and loved the wild man for his rough gratitude; but it never occurred to the poor young clergyman, lying on his sick-bed, and praying, as Miss Galindo had told us he did, to be forgiven for his unprofitable life, to think of Gregson's reclaimed soul as anything with which he had had to do. It was now more than three months since Mr. Gray had been at Hanbury Court. During all that time he had been confined to his house, if not to his sick-bed, and he and my lady had never met since their last discussion and difference about Farmer Hale's barn.

This was not my dear lady's fault; no one could have been more attentive in every way to the slightest possible want of either of the invalids, especially of Mr. Gray. And she would have gone to see him at his own house, as she sent him word, but that her foot had slipped upon the polished oak staircase, and her ankle had been sprained.

So we had never seen Mr. Gray since his illness, when one November day he was announced as wishing to speak to my lady. She was sitting in her room—the room in which I lay now pretty constantly—and I remember she looked startled, when word was brought to her of Mr. Gray's being at the Hall.

She could not go to him, she was too lame for that, so she bade him be shown into where she sat.

"Such a day for him to go out!" she exclaimed, looking at the fog which had crept up to the windows, and was sapping the little remaining life in the brilliant Virginian creeper leaves that draperied the house on the terrace side.

He came in white, trembling, his large eyes wild and dilated. He hastened up to Lady Ludlow's chair, and, to my surprise, took one of her hands and kissed it, without speaking, yet shaking all over.

"Mr. Gray!" said she, quickly, with sharp, tremulous apprehension of some unknown evil. "What is it? There is something unusual about you."

"Something unusual has occurred," replied he, forcing his words to be calm, as with a great effort. "A gentleman came to my house, not half an hour ago—a Mr. Howard. He came straight from Vienna."

"My son!" said my dear lady, stretching out her arms in dumb questioning attitude.

"The Lord gave and the Lord taketh away. Blessed be the name of the Lord."

But my poor lady could not echo the words. He was the last remaining child. And once she had been the joyful mother of nine.

CHAPTER XII

I AM ashamed to say what feeling became strongest in my mind about this time; next to the sympathy we all of us felt for my dear lady in her deep sorrow, I mean; for that was greater and stronger than anything else, however contradictory you may think it, when you hear all.

It might arise from my being so far from well at the time, which produced a diseased mind in a diseased body; but I was absolutely jealous for my father's memory, when I saw how many signs of grief there were for my lord's death, he having done next to nothing for the village and parish, which now changed, as it were, its daily course of life, because his lordship died in a far-off city. My father had spent the best years of his manhood in labouring hard, body and soul, for the people amongst whom he lived. His family, of course, claimed the first place in his heart; he would have been good for little, even in the way of benevolence, if they had not. But close after them he cared for his parishioners, and neighbours. And yet, when he died, though the church-bells tolled, and smote upon our hearts with hard, fresh pain at every beat, the sounds of every-day life still went on, close pressing around us,—carts and carriages, street-cries, distant barrel-organs (the kindly neighbours kept them out of our street): life, active, noisy life, pressed on our acute consciousness of Death, and jarred upon it as on a quick nerve.

And when we went to church,—my father's own church,— though the pulpit cushions were black, and many of the congregation had put on some humble sign of mourning, yet it did not alter the whole material aspect of the place. And yet what was Lord Ludlow's relation to Hanbury, compared to my father's work and place in ——?

O! it was very wicked in me! I think if I had seen my lady, —if I had dared to ask to go to her, I should not have felt so miserable, so discontented. But she sat in her own room, hung with black, all, even over the shutters. She saw no light but that which was artificial—candles, lamps, and the like—for more than a month. Only Adams went near her. Mr. Gray was not admitted, though he called daily. Even Mrs. Medlicott did not see her for near a fortnight. The sight of my lady's griefs, or rather the recollection of it, made Mrs. Medlicott talk far more than was her wont. She told us, with many tears, and much gesticulation, even speaking German at times, when her English would not flow, that my lady sat there, a white figure in the middle of the darkened room; a shaded lamp near her, the light of which fell on an open Bible,—the great family Bible. It was not open at any chapter or consoling verse; but at the page whereon were registered the births of her nine children. Five had died in infancy,—sacrificed to the cruel system which forbade the mother to suckle her babies. Four had lived longer; Urian had been the first to die, Ughtred-Mortimar, Earl Ludlow, the last.

My lady did not cry, Mrs. Medlicott said. She was quite composed; very still, very silent. She put aside everything that savoured of mere business: sent people to Mr. Horner for that. But she was proudly alive to every possible form which might do honour to the last of her race.

In those days, expresses were slow things, and forms still slower. Before my lady's directions could reach Vienna, my lord was buried. There was some talk (so Mrs. Medlicott said) about taking the body up, and bringing him to Hanbury. But his executors,—connections on the Ludlow side,—demurred to this. If he were removed to England, he must be carried on to Scotland, and interred with his Monkshaven forefathers. My lady, deeply hurt, withdrew from the discussion, before it degenerated to an unseemly contest. But all the more, for this understood mortification of my lady's, did the whole village and estate of Hanbury assume every outward sign of mourning. The church bells tolled morning and evening. The church itself was draped in black inside. Hatchments were placed everywhere, where hatchments could be put. All the tenantry spoke in hushed voices for more than a week, scarcely daring to observe that all flesh, even that of an Earl Ludlow, and the last of the Hanburys, was but grass after all. The very Fighting Lion closed its front door, front shutters it had none, and those who needed drink stole in at the back, and were silent and maudlin over their cups, instead of riotous and noisy. Miss Galindo's eyes were swollen up with crying, and she told me, with a fresh burst of tears, that even humpbacked Sally had been found sobbing over her Bible, and using a pocket-handkerchief for the first time in her life; her aprons having hitherto stood her in the necessary stead, but not being sufficiently in accordance with etiquette to be used when mourning over an earl's premature decease.

If it was this way out of the Hall, " you might work it by the rule of three," as Miss Galindo used to say, and judge what it was in the Hall. We none of us spoke but in a whisper: we tried not to eat; and indeed the shock had been so really great, and we did really care so much for my lady, that for some days we had but little appetite. But after that I fear our sympathy grew weaker, while our flesh grew stronger. But we still spoke low, and our hearts ached whenever we thought of my lady sitting there alone in the darkened room, with the light ever falling on that one solemn page.

We wished, O how I wished that she would see Mr. Gray! But Adams said, she thought my lady ought to have a bishop come to see her. Still no one had authority enough to send for one.

Mr. Horner all this time was suffering as much as any one. He was too faithful a servant of the great Hanbury family, though now the family had dwindled down to a fragile old lady, not to mourn acutely over its probable extinction. He had, besides, a deeper sympathy and reverence with, and for, my lady in all things, than probably he ever cared to show, for his manners were always measured and cold. He suffered from sorrow. He also suffered from wrong. My lord's executors kept writing to him continually. My lady refused to listen to mere business, saying she intrusted all to him. But the " all " was more complicated than I ever thoroughly understood. As far as I comprehended the case, it was something of this kind:—There had been a mortgage raised on my lady's property of Hanbury, to enable my lord, her husband, to spend money in cultivating his Scotch estates, after some new fashion that required capital. As long as my lord, her son, lived, who was to succeed to both the estates after her death, this did not signify; so she had said and felt; and she had refused to take any steps to secure the repayment of capital, or even the payment of the interest of the mortgage from the possible representatives and possessors of the Scotch estates, to the possible owner of the Hanbury property; saying it ill became her to calculate on the contingency of her son's death.

But he had died childless, unmarried. The heir of the Monkshaven property was an Edinburgh advocate, a far-away kinsman of my lord's: the Hanbury property, at my lady's death, would go to the descendants of a third son of the Squire Hanbury in the days of Queen Anne.

This complication of affairs was most grievous to Mr. Horner. He had always been opposed to the mortgage; had hated the payment of the interest, as obliging my lady to practise certain economies which, though she took care to make them as personal as possible, he disliked as derogatory to the family. Poor Mr. Horner! He was so cold and hard in his manner, so curt and decisive in his speech, that I don't think we any of us did him justice. Miss Galindo was almost the first, at this time, to speak a kind word of him, or to take thought of him at all, any farther than to get out of his way when we saw him approaching.

"I don't think Mr. Horner is well," she said one day, about three weeks after we had heard of my lord's death. "He sits resting his head on his hand, and hardly hears me when I speak to him."

But I thought no more of it, as Miss Galindo did not name it again. My lady came amongst us once more. From elderly she had become old; a little, frail, old lady, in heavy black drapery, never speaking about nor alluding to her great sorrow; quieter, gentler, paler, than ever before; and her eyes dim with much weeping, never witnessed by mortal.

She had seen Mr. Gray at the expiration of the month of deep retirement. But I do not think that even to him she had said one word of her own particular individual sorrow. All mention of it seemed buried deep for evermore. One day, Mr. Horner sent word that he was too much indisposed to attend to his usual business at the Hall; but he wrote down some directions and requests to Miss Galindo, saying that he would be at his office early the next morning. The next morning he was dead.

Miss Galindo told my lady. Miss Galindo herself cried plentifully, but my lady, although very much distressed, could not cry. It seemed a physical impossibility, as if she had shed all the tears in her power. Moreover, I almost think her wonder was far greater that she herself lived than that Mr. Horner died. It was almost natural that so faithful a servant should break his heart, when the family he belonged to lost their stay, their heir, and their last hope.

Yes! Mr. Horner was a faithful servant. I do not think there are many so faithful now; but perhaps that is an old woman's fancy of mine. When his will came to be examined, it was discovered that, soon after Harry Gregson's accident, Mr. Horner had left the few thousands (three, I think), of which he was possessed, in trust for Harry's benefit, desiring his executors to see that the lad was well educated in certain things, for which Mr. Horner had thought that he had shown especial aptitude; and there was a kind of implied apology to my lady in one sentence, where he stated that Harry's lameness would prevent his being ever able to gain his living by the exercise of any mere bodily faculties, " as had been wished by a lady whose wishes " he, the testator, " was bound to regard."

But there was a codicil in the will, dated since Lord Ludlow's death—feebly written by Mr. Horner himself, as if in preparation only for some more formal manner of bequest: or, perhaps, only as a mere temporary arrangement till he could see a lawyer, and have a fresh will made. In this he revoked his previous bequest to Harry Gregson. He only left two hundred pounds to Mr. Gray to be used, as that gentleman thought best, for Henry Gregson's benefit. With this one exception, he bequeathed all the rest of his savings to my lady, w th a hope that they might form a nest-egg, as it were, towards the paying off of the mortgage which had been such a grief to him during his life. I may not repeat all this in lawyer's phrase; I heard it through Miss Galindo, and she might make mistakes. Though, indeed, she was very clear-headed, and soon earned the respect of Mr. Smithson, my lady's lawyer from Warwick. Mr. Smithson knew Miss Galindo a little before, both personally and by reputation; but I don't think he was prepared to find her installed as steward's clerk, and, at first, he was inclined to treat her, in this capacity, with polite contempt. But Miss Galindo was both a lady and a spirited, sensible woman, and she could put aside her self-indulgence in eccentricity of speech and manner whenever she chose. Nay more; she was usually so talkative, that if she had not been amusing and warm-hearted, one might have thought her wearisome occasionally. But to meet Mr. Smithson she came out daily in her Sunday gown; she said no more than was required in answer to his questions; her books and papers were in thorough order and methodically kept; her statements of matters-of-fact accurate and to be relied on. She was amusingly conscious of her victory over his contempt of a woman-clerk and his preconceived opinion of her unpractical eccentricity.

"Let me alone," said she, one day when she came in to sit awhile with me. "That man is a good man—a sensible man—and I have no doubt he is a good lawyer; but he can't fathom women yet. I make no doubt he'll go back to Warwick, and never give credit again to those people who made him think me half-cracked to begin with. O, my dear, he did! He showed it twenty times worse than my poor dear master ever did. It was a form to be gone through to please my lady, and, for her sake, he would hear my statements and see my books. It was eeping a woman out of harm's way, at any rate, to let her fancy herself useful. I read the man. And, I am thinkful to say, he cannot read me. At least, only one side of me. When I see an end to be gained, I can behave myself accordingly. Here was a man who thought that a woman in a black silk gown was a respectable, orderly kind of person; and I was a woman in a black silk gown. He believed that a woman could not write straight lines, and required a man to tell her that two and two made four. I was not above ruling my books, and had Cocker a little more at my finger's ends than he had. But my greatest triumph has been holding my tongue. He would have thought nothing of my books, or my sums, or my black silk gown, if I had spoken unasked. So I have buried more sense in my bosom these ten days than ever I have uttered in the whole course of my life before. I have been so curt, so abrupt, so abominably dull, that I'll answer for it he thinks me worthy to be a man. But I must go back to him, my dear, so good-bye to conversation and you."

But though Mr. Smithson might be satisfied with Miss Galindo, I am afraid she was the only part of the affair with which he was content. Everything else went wrong. I could not say who told me so—but the conviction of this seemed to pervade the house. I never knew how much we had all looked up to the silent, gruff Mr. Horner for decisions, until he was gone. My lady herself was a pretty good woman of business, as women of business go. Her father, seeing that she would be the heiress of the Hanbury property, had given her a training which was thought unusual in those days, and she liked to feel herself queen regnant, and to have to decide in all cases between herself and her tenantry. But, perhaps, Mr. Horner would have done it more wisely; not but what she always attended to him at last. She would begin by saying, pretty clearly and promptly, what she would have done, and what she would not have done. If Mr. Horner approved of it, he bowed, and set about obeying her directly; if he disapproved of it, he bowed, and lingered so long before he obeyed her, that she forced his opinion out of him with her " Well, Mr. Horner! and what have you to say against it? " For she always understood his silence as well as if he had spoken. But the estate was pressed for ready money, and Mr. Horner had grown gloomy and languid since the death of his wife, and even his own personal affairs were not in the order in which they had been a year or two before, for his old clerk had gradually become superannuated, or, at any rate, unable by the superfluity of his own energy and wit to supply the spirit that was wanting in Mr. Horner.

Day after day, Mr. Smithson seemed to grow more fidgety, more annoyed at the state of affairs. Like every one else employed by Lady Ludlow, as far as I could learn, he had an hereditary tie to the Hanbury family. As long as the Smithsons had been lawyers, they had been lawyers to the Hanburys; always coming in on all great family occasions, and better able to understand the characters, and connect the links of what had once been a large and scattered family, than any individual thereof had ever been.

As long as a man was at the head of the Hanburys, the lawyers had simply acted as servants, and had only given their advice when it was required. But they had assumed a different position on the memorable occasion of the mortgage: they had remonstrated against it. My lady had resented this remonstrance, and a slight, unspoken coolness had existed between her and the father of this Mr. Smithson ever since.

I was very sorry for my lady. Mr. Smithson was inclined to blame Mr. Horner for the disorderly state in which he found some of the outlying farms, and for the deficiencies in the annual payment of rents. Mr. Smithson had too much good feeling to put this blame into words; but my lady's quick instinct led her to reply to a thought, the existence of which she perceived; and she quietly told the truth, and explained how she had interfered repeatedly to prevent Mr. Horner from taking certain desirable steps, which were discordant to her hereditary sense of right and wrong between landlord and tenant. She also spoke of the want of ready money as a misfortune that could be remedied, by more economical personal expenditure on her own part; by which individual saving it was possible that a reduction of fifty pounds a year might have been accomplished. But as soon as Mr. Smithson touched on larger economies, such as either affected the welfare of others, or the honour and standing of the great House of Hanbury, she was inflexible. Her establishment consisted of somewhere about forty servants, of whom nearly as many as twenty were unable to perform their work properly, and yet would have been hurt if they had been dismissed; so they had the credit of fulfilling duties, while my lady paid and kept their substitutes. Mr. Smithson made a calculation, and would have saved some hundreds a year by pensioning off these old servants. But my lady would not hear of it. Then, again, I know privately that he urged her to allow some of us to return to our homes. Bitterly we should have regretted the separation from Lady Ludlow; but we would have gone back gladly, had we known at the time that her circumstances required it: but she would not listen to the proposal for a moment.

"If I cannot act justly towards every one, I will give up a plan which has been a source of much satisfaction; at least, I will not carry it out to such an extent in future. But to these young ladies, who do me the favour to live with me at present, I stand pledged. I cannot go back from my word, Mr. Smithson. We had better talk no more of this."

As she spoke, she entered the room where I lay. She and Mr. Smithson were coming for some papers contained in the bureau. They did not know I was there, and Mr. Smithson started a little when he saw me, as he must have been aware that I had overheard something. But my lady did not change a muscle of her face. All the world might overhear her kind, just, pure sayings, and she had no fear of their misconstruction. She came up to me, and kissed me on the forehead, and then went to search for the required papers.

"I rode over the Conington farms yesterday, my lady. I must say I was quite grieved to see the condition they are in; all the land that is not waste is utterly exhausted with working successive white crops. Not a pinch of manure laid on the ground for years. I must say that a greater contrast could never have been presented than that between Harding's farm and the next fields—fences in perfect order, rotation crops, sheep eating down the turnips on the waste lands—everything that could be desired."

"Whose farm is that?" asked my lady.

"Why, I am sorry to say, it was on none of your ladyship's that I saw such good methods adopted. I hoped it was, I stopped my horse to inquire. A queer-looking man, sitting on his horse like a tailor, watching his men with a couple of the sharpest eyes I ever saw, and dropping his h's at every word, answered my question, and told me it was his. I could not go on asking him who he was; but I fell into conversation with him, and I gathered that he had earned some money in trade in Birmingham, and had bought the estate (five hundred acres, I think he said), on which he was born, and now was setting himself to cultivate it in downright earnest, going to Holkham and Woburn, and half the country over, to get himself up on the subject."

"It would be Brooke, that dissenting baker from Birmingham," said my lady in her most icy tone. "Mr. Smithson, I am sorry I have been detaining you so long, but I think these are the letters you wished to see."

If her ladyship thought by this speech to quench Mr.

Smithson she was mistaken. Mr. Smithson just looked at the letters, and went on with the old subject.

"Now, my lady, it struck me that if you had such a man to take poor Horner's place, he would work the rents and the land round most satisfactorily. I should not despair of inducing this very man to undertake the work. I should not mind speaking to him myself on the subject, for we got capital friends over a snack of luncheon that he asked me to share with him."

Lady Ludlow fixed her eyes on Mr. Smithson as he spoke, and never took them off his face until he had ended. She was silent a minute before she answered.

"You are very good, Mr. Smithson, but I need not trouble you with any such arrangements. I am going to write this afternoon to Captain James, a friend of one of my sons, who has, I hear, been severely wounded at Trafalgar, to request him to honour me by accepting Mr. Horner's situation."

"A Captain James! A captain in the navy! going to manage your ladyship's estate!"

"If he will be so kind. I shall esteem it a condescension on his part; but I hear that he will have to resign his profession, his state of health is so bad, and a country life is especially prescribed for him. I am in some hopes of tempting him here, as I learn he has but little to depend on if he gives up his profession."

"A Captain James! an invalid captain!"

"You think I am asking too great a favour," continued my lady. (I never could tell how far it was simplicity, or how far a kind of innocent malice, that made her misinterpret Mr. Smithson's words and looks as she did.) "But he is not a post-captain, only a commander, and his pension will be but small. I may be able, by offering him country air and a healthy occupation, to restore him to health."

"Occupation! My lady, may I ask how a sailor is to manage land? Why, your tenants will laugh him to scorn."

"My tenants, I trust, will not behave so ill as to laugh at any one I choose to set over them. Captain James has had experience in managing men. He has remarkable practical talents, and great common sense, as I hear from every one. But, whatever he may be, the affair rests between him and myself. I can only say I shall esteem myself fortunate if he comes."

There was no more to be said, after my lady spoke in this manner. I had heard her mention Captain James before, as a

middy who had been very kind to her son Urian. I thought
I remembered then that she had mentioned that his family
circumstances were not very prosperous. But, I confess, that
little as I knew of the management of land, I quite sided with Mr.
Smithson. He, silently prohibited from again speaking to my
lady on the subject, opened his mind to Miss Galindo, from
whom I was pretty sure to hear all the opinions and news of the
household and village. She had taken a great fancy to me,
because she said I talked so agreeably. I believe it was because
I listened so well.

"Well, have you heard the news," she began, "about this
Captain James? A sailor—with a wooden leg, I have no doubt.
What would the poor, dear, deceased master have said to it, if he
had known who was to be his successor! My dear, I have often
thought of the postman's bringing me a letter as one of the
pleasures I shall miss in heaven. But, really, I think Mr. Horner
may be thankful he has got out of the reach of news; or else he
would hear of Mr. Smithson's having made up to the Birmingham baker, and of this one-legged captain, coming to dot-and-go-
one over the estate. I suppose he will look after the labourers
through a spy-glass. I only hope he won't stick in the mud with
his wooden leg; for I, for one, won't help him out. Yes, I
would," said she, correcting herself; "I would, for my lady's
sake."

"But are you sure he has a wooden leg?" asked I. "I heard
Lady Ludlow tell Mr. Smithson about him, and she only spoke
of him as wounded."

"Well, sailors are almost always wounded in the leg. Look
at Greenwich Hospital! I should say there were twenty one-
legged pensioners to one without an arm there. But say he has
got half-a-dozen legs: what has he to do with managing land?
I shall think him very impudent if he comes, taking advantage of
my lady's kind heart."

However, come he did. In a month from that time, the
carriage was sent to meet Captain James; just as three years
before it had been sent to meet me. His coming had been so
much talked about that we were all as curious as possible to see
him, and to know how so unusual an experiment, as it seemed
to us, would answer. But, before I tell you anything about our
new agent, I must speak of something quite as interesting, and
I really think quite as important. And this was my lady's
making friends with Harry Gregson. I do believe she did it for
Mr. Horner's sake; but, of course, I can only conjecture why

my lady did anything. But I heard one day, from Mary Legard, that my lady had sent for Harry to come and see her, if he was well enough to walk so far; and the next day he was shown into the room he had been in once before under such unlucky circumstances.

The lad looked pale enough, as he stood propping himself up on his crutch, and the instant my lady saw him, she bade John Footman place a stool for him to sit down upon while she spoke to him. It might be his paleness that gave his whole face a more refined and gentle look; but I suspect it was that the boy was apt to take impressions, and that Mr. Horner's grave, dignified ways, and Mr. Gray's tender and quiet manners, had altered him; and then the thoughts of illness and death seem to turn many of us into gentlemen and gentlewomen, as long as such thoughts are in our minds. We cannot speak loudly or angrily at such times; we are not apt to be eager about mere worldly things, for our very awe at our quickened sense of the nearness of the invisible world, makes us calm and serene about the petty trifles of to-day. At least, I know that was the explanation Mr. Gray once gave me of what we all thought the great improvement in Harry Gregson's way of behaving.

My lady hesitated so long about what she had best say, that Harry grew a little frightened at her silence. A few months ago it would have surprised me more than it did now; but since my lord her son's death, she had seemed altered in many ways— more uncertain and distrustful of herself, as it were.

At last she said, and I think the tears were in her eyes: " My poor little fellow, you have had a narrow escape with your life since I saw you last."

To this there was nothing to be said but " Yes; " and again there was silence.

" And you have lost a good, kind friend, in Mr. Horner."

The boy's lips worked, and I think he said, " Please, don't." But I can't be sure; at any rate, my lady went on:

" And so have I—a good, kind friend, he was to both of us; and to you he wished to show his kindness in even a more generous way than he has done. Mr. Gray has told you about his legacy to you, has he not? "

There was no sign of eager joy on the lad's face, as if he realised the power and pleasure of having what to him must have seemed like a fortune.

" Mr. Gray said as how he had left me a matter of money."

" Yes, he has left you two hundred pounds."

"But I would rather have had him alive, my lady," he burst out, sobbing as if his heart would break.

"My lad, I believe you. We would rather have had our dead alive, would we not? and there is nothing in money that can comfort us for their loss. But you know—Mr. Gray has told you—who has appointed all our times to die. Mr. Horner was a good, just man; and has done well and kindly, both by me and you. You perhaps do not know" (and now I understood what my lady had been making up her mind to say to Harry, all the time she was hesitating how to begin) "that Mr. Horner, at one time, meant to leave you a great deal more; probably all he had, with the exception of a legacy to his old clerk, Morrison. But he knew that this estate—on which my forefathers had lived for six hundred years—was in debt, and that I had no immediate chance of paying off this debt; and yet he felt that it was a very sad thing for an old property like this to belong in part to those other men, who had lent the money. You understand me, I think, my little man?" said she, questioning Harry's face.

He had left off crying, and was trying to understand, with all his might and main; and I think he had got a pretty good general idea of the state of affairs; though probably he was puzzled by the term "the estate being in debt." But he was sufficiently interested to want my lady to go on; and he nodded his head at her, to signify this to her.

"So Mr. Horner took the money which he once meant to be yours, and has left the greater part of it to me, with the intention of helping me to pay off this debt I have told you about. It will go a long way, and I shall try hard to save the rest, and then I shall die happy in leaving the land free from debt." She paused. "But I shall not die happy in thinking of you. I do not know if having money, or even having a great estate and much honour, is a good thing for any of us. But God sees fit that some of us should be called to this condition, and it is our duty then to stand by our posts, like brave soldiers. Now, Mr. Horner intended you to have this money first. I shall only call it borrowing from you, Harry Gregson, if I take it and use it to pay off the debt. I shall pay Mr. Gray interest on this money, because he is to stand as your guardian, as it were, till you come of age; and he must fix what ought to be done with it, so as to fit you for spending the principal rightly when the estate can repay it you. I suppose, now, it will be right for you to be educated. That will be another snare that will come with your money. But have courage, Harry. Both education and money may be used rightly, if we only pray against the temptations they bring with them."

Harry could make no answer, though I am sure he understood it all. My lady wanted to get him to talk to her a little, by way of becoming acquainted with what was passing in his mind; and she asked him what he would like to have done with his money, if he could have part of it now? To such a simple question, involving no talk about feelings, his answer came readily enough.

"Build a cottage for father, with stairs in it, and give Mr. Gray a school-house. O, father does so want Mr. Gray for to have his wish! Father saw all the stones lying quarried and hewn on Farmer Hale's land; Mr. Gray had paid for them all himself. And father said he would work night and day, and little Tommy should carry mortar, if the parson would let him, sooner than that he should be fretted and frabbed as he was, with no one giving him a helping hand or a kind word."

Harry knew nothing of my lady's part in the affair; that was very clear. My lady kept silence.

"If I might have a piece of my money, I would buy land from Mr. Brooke; he has got a bit to sell just at the corner of Hendon Lane, and I would give it to Mr. Gray; and, perhaps, if your ladyship thinks I may be learned again, I might grow up into the schoolmaster."

"You are a good boy," said my lady. "But there are more things to be thought of, in carrying out such a plan, than you are aware of. However, it shall be tried."

"The school, my lady?" I exclaimed, almost thinking she did not know what she was saying.

"Yes, the school. For Mr. Horner's sake, for Mr. Gray's sake, and last, not least, for this lad's sake, I will give the new plan a trial. Ask Mr. Gray to come up to me this afternoon about the land he wants. He need not go to a Dissenter for it. And tell your father he shall have a good share in the building of it, and Tommy shall carry the mortar."

"And I may be schoolmaster?" asked Harry, eagerly.

"We'll see about that," said my lady, amused. "It will be some time before that plan comes to pass, my little fellow."

And now to return to Captain James. My first account of him was from Miss Galindo.

"He's not above thirty; and I must just pack up my pens and my paper, and be off; for it would be the height of impropriety for me to be staying here as his clerk. It was all very well in the old master's days. But here am I, not fifty till next May, and this young, unmarried man, who is not even a widower! O, there would be no end of gossip. Besides he looks as askance at me as I do at him. My black silk gown had no effect. He's afraid I shall marry him. But I won't; he may feel himself quite safe from that. And Mr. Smithson has been recommending a clerk to my lady. She would far rather keep me on; but I can't stop. I really could not think it proper."

"What sort of a looking man is he?"

"O, nothing particular. Short, and brown, and sunburnt. I did not think it became me to look at him. Well, now for the nightcaps. I should have grudged any one else doing them, for I have got such a pretty pattern!"

But when it came to Miss Galindo's leaving, there was a great misunderstanding between her and my lady. Miss Galindo had imagined that my lady had asked her as a favour to copy the letters, and enter the accounts, and had agreed to do the work without the notion of being paid for so doing. She had, now and then, grieved over a very profitable order for needlework passing out of her hands on account of her not having time to do it, because of her occupation at the Hall; but she had never hinted this to my lady, but gone on cheerfully at her writing as long as her clerkship was required. My lady was annoyed that she had not made her intention of paying Miss Galindo more clear, in the first conversation she had had with her; but I suppose that she had been too delicate to be very explicit with regard to money matters; and now Miss Galindo was quite hurt at my lady's wanting to pay her for what she had done in such right-down good-will.

"No," Miss Galindo said; "my own dear lady, you may be as angry with me as you like, but don't offer me money. Think of six-and-twenty years ago, and poor Arthur, and as you were to me then! Besides, I wanted money—I don't disguise it—for a particular purpose; and when I found that (God bless you for asking me!) I could do you a service, I turned it over in my mind, and I gave up one plan and took up another, and it's all settled now. Bessy is to leave school and come and live with me. Don't, please, offer me money again. You don't know how glad I have been to do anything for you. Have not I, Margaret Dawson? Did you not hear me say, one day, I would cut off my hand for my lady; for am I a stock or a stone, that I should forget kindness? O, I have been so glad to work for you. And now Bessy is coming here; and no one knows anything about her—as if she had done anything wrong, poor child!"

"Dear Miss Galindo," replied my lady, "I will never ask you to take money again. Only I thought it was quite understood between us. And you know you have taken money for a set of morning wrappers, before now."

"Yes, my lady; but that was not confidential. Now I was so proud to have something to do for you confidentially."

"But who is Bessy?" asked my lady. "I do not understand who she is, or why she is to come and live with you. Dear Miss Galindo, you must honour me by being confidential with me in your turn!"

CHAPTER XIII

I HAD always understood that Miss Galindo had once been in much better circumstances, but I had never liked to ask any questions respecting her. But about this time many things came out respecting her former life, which I will try and arrange: not, however, in the order in which I heard them, but rather as they occurred.

Miss Galindo was the daughter of a clergyman in Westmoreland. Her father was the younger brother of a baronet, his ancestor having been one of those of James the First's creation. This baronet-uncle of Miss Galindo was one of the queer, out-of-the-way people who were bred at that time, and in that northern district of England. I never heard much of him from any one, besides this one great fact: that he had early disappeared from his family, which indeed only consisted of a brother and sister who died unmarried, and lived no one knew where—somewhere on the Continent, it was supposed, for he had never returned from the grand tour which he had been sent to make, according to the general fashion of the day, as soon as he had left Oxford. He corresponded occasionally with his brother the clergyman; but the letters passed through a banker's hands; the banker being pledged to secrecy, and, as he told Mr. Galindo, having the penalty, if he broke his pledge, of losing the whole profitable business, and of having the management of the baronet's affairs taken out of his hands, without any advantage accruing to the inquirer, for Sir Lawrence had told Messrs. Graham that, in case his place of residence was revealed by them, not only would he cease to bank with them, but instantly take measures to baffle any future inquiries as to his whereabouts, by removing to some distant country.

Sir Lawrence paid a certain sum of money to his brother's account every year; but the time of this payment varied, and it was sometimes eighteen or nineteen months between the deposits; then, again, it would not be above a quarter of the time, showing that he intended it to be annual, but, as this intention was never expressed in words, it was impossible to rely upon it, and a great deal of this money was swallowed up by the necessity Mr. Galindo felt himself under of living in the large, old, rambling family mansion, which had been one of Sir Lawrence's rarely expressed desires. Mr. and Mrs. Galindo often planned to live upon their own small fortune and the income derived from the living (a vicarage, of which the great tithes went to Sir Lawrence as lay impropriator), so as to put by the payments made by the baronet, for the benefit of Laurentia—our Miss Galindo. But I suppose they found it difficult to live economically in a large house, even though they had it rent free. They had to keep up with hereditary neighbours and friends, and could hardly help doing it in the hereditary manner.

One of these neighbours, a Mr. Gibson, had a son a few years older than Laurentia. The families were sufficiently intimate for the young people to see a good deal of each other: and I was told that this young Mr. Mark Gibson was an unusually prepossessing man (he seemed to have impressed every one who spoke of him to me as being a handsome, manly, kind-hearted fellow), just what a girl would be sure to find most agreeable. The parents either forgot that their children were growing up to man's and woman's estate, or thought that the intimacy and probable attachment would be no bad thing, even if it did lead to a marriage. Still, nothing was ever said by young Gibson till later on, when it was too late, as it turned out. He went to and from Oxford; he shot and fished with Mr. Galindo, or came to the Mere to skate in winter-time; was asked to accompany Mr. Galindo to the Hall, as the latter returned to the quiet dinner with his wife and daughter; and so, and so, it went on, nobody much knew how, until one day, when Mr. Galindo received a formal letter from his brother's bankers, announcing Sir Lawrence's death, of malaria fever, at Albano, and congratulating Sir Hubert on his accession to the estates and the baronetcy. The king is dead—" Long live the king!" as I have since heard that the French express it.

Sir Hubert and his wife were greatly surprised. Sir Lawrence was but two years older than his brother; and they had never heard of any illness till they heard of his death. They were sorry; very much shocked; but still a little elated at the succession to the baronetcy and estates. The London bankers had managed everything well. There was a large sum of ready money in their hands, at Sir Hubert's service, until he should touch his rents, the rent-roll being eight thousand a year. And only Laurentia to inherit it all! Her mother, a poor clergyman's daughter, began to plan all sorts of fine marriages for her; nor was her father much behind his wife in his ambition. They took her up to London, when they went to buy new carriages, and dresses, and furniture. And it was then and there she made my lady's acquaintance. How it was that they came to take a fancy to each other, I cannot say. My lady was of the old nobility—grand, composed, gentle, and stately in her ways. Miss Galindo must always have been hurried in her manner, and her energy must have shown itself in inquisitiveness and oddness even in her youth. But I don't pretend to account for things: I only narrate them. And the fact was this:—that the elegant, fastidious countess was attracted to the country girl, who on her part almost worshipped my lady. My lady's notice of their daughter made her parents think, I suppose, that there was no match that she might not command; she, the heiress of eight thousand a year, and visiting about among earls and dukes. So when they came back to their old Westmoreland Hall, and Mark Gibson rode over to offer his hand and his heart, and prospective estate of nine hundred a year, to his old companion and playfellow, Laurentia, Sir Hubert and Lady Galindo made very short work of it. They refused him plumply themselves; and when he begged to be allowed to speak to Laurentia, they found some excuse for refusing him the opportunity of so doing, until they had talked to her themselves, and brought up every argument and fact in their power to convince her—a plain girl, and conscious of her plainness—that Mr. Mark Gibson had never thought of her in the way of marriage till after her father's accession to his fortune; and that it was the estate—not the young lady—that he was in love with. I suppose it will never be known in this world how far this supposition of theirs was true. My Lady Ludlow had always spoken as if it was; but perhaps events, which came to her knowledge about this time, altered her opinion. At any rate, the end of it was, Laurentia refused Mark, and almost broke her heart in doing so. He discovered the suspicions of Sir Hubert and Lady Galindo, and that they had persuaded their daughter to share in them. So he flung off with high words, saying that they did not know a true heart

when they met with one; and that although he had never
offered till after Sir Lawrence's death, yet that his father knew
all along that he had been attached to Laurentia, only that
he, being the eldest of five children, and having as yet no profession, had had to conceal, rather than to express, an attachment, which, in those days, he had believed was reciprocated.
He had always meant to study for the bar, and the end of all
he had hoped for had been to earn a moderate income, which he
might ask Laurentia to share. This, or something like it, was
what he said. But his reference to his father cut two ways.
Old Mr. Gibson was known to be very keen about money. It
was just as likely that he would urge Mark to make love to the
heiress, now she was an heiress, as that he would have restrained
him previously, as Mark said he had done. When this was
repeated to Mark, he became proudly reserved, or sullen, and
said that Laurentia, at any rate, might have known him better.
He left the country, and went up to London to study law soon
afterwards; and Sir Hubert and Lady Galindo thought they were
well rid of him. But Laurentia never ceased reproaching herself, and never did to her dying day, as I believe. The words,
" She might have known me better," told to her by some kind
friend or other, rankled in her mind, and were never forgotten.
Her father and mother took her up to London the next year;
but she did not care to visit—dreaded going out even for a drive,
lest she should see Mark Gibson's reproachful eyes—-pined and
lost her health. Lady Ludlow saw this change with regret, and
was told the cause by Lady Galindo, who, of course, gave her own
version of Mark's conduct and motives. My lady never spoke
to Miss Galindo about it, but tried constantly to interest and
please her. It was at this time that my lady told Miss Galindo
so much about her own early life, and about Hanbury, that
Miss Galindo resolved, if ever she could, she would go and see
the old place which her friend loved so well. The end of it all
was, that she came to live there, as we know.

But a great change was to come first. Before Sir Hubert and
Lady Galindo had left London on this, their second visit, they
had a letter from the lawyer, whom they employed, saying that
Sir Lawrence had left an heir, his legitimate child by an Italian
woman of low rank; at least, legal claims to the title and
property had been sent into him on the boy's behalf. Sir
Lawrence had always been a man of adventurous and artistic,
rather than of luxurious tastes; and it was supposed, when all
came to be proved at the trial, that he was captivated by the

free, beautiful life they lead in Italy, and had married this Neapolitan fisherman's daughter, who had people about her shrewd enough to see that the ceremony was legally performed. She and her husband had wandered about the shores of the Mediterranean for years, leading a happy, careless, irresponsible life, unencumbered by any duties except those connected with a rather numerous family. It was enough for her that they never wanted money, and that her husband's love was always continued to her. She hated the name of England—wicked, cold, heretic England—and avoided the mention of any subjects connected with her husband's early life. So that, when he died at Albano, she was almost roused out of her vehement grief to anger with the Italian doctor, who declared that he must write to a certain address to announce the death of Lawrence Galindo. For some time, she feared lest English barbarians might come down upon her, making a claim to the children. She hid herself and them in the Abruzzi, living upon the sale of what furniture and jewels Sir Lawrence had died possessed of. When these failed, she returned to Naples, which she had not visited since her marriage. Her father was dead; but her brother inherited some of his keenness. He interested the priests, who made inquiries and found that the Galindo succession was worth securing to an heir of the true faith. They stirred about it, obtained advice at the English Embassy; and hence that letter to the lawyers, calling upon Sir Hubert to relinquish title and property, and to refund what money he had expended. He was vehement in his opposition to this claim. He could not bear to think of his brother having married a foreigner—a papist, a fisherman's daughter; nay, of his having become a papist himself. He was in despair at the thought of his ancestral property going to the issue of such a marriage. He fought tooth and nail, making enemies of his relations, and losing almost all his own private property; for he would go on against the lawyer's advice, long after every one was convinced except himself and his wife. At last he was conquered. He gave up his living in gloomy despair. He would have changed his name if he could, so desirous was he to obliterate all tie between himself and the mongrel papist baronet and his Italian mother, and all the succession of children and nurses who came to take possession of the Hall soon after Mr. Hubert Galindo's departure, stayed there one winter, and then flitted back to Naples with gladness and delight. Mr. and Mrs. Hubert Galindo lived in London. He had obtained a curacy somewhere in the city. They would have been thankful now if Mr. Mark Gibson had renewed his offer. No one could accuse him of mercenary motives if he had done so. Because he did not come forward, as they wished, they brought his silence up as a justification of what they had previously attributed to him. I don't know what Miss Galindo thought herself; but Lady Ludlow has told me how she shrank from hearing her parents abuse him. Lady Ludlow supposed that he was aware that they were living in London. His father must have known the fact, and it was curious if he had never named it to his son. Besides, the name was very uncommon; and it was unlikely that it should never come across him, in the advertisements of charity sermons which the new and rather eloquent curate of Saint Mark's East was asked to preach. All this time Lady Ludlow never lost sight of them, for Miss Galindo's sake. And when the father and mother died, it was my lady who upheld Miss Galindo in her determination not to apply for any provision to her cousin, the Italian baronet, but rather to live upon the hundred a year which had been settled on her mother and the children of his son Hubert's marriage by the old grandfather, Sir Lawrence.

Mr. Mark Gibson had risen to some eminence as a barrister on the Northern Circuit, but had died unmarried in the lifetime of his father, a victim (so people said) to intemperance. Doctor Trevor, the physician who had been called in to Mr. Gray and Harry Gregson, had married a sister of his. And that was all my lady knew about the Gibson family. But who was Bessy?

That mystery and secret came out, too, in process of time. Miss Galindo had been to Warwick, some years before I arrived at Hanbury, on some kind of business or shopping, which can only be transacted in a county town. There was an old West-moreland connection between her and Mrs. Trevor, though I believe the latter was too young to have been made aware of her brother's offer to Miss Galindo at the time when it took place; and such affairs, if they are unsuccessful, are seldom spoken about in the gentleman's family afterwards. But the Gibsons and Galindos had been county neighbours too long for the con-nection not to be kept up between two members settled far away from their early homes. Miss Galindo always desired her parcels to be sent to Dr. Trevor's, when she went to Warwick for shopping purchases. If she were going any journey, and the coach did not come through Warwick as soon as she arrived (in my lady's coach or otherwise) from Hanbury, she went to Doctor Trevor's to wait. She was as much expected to sit down to the household meals as if she had been one of the family; and in after years it was Mrs. Trevor who managed her repository business for her.

So, on the day I spoke of, she had gone to Doctor Trevor's to rest, and possibly to dine. The post in those times came in at all hours of the morning; and Doctor Trevor's letters had not arrived until after his departure on his morning round. Miss Galindo was sitting down to dinner with Mrs. Trevor and her seven children, when the Doctor came in. He was flurried and uncomfortable, and hurried the children away as soon as he decently could. Then (rather feeling Miss Galindo's presence an advantage, both as a present restraint on the violence of his wife's grief, and as a consoler when he was absent on his after-noon round), he told Mrs. Trevor of her brother's death. He had been taken ill on circuit, and had hurried back to his chambers in London only to die. She cried terribly; but Doctor Trevor said afterwards, he never noticed that Miss Galindo cared much about it one way or another. She helped him to soothe his wife, promised to stay with her all the afternoon instead of returning to Hanbury, and afterwards offered to remain with her while the Doctor went to attend the funeral. When they heard of the old love-story between the dead man and Miss Galindo—brought up by mutual friends in Westmore-land, in the review which we are all inclined to take of the events of a man's life when he comes to die—they tried to remember Miss Galindo's speeches and ways of going on during this visit. She was a little pale, a little silent; her eyes were sometimes swollen, and her nose red; but she was at an age when such appearances are generally attributed to a bad cold in the head, rather than to any more sentimental reason. They felt towards her as towards an old friend, a kindly, useful, eccentric old maid. She did not expect more, or wish them to remember that she might once have had other hopes, and more youthful feelings. Doctor Trevor thanked her very warmly for staying with his wife, when he returned home from London (where the funeral had taken place). He begged Miss Galindo to stay with them, when the children were gone to bed, and she was preparing to leave the husband and wife by themselves. He told her and his wife many particulars—then paused—then went on—

" And Mark has left a child—a little girl——"

" But he never was married! " exclaimed Mrs. Trevor.

" A little girl," continued her husband, " whose mother, I conclude, is dead. At any rate, the child was in possession of his chambers; she and an old nurse, who seemed to have the charge of everything, and has cheated poor Mark, I should fancy, not a little."

" But the child!" asked Mrs. Trevor, still almost breathless with astonishment. "How do you know it is his?"

" The nurse told me it was, with great appearance of indignation at my doubting it. I asked the little thing her name, and all I could get was 'Bessy!' and a cry of 'Me wants papa!' The nurse said the mother was dead, and she knew no more about it than that Mr. Gibson had engaged her to take care of the little girl, calling it his child. One or two of his lawyer friends, whom I met with at the funeral, told me they were aware of the existence of the child."

" What is to be done with her?" asked Mrs. Gibson.

" Nay, I don't know," replied he. " Mark has hardly left assets enough to pay his debts, and your father is not inclined to come forward."

That night, as Doctor Trevor sat in his study, after his wife had gone to bed, Miss Galindo knocked at his door. She and he had a long conversation. The result was that he accompanied Miss Galindo up to town the next day; that they took possession of the little Bessy, and she was brought down, and placed at nurse at a farm in the country near Warwick, Miss Galindo undertaking to pay one-half of the expense, and to furnish her with clothes, and Dr. Trevor undertaking that the remaining half should be furnished by the Gibson family, or by himself in their default.

Miss Galindo was not fond of children; and I dare say she dreaded taking this child to live with her for more reasons than one. My Lady Ludlow could not endure any mention of illegitimate children. It was a principle of hers that society ought to ignore them. And I believe Miss Galindo had always agreed with her until now, when the thing came home to her womanly heart. Still she shrank from having this child of some strange woman under her roof. She went over to see it from time to time; she worked at its clothes long after every one thought she was in bed; and, when the time came for Bessy to be sent to school, Miss Galindo laboured away more diligently than ever, in order to pay the increased expense. For the Gibson family had, at first, paid their part of the compact, but with unwillingness and grudging hearts; then they had left it off altogether, and it fell hard on Dr. Trevor with his twelve children; and, latterly, Miss Galindo had taken upon herself almost all the burden. One can hardly live and labour, and plan and make sacrifices, for any human creature, without learning to love it. And Bessy loved Miss Galindo, too, for all the poor girl's scanty pleasures came from her, and Miss Galindo had always a kind word, and, latterly, many a kind caress, for Mark Gibson's child; whereas, if she went to Dr. Trevor's for her holiday, she was overlooked and neglected in that bustling family, who seemed to think that if she had comfortable board and lodging under their roof, it was enough.

I am sure, now, that Miss Galindo had often longed to have Bessy to live with her; but, as long as she could pay for her being at school, she did not like to take so bold a step as bringing her home, knowing what the effect of the consequent explanation would be on my lady. And as the girl was now more than seventeen, and past the age when young ladies are usually kept at school, and as there was no great demand for governesses in those days, and as Bessy had never been taught any trade by which to earn her own living, why I don't exactly see what could have been done but for Miss Galindo to bring her to her own home in Hanbury. For, although the child had grown up lately, in a kind of unexpected manner, into a young woman, Miss Galindo might have kept her at school for a year longer, if she could have afforded it; but this was impossible when she became Mr. Horner's clerk, and relinquished all the payment of her repository work; and perhaps, after all, she was not sorry to be compelled to take the step she was longing for. At any rate, Bessy came to live with Miss Galindo, in a very few weeks from the time when Captain James set Miss Galindo free to superintend her own domestic economy again.

For a long time I knew nothing about this new inhabitant of Hanbury. My lady never mentioned her in any way. This was in accordance with Lady Ludlow's well-known principles. She neither saw nor heard, nor was in any way cognisant of the existence of those who had no legal right to exist at all. If Miss Galindo had hoped to have an exception made in Bessy's favour, she was mistaken. My lady sent a note inviting Miss Galindo herself to tea one evening, about a month after Bessy came; but Miss Galindo "had a cold and could not come." The next time she was invited, she "had an engagement at home,"—a step nearer to the absolute truth. And the third time, she "had a young friend staying with her whom she was unable to leave." My lady accepted every excuse as *bonâ fide*, and took no further notice. I missed Miss Galindo very much; we all did; for, in the days when she was clerk, she was sure to come in and find the opportunity of saying something amusing to some of us before she went away. And I, as an invalid, or perhaps from natural tendency, was particularly fond of little bits of village gossip. There was no Mr. Horner—he even had come in, now and then, with formal, stately pieces of intelligence—and there was no Miss Galindo in these days. I missed her much. And so did my lady, I am sure. Behind all her quiet, sedate manner, I am certain her heart ached sometimes for a few words from Miss Galindo, who seemed to have absented herself altogether from the Hall now Bessy was come.

Captain James might be very sensible, and all that; but not even my lady could call him a substitute for the old familiar friends. He was a thorough sailor, as sailors were in those days—swore a good deal, drank a good deal (without its ever affecting him in the least), and was very prompt and kind-hearted in all his actions; but he was not accustomed to women, as my lady once said, and would judge in all things for himself. My lady had expected, I think, to find some one who would take his notions on the management of her estate from her ladyship's own self; but he spoke as if he were reponsible for the good management of the whole, and must, consequently, be allowed full liberty of action. He had been too long in command over men at sea to like to be directed by a woman in anything he undertook, even though that woman was my lady. I suppose this was the common-sense my lady spoke of; but when common-sense goes against us, I don't think we value it quite so much as we ought to do.

Lady Ludlow was proud of her personal superintendence of her own estate. She liked to tell us how her father used to take her with him in his rides, and bid her observe this and that, and on no account to allow such and such things to be done. But I have heard that the first time she told all this to Captain James, he told her point-blank that he had heard from Mr. Smithson that the farms were much neglected and the rents sadly behind-hand, and that he meant to set to in good earnest and study agriculture, and see how he could remedy the state of things. My lady would, I am sure, be greatly surprised, but what could she do? Here was the very man she had chosen herself, setting to with all his energy to conquer the defect of ignorance, which was all that those who had presumed to offer her ladyship advice had ever had to say against him. Captain James read Arthur Young's *Tours* in all his spare time, as long as he was an invalid; and shook his head at my lady's accounts as to how the land had been cropped or left fallow from time immemorial. Then he set to, and tried too many new experiments at once. My lady looked on in dignified silence; but all the farmers and tenants were in an uproar, and prophesied a hundred failures. Perhaps fifty did occur; they were only half as many as Lady Lud ow had feared; but they were twice as many, four, eight times as many as the captain had anticipated. His openly-expressed disappointment made him popular again. The rough country people could not have understood silent and dignified regret at the failure of his plans; but they sympathised with a man who swore at his ill success—sympathised, even while they chuckled over his discomfiture. Mr. Brooke, the retired tradesman, did not cease blaming him for not succeeding, and for swearing. " But what could you expect from a sailor? " Mr. Brooke asked, even in my lady's hearing; though he might have known Captain James was my lady's own personal choice, from the old friendship Mr. Urian had always shown for him. I think it was this speech of the Birmingham baker's that made my lady determine to stand by Captain James, and encourage him to try again. For she would not allow that her choice had been an unwise one, at the bidding (as it were) of a dissenting tradesman; the only person in the neighbourhood, too, who had flaunted about in coloured clothes, when all the world was in mourning for my lady's only son.

Captain James would have thrown the agency up at once, if my lady had not felt herself bound to justify the wisdom of her choice, by urging him to stay. He was much touched by her confidence in him, and swore a great oath, that the next year he would make the land such as it had never been before for produce. It was not my lady's way to repeat anything she had heard, especially to another person's disadvantage. So I don't think she ever told Captain James of Mr. Brooke's speech about a sailor's being likely to mismanage the property; and the captain was too anxious to succeed in this, the second year of his trial, to be above going to the flourishing, shrewd Mr. Brooke, and asking for his advice as to the best method of working the estate. I dare say, if Miss Galindo had been as intimate as formerly at the Hall, we should all of us have heard of this new acquaintance of the agent's long before we did. As it was, I am sure my lady never dreamed that the captain, who held opinions that were even more Church and King than her own, could ever have made friends with a Baptist baker from Birmingham, even to serve her ladyship's own interests in the most loyal m inner.

We heard of it first from Mr. Gray, who came now often to see my lady, for neither he nor she could forget the solemn tie which the fact of his being the person to acquaint her with my lord's death had created between them. For true and holy words spoken at that time, though having no reference to aught below the solemn subjects of life and death, had made her withdraw her opposition to Mr. Gray's wish about establishing a village school. She had sighed a little, it is true, and was even yet more apprehensive than hopeful as to the result; but almost as if as a memorial to my lord, she had allowed a kind of rough school-house to be built on the green, just by the church; and had gently used the power she undoubtedly had, in expressing her strong wish that the boys might only be taught to read and write, and the first four rules of arithmetic; while the girls were only to learn to read, and to add up in their heads, and the rest of the time to work at mending their own clothes, knitting stockings and spinning. My lady presented the school with more spinning-wheels than there were girls, and requested that there might be a rule that they should have spun so many hanks of flax, and knitted so many pairs of stockings, before they ever were taught to read at all. After all, it was but making the best of a bad job with my poor lady—but life was not what it had been to her. I remember well the day that Mr. Gray pulled some delicately fine yarn (and I was a good judge of those things) out of his pocket, and laid it and a capital pair of knitted stockings before my lady, as the first-fruits, so to say, of his school. I recollect seeing her put on her spectacles, and carefully examine both productions. Then she passed them to me.

"This is well, Mr. Gray. I am much pleased. You are fortunate in your schoolmistress. She has had both proper knowledge of womanly things and much patience. Who is she? One out of our village?"

"My lady," said Mr. Gray, stammering and colouring in his old fashion, "Miss Bessy is so very kind as to teach all those sorts of things—Miss Bessy, and Miss Galindo, sometimes."

My lady looked at him over her spectacles: but she only repeated the words "Miss Bessy," and paused, as if trying to remember who such a person could be; and he, if he had then intended to say more, was quelled by her manner, and dropped the subject. He went on to say, that he had thought it his duty to decline the subscription to his school offered by Mr. Brooke, because he was a Dissenter; that he (Mr. Gray) feared that Captain James, through whom Mr. Brooke's offer of money had been made, was offended at his refusing to accept it from a man who held heterodox opinions; nay, whom Mr. Gray suspected of being infected by Dodwell's heresy.

"I think there must be some mistake," said my lady, "or I have misunderstood you. Captain James would never be sufficiently with a schismatic to be employed by that man Brooke in distributing his charities. I should have doubted, until now, if Captain James knew him."

"Indeed, my lady, he not only knows him, but is intimate with him, I regret to say. I have repeatedly seen the captain and Mr. Brooke walking together; going through the fields together; and people do say——"

My lady looked up in interrogation at Mr. Gray's pause.

"I disapprove of gossip, and it may be untrue; but people do say that Captain James is very attentive to Miss Brooke."

"Impossible!" said my lady, indignantly. "Captain James is a loyal and religious man. I beg your pardon, Mr. Gray, but it is impossible."

CHAPTER XIV

LIKE many other things which have been declared to be impossible, this report of Captain James being attentive to Miss Brooke turned out to be very true.

The mere idea of her agent being on the slightest possible terms of acquaintance with the Dissenter, the tradesman, the Birmingham democrat, who had come to settle in our good, orthodox, aristocratic, and agricultural Hanbury, made my lady very uneasy. Miss Galindo's misdemeanour in having taken Miss Bessy to live with her, faded into a mistake, a mere error of judgment, in comparison with Captain James's intimacy at Yeast House, as the Brookes called their ugly square-built farm. My lady talked herself quite into complacency with Miss Galindo, and even Miss Bessy was named by her, the first time I had ever been aware that my lady recognised her existence; but—I recollect it was a long rainy afternoon, and I sat with her ladyship, and we had time and opportunity for a long uninterrupted talk—whenever we had been silent for a little while she began again, with something like a wonder how it was that Captain James could ever have commenced an acquaintance with "that man Brooke." My lady recapitulated all the times she could remember, that anything had occurred, or been said by Captain James which she could now understand as throwing light upon the subject.

"He said once that he was anxious to bring in the Norfolk system of cropping, and spoke a good deal about Mr. Coke of Holkham (who, by the way, was no more a Coke than I am— collateral in the female line—which counts for little or nothing among the great old commoners' families of pure blood), and his new ways of cultivation; of course new men bring in new ways, but it does not follow that either are better than the old ways. However, Captain James has been very anxious to try turnips and bone manure, and he really is a man of such good sense and energy, and was so sorry last year about the failure, that I consented; and now I begin to see my error. I have always heard that town bakers adulterate their flour with bone-dust; and, of course, Captain James would be aware of this, and go to Brooke to inquire where the article was to be purchased."

My lady always ignored the fact which had sometimes, I suspect, been brought under her very eyes during her drives, that Mr. Brooke's few fields were in a state of far higher cultivation than her own; so she could not, of course, perceive that there was any wisdom to be gained from asking the advice of the tradesman turned farmer.

But by-and-by this fact of her agent's intimacy with the person whom in the whole world she most disliked (with that sort of dislike in which a large amount of uncomfortableness is combined —the dislike which conscientious people sometimes feel to another without knowing why, and yet which they cannot indulge in with comfort to themselves without having a moral reason why), came before my lady in many shapes. For, indeed, I am sure that Captain James was not a man to conceal or be ashamed of one of his actions. I cannot fancy his ever lowering his strong loud clear voice, or having a confidential conversation with any one. When his crops had failed, all the village had known it. He complained, he regretted, he was angry, or owned himself a —— fool, all down the village street; and the consequence was that, although he was a far more passionate man than Mr. Horner, all the tenants liked him far better. People, in general, take a kindlier interest in any one, the workings of whose mind and heart they can watch and understand, than in a man who only lets you know what he has been thinking about and feeling, by what he does. But Harry Gregson was faithful to the memory of Mr. Horner. Miss Galindo has told me that

she used to watch him hobble out of the way of Captain James, as
if to accept his notice, however good-naturedly given, would have
been a kind of treachery to his former benefactor. But Gregson
(the father) and the new agent rather took to each other; and
one day, much to my surprise, I heard that the " poaching,
tinkering vagabond," as the people used to call Gregson when I
first had come to live at Hanbury, had been appointed gamekeeper; Mr. Gray standing godfather, as it were, to his trust-
worthiness, if he were trusted with anything; which I thought
at the time was rather an experiment, only it answered, as many
of Mr. Gray's deeds of daring did. It was curious how he was
growing to be a kind of autocrat in the village; and how unconscious he was of it. He was as shy and awkward and nervous
as ever in any affair that was not of some moral consequence to
him. But as soon as he was convinced that a thing was right,
he " shut his eyes and ran and butted at it like a ram," as
Captain James once expressed it, in talking over something Mr.
Gray had done. People in the village said, " they never knew
what the parson would be at next;" or they might have said,
" where his reverence would next turn up." For I have heard of
his marching right into the middle of a set of poachers, gathered
together for some desperate midnight enterprise, or walking into
a public-house that lay just beyond the bounds of my lady's
estate, and in that extra-parochial piece of ground I named long
ago, and which was considered the rendezvous of all the ne'er-
do-weel characters for miles round, and where a parson and
a constable were held in much the same kind of esteem as
unwelcome visitors. And yet Mr. Gray had his long fits of
depression, in which he felt as if he were doing nothing, making
no way in his work, useless and unprofitable, and better out of the
world than in it. In comparison with the work he had set himself to do, what he did seemed to be nothing. I suppose it was
constitutional, those attacks of lowness of spirits which he had
about this time; perhaps a part of the nervousness which made
him always so awkward when he came to the Hall. Even Mrs.
Medlicott, who almost worshipped the ground he trod on, as the
saying is, owned that Mr. Gray never entered one of my lady's
rooms without knocking down something, and too often breaking
it. He would much sooner have faced a desperate poacher than
a young lady any day. At least so we thought.

I do not know how it was that it came to pass that my lady
became reconciled to Miss Galindo about this time. Whether
it was that her ladyship was weary of the unspoken coolness

with her old friend; or that the specimens of delicate sewing and fine spinning at the school had mollified her towards Miss Bessy; but I was surprised to learn one day that Miss Galindo and her young friend were coming that very evening to tea at the Hall. This information was given me by Mrs. Medlicott, as a message from my lady, who further went on to desire that certain little preparations should be made in her own private sitting-room, in which the greater part of my days were spent. From the nature of these preparations, I became quite aware that my lady intended to do honour to her expected visitors. Indeed, Lady Ludlow never forgave by halves, as I have known some people do. Whoever was coming as a visitor to my lady, peeress, or poor nameless girl, there was a certain amount of preparation required in order to do them fitting honour. I do not mean to say that the preparation was of the same degree of importance in each case. I dare say, if a peeress had come to visit us at the Hall, the covers would have been taken off the furniture in the white drawing-room (they never were uncovered all the time I stayed at the Hall), because my lady would wish to offer her the ornaments and luxuries which this grand visitor (who never came—I wish she had! I did so want to see that furniture uncovered!) was accustomed to at home, and to present them to her in the best order in which my lady could. The same rule, mollified, held good with Miss Galindo. Certain things, in which my lady knew she took an interest, were laid out ready for her to examine on this very day; and, what was more, great books of prints were laid out, such as I remembered my lady had had brought forth to beguile my own early days of illness,—Mr. Hogarth's works, and the like,—which I was sure were put out for Miss Bessy.

No one knows how curious I was to see this mysterious Miss Bessy—twenty times more mysterious, of course, for want of her surname. And then again (to try and account for my great curiosity, of which in recollection I am more than half ashamed), I had been leading the quiet monotonous life of a crippled invalid for many years,—shut up from any sight of new faces; and this was to be the face of one whom I had thought about so much and so long,—Oh! I think I might be excused.

Of course they drank tea in the great hall, with the four young gentlewomen, who, with myself, formed the small bevy now under her ladyship's charge. Of those who were at Hanbury when first I came, none remained; all were married, or gone once more to live at some home which could be called their own, whether the ostensible head were father or brother. I myself was not without some hopes of a similar kind. My brother Harry was now a curate in Westmoreland, and wanted me to go and live with him, as eventually I did for a time. But that is neither here nor there at present. What I am talking about is Miss Bessy.

After a reasonable time had elapsed, occupied as I well knew by the meal in the great hall,—the measured, yet agreeable conversation afterwards,—and a certain promenade around the hall, and through the drawing-rooms, with pauses before different pictures, the history or subject of each of which was invariably told by my lady to every new visitor,—a sort of giving them the freedom of the old family-seat, by describing the kind and nature of the great progenitors who had lived there before the narrator, —I heard the steps approaching my lady's room, where I lay. I think I was in such a state of nervous expectation, that if I could have moved easily, I should have got up and run away. And yet I need not have been, for Miss Galindo was not in the least altered (her nose a little redder, to be sure, but then that might only have had a temporary cause in the private crying I know she would have had before coming to see her dear Lady Ludlow once again). But I could almost have pushed Miss Galindo away, as she intercepted me in my view of the mysterious Miss Bessy.

Miss Bessy was, as I knew, only about eighteen, but she looked older. Dark hair, dark eyes, a tall, firm figure, a good, sensible face, with a serene expression, not in the least disturbed by what I had been thinking must be such awful circumstances as a first introduction to my lady, who had so disapproved of her very existence: those are the clearest impressions I remember of my first interview with Miss Bessy. She seemed to observe us all, in her quiet manner, quite as much as I did her; but she spoke very little; occupied herself, indeed, as my lady had planned, with looking over the great books of engravings. I think I must have (foolishly) intended to make her feel at her ease, by my patronage; but she was seated far away from my sofa, in order to command the light, and really seemed so unconcerned at her unwonted circumstances, that she did not need my countenance or kindness. One thing I did like—her watchful look at Miss Galindo from time to time: it showed that her thoughts and sympathy were ever at Miss Galindo's service, as indeed they well might be. When Miss Bessy spoke, her voice was full and clear, and what she said to the purpose, though there was a slight provincial accent in her way of speaking. After a while, my lady set us two to play at chess, a game which I had lately learnt at Mr. Gray's suggestion. Still we did not talk much together, though we were becoming attracted towards each other, I fancy.

" You will play well," said she. " You have only learnt about six months, have you? And yet you can nearly beat me, who have been at it as many years."

" I began to learn last November. I remember Mr. Gray's bringing me *Philidor on Chess*, one very foggy, dismal day."

What made her look up so suddenly, with bright inquiry in her eyes? What made her silent for a moment, as if in thought, and then go on with something, I know not what, in quite an altered tone?

My lady and Miss Galindo went on talking, while I sat thinking. I heard Captain James's name mentioned pretty frequently; and at last my lady put down her work, and said, almost with tears in her eyes:

" I could not—I cannot believe it. He must be aware she is a schismatic; a baker's daughter; and he is a gentleman by virtue and feeling, as well as by his profession, though his manners may be at times a little rough. My dear Miss Galindo, what will this world come to? "

Miss Galindo might possibly be aware of her own share in bringing the world to the pass which now dismayed my lady,— for of course, though all was now over and forgiven, yet Miss Bessy's being received into a respectable maiden lady's house, was one of the portents as to the world's future which alarmed her ladyship; and Miss Galindo knew this,—but, at any rate, she had too lately been forgiven herself not to plead for mercy for the next offender against my lady's delicate sense of fitness and propriety,—so she replied:

" Indeed, my lady, I have long left off trying to conjecture what makes Jack fancy Gill, or Gill Jack. It's best to sit down quiet under the belief that marriages are made for us, some- where out of this world, and out of the range of this world's reason and laws. I'm not so sure that I should settle it down that they were made in heaven; t'other place seems to me as likely a workshop; but at any rate, I've given up troubling my head as to why they take place. Captain James is a gentleman; I make no doubt of that ever since I saw him stop to pick up old Goody Blake (when she tumbled down on the slide last winter) and then swear at a little lad who was laughing at her, and cuff him till he tumbled down crying; but we must have bread somehow, and though I like it better baked at home in a good sweet brick oven, yet, as some folks never can get it to rise, I don't see why a man may not be a baker. You see, my lady, I look upon baking as a simple trade, and as such lawful. There is no machine comes in to take away a man's or woman's power of earning their living, like the spinning-jenny (the old busybody that she is), to knock up all our good old women's livelihood, and send them to their graves before their time. There's an invention of the enemy, if you will!"

" That's very true! " said my lady, shaking her head.

" But baking bread is wholesome, straight-forward elbow-work. They have not got to inventing any contrivance for that yet, thank Heaven! It does not seem to me natural, nor according to Scripture, that iron and steel (whose brows can't sweat) should be made to do man's work. And so I say, all those trades where iron and steel do the work ordained to man at the Fall, are unlawful, and I never stand up for them. But say this baker Brooke did knead his bread, and make it rise, and then that people, who had, perhaps, no good ovens, came to him, and bought his good light bread, and in this manner he turned an honest penny and got rich; why, all I say, my lady, is this,— I dare say he would have been born a Hanbury, or a lord if he could; and if he was not, it is no fault of his, that I can see, that he made good bread (being a baker by trade), and got money, and bought his land. It was his misfortune, not his fault, that he was not a person of quality by birth."

" That's very true," said my lady, after a moment's pause for consideration. " But, although he was a baker, he might have been a Churchman. Even your eloquence, Miss Galindo, shan't convince me that that is not his own fault."

" I don't see even that, begging your pardon, my lady," said Miss Galindo, emboldened by the first success of her eloquence. " When a Baptist is a baby, if I understand their creed aright, he is not baptised; and, consequently, he can have no godfathers and godmothers to do anything for him in his baptism; you agree to that, my lady? "

My lady would rather have known what her acquiescence would lead to, before acknowledging that she could not dissent from this first proposition; still she gave her tacit agreement by bowing her head.

" And you know, our godfathers and godmothers are expected to promise and vow three things in our name, when we are little babies, and can do nothing but squall for ourselves. It is a great privilege, but don't let us be hard upon those who have not had the chance of godfathers and godmothers. Some people, we know, are born with silver spoons,—that's to say, a godfather to give one things, and teach one's catechism, and see that we're confirmed into good church-going Christians,—and others with wooden ladles in their mouths. These poor last folks must just be content to be godfatherless orphans, and Dissenters, all their lives; and if they are tradespeople into the bargain, so much the worse for them; but let us be humble Christians, my dear lady, and not hold our heads too high because we were born orthodox quality."

"You go on too fast, Miss Galindo! I can't follow you. Besides, I do believe dissent to be an invention of the Devil's. Why can't they believe as we do? It's very wrong. Besides, it's schism and heresy, and, you know, the Bible says that's as bad as witchcraft."

My lady was not convinced, as I could see. After Miss Galindo had gone, she sent Mrs. Medlicott for certain books out of the great old library up stairs, and had them made up into a parcel under her own eye.

"If Captain James comes to-morrow, I will speak to him about these Brookes. I have not hitherto liked to speak to him, because I did not wish to hurt him, by supposing there could be any truth in the reports about his intimacy with them. But now I will try and do my duty by him and them. Surely, this great body of divinity will bring them back to the true church."

" I could not tell, for though my lady read me over the titles, I was not any the wiser as to their contents. Besides, I was much more anxious to consult my lady as to my own change of place. I showed her the letter I had that day received from Harry; and we once more talked over the expediency of my going to live with him, and trying what entire change of air would do to re-establish my failing health. I could say anything to my lady, she was so sure to understand me rightly. For one thing, she never thought of herself, so I had no fear of hurting her by stating the truth. I told her how happy my years had been while passed under her roof; but that now I had begun to wonder whether I had not duties elsewhere, in making a home for Harry,—and whether the fulfilment of these duties, quiet ones they must needs be in the case of such a cripple as myself, would not prevent my sinking into the querulous habit of thinking and talking, into which I found myself occasionally falling. Add to which, there was the prospect of benefit from the more bracing air of the north.

It was then settled that my departure from Hanbury, my happy home for so long, was to take place before many weeks had passed. And as, when one period of life is about to be shut up for ever, we are sure to look back upon it with fond regret, so I, happy enough in my future prospects, could not avoid recurring to all the days of my life in the Hall, from the time when I came to it, a shy awkward girl, scarcely past childhood, to now, when a grown woman,—past childhood—almost, from the very character of my illness, past youth,—I was looking forward to leaving my lady's house (as a residence) for ever. As it has turned out, I never saw either her or it again. Like a piece of sea-wreck, I have drifted away from those days: quiet, happy, eventless days,—very happy to remember!

I thought of good, jovial Mr. Mountford,—and his regrets that he might not keep a pack, " a very small pack," of harriers, and his merry ways, and his love of good eating; of the first coming of Mr. Gray, and my lady's attempt to quench his sermons, when they tended to enforce any duty connected with education. And now we had an absolute school-house in the village; and since Miss Bessy's drinking tea at the Hall, my lady had been twice inside it, to give directions about some fine yarn she was having spun for table-napery. And her ladyship had so outgrown her old custom of dispensing with sermon or discourse, that even during the temporary preaching of Mr. Crosse, she had never had recourse to it, though I believe she would have had all the congregation on her side if she had.

And Mr. Horner was dead, and Captain James reigned in his stead. Good, steady, severe, silent Mr. Horner! with his clock-like regularity, and his snuff-coloured clothes, and silver buckles! I have often wondered which one misses most when they are dead and gone,—the bright creatures full of life, who are hither and thither and everywhere, so that no one can reckon upon their coming and going, with whom stillness and the long quiet of the grave, seems utterly irreconcilable, so full are they of vivid motion and passion,—or the slow, serious people, whose movements—nay, whose very words, seem to go by clockwork; who never appear much to affect the course of our life while they are with us, but whose methodical ways show themselves, when they are gone, to have been intertwined with our very roots of daily existence. I think I miss these last the

most, although I may have loved the former best. Captain
James never was to me what Mr. Horner was, though the latter
had hardly changed a dozen words with me at the day of his
death. Then Miss Galindo! I remembered the time as if it
had been only yesterday, when she was but a name—and a very
odd one—to me; then she was a queer, abrupt, disagreeable,
busy old maid. Now I loved her dearly, and I found out that
I was almost jealous of Miss Bessy.

Mr. Gray I never thought of with love; the feeling was
almost reverence with which I looked upon him. I have not
wished to speak much of myself, or else I could have told you
how much he had been to me during these long, weary years of
illness. But he was almost as much to every one, rich and
poor, from my lady down to Miss Galindo's Sally.

The village, too, had a different look about it. I am sure I
could not tell you what caused the change; but there were no
more lounging young men to form a group at the cross-road, at
a time of day when young men ought to be at work. I don't
say this was all Mr. Gray's doing, for there really was so much
to do in the fields that there was but little time for lounging
now-a-days. And the children were hushed up in school,
and better behaved out of it, too, than in the days when I used
to be able to go my lady's errands in the village. I went so
little about now, that I am sure I can't tell who Miss Galindo
found to scold; and yet she looked so well and so happy that
I think she must have had her accustomed portion of that
wholesome exercise.

Before I left Hanbury, the rumour that Captain James was
going to marry Miss Brooke, Baker Brooke's eldest daughter,
who had only a sister to share his property with her, was confirmed. He himself announced it to my lady; nay, more, with
a courage, gained, I suppose, in his former profession, where,
as I have heard, he had led his ship into many a post of danger,
he asked her ladyship, the Countess Ludlow, if he might bring
his bride elect (the Baptist baker's daughter!) and present her
to my lady!

I am glad I was not present when he made this request; I
should have felt so much ashamed for him, and I could not
have helped being anxious till I heard my lady's answer, if
I had been there. Of course she acceded; but I can fancy
the grave surprise of her look. I wonder if Captain James
noticed it.

I hardly dared ask my lady, after the interview had taken

place, what she thought of the bride elect; but I hinted my curiosity, and she told me, that if the young person had applied to Mrs. Medlicott, for the situation of cook, and Mrs. Medlicott had engaged her, she thought that it would have been a very suitable arrangement. I understood from this how little she thought a marriage with Captain James, R.N., suitable.

About a year after I left Hanbury, I received a letter from Miss Galindo; I think I can find it—Yes, this is it.

"HANBURY, *May* 4, 1811.

"DEAR MARGARET,—You ask for news of us all. Don't you know there is no news in Hanbury? Did you ever hear of an event here? Now, if you have answered 'Yes,' in your own mind to these questions, you have fallen into my trap, and never were more mistaken in your life. Hanbury is full of news; and we have more events on our hands than we know what to do with I will take them in the order of the newspapers—births, deaths, and marriages. In the matter of births, Jenny Lucas has had twins not a week ago. Sadly too much of a good thing, you'll say. Very true: but then they died; so their birth did not much signify. My cat has kittened, too; she has had three kittens, which again you may observe is too much of a good thing; and so it would be, if it were not for the next item of intelligence I shall lay before you. Captain and Mrs. James have taken the old house next Pearson's; and the house is overrun with mice, which is just as fortunate for me as the King of Egypt's rat-ridden kingdom was to Dick Whittington. For my cat's kittening decided me to go and call on the bride, in hopes she wanted a cat; which she did, like a sensible woman, as I do believe she is, in spite of Baptism, Bakers, Bread, and Birmingham, and something worse than all, which you shall hear about, if you'll only be patient. As I had got my best bonnet on, the one I bought when poor Lord Ludlow was last at Hanbury in '99—I thought it a great condescension in myself (always remembering the date of the Galindo baronetcy) to go and call on the bride; though I don't think so much of myself in my every-day clothes, as you know. But who should I find there but my Lady Ludlow! She looks as frail and delicate as ever, but is, I think, in better heart ever since that old city merchant of a Hanbury took it into his head that he was a cadet of the Hanburys of Hanbury, and left her that handsome legacy. I'll warrant you that the mortgage was paid off pretty fast; and Mr. Horner's money—or my lady's money, or Harry Gregson's money, call it which you will—is invested in his name, all right and tight; and they do talk of his being captain of his school, or Grecian, or something, and going to college, after all! Harry Gregson the poacher's son! Well! to be sure, we are living in strange times!

"But I have not done with the marriages yet. Captain James's is all very well, but no one cares for it now, we are so full of Mr. Gray's. Yes, indeed, Mr. Gray is going to be married, and to nobody else but my little Bessy! I tell her she will have to nurse him half the days of her life, he is such a frail little body. But she says she does not care for that; so that his body holds his soul, it is enough for her. She has a good spirit and a brave heart, has my Bessy! It is a great advantage that she won't have to mark her clothes over again; for when she had knitted herself her last set of stockings, I told her to put G for Galindo, if she did not choose to put it for Gibson, for she should be my child if she was no one else's. And now you see it stands for Gray. So there are two marriages, and what more would you have? And she promises to take another of my kittens.

"Now, as to deaths, old Farmer Hale is dead—poor old man, I should think his wife thought it a good riddance, for he beat her every day that he was drunk, and he was never sober, in spite of Mr. Gray. I don't think (as I tell him) that Mr. Gray would ever have found courage to speak to Bessy as long as Farmer Hale lived, he took the old gentleman's sins so much to heart, and seemed to think it was all his fault for not being able to make a sinner into a saint. The parish bull is dead too. I never was so glad in my life. But they say we are to have a new one in his place. In the meantime I cross the common in peace, which is very convenient just now, when I have so often to go to Mr. Gray's to see about furnishing.

"Now you think I have told you all the Hanbury news, don't you? Not so. The very greatest thing of all is to come. I won't tantalise you, but just out with it, for you would never guess it. My Lady Ludlow has given a party, just like any plebeian amongst us. We had tea and toast in the blue drawing-room, old John Footman waiting with Tom Diggles, the lad that used to frighten away crows in Farmer Hale's fields, following in my lady's livery, hair powdered and everything. Mrs. Medlicott made tea in my lady's own room. My lady looked like a splendid fairy queen of mature age, in black velvet, and the old lace, which I have never seen her wear before since my lord's death. But the company? you'll say. Why, we had the parson of Clover, and the parson of Headleigh, and the parson of Merribank, and the three parsonesses; and Farmer Donkin, and two Miss Donkins; and Mr. Gray (of course), and myself and Bessy; and Captain and Mrs. James; yes, and Mr. and Mrs. Brooke; think of that! I am not sure the parsons liked it; but he was there. For he has been helping Captain James to get my lady's land into order; and then his daughter married the agent; and Mr. Gray (who ought to know) says that, after all, Baptists are not such bad people; and he was right against them at one time, as you may remember. Mrs. Brooke is a rough diamond, to be sure. People have said that of me, I know. But, being a Galindo, I learnt manners in my youth and can take them up when I choose. But Mrs. Brooke never learnt manners, I'll be bound. When John Footman handed her the tray with the tea-cups, she looked up at him as if she were sorely puzzled by that way of going on. I was sitting next to her, so I pretended not to see her perplexity, and put her cream and sugar in for her, and was all ready to pop it into her hands—when who should come up, but that impudent lad Tom Diggles (I call him lad, for all his hair is powdered, for you know that it is not natural grey hair), with his tray full of cakes and what not, all as good as Mrs. Medlicott could make them. By this time, I should tell you, all the parsonesses were looking at Mrs. Brooke, for she had shown her want of breeding before; and the parsonesses, who were just a step above her in manners, were very much inclined to smile at her doings and sayings. Well! what does she do, but pull out a clean Bandanna pocket-handkerchief, all red and yellow silk, spread it over her best silk gown; it was, like enough, a new one, for I had it from Sally, who had it from her cousin Molly, who is dairy-woman at the Brookes', that the Brookes were mighty set-up with an invitation to drink tea at the Hall. There we were, Tom Diggles even on the grin (I wonder how long it is since he was own brother to a scarecrow, only not so decently dressed) and Mrs. Parsoness of Headleigh—I forget her name, and it's no matter, for she's an ill-bred creature, I hope Bessy will behave herself better—was right-down bursting with laughter, and as near a hee-haw as ever a donkey was, when what does my lady do? Ay! there's my own dear Lady Ludlow, God bless her! She takes out her own pocket-handkerchief, all snowy cambric, and lays it softly down on her velvet lap, for all the world as if she did it every day of her life, just like Mrs. Brooke, the baker's wife; and when the one got up to shake the crumbs into the fire-place, the other did just the same. But with such a grace! and such a look at us all! Tom Diggles went red all over; and Mrs. Parsoness of Headleigh scarce spoke for the rest of the evening; and the tears came into my old silly eyes; and Mr. Gray, who was before silent and awkward in a way which I tell Bessy she must cure him of, was made so happy by this pretty action of my lady's, that he talked away all the rest of the evening, and was the life of the company.

"Oh, Margaret Dawson! I sometimes wonder if you're the better off for leaving us. To be sure you're with your brother, and blood is blood. But when I look at my lady and Mr. Gray, for all they're so different, I would not change places with any in England."

Alas! alas! I never saw my dear lady again. She died in eighteen hundred and fourteen, and Mr. Gray did not long survive her. As I dare say you know, the Reverend Henry Gregson is now vicar of Hanbury, and his wife is the daughter of Mr. Gray and Miss Bessy.

HALF A LIFE-TIME AGO

CHAPTER I

HALF a life-time ago, there lived in one of the Westmoreland dales a single woman, of the name of Susan Dixon. She was owner of the small farm-house where she resided, and of some thirty or forty acres of land by which it was surrounded. She had also an hereditary right to a sheep-walk, extending to the wild fells that overhang Blea Tarn. In the language of the country she was a Stateswoman. Her house is yet to be seen on the Oxenfell road, between Skelwith and Coniston. You go along a moorland track, made by the carts that occasionally came for turf from the Oxenfell. A b ook babbles and brattles by the wayside, giving you a sense of companionship, which relieves the deep solitude in which this way is usually traversed. Some miles on this side of Coniston there is a farmstead—a grey stone house, and a square of farm-buildings surrounding a green space of rough turf, in the midst of which stands a mighty, funereal, umbrageous yew, making a solemn shadow, as of death, in the very heart and centre of the light and heat of the brightest summer day. On the side away from the house, this yard slopes down to a dark-brown pool, which is supplied with fresh water from the overflowings of a stone cistern, into which some rivulet of the brook before mentioned continually and melodiously falls bubbling. The cattle drink out of this cistern. The household bring their pitchers and fill them with drinking-water by a dilatory, yet pretty, process. The water-carrier brings with her a leaf of the hound's-tongue fern, and, inserting it in the crevice of the grey rock, makes a cool, green spout for the sparkling stream.

The house is no specimen, at the present day, of what it was in the lifetime of Susan Dixon. Then, every small diamond pane in the windows glittered with cleanliness. You might have eaten off the floor; you could see yourself in the pewter plates and the polished oaken awmry, or dresser, of the state kitchen into which you entered. Few strangers penetrated further than this room. Once or twice, wandering tourists, attracted by the lonely picturesqueness of the situation, and the exquisite cleanliness of the house itself, made their way into this house-place, and offered money enough (as they thought) to tempt the hostess to receive them as lodgers. They would give no trouble, they said; they would be out rambling or sketching all day long; would be perfectly content with a share of the food which she provided for herself; or would procure what they required from the Waterhead Inn at Coniston. But no liberal sum—no fair words—moved her from her stony manner, or her monotonous tone of indifferent refusal. No persuasion could induce her to show any more of the house than that first room; no appearance of fatigue procured for the weary an invitation to sit down and rest; and if one more bold and less delicate did so without being asked, Susan stood by, cold and apparently deaf, or only replying by the briefest monosyllables, till the unwelcome visitor had departed. Yet those with whom she had dealings, in the way of selling her cattle or her farm produce, spoke of her as keen after a bargain—a hard one to have to do with; and she never spared herself exertion or fatigue, at market or in the field, to make the most of her produce. She led the hay-makers with her swift, steady rake, and her noiseless evenness of motion. She was about among the earliest in the market, examining samples of oats, pricing them, and then turning with grim satisfaction to her own cleaner corn.

She was served faithfully and long by those who were rather her fellow-labourers than her servants. She was even and just in her dealings with them. If she was peculiar and silent, they knew her, and knew that she might be relied on. Some of them had known her from her childhood; and deep in their hearts was an unspoken—almost unconscious—pity for her, for they knew her story, though they never spoke of it.

Yes; the time had been when that tall, gaunt, hard-featured, angular woman—who never smiled, and hardly ever spoke an unnecessary word—had been a fine-looking girl, bright-spirited and rosy; and when the hearth at the Yew Nook had been as bright as she, with family love and youthful hope and mirth. Fifty or fifty-one years ago, William Dixon and his wife Margaret were alive; and Susan, their daughter, was about eighteen years old—ten years older than the only other child, a boy named after his father. William and Margaret Dixon were rather superior people, of a character belonging—as far as I have seen—exclusively to the class of Westmoreland and Cumberland statesmen—just, independent, upright; not given to much speaking; kind-hearted, but not demonstrative; disliking change, and new ways, and new people; sensible and shrewd; each household self-contained, and its members having little curiosity as to their neighbours, with whom they rarely met for any social intercourse, save at the stated times of sheep-shearing and Christmas; having a certain kind of sober pleasure in amassing money, which occasionally made them miserable (as they call miserly people up in the north) in their old age; reading no light or ephemeral literature, but the grave, solid books brought round by the pedlars (such as the *Paradise Lost* and *Regained*, *The Death of Abel*, *The Spiritual Quixote*, and *The Pilgrim's Progress*), were to be found in nearly every house: the men occasionally going off laking, *i.e.* playing, *i.e.* drinking for days together, and having to be hunted up by anxious wives, who dared not leave their husbands to the chances of the wild precipitous roads, but walked miles and miles, lantern in hand, in the dead of night, to discover and guide the solemnly-drunken husband home; who had a dreadful headache the next day, and the day after that came forth as grave, and sober, and virtuous looking as if there were no such thing as malt and spirituous liquors in the world; and who were seldom reminded of their misdoings by their wives, to whom such occasional outbreaks were as things of course, when once the immediate anxiety produced by them was over. Such were—such are—the characteristics of a class now passing away from the face of the land, as their compeers, the yeomen, have done before them. Of such was William Dixon. He was a shrewd clever farmer, in his day and generation, when shrewdness was rather shown in the breeding and rearing of sheep and cattle than in the cultivation of land. Owing to this character of his, statesmen from a distance from beyond Kendal, or from Borrowdale, of greater wealth than he, would send their sons to be farm-servants for a year or two with him, in order to learn some of his methods before setting up on land of their own. When Susan, his daughter, was about seventeen, one Michael Hurst was farm-servant at Yew Nook. He worked with the master, and lived with the family, and was in all respects treated as an equal, except in the field. His father was a wealthy statesman at Wythburne, up beyond Grasmere; and through Michael's servitude the families had become acquainted, and the Dixons went over to the High Beck sheep-shearing, and the Hursts came down by Red Bank and Loughrig Tarn and across the Oxenfell when there was the Christmastide feasting at Yew Nook. The fathers strolled round the fields together, examined cattle and sheep, and looked knowing over each other's horses. The mothers inspected the dairies and household arrangements, each openly admiring the plans of the other, but secretly preferring their own. Both fathers and mothers cast a glance from time to time at Michael and Susan, who were thinking of nothing less than farm or dairy, but whose unspoken attachment was, in all ways, so suitable and natural a thing that each parent rejoiced over it, although with characteristic reserve it was never spoken about—not even between husband and wife.

Susan had been a strong, independent, healthy girl; a clever help to her mother, and a spirited companion to her father; more of a man in her (as he often said) than her delicate little brother would have. He was his mother's darling, although she loved Susan well. There was no positive engagement between Michael and Susan—I doubt whether even plain words of love had been spoken; when one winter-time Margaret Dixon was seized with inflammation consequent upon a neglected cold. She had always been strong and notable, and had been too busy to attend to the early symptoms of illness. It would go off, she said to the woman who helped in the kitchen; or if she did not feel better when they had got the hams and bacon out of hand, she would take some herb-tea and nurse up a bit. But Death could not wait till the hams and bacon were cured: he came on with rapid strides, and shooting arrows of portentous agony. Susan had never seen illness—never knew how much she loved her mother till now, when she felt a dreadful, instinctive certainty that she was losing her. Her mind was thronged with recollections of the many times she had slighted her mother's wishes; her heart was full of the echoes of careless and angry replies that she had spoken. What would she not now give to have opportunities of service and obedience, and trials of her patience and love, for that dear mother who lay gasping in torture! And yet Susan had been a good girl and an affectionate daughter.

The sharp pain went off, and delicious ease came on; yet still her mother sunk. In the midst of this languid peace she was dying. She motioned Susan to her bedside, for she could only whisper; and then, while the father was out of the room, she spoke as much to the eager, hungering eyes of her daughter by the motion of her lips, as by the slow, feeble sounds of her voice.

" Susan, lass, thou must not fret. It is God's will, and thou
wilt have a deal to do. Keep father straight if thou canst; and
if he goes out Ulverstone ways, see that thou meet him before he
gets to the Old Quarry. It's a dree bit for a man who has had
a drop. As for lile Will "—Here the poor woman's face began
to work and her fingers to move nervously as they lay on the
bed-quilt—" lile Will will miss me most of all. Father's often
vexed with him because he's not a quick strong lad; he is not,
my poor lile chap. And father thinks he's saucy, because he
cannot always stomach oat-cake and porridge. There's better
than three pound in th' old black tea-pot on the top shelf of the
cupboard. Just keep a piece of loaf-bread by you, Susan dear,
for Will to come to when he's not taken his breakfast. I have,
may be, spoilt him; but there'll be no one to spoil him now."

She began to cry a low, feeble cry, and covered up her face
that Susan might not see her. That dear face! those precious
moments while yet the eyes could look out with love and
intelligence. Susan laid her head down close by her mother's
ear.

" Mother, I'll take tent of Will. Mother, do you hear? He
shall not want ought I can give or get for him, least of all the
kind words which you had ever ready for us both. Bless you!
bless you! my own mother."

" Thou'lt promise me that, Susan, wilt thou? I can die easy
if thou'lt take charge of him. But he's hardly like other folk;
he tries father at times, though I think father'll be tender of him
when I'm gone, for my sake. And, Susan, there's one thing
more. I never spoke on it for fear of the bairn being called a
tell-tale, but I just comforted him up. He vexes Michael at
times, and Michael has struck him before now. I did not want
to make a stir; but he's not strong, and a word from thee,
Susan, will go a long way with Michael."

Susan was as red now as she had been pale before; it was
the first time that her influence over Michael had been openly
acknowledged by a third person, and a flash of joy came athwart
the solemn sadness of the moment. Her mother had spoken too
much, and now came on the miserable faintness. She never
spoke again coherently; but when her children and her husband
stood by her bedside, she took lile Will's hand and put it into
Susan's, and looked at her with imploring eyes. Susan clasped
her arms round Will, and leaned her head upon his little curly
one, and vowed within herself to be as a mother to him.

Henceforward she was all in all to her brother. She was a

more spirited and amusing companion to him than his mother
had been, from her greater activity, and perhaps, also, from her
originality of character, which often prompted her to perform
her habitual actions in some new and racy manner. She was
tender to lile Will when she was prompt and sharp with everybody else—with Michael most of all; for somehow the girl
felt that, unprotected by her mother, she must keep up her
own dignity, and not allow her lover to see how strong a hold
he had upon her heart. He called her hard and cruel, and left
her so; and she smiled softly to herself, when his back was
turned, to think how little he guessed how deeply he was loved.
For Susan was merely comely and fine looking; Michael was
strikingly handsome, admired by all the girls for miles round, and
quite enough of a country coxcomb to know it and plume himself
accordingly. He was the second son of his father; the eldest
would have High Beck farm, of course, but there was a good
penny in the Kendal bank in store for Michael. When harvest
was over, he went to Chapel Langdale to learn to dance; and at
night, in his merry moods, he would do his steps on the flag
floor of the Yew Nook kitchen, to the secret admiration of
Susan, who had never learned dancing, but who flouted him perpetually, even while she admired, in accordance with the rule she
seemed to have made for herself about keeping him at a distance
so long as he lived under the same roof with her. One evening he
sulked at some saucy remark of hers; he sitting in the chimney-
corner with his arms on his knees, and his head bent forwards,
lazily gazing into the wood-fire on the hearth, and luxuriating
in rest after a hard day's labour; she sitting among the
geraniums on the long, low window-seat, trying to catch the
last slanting rays of the autumnal light to enable her to finish
stitching a shirt-collar for Will, who lounged full length on the
flags at the other side of the hearth to Michael, poking the
burning wood from time to time with a long hazel-stick to bring
out the leap of glittering sparks.

" And if you can dance a threesome reel, what good does it
do ye?" asked Susan, looking askance at Michael, who had just
been vaunting his proficiency. "Does it help you plough, or
reap, or even climb the rocks to take a raven's nest? If I
were a man, I'd be ashamed to give in to such softness."

" If you were a man, you'd be glad to do anything which
made the pretty girls stand round and admire."

" As they do to you, eh! Ho, Michael, that would not be my
way o' being a man!"

"What would then?" asked he, after a pause, during which he had expected in vain that she would go on with her sentence. No answer.

"I should not like you as a man, Susy; you'd be too hard and headstrong."

"Am I hard and headstrong?" asked she, with as indifferent a tone as she could assume, but which yet had a touch of pique in it. His quick ear detected the inflexion.

"No, Susy! You're wilful at times, and that's right enough. I don't like a girl without spirit. There's a mighty pretty girl comes to the dancing class; but she is all milk and water. Her eyes never flash like yours when you're put out; why, I can see them flame across the kitchen like a cat's in the dark. Now, if you were a man, I should feel queer before those looks of yours; as it is, I rather like them, because——"

"Because what?" asked she, looking up and perceiving that he had stolen close up to her.

"Because I can make all right in this way," said he, kissing her suddenly.

"Can you?" said she, wrenching herself out of his grasp and panting, half with rage. "Take that, by way of proof that making right is none so easy." And she boxed his ears pretty sharply. He went back to his seat discomfited and out of temper. She could no longer see to look, even if her face had not burnt and her eyes dazzled, but she did not choose to move her seat, so she still preserved her stooping attitude and pretended to go on sewing.

"Eleanor Hebthwaite may be milk and water," muttered he, "but— Confound thee, lad! what art thou doing?" exclaimed Michael, as a great piece of burning wood was cast into his face by an unlucky poke of Will's. "Thou great lounging, clumsy chap, I'll teach thee better!" and with one or two good round kicks he sent the lad whimpering away into the back-kitchen. When he had a little recovered himself from his passion, he saw Susan standing before him, her face looking strange and almost ghastly by the reversed position of the shadows, arising from the firelight shining upwards right under it.

"I tell thee what, Michael," said she, "that lad's motherless, but not friendless."

"His own father leathers him, and why should not I, when he's given me such a burn on my face?" said Michael, putting up his hand to his cheek as if in pain.

"His father's his father, and there is nought more to be said.

But if he did burn thee, it was by accident, and not o' purpose; as thou kicked him, it's a mercy if his ribs are not broken."

" He howls loud enough, I'm sure. I might ha' kicked many a lad twice as hard, and they'd ne'er ha' said ought but ' damn ye;' but yon lad must needs cry out like a stuck pig if one touches him;" replied Michael, sullenly.

Susan went back to the window-seat, and looked absently out of the window at the drifting clouds for a minute or two, while her eyes filled with tears. Then she got up and made for the outer door which led into the back-kitchen. Before she reached it, however, she heard a low voice, whose music made her thrill, say—

" Susan, Susan !"

Her heart melted within her, but it seemed like treachery to her poor boy, like faithlessness to her dead mother, to turn to her lover while the tears which he had caused to flow were yet unwiped on Will's cheeks. So she seemed to take no heed, but passed into the darkness, and, guided by the sobs, she found her way to where Willie sat crouched among the disused tubs and churns.

" Come out wi' me, lad;" and they went out into the orchard, where the fruit-trees were bare of leaves, but ghastly in their tattered covering of grey moss: and the soughing November wind came with long sweeps over the fells till it rattled among the crackling boughs, underneath which the brother and sister sat in the dark; he in her lap, and she hushing his head against her shoulder.

" Thou should'st na' play wi' fire. It's a naughty trick. Thou'lt suffer for it in worse ways nor this before thou'st done, I'm afeared. I should ha' hit thee twice as lungeous kicks as Mike, if I'd been in his place. He did na' hurt thee, I am sure," she assumed, half as a question.

" Yes, but he did. He turned me quite sick." And he let his head fall languidly down on his sister's breast.

" Come, lad ! come, lad !" said she anxiously. " Be a man. It was not much that I saw. Why, when first the red cow came she kicked me far harder for offering to milk her before her legs were tied. See thee ! here's a peppermint-drop, and I'll make thee a pasty to-night; only don't give way so, for it hurts me sore to think that Michael has done thee any harm, my pretty."

Willie roused himself up, and put back the wet and ruffled hair from his heated face; and he and Susan rose up, and hand-in-hand went towards the house, walking slowly and quietly except for a kind of sob which Willie could not repress. Susan took him to the pump and washed his tear-stained face, till she thought she had obliterated all traces of the recent disturbance, arranging his curls for him, and then she kissed him tenderly, and led him in, hoping to find Michael in the kitchen, and make all straight between them. But the blaze had dropped down into darkness; the wood was a heap of grey ashes in which the sparks ran hither and thither; but even in the groping darkness Susan knew by the sinking at her heart that Michael was not there. She threw another brand on the hearth and lighted the candle, and sat down to her work in silence. Willie cowered on his stool by the side of the fire, eyeing his sister from time to time, and sorry and oppressed, he knew not why, by the sight of her grave, almost stern face. No one came. They two were in the house alone. The old woman who helped Susan with the household work had gone out for the night to some friend's dwelling. William Dixon, the father, was up on the fells seeing after his sheep. Susan had no heart to prepare the evening meal.

"Susy, darling, are you angry with me?" said Willie, in his little piping, gentle voice. He had stolen up to his sister's side. "I won't never play with the fire again; and I'll not cry if Michael does kick me. Only don't look so like dead mother —don't—don't—please don't!" he exclaimed, hiding his face on her shoulder.

"I'm not angry, Willie," said she. "Don't be feared on me. You want your supper, and you shall have it; and don't you be feared on Michael. He shall give reason for every hair of your head that he touches—he shall."

When William Dixon came home he found Susan and Willie sitting together, hand-in-hand, and apparently pretty cheerful. He bade them go to bed, for that he would sit up for Michael; and the next morning, when Susan came down, she found that Michael had started an hour before with the cart for lime. It was a long day's work; Susan knew it would be late, perhaps later than on the preceding night, before he returned—at any rate, past her usual bed-time; and on no account would she stop up a minute beyond that hour in the kitchen, whatever she might do in her bed-room. Here she sat and watched till past midnight; and when she saw him coming up the brow with the carts, she knew full well, even in that faint moonlight, that his gait was the gait of a man in liquor. But though she was annoyed and mortified to find in what way he had chosen to forget her, the fact did not disgust or shock her as it would have done many a girl, even at that day, who had not been brought up as Susan had, among a class who considered it no crime, but rather a mark of spirit, in a man to get drunk occasionally. Nevertheless, she chose to hold herself very high all the next day when Michael was, perforce, obliged to give up any attempt to do heavy work, and hung about the out-buildings and farm in a very disconsolate and sickly state. Willie had far more pity on him than Susan. Before evening, Willie and he were fast, and, on his side, ostentatious friends. Willie rode the horses down to water; Willie helped him to chop wood. Susan sat gloomily at her work, hearing an indistinct but cheerful conversation going on in the shippon, while the cows were being milked. She almost felt irritated with her little brother, as if he were a traitor, and had gone over to the enemy in the very battle that she was fighting in his cause. She was alone with no one to speak to, while they prattled on regardless if she were glad or sorry.

Soon Willie burst in. " Susan! Susan! come with me; I've something so pretty to show you. Round the corner of the barn —run! run! " He was dragging her along, half reluctant, half desirous of some change in that weary day. Round the corner of the barn; and caught hold of by Michael, who stood there awaiting her.

" O Willie! " cried she, " you naughty boy. There is nothing pretty—what have you brought me here for? Let me go; I won't be held."

" Only one word. Nay, if you wish it so much, you may go," said Michael, suddenly loosing his hold as she struggled. But now she was free, she only drew off a step or two, murmuring something about Willie.

" You are going, then? " said Michael, with seeming sadness. " You won't hear me say a word of what is in my heart."

" How can I tell whether it is what I should like to hear? " replied she, still drawing back.

" That is just what I want you to tell me; I want you to hear it and then to tell me whether you like it or not."

" Well, you may speak," replied she, turning her back, and beginning to plait the hem of her apron.

He came close to her ear.

" I'm sorry I hurt Willie the other night. He has forgiven me. Can you? "

" You hurt him very badly," she replied. " But you are right to be sorry. I forgive you."

" Stop, stop! " said he, laying his hand upon her arm.

" There is something more I've got to say. I want you to be my——what is it they call it, Susan? "

" I don't know," said she, half laughing, but trying to get away with all her might now; and she was a strong girl, but she could not manage it.

" You do. My——what is it I want you to be? "

" I tell you I don't know, and you had best be quiet, and just let me go in, or I shall think you're as bad now as you were last night."

" And how did you know what I was last night? It was past twelve when I came home. Were you watching? Ah, Susan! be my wife, and you shall never have to watch for a drunken husband. If I were your husband, I would come straight home, and count every minute an hour till I saw your bonny face. Now you know what I want you to be. I ask you to be my wife. Will you, my own dear Susan? "

She did not speak for some time. Then she only said " Ask father." And now she was really off like a lapwing round the corner of the barn, and up in her own little room, crying with all her might, before the triumphant smile had left Michael s face where he stood.

The " Ask father " was a mere form to be gone through. Old Daniel Hurst and William Dixon had talked over what they could respectively give their children before this; and that was the parental way of arranging such matters. When the probable amount of worldly gear that he could give his child had been named by each father, the young folk, as they said, might take their own time in coming to the point which the old men, with the prescience of experience, saw they were drifting to; no need to hurry them, for they were both young, and Michael, though active enough, was too thoughtless, old Daniel said, to be trusted with the entire management of a farm. Meanwhile, his father would look about him, and see after all the farms that were to be let.

Michael had a shrewd notion of this preliminary understanding between the fathers, and so felt less daunted than he might otherwise have done at making the application for Susan's hand. It was all right, there was not an obstacle; only a deal of good advice, which the lover thought might have as well been spared, and which it must be confessed he did not much attend to, although he assented to every part of it. Then Susan was called downstairs, and slowly came dropping into view down the steps which led from the two family apartments into the house-place.

She tried to look composed and quiet, but it could not be done. She stood side by side with her lover, with her head drooping, her cheeks burning, not daring to look up or move, while her father made the newly-betrothed a somewhat formal address in which he gave his consent, and many a piece of worldly wisdom beside. Susan listened as well as she could for the beating of her heart; but when her father solemnly and sadly referred to his own lost wife, she could keep from sobbing no longer; but throwing her apron over her face, she sat down on the bench by the dresser, and fairly gave way to pent-up tears. Oh, how strangely sweet to be comforted as she was comforted, by tender caress, and many a low-whispered promise of love! Her father sat by the fire, thinking of the days that were gone; Willie was still out of doors; but Susan and Michael felt no one's presence or absence—they only knew they were together as betrothed husband and wife.

In a week or two, they were formally told of the arrangements to be made in their favour. A small farm in the neighbourhood happened to fall vacant; and Michael's father offered to take it for him, and be responsible for the rent for the first year, while William Dixon was to contribute a certain amount of stock, and both fathers were to help towards the furnishing of the house. Susan received all this information in a quiet, indifferent way; she did not care much for any of these preparations, which were to hurry her through the happy hours; she cared least of all for the money amount of dowry and of substance. It jarred on her to be made the confidante of occasional slight repinings of Michael's, as one by one his future father-in-law set aside a beast or a pig for Susan's portion, which were not always the best animals of their kind upon the farm. But he also complained of his own father's stinginess, which somewhat, though not much, alleviated Susan's dislike to being awakened out of her pure dream of love to the consideration of worldly wealth.

But in the midst of all this bustle, Willie moped and pined. He had the same chord of delicacy running through his mind that made his body feeble and weak. He kept out of the way, and was apparently occupied in whittling and carving uncouth heads on hazel-sticks in an out-house. But he positively avoided Michael, and shrunk away even from Susan. She was too much occupied to notice this at first. Michael pointed it out to her, saying, with a laugh—

"Look at Willie! he might be a cast-off lover and jealous of me, he looks so dark and downcast at me." Michael spoke this jest out loud, and Willie burst into tears, and ran out of the house.

"Let me go. Let me go!" said Susan (for her lover's arm was round her waist). "I must go to him if he's fretting. I promised mother I would!" She pulled herself away, and went in search of the boy. She sought in byre and barn, through the orchard, where indeed in this leafless winter-time there was no great concealment; up into the room where the wool was usually stored in the later summer, and at last she found him, sitting at bay, like some hunted creature, up behind the wood-stack.

"What are ye gone for, lad, and me seeking you everywhere?" asked she, breathless.

"I did not know you would seek me. I've been away many a time, and no one has cared to seek me," said he, crying afresh.

"Nonsense," replied Susan, "don't be so foolish, ye little good-for-nought." But she crept up to him in the hole he had made underneath the great, brown sheaves of wood, and squeezed herself down by him. "What for should folk seek after you, when you get away from them whenever you can?" asked she.

"They don't want me to stay. Nobody wants me. If I go with father, he says I hinder more than I help. You used to like to have me with you. But now, you've taken up with Michael, and you'd rather I was away; and I can just bide away; but I cannot stand Michael jeering at me. He's got you to love him and that might serve him."

"But I love you, too, dearly, lad!" said she, putting her arm round his neck.

"Which on us do you like best?" said he, wistfully, after a little pause, putting her arm away, so that he might look in her face, and see if she spoke truth.

She went very red.

"You should not ask such questions. They are not fit for you to ask, nor for me to answer."

"But mother bade you love me!" said he, plaintively.

"And so I do. And so I ever will do. Lover nor husband shall come betwixt thee and me, lad—ne'er a one of them. That I promise thee (as I promised mother before), in the sight of God and with her hearkening now, if ever she can hearken to earthly word again. Only I cannot abide to have thee fretting, just because my heart is large enough for two."

"And thou'lt love me always?"

"Always, and ever. And the more—the more thou'lt love Michael," said she, dropping her voice.

" I'll try," said the boy, sighing, for he remembered many a harsh word and blow of which his sister knew nothing. She would have risen up to go away, but he held her tight, for here and now she was all his own, and he did not know when such a time might come again. So the two sat crouched up and silent, till they heard the horn blowing at the field-gate, which was the summons home to any wanderers belonging to the farm, and at this hour of the evening, signified that supper was ready. Then the two went in.

CHAPTER II

SUSAN and Michael were to be married in April. He had already gone to take possession of his new farm, three or four miles away from Yew Nook—but that is neighbouring, according to the acceptation of the word in that thinly-populated district—when William Dixon fell ill. He came home one evening, complaining of head-ache and pains in his limbs, but seemed to loathe the posset which Susan prepared for him; the treacle-posset which was the homely country remedy against an incipient cold. He took to his bed with a sensation of exceeding weariness, and an odd, unusual looking-back to the days of his youth, when he was a lad living with his parents, in this very house.

The next morning he had forgotten all his life since then, and did not know his own children; crying, like a newly-weaned baby, for his mother to come and soothe away his terrible pain. The doctor from Coniston said it was the typhus-fever, and warned Susan of its infectious character, and shook his head over his patient. There were no near friends to come and share her anxiety; only good, kind old Peggy, who was faithfulness itself, and one or two labourers' wives, who would fain have helped her, had not their hands been tied by their responsibility to their own families. But, somehow, Susan neither feared nor flagged. As for fear, indeed, she had no time to give way to it, for every energy of both body and mind was required. Besides, the young have had too little experience of the danger of infection to dread it much. She did indeed wish, from time to time, that Michael had been at home to have taken Willie over to his father's at High Beck; but then, again, the lad was docile and useful to her, and his fecklessness in many things might make him harshly treated by strangers; so, perhaps, it was as well that Michael was away at Appleby fair, or even beyond that—gone into Yorkshire after horses.

Her father grew worse; and the doctor insisted on sending over a nurse from Coniston. Not a professed nurse—Coniston could not have supported such a one; but a widow who was ready to go where the doctor sent her for the sake of the payment. When she came, Susan suddenly gave way; she was felled by the fever herself, and lay unconscious for long weeks. Her consciousness returned to her one spring afternoon; early spring; April—her wedding-month. There was a little fire burning in the small corner-grate, and the flickering of the blaze was enough for her to notice in her weak state. She felt that there was some one sitting on the window-side of her bed, behind the curtain, but she did not care to know who it was; it was even too great a trouble for her languid mind to consider who it was likely to be. She would rather shut her eyes, and melt off again into the gentle luxury of sleep. The next time she wakened, the Coniston nurse perceived her movement, and made her a cup of tea, which she drank with eager relish; but still they did not speak, and once more Susan lay motionless—not asleep, but strangely, pleasantly conscious of all the small chamber and household sounds; the fall of a cinder on the hearth, the fitful singing of the half-empty kettle, the cattle tramping out to field again after they had been milked, the aged step on the creaking stair—old Peggy's, as she knew. It came to her door; it stopped; the person outside listened for a moment, and then lifted the wooden latch, and looked in. The watcher by the bedside arose, and went to her. Susan would have been glad to see Peggy's face once more, but was far too weak to turn, so she lay and listened.

" How is she? " whispered one trembling, aged voice.

" Better," replied the other. " She's been awake, and had a cup of tea. She'll do now."

" Has she asked after him? "

" Hush! No; she has not spoken a word."

" Poor lass! poor lass! "

The door was shut. A weak feeling of sorrow and self-pity came over Susan. What was wrong? Whom had she loved? And dawning, dawning, slowly rose the sun of her former life, and all particulars were made distinct to her. She felt that some sorrow was coming to her, and cried over it before she knew what it was, or had strength enough to ask. In the dead of night—and she had never slept again—she softly called to the watcher, and asked—

" Who? "

" Who what? " replied the woman, with a conscious affright, ill-veiled by a poor assumption of ease. " Lie still, there's a darling, and go to sleep. Sleep's better for you than all the doctor's stuff."

" Who? " repeated Susan. " Something is wrong. Who? "

" Oh, dear! " said the woman. " There's nothing wrong. Willie has taken the turn and is doing nicely."

" Father? "

" Well! he's all right now," she answered, looking another way, as if seeking for something.

" Then it's Michael! Oh, me! oh, me! " She set up a succession of weak, plaintive, hysterical cries before the nurse could pacify her, by declaring that Michael had been at the house not three hours before to ask after her, and looked as well and as hearty as ever man did.

" And you heard of no harm to him since? " inquired Susan.

" Bless the lass, no, for sure! I've ne'er heard his name named since I saw him go out of the yard as stout a man as ever trod shoe-leather."

It was well, as the nurse said afterwards to Peggy, that Susan had been so easily pacified by the equivocating answer in respect to her father. If she had pressed the questions home in his case as she did in Michael's, she would have learnt that he was dead and buried more than a month before. It was well, too, that in her weak state of convalescence (which lasted long after this first day of consciousness) her perceptions were not sharp enough to observe the sad change that had taken place in Willie. His bodily strength returned, his appetite was something enormous, but his eyes wandered continually; his regard could not be arrested; his speech became slow, impeded, and incoherent. People began to say, that the fever had taken away the little wit Willie Dixon had ever possessed, and that they feared that he would end in being a " natural," as they call an idiot in the Dales.

The habitual affection and obedience to Susan lasted longer than any other feeling that the boy had had previous to his illness; and, perhaps, this made her be the last to perceive what every one else had long anticipated. She felt the awakening rude when it did come. It was in this wise:—

One June evening, she sat out of doors under the yew-tree,

knitting. She was pale still from her recent illness; and her languor, joined to the fact of her black dress, made her look more than usually interesting. She was no longer the buoyant self-sufficient Susan, equal to every occasion. The men were bringing in the cows to be milked, and Michael was about in the yard giving orders and directions with somewhat the air of a master, for the farm belonged of right to Willie, and Susan had succeeded to the guardianship of her brother. Michael and she were to be married as soon as she was strong enough—so, perhaps, his authoritative manner was justified; but the labourers did not like it, although they said little. They remembered him a stripling on the farm, knowing far less than they did, and often glad to shelter his ignorance of all agricultural matters behind their superior knowledge. They would have taken orders from Susan with far more willingness; nay, Willie himself might have commanded them; and from the old hereditary feeling towards the owners of land, they would have obeyed him with far greater cordiality than they now showed to Michael. But Susan was tired with even three rounds of knitting, and seemed not to notice, or to care, how things went on around her; and Willie—poor Willie!—there he stood lounging against the door-sill, enormously grown and developed, to be sure, but with restless eyes and ever-open mouth, and every now and then setting up a strange kind of howling cry, and then smiling vacantly to himself at the sound he had made. As the two old labourers passed him, they looked at each other ominously, and shook their heads.

"Willie, darling," said Susan, "don't make that noise—it makes my head ache."

She spoke feebly, and Willie did not seem to hear; at any rate, he continued his howl from time to time.

"Hold thy noise, wilt'a?" said Michael, roughly, as he passed near him, and threatening him with his fist. Susan's back was turned to the pair. The expression of Willie's face changed from vacancy to fear, and he came shambling up to Susan, who put her arm round him, and, as if protected by that shelter, he began making faces at Michael. Susan saw what was going on, and, as if now first struck by the strangeness of her brother's manner, she looked anxiously at Michael for an explanation. Michael was irritated at Willie's defiance of him, and did not mince the matter.

"It's just that the fever has left him silly—he never was as wise as other folk, and now I doubt if he will ever get right."

Susan did not speak, but she went very pale, and her lip quivered. She looked long and wistfully at Willie's face, as he watched the motion of the ducks in the great stable-pool. He laughed softly to himself every now and then.

"Willie likes to see the ducks go overhead," said Susan, instinctively adopting the form of speech she would have used to a young child.

"Willie, boo! Willie, boo!" he replied, clapping his hands, and avoiding her eye.

"Speak properly, Willie," said Susan, making a strong effort at self-control, and trying to arrest his attention.

"You know who I am—tell me my name!" She grasped his arm almost painfully tight to make him attend. Now he looked at her, and, for an instant, a gleam of recognition quivered over his face; but the exertion was evidently painful, and he began to cry at the vainness of the effort to recall her name. He hid his face upon her shoulder with the old affectionate trick of manner. She put him gently away, and went into the house into her own little bedroom. She locked the door, and did not reply at all to Michael's calls for her, hardly spoke to old Peggy, who tried to tempt her out to receive some homely sympathy, and through the open casement there still came the idiotic sound of "Willie, boo! Willie, boo!"

CHAPTER III

After the stun of the blow came the realisation of the consequences. Susan would sit for hours trying patiently to recall and piece together fragments of recollection and consciousness in her brother's mind. She would let him go and pursue some senseless bit of play, and wait until she could catch his eye or his attention again, when she would resume her self-imposed task. Michael complained that she never had a word for him, or a minute of time to spend with him now; but she only said she must try, while there was yet a chance, to bring back her brother's lost wits. As for marriage in this state of uncertainty, she had no heart to think of it. Then Michael stormed, and absented himself for two or three days; but it was of no use. When he came back, he saw that she had been crying till her eyes were all swollen up, and he gathered from Peggy's scoldings (which she did not spare him) that Susan had eaten nothing since he went away. But she was as inflexible as ever.

"Not just yet. Only not just yet. And don't say again that I do not love you," said she, suddenly hiding herself in his arms.

And so matters went on through August. The crop of oats was gathered in; the wheat-field was not ready as yet, when one fine day Michael drove up in a borrowed shandry, and offered to take Willie a ride. His manner, when Susan asked him where he was going to, was rather confused; but the answer was straight and clear enough.

He had business in Ambleside. He would never lose sight of the lad, and have him back safe and sound before dark. So Susan let him go.

Before night they were at home again: Willie in high delight at a little rattling paper windmill that Michael had bought for him in the street, and striving to imitate this new sound with perpetual buzzings. Michael, too, looked pleased. Susan knew the look, although afterwards she remembered that he had tried to veil it from her, and had assumed a grave appearance of sorrow whenever he caught her eye. He put up his horse; for, although he had three miles further to go, the moon was up— the bonny harvest-moon—and he did not care how late he had to drive on such a road by such a light. After the supper which Susan had prepared for the travellers was over, Peggy went upstairs to see Willie safe in bed; for he had to have the same care taken of him that a little child of four years old requires.

Michael drew near to Susan.

"Susan," said he, "I took Will to see Dr. Preston, at Kendal. He's the first doctor in the county. I thought it were better for us—for you—to know at once what chance there were for him."

"Well!" said Susan, looking eagerly up. She saw the same strange glance of satisfaction, the same instant change to apparent regret and pain. "What did he say?" said she. "Speak! can't you?"

"He said he would never get better of his weakness."

"Never!"

"No; never. It's a long word, and hard to bear. And there's worse to come, dearest. The doctor thinks he will get badder from year to year. And he said, if he was us—you— he would send him off in time to Lancaster Asylum. They've ways there both of keeping such people in order and making them happy. I only tell you what he said," continued he, seeing the gathering storm in her face.

" There was no harm in his saying it," she replied, with great self-constraint, forcing herself to speak coldly instead of angrily. " Folk is welcome to their opinions."

They sat silent for a minute or two, her breast heaving with suppressed feeling.

" He's counted a very clever man," said Michael at length.

" He may be. He's none of my clever men, nor am I going to be guided by him, whatever he may think. And I don't thank them that went and took my poor lad to have such harsh notions formed about him. If I'd been there, I could have called out the sense that is in him."

" Well! I'll not say more to-night, Susan. You're not taking it rightly, and I'd best be gone, and leave you to think it over. I'll not deny they are hard words to hear, but there's sense in them, as I take it; and I reckon you'll have to come to 'em. Anyhow, it's a bad way of thanking me for my pains, and I don't take it well in you, Susan," said he, getting up, as if offended.

" Michael, I'm beside myself with sorrow. Don't blame me if I speak sharp. He and me is the only ones, you see. And mother did so charge me to have a care of him! And this is what he's come to, poor lile chap!" She began to cry, and Michael to comfort her with caresses.

" Don't," said she. " It's no use trying to make me forget poor Willie is a natural. I could hate myself for being happy with you, even for just a little minute. Go away, and leave me to face it out."

" And you'll think it over, Susan, and remember what the doctor says? "

" I can't forget," said she. She meant she could not forget what the doctor had said about the hopelessness of her brother's case; Michael had referred to the plan of sending Willie to an asylum, or madhouse, as they were called in that day and place. The idea had been gathering force in Michael's mind for some time; he had talked it over with his father, and secretly rejoiced over the possession of the farm and land which would then be his in fact, if not in law, by right of his wife. He had always considered the good penny her father could give her in his catalogue of Susan's charms and attractions. But of late he had grown to esteem her as the heiress of Yew Nook. He, too, should have land like his brother—land to possess, to cultivate, to make profit from, to bequeath. For some time he had wondered that Susan had been so much absorbed in Willie's present, that she had never seemed to look forward to his future, state. Michael had long felt the boy to be a trouble; but of late he had absolutely loathed him. His gibbering, his uncouth gestures, his loose, shambling gait, all irritated Michael inexpressibly. He did not come near the Yew Nook for a couple of days. He thought that he would leave her time to become anxious to see him and reconciled to his plan. They were strange lonely days to Susan. They were the first she had spent face to face with the sorrows that had turned her from a girl into a woman; for hitherto Michael had never let twenty-four hours pass by without coming to see her since she had had the fever. Now that he was absent, it seemed as though some cause of irritation was removed from Will, who was much more gentle and tractable than he had been for many weeks. Susan thought that she observed him making efforts at her bidding, and there was something piteous in the way in which he crept up to her, and looked wistfully in her face, as if asking her to restore him the faculties that he felt to be wanting.

"I never will let thee go, lad. Never! There's no knowing where they would take thee to, or what they would do with thee. As it says in the Bible, 'Nought but death shall part thee and me!'"

The country-side was full, in those days, of stories of the brutal treatment offered to the insane; stories that were, in fact, but too well founded, and the truth of one of which only would have been a sufficient reason for the strong prejudice existing against all such places. Each succeeding hour that Susan passed, alone, or with the poor affectionate lad for her sole companion, served to deepen her solemn resolution never to part with him. So, when Michael came, he was annoyed and surprised by the calm way in which she spoke, as if following Dr. Preston's advice was utterly and entirely out of the question. He had expected nothing less than a consent, reluctant it might be, but still a consent; and he was extremely irritated. He could have repressed his anger, but he chose rather to give way to it; thinking that he could thus best work upon Susan's affection, so as to gain his point. But, somehow, he over-reached himself; and now he was astonished in his turn at the passion of indignation that she burst into.

"Thou wilt not bide in the same house with him, say'st thou? There's no need for thy biding, as far as I can tell. There's solemn reason why I should bide with my own flesh and blood, and keep to the word I pledged my mother on her death-bed;

but, as for thee, there's no tie that I know on to keep thee fro' going to America or Botany Bay this very night, if that were thy inclination. I will have no more of your threats to make me send my bairn away. If thou marry me, thou'lt help me to take charge of Willie. If thou doesn't choose to marry me on those terms—why, I can snap my fingers at thee, never fear. I'm not so far gone in love as that. But I will not have thee, if thou say'st in such a hectoring way that Willie must go out of the house—and the house his own too—before thou'lt set foot in it. Willie bides here, and I bide with him."

"Thou hast maybe spoken a word too much," said Michael, pale with rage. "If I am free, as thou say'st, to go to Canada, or Botany Bay, I reckon I'm free to live where I like, and that will not be with a natural who may turn into a madman some day, for aught I know. Choose between him and me, Susy, for I swear to thee, thou shan't have both."

"I have chosen," said Susan, now perfectly composed and still. "Whatever comes of it, I bide with Willie."

"Very well," replied Michael, trying to assume an equal composure of manner. "Then I'll wish you a very good night." He went out of the house door, half-expecting to be called back again; but, instead, he heard a hasty step inside, and a bolt drawn.

"Whew!" said he to himself, "I think I must leave my lady alone for a week or two, and give her time to come to her senses. She'll not find it so easy as she thinks to let me go."

So he went past the kitchen-window in nonchalant style, and was not seen again at Yew Nook for some weeks. How did he pass the time? For the first day or two, he was unusually cross with all things and people that came athwart him. Then wheat-harvest began, and he was busy, and exultant about his heavy crop. Then a man came from a distance to bid for the lease of his farm, which, by his father's advice, had been offered for sale, as he himself was so soon likely to remove to the Yew Nook. He had so little idea that Susan really would remain firm to her determination, that he at once began to haggle with the man who came after his farm, showed him the crop just got in, and managed skilfully enough to make a good bargain for himself. Of course, the bargain had to be sealed at the public-house; and the companions he met with there soon became friends enough to tempt him into Langdale, where again he met with Eleanor Hebthwaite.

How did Susan pass the time? For the first day or so, she

was too angry and offended to cry. She went about her household duties in a quick, sharp, jerking, yet absent way; shrinking one moment from Will, overwhelming him with remorseful caresses the next. The third day of Michael's absence, she had the relief of a good fit of crying; and after that, she grew softer and more tender; she felt how harshly she had spoken to him, and remembered how angry she had been. She made excuses for him. " It was no wonder," she said to herself, " that he had been vexed with her; and no wonder he would not give in, when she had never tried to speak gently or to reason with him. She was to blame, and she would tell him so, and tell him once again all that her mother had bade her to be to Willie, and all the horrible stories she had heard about madhouses, and he would be on her side at once."

And so she watched for his coming, intending to apologise as soon as ever she saw him. She hurried over her household work, in order to sit quietly at her sewing, and hear the first distant sound of his well-known step or whistle. But even the sound of her flying needle seemed too loud—perhaps she was losing an exquisite instant of anticipation; so she stopped sewing, and looked longingly out through the geranium leaves, in order that her eye might catch the first stir of the branches in the wood-path by which he generally came. Now and then a bird might spring out of the covert; otherwise the leaves were heavily still in the sultry weather of early autumn. Then she would take up her sewing, and, with a spasm of resolution, she would determine that a certain task should be fulfilled before she would again allow herself the poignant luxury of expectation. Sick at heart was she when the evening closed in, and the chances of that day diminished. Yet she stayed up longer than usual, thinking that if he were coming—if he were only passing along the distant road—the sight of a light in the window might encourage him to make his appearance even at that late hour, while seeing the house all darkened and shut up might quench any such intention.

Very sick and weary at heart, she went to bed; too desolate and despairing to cry, or make any moan. But in the morning hope came afresh. Another day—another chance! And so it went on for weeks. Peggy understood her young mistress's sorrow full well, and respected it by her silence on the subject. Willie seemed happier now that the irritation of Michael's presence was removed; for the poor idiot had a sort of antipathy to Michael, which was a kind of heart's echo to the repugnance in which the latter held him. Altogether, just at this time, Willie was the happiest of the three.

As Susan went into Coniston, to sell her butter, one Saturday, some inconsiderate person told her that she had seen Michael Hurst the night before. I said inconsiderate, but I might rather have said unobservant; for any one who had spent half-an-hour in Susan Dixon's company might have seen that she disliked having any reference made to the subjects nearest her heart, were they joyous or grievous. Now she went a little paler than usual (and she had never recovered her colour since she had had the fever), and tried to keep silence. But an irrepressible pang forced out the question—

" Where? "

" At Thomas Applethwaite's, in Langdale. They had a kind of harvest-home, and he were there among the young folk, and very thick wi' Nelly Hebthwaite, old Thomas's niece. Thou'lt have to look after him a bit, Susan! "

She neither smiled nor sighed. The neighbour who had been speaking to her was struck with the grey stillness of her face. Susan herself felt how well her self-command was obeyed by every little muscle, and said to herself in her Spartan manner, " I can bear it without either wincing or blenching." She went home early, at a tearing, passionate pace, trampling and breaking though all obstacles of briar or bush. Willie was moping in her absence—hanging listlessly on the farm-yard gate to watch for her. When he saw her, he set up one of his strange, inarticulate cries, of which she was now learning the meaning, and came towards her with his loose, galloping run, head and limbs all shaking and wagging with pleasant excitement. Suddenly she turned from him, and burst into tears. She sat down on a stone by the wayside, not a hundred yards from home, and buried her face in her hands, and gave way to a passion of pent-up sorrow; so terrible and full of agony were her low cries that the idiot stood by her, aghast and silent. All his joy gone for the time, but not, like her joy, turned into ashes. Some thought struck him. Yes! the sight of her woe made him think, great as the exertion was. He ran, and stumbled, and shambled home, buzzing with his lips all the time. She never missed him. He came back in a trice, bringing with him his cherished paper windmill, bought on that fatal day when Michael had taken him into Kendal to have his doom of perpetual idiotcy pronounced. He thrust it into Susan's face, her hands, her lap, regardless of the injury his frail plaything thereby received. He leapt before her to think how he had cured all heart-sorrow, buzzing louder than ever. Susan looked up at him, and that glance of her sad eyes sobered him. He began to whimper, he knew not why: and she now, comforter in her turn, tried to soothe him by twirling his windmill. But it was broken; it made no noise; it would not go round. This seemed to afflict Susan more than him. She tried to make it right, although she saw the task was hopeless; and while she did so, the tears rained down unheeded from her bent head on the paper toy.

" It won't do," said she, at last. " It will never do again." And, somehow, she took the accident and her words as omens of the love that was broken, and that she feared could never be pieced together more. She rose up and took Willie's hand, and the two went slowly into the house.

To her surprise, Michael Hurst sat in the house-place. House-place is a sort of better kitchen, where no cookery is done, but which is reserved for state occasions. Michael had gone in there because he was accompanied by his only sister, a woman older than himself, who was well married beyond Keswick, and who now came for the first time to make acquaintance with Susan. Michael had primed his sister with his wishes regarding Will, and the position in which he stood with Susan; and arriving at Yew Nook in the absence of the latter, he had not scrupled to conduct his sister into the guest-room, as he held Mrs. Gale's worldly position in respect and admiration, and therefore wished her to be favourably impressed with all the signs of property which he was beginning to consider as Susan's greatest charms. He had secretly said to himself, that if Eleanor Hebthwaite and Susan Dixon were equal in point of riches, he would sooner have Eleanor by far. He had begun to consider Susan as a termagant, and when he thought of his intercourse with her, recollections of her somewhat warm and hasty temper came far more readily to his mind than any remembrance of her generous, loving nature.

And now she stood face to face with him; her eyes tear-swollen, her garments dusty, and here and there torn in consequence of her rapid progress through the bushy by-paths. She did not make a favourable impression on the well-clad Mrs. Gale, dressed in her best silk gown, and therefore unusually susceptible to the appearance of another. Nor were Susan's manners gracious or cordial. How could they be, when she remembered what had passed between Michael and herself the last time they met? For her penitence had faded away under the daily disappoint-ment of these last weary weeks.

But she was hospitable in substance. She bade Peggy hurry on the kettle, and busied herself among the tea-cups, thankful that the presence of Mrs. Gale, as a stranger, would prevent the immediate recurrence to the one subject which she felt must be present in Michael's mind as well as in her own. But Mrs. Gale was withheld by no such feelings of delicacy. She had come ready-primed with the case, and had undertaken to bring the girl to reason. There was no time to be lost. It had been pre-arranged between the brother and sister that he was to stroll out into the farm-yard before his sister introduced the subject; but she was so confident in the success of her arguments, that she must needs have the triumph of a victory as soon as possible; and, accordingly, she brought a hail-storm of good reasons to bear upon Susan. Susan did not reply for a long time; she was so indignant at this intermeddling of a stranger in the deep family sorrow and shame. Mrs Gale thought she was gaining the day, and urged her arguments more pitilessly. Even Michael winced for Susan, and wondered at her silence. He shrunk out of sight, and into the shadow, hoping that his sister might prevail, but annoyed at the hard way in which she kept putting the case.

Suddenly Susan turned round from the occupation she had pretended to be engaged in, and said to him in a low voice, which yet not only vibrated itself, but made its hearers thrill through all their obtuseness:

" Michael Hurst! does your sister speak truth, think you? "

Both women looked at him for his answer; Mrs. Gale without anxiety, for had she not said the very words they had spoken together before? had she not used the very arguments that he himself had suggested? Susan, on the contrary, looked to his answer as settling her doom for life; and in the gloom of her eyes you might have read more despair than hope.

He shuffled his position. He shuffled in his words.

" What is it you ask? My sister has said many things."

" I ask you," said Susan, trying to give a crystal clearness both to her expressions and her pronunciations, " if, knowing as you do how Will is afflicted, you will help me to take that charge of him which I promised my mother on her death-bed that I would do; and which means, that I shall keep him always with me, and do all in my power to make his life happy. If you will do this, I will be your wife; if not, I remain unwed."

" But he may get dangerous; he can be but a trouble; his being here is a pain to you, Susan, not a pleasure."

" I ask you for either yes or no," said she, a little contempt at his evading her question mingling with her tone. He perceived it, and it nettled him.

" And I have told you. I answered your question the last time I was here. I said I would ne'er keep house with an idiot; no more I will. So now you've gotten your answer."

" I have," said Susan. And she sighed deeply.

" Come, now," said Mrs. Gale, encouraged by the sigh; " one would think you don't love Michael, Susan, to be so stubborn in yielding to what I'm sure would be best for the lad."

" Oh! she does not care for me," said Michael. " I don't believe she ever did."

" Don't I? Haven't I? " asked Susan, her eyes blazing out fire. She left the room directly, and sent Peggy in to make the tea; and catching at Will, who was lounging about in the kitchen, she went upstairs with him and bolted herself in, straining the boy to her heart, and keeping almost breathless, lest any noise she made might cause him to break out into the howls and sounds which she could not bear that those below should hear.

A knock at the door. It was Peggy.

" He wants for to see you, to wish you good-bye."

" I cannot come. Oh, Peggy, send them away."

It was her only cry for sympathy; and the old servant understood it. She sent them away, somehow; not politely, as I have been given to understand.

" Good go with them," said Peggy, as she grimly watched their retreating figures. " We're rid of bad rubbish, anyhow." And she turned into the house, with the intention of making ready some refreshment for Susan, after her hard day at the market, and her harder evening. But in the kitchen, to which she passed through the empty house-place, making a face of contemptuous dislike at the used teacups and fragments of a meal yet standing there, she found Susan, with her sleeves tucked up and her working apron on, busied in preparing to make clap-bread, one of the hardest and hottest domestic tasks of a Daleswoman. She looked up, and first met, and then avoided Peggy's eye; it was too full of sympathy. Her own cheeks were flushed, and her own eyes were dry and burning.

" Where's the board, Peggy? We need clap-bread; and, I reckon, I've time to get through with it to-night." Her voice had a sharp, dry tone in it, and her motions a jerking angularity about them.

Peggy said nothing, but fetched her all that she needed. Susan beat her cakes thin with vehement force. As she stooped over them, regardless even of the task in which she seemed so much occupied, she was surprised by a touch on her mouth of something—what she did not see at first. It was a cup of tea, delicately sweetened and cooled, and held to her lips, when exactly ready, by the faithful old woman. Susan held it off a hand's-breadth, and looked into Peggy's eyes, while her own filled with the strange relief of tears.

" Lass! " said Peggy, solemnly, " thou hast done well. It is not long to bide, and then the end will come."

" But you are very old, Peggy," said Susan, quivering.

" It is but a day sin' I were young," replied Peggy; but she stopped the conversation by again pushing the cup with gentle force to Susan's dry and thirsty lips. When she had drunken she fell again to her labour, Peggy heating the hearth, and doing all that she knew would be required, but never speaking another word. Willie basked close to the fire, enjoying the animal luxury of warmth, for the autumn evenings were beginning to be chilly. It was one o'clock before they thought of going to bed on that memorable night.

CHAPTER IV

THE vehemence with which Susan Dixon threw herself into occupation could not last for ever. Times of languor and remembrance would come—times when she recurred with a passionate yearning to bygone days, the recollection of which was so vivid and delicious that it seemed as though it were the reality, and the present bleak bareness the dream. She smiled anew at the magical sweetness of some touch or tone which in memory she felt and heard, and drank the delicious cup of poison, although at the very time she knew what the consequences of racking pain would be.

"This time, last year," thought she, "we went nutting together —this very day last year; just such a day as to-day. Purple and gold were the lights on the hills; the leaves were just turning brown; here and there on the sunny slopes the stubble-fields looked tawny; down in a cleft of yon purple slate-rock the beck fell like a silver glancing thread; all just as it is to-day. And he climbed the slender, swaying nut-trees, and bent the branches for me to gather; or made a passage through the hazel copses, from time to time claiming a toll. Who could have thought he loved me so little?—who?—who?"

Or, as the evening closed in, she would allow herself to imagine that she heard his coming step, just that she might recall the feeling of exquisite delight which had passed by without the due and passionate relish at the time. Then she would wonder how she could have had strength, the cruel, self-piercing strength, to say what she had done; to stab herself with that stern resolution, of which the scar would remain till her dying day. It might have been right; but, as she sickened, she wished she had not instinctively chosen the right. How luxurious a life haunted by no stern sense of duty must be! And many led this kind of life; why could not she? O, for one hour again of his sweet company! If he came now, she would agree to whatever he proposed.

It was a fever of the mind. She passed through it, and came out healthy, if weak. She was capable once more of taking pleasure in following an unseen guide through briar and brake. She returned with tenfold affection to her protecting care of Willie. She acknowledged to herself that he was to be her all-in-all in life. She made him her constant companion. For his sake, as the real owner of Yew Nook, and she as his steward and guardian, she began that course of careful saving, and that love of acquisition, which afterwards gained for her the reputation of being miserly. She still thought that he might regain a scanty portion of sense—enough to require some simple pleasures and excitement, which would cost money. And money should not be wanting. Peggy rather assisted her in the formation of her parsimonious habits than otherwise; economy was the order of the district, and a certain degree of respectable avarice the characteristic of her age. Only Willie was never stinted nor hindered of anything that the two women thought could give him pleasure, for want of money.

There was one gratification which Susan felt was needed for the restoration of her mind to its more healthy state, after she had passed through the whirling fever, when duty was as nothing, and anarchy reigned; a gratification that, somehow, was to be her last burst of unreasonableness; of which she knew and recognised pain as the sure consequence. She must see him once more,—herself unseen.

The week before the Christmas of this memorable year, she went out in the dusk of the early winter evening, wrapped close in shawl and cloak. She wore her dark shawl under her cloak, putting it over her head in lieu of a bonnet; for she knew that she might have to wait long in concealment. Then she tramped over the wet fell-path, shut in by misty rain for miles and miles, till she came to the place where he was lodging; a farm-house in Langdale, with a steep, stony lane leading up to it: this lane was entered by a gate out of the main road, and by the gate were a few bushes—thorns; but of them the leaves had fallen, and they offered no concealment: an old wreck of a yew-tree grew among them, however, and underneath that Susan cowered down, shrouding her face, of which the colour might betray her, with a corner of her shawl. Long did she wait; cold and cramped she became, too damp and stiff to change her posture readily. And after all, he might never come! But, she would wait till daylight, if need were; and she pulled out a crust, with which she had providently supplied herself. The rain had ceased,—a dull, still, brooding weather had succeeded; it was a night to hear distant sounds. She heard horses' hoofs striking and splashing in the stones, and in the pools of the road at her back. Two horses; not well ridden, or evenly guided, as she could tell.

Michael Hurst and a companion drew near; not tipsy, but not sober. They stopped at the gate to bid each other a maudlin farewell. Michael stooped forward to catch the latch with the hook of the stick which he carried; he dropped the stick, and it fell with one end close to Susan,—indeed, with the slightest change of posture she could have opened the gate for him. He swore a great oath, and struck his horse with his closed fist, as if that animal had been to blame; then he dismounted, opened the gate, and fumbled about for his stick. When he had found it (Susan had touched the other end) his first use of it was to flog his horse well, and she had much ado to avoid its kicks and plunges. Then, still swearing, he staggered up the lane, for it was evident he was not sober enough to remount.

By daylight Susan was back and at her daily labours at Yew Nook. When the spring came, Michael Hurst was married to Eleanor Hebthwaite. Others, too, were married, and christenings made their firesides merry and glad; or they travelled, and came back after long years with many wondrous tales. More rarely, perhaps, a Dalesman changed his dwelling. But to all households more change came than to Yew Nook. There the seasons came round with monotonous sameness; or, if they brought mutation, it was of a slow, and decaying, and depressing kind. Old Peggy died. Her silent sympathy, concealed under much roughness, was a loss to Susan Dixon. Susan was not yet thirty when this happened, but she looked a middle-aged, not to say an elderly woman. People affirmed that she had never recovered her complexion since that fever, a dozen years ago, which killed her father, and left Will Dixon an idiot. But besides her grey sallowness, the lines in her face were strong, and deep, and hard. The movements of her eyeballs were slow and heavy; the wrinkles at the corners of her mouth and eyes were planted firm and sure; not an ounce of unnecessary flesh was there on her bones—every muscle started strong and ready for use. She needed all this bodily strength, to a degree that no human creature, now Peggy was dead, knew of: for Willie had grown up large and strong in body, and, in general, docile enough in mind; but, every now and then, he became first moody, and then violent. These paroxysms lasted but a day or two; and it was Susan's anxious care to keep their very existence hidden and unknown. It is true, that occasional passers-by on that lonely road heard sounds at night of knocking about of furniture, blows, and cries, as of some tearing demon within the solitary farm-house; but these fits of violence usually occurred in the night; and whatever had been their consequence, Susan had tidied and redded up all signs of aught unusual before the morning. For, above all, she dreaded lest some one might find out in what danger and peril she occasionally was, and might assume a right to take away her brother from her care. The one idea of taking charge of him had deepened and deepened with years. It was graven into her mind as the object for which she lived. The sacrifice she had made for this object only made it more precious to her. Besides, she separated the idea of the docile, affectionate, loutish, indolent Will, and kept it distinct from the terror which the demon that occasionally possessed him inspired her with. The one was her flesh and her blood—the child of her dead mother; the other was some fiend who came to torture and convulse the creature she so loved. She believed that she fought her brother's battle in holding down those tearing hands, in binding whenever she could those uplifted restless arms prompt and prone to do mischief. All the time she subdued him with her cunning or her strength, she spoke to him in pitying murmurs, or abused the third person, the fiendish enemy, in no unmeasured tones. Towards morning the paroxysm was exhausted, and he would fall asleep, perhaps only to waken with evil and renewed vigour. But when he was laid down, she would sally out to taste the fresh air, and to work off her wild sorrow in cries and mutterings to herself. The early labourers saw her gestures at a distance, and thought her as crazed as the idiot-brother who made the neighbourhood a haunted place. But did any chance person call at Yew Nook later on in the day, he would find Susan Dixon cold, calm, collected; her manner curt, her wits keen.

Once this fit of violence lasted longer than usual. Susan's strength both of mind and body was nearly worn out; she wrestled in prayer that somehow it might end before she, too, was driven mad; or, worse, might be obliged to give up life's aim, and consign Willie to a madhouse. From that moment of prayer (as she afterwards superstitiously thought) Willie calmed—and then he drooped—and then he sank—and, last of all, he died in reality from physical exhaustion.

But he was so gentle and tender as he lay on his dying bed; such strange, child-like gleams of returning intelligence came over his face, long after the power to make his dull, inarticulate sounds had departed, that Susan was attracted to him by a stronger tie than she had ever felt before. It was something to have even an idiot loving her with dumb, wistful, animal affection; something to have any creature looking at her with such beseeching eyes, imploring protection from the insidious enemy stealing on. And yet she knew that to him death was no enemy, but a true friend, restoring light and health to his poor clouded mind. It was to her that death was an enemy; to her, the survivor, when Willie died; there was no one to love her. Worse doom still, there was no one left on earth for her to love.

You now know why no wandering tourist could persuade her to receive him as a lodger; why no tired traveller could melt her heart to afford him rest and refreshment; why long habits of seclusion had given her a moroseness of manner, and how care for the interests of another had rendered her keen and miserly.

But there was a third act in the drama of her life.

CHAPTER V

IN spite of Peggy's prophecy that Susan's life should not seem long, it did seem wearisome and endless, as the years slowly uncoiled their monotonous circles. To be sure, she might have made change for herself, but she did not care to do it. It was, indeed, more than " not caring," which merely implies a certain degree of *vis inertiæ* to be subdued before an object can be attained, and that the object itself does not seem to be of sufficient importance to call out the requisite energy. On the contrary, Susan exerted herself to avoid change and variety. She had a morbid dread of new faces, which originated in her desire to keep poor dead Willie's state a profound secret. She had a contempt for new customs; and, indeed, her old ways prospered so well under her active hand and vigilant eye, that it was difficult to know how they could be improved upon. She was regularly present in Coniston market with the best butter and the earliest chickens of the season. Those were the common farm produce that every farmer's wife about had to sell; but Susan, after she had disposed of the more feminine articles, turned to on the man's side. A better judge of a horse or cow there was not in all the country round. Yorkshire itself might have attempted to jockey her, and would have failed. Her corn was sound and clean; her potatoes well preserved to the latest spring. People began to talk of the hoards of money Susan Dixon must have laid up somewhere; and one young ne'er-do-weel of a farmer's son undertook to make lo e to the woman of forty, who looked fifty-five, if a day. He made up to her by opening a gate on the road-path home, as she was riding on a bare-backed horse, her purchase not an hour ago. She was off before him, refusing his civility; but the remounting was not so easy, and rather than fail she did not choose to attempt it. She walked, and he walked alongside, improving his opportunity, which, as he vainly thought, had been consciously granted to him. As they drew near Yew Nook, he ventured on some expression of a wish to keep company with her. His words were vague and clumsily arranged. Susan turned round and coolly asked him to explain himself. He took courage, as he thought of her reputed wealth, and expressed his wishes this second time pretty plainly. To his surprise, the reply she made was in a series of smart strokes across his shoulders, administered through the medium of a supple hazel-switch.

"Take that!" said she, almost breathless, "to teach thee how thou darest make a fool of an honest woman old enough to be thy mother. If thou com'st a step nearer the house, there's a good horse-pool, and there's two stout fellows who'll like no better fun than ducking thee. Be off wi' thee!"

And she strode into her own premises, never looking round to see whether he obeyed her injunction or not.

Sometimes three or four years would pass over without her hearing Michael Hurst's name mentioned. She used to wonder at such times whether he were dead or alive. She would sit for hours by the dying embers of her fire on a winter's evening, trying to recall the scenes of her youth; trying to bring up living pictures of the faces she had then known—Michael's most especially. She thought it was possible, so long had been the lapse of years, that she might now pass by him in the street unknowing and unknown. His outward form she might not recognise, but himself she should feel in the thrill of her whole being. He could not pass her unawares.

What little she did hear about him, all testified a downward tendency. He drank—not at stated times when there was no other work to be done, but continually, whether it was seed-time or harvest. His children were all ill at the same time; then one died, while the others recovered, but were poor sickly things. No one dared to give Susan any direct intelligence of her former lover; many avoided all mention of his name in her presence; but a few spoke out either in indifference to, or ignorance of, those bygone days. Susan heard every word, every whisper, every sound that related to him. But her eye never changed, nor did a muscle of her face move.

Late one November night she sat over her fire; not a human being besides herself in the house; none but she had ever slept there since Willie's death. The farm-labourers had foddered the cattle and gone home hours before. There were crickets chirping all round the warm hearth-stones; there was the clock ticking with the peculiar beat Susan had known from her child-hood, and which then and ever since she had oddly associated with the idea of a mother and child talking together, one loud tick, and quick—a feeble, sharp one following.

The day had been keen, and piercingly cold. The whole lift of heaven seemed a dome of iron. Black and frost-bound was the earth under the cruel east wind. Now the wind had dropped, and as the darkness gathered in, the weather-wise old labourers prophesied snow. The sounds in the air arose again, as Susan sat still and silent. They were of a different character to what they had been during the prevalence of the east wind. Then they had been shrill and piping; now they were like low distant growling; not unmusical, but strangely threatening. Susan went to the window, and drew aside the little curtain. The whole world was white—the air was blinded with the swift and heavy fall of snow. At present it came down straight, but

Susan knew those distant sounds in the hollows and gulleys of the hills portended a driving wind and a more cruel storm. She thought of her sheep; were they all folded? the new-born calf, was it bedded well? Before the drifts were formed too deep for her to pass in and out—and by the morning she judged that they would be six or seven feet deep—she would go out and see after the comfort of her beasts. She took a lantern, and tied a shawl over her head, and went out into the open air. She had tenderly provided for all her animals, and was returning, when, borne on the blast as if some spirit-cry—for it seemed to come rather down from the skies than from any creature standing on earth's level—she heard a voice of agony; she could not distinguish words; it seemed rather as if some bird of prey was being caught in the whirl of the icy wind, and torn and tortured by its violence. Again! up high above! Susan put down her lantern, and shouted loud in return; it was an instinct, for if the creature were not human, which she had doubted but a moment before, what good could her responding cry do? And her cry was seized on by the tyrannous wind, and borne farther away in the opposite direction to that from which the call of agony had proceeded. Again she listened; no sound: then again it rang through space; and this time she was sure it was human. She turned into the house, and heaped turf and wood on the fire, which, careless of her own sensations, she had allowed to fade and almost die out. She put a new candle in her lantern; she changed her shawl for a maud, and leaving the door on latch, she sallied out. Just at the moment when her ear first encountered the weird noises of the storm, on issuing forth into the open air, she thought she heard the words, "O God! O help!" They were a guide to her, if words they were, for they came straight from a rock not a quarter of a mile from Yew Nook, but only to be reached, on account of its precipitous character, by a round-about path. Thither she steered, defying wind and snow, guided by here a thorn-tree, there an old, doddered oak, which had not quite lost their identity under the whelming mask of snow. Now and then she stopped to listen; but never a word or sound heard she, till right from where the copse-wood grew thick and tangled at the base of the rock, round which she was winding, she heard a moan. Into the brake —all snow in appearance—almost a plain of snow looked on from the little eminence where she stood—she plunged, breaking down the bush, stumbling, bruising herself, fighting her way; her lantern held between her teeth, and she herself using head as well as hands to butt away a passage, at whatever cost of bodily injury. As she climbed or staggered, owing to the uneven-ness of the snow-covered ground, where the briars and weeds of years were tangled and matted together, her foot felt some-thing strangely soft and yielding. She lowered her lantern; there lay a man, prone on his face, nearly covered by the fast-falling flakes; he must have fallen from the rock above, as, not knowing of the circuitous path, he had tried to descend its steep, slippery face. Who could tell? it was no time for thinking. Susan lifted him up with her wiry strength; he gave no help—no sign of life; but for all that he might be alive: he was still warm; she tied her maud round him; she fastened the lantern to her apron-string; she held him tight: half-carrying, half-dragging—what did a few bruises signify to him, compared to dear life, to precious life! She got him through the brake and down the path. There, for an instant, she stopped to take breath; but, as if stung by the Furies, she pushed on again with almost superhuman strength. Clasping him round the waist, and lean-ing his dead weight against the lintel of the door, she tried to undo the latch; but now, just at this moment, a trembling faintness came over her, and a fearful dread took possession of her—that here, on the very threshold of her home, she might be found dead, and buried under the snow, when the farm-servants came in the morning. This terror stirred her up to one more effort. Then she and her companion were in the warmth of the quiet haven of that kitchen; she laid him on the settle, and sank on the floor by his side. How long she remained in this swoon she could not tell; not very long she judged by the fire, which was still red and sullenly glowing when she came to herself. She lighted the candle, and bent over her late burden to ascertain if indeed he were dead. She stood long gazing. The man lay dead. There could be no doubt about it. His filmy eyes glared at her, unshut. But Susan was not one to be affrighted by the stony aspect of death. It was not that; it was the bitter, woeful recognition of Michael Hurst!

She was convinced he was dead; but after a while she refused to believe in her conviction. She stripped off his wet outer garments with trembling, hurried hands. She brought a blanket down from her own bed; she made up the fire. She swathed him in fresh, warm wrappings, and laid him on the flags before the fire, sitting herself at his head, and holding it in her lap, while she tenderly wiped his loose, wet hair, curly still, although its colour had changed from nut-brown to iron-grey since she had seen it last. From time to time she bent over the face afresh, sick, and fain to believe that the flicker of the fire-light was some slight convulsive motion. But the dim, staring eyes struck chill to her heart. At last she ceased her delicate, busy cares; but she still held the head softly, as if caressing it. She thought over all the possibilities and chances in the mingled yarn of their lives that might, by so slight a turn, have ended far otherwise. If her mother's cold had been early tended, so that the responsibility as to her brother's weal or woe had not fallen upon her; if the fever had not taken such rough, cruel hold on Will; nay, if Mrs. Gale, that hard, worldly sister, had not accompanied him on his last visit to Yew Nook—his very last before this fatal, stormy night; if she had heard his cry— cry uttered by those pale, dead lips with such wild, despairing agony, not yet three hours ago!—O! if she had but heard it sooner, he might have been saved before that blind, false step had precipitated him down the rock! In going over this weary chain of unrealised possibilities, Susan learnt the force of Peggy's words. Life was short, looking back upon it. It seemed but yesterday since all the love of her being had been poured out, and run to waste. The intervening years—the long monotonous years that had turned her into an old woman before her time—were but a dream.

The labourers coming in the dawn of the winter's day were surprised to see the fire-light through the low kitchen-window. They knocked, and hearing a moaning answer, they entered, fearing that something had befallen their mistress. For all explanation they got these words:

"It is Michael Hurst. He was belated, and fell down the Raven's Crag. Where does Eleanor, his wife, live?"

How Michael Hurst got to Yew Nook no one but Susan ever knew. They thought he had dragged himself there, with some sore internal bruise sapping away his minuted life. They could not have believed the superhuman exertion which had first sought him out, and then dragged him hither. Only Susan knew of that.

She gave him into the charge of her servants, and went out and saddled her horse. Where the wind had drifted the snow on one side, and the road was clear and bare, she rode, and rode fast; where the soft, deceitful heaps were massed up, she dismounted and led her steed, plunging in deep, with fierce energy, the pain at her heart urging her onwards with a sharp, digging spur.

The grey, solemn, winter's noon was more night-like than the depth of summer's night; dim-purple brooded the low skies over the white earth, as Susan rode up to what had been Michael Hurst's abode while living. It was a small farm-house carelessly kept outside, slatternly tended within. The pretty Nelly Hebthwaite was pretty still; her delicate face had never suffered from any long-enduring feeling. If anything, its expression was that of plaintive sorrow; but the soft, light hair had scarcely a tinge of grey; the wood-rose tint of complexion yet remained, if not so brilliant as in youth; the straight nose, the small mouth were untouched by time. Susan felt the contrast even at that moment. She knew that her own skin was weather-beaten, furrowed, brown—that her teeth were gone, and her hair grey and ragged. And yet she was not two years older than Nelly—she had not been, in youth, when she took account of these things. Nelly stood wondering at the strange-enough horse-woman, who stopped and panted at the door, holding her horse's bridle, and refusing to enter.

"Where is Michael Hurst?" asked Susan, at last.

"Well, I can't rightly say. He should have been at home last night, but he was off, seeing after a public-house to be let at Ulverstone, for our farm does not answer, and we were thinking——"

"He did not come home last night?" said Susan, cutting short the story, and half-affirming, half-questioning, by way of letting in a ray of the awful light before she let it full in, in its consuming wrath.

"No! he'll be stopping somewhere out Ulverstone ways. I'm sure we've need of him at home, for I've no one but lile Tommy to help me tend the beasts. Things have not gone well with us, and we don't keep a servant now. But you're trembling all over, ma'am. You'd better come in, and take something warm, while your horse rests. That's the stable-door, to your left."

Susan took her horse there; loosened his girths, and rubbed him down with a wisp of straw. Then she looked about her for hay; but the place was bare of food, and smelt damp and unused. She went to the house, thankful for the respite, and got some clap-bread, which she mashed up in a pailful of luke-warm water. Every moment was a respite, and yet every moment made her dread the more the task that lay before her. It would be longer than she thought at first. She took the saddle off, and hung about her horse, which seemed, somehow, more like a friend than anything else in the world. She laid her cheek against its neck, and rested there, before returning to the house for the last time.

Eleanor had brought down one of her own gowns, which hung on a chair against the fire, and had made her unknown visitor a cup of hot tea. Susan could hardly bear all these little attentions: they choked her, and yet she was so wet, so weak with fatigue and excitement, that she could neither resist by voice or by action. Two children stood awkwardly about, puzzled at the scene, and even Eleanor began to wish for some explanation of who her strange visitor was.

" You've, maybe, heard him speaking of me? I'm called Susan Dixon."

Nelly coloured, and avoided meeting Susan's eye.

" I've heard other folk speak of you. He never named your name."

This respect of silence came like balm to Susan: balm not felt or heeded at the time it was applied, but very grateful in its effects for all that.

" He is at my house," continued Susan, determined not to stop or quaver in the operation—the pain which must be inflicted.

" At your house? Yew Nook? " questioned Eleanor, surprised. " How came he there? "—half jealously. " Did he take shelter from the coming storm? Tell me—there is something—tell me, woman! "

" He took no shelter. Would to God he had! "

" O! would to God! would to God! " shrieked out Eleanor, learning all from the woful import of those dreary eyes. Her cries thrilled through the house; the children's piping wailings and passionate cries on " Daddy! Daddy! " pierced into Susan's very marrow. But she remained as still and tearless as the great round face upon the clock.

At last, in a lull of crying, she said—not exactly questioning, but as if partly to herself——

" You loved him, then? "

" Loved him! he was my husband! He was the father of three bonny bairns that lie dead in Grasmere churchyard. I wish you'd go, Susan Dixon, and let me weep without your watching me! I wish you'd never come near the place."

" Alas! alas! it would not have brought him to life. I would have laid down my own to save his. My life has been so very sad! No one would have cared if I had died. Alas! alas! "

The tone in which she said this was so utterly mournful and despairing that it awed Nelly into quiet for a time. But by-and-by she said, " I would not turn a dog out to do it harm; but the night is clear, and Tommy shall guide you to the Red Cow. But, oh, I want to be alone! If you'll come back to-morrow, I'll be better, and I'll hear all, and thank you for every kindness you have shown him—and I do believe you've showed him kindness—though I don't know why."

Susan moved heavily and strangely.

She said something—her words came thick and unintelligible. She had had a paralytic stroke since she had last spoken. She could not go, even if she would. Nor did Eleanor, when she became aware of the state of the case, wish her to leave. She had her laid on her own bed, and weeping silently all the while for her lost husband, she nursed Susan like a sister. She did not know what her guest's worldly position might be; and she might never be repaid. But she sold many a little trifle to purchase such small comforts as Susan needed. Susan, lying still and motionless, learnt much. It was not a severe stroke; it might be the forerunner of others yet to come, but at some distance of time. But for the present she recovered, and regained much of her former health. On her sick-bed she matured her plans. When she returned to Yew Nook, she took Michael Hurst's widow and children with her to live there, and fill up the haunted hearth with living forms that should banish the ghosts.

And so it fell out that the latter days of Susan Dixon's life were better than the former.

RIGHT AT LAST

DOCTOR BROWN was poor, and had to make his way in the world. He had gone to study his profession in Edinburgh, and his energy, ability, and good conduct had entitled him to some notice on the part of the professors. Once introduced to the ladies of their families, his prepossessing appearance and pleasing manners made him a universal favourite; and perhaps no other student received so many invitations to dancing- and evening-parties, or was so often singled out to fill up an odd vacancy at the last moment at the dinner-table. No one knew particularly who he was, or where he sprang from; but then he had no near relations, as he had once or twice observed; so he was evidently not hampered with low-born or low-bred connections. He had been in mourning for his mother when he first came to college.

All this much was recalled to the recollection of Professor Frazer by his niece Margaret, as she stood before him one morning in his study; telling him, in a low, but resolute voice that, the night before, Doctor James Brown had offered her marriage—that she had accepted him—and that he was intending to call on Professor Frazer (her uncle and natural guardian) that very morning, to obtain his consent to their engagement. Professor Frazer was perfectly aware, from Margaret's manner, that his consent was regarded by her as a mere form, for that her mind was made up: and he had more than once had occasion to find out how inflexible she could be. Yet he, too, was of the same blood, and held to his own opinions in the same obdurate manner. The consequence of which frequently was, that uncle and niece had argued themselves into mutual bitterness of feeling, without altering each other's opinions one jot. But Professor Frazer could not restrain himself on this occasion, of all others.

"Then, Margaret, you will just quietly settle down to be a beggar, for that lad Brown has little or no money to think of marrying upon: you that might be my Lady Kennedy, if you would!"

"I could not, uncle."

" Nonsense, child! Sir Alexander is a personable and agreeable man—middle-aged, if you will—well, a wilful woman maun have her way; but, if I had had a notion that this youngster was sneaking into my house to cajole you into fancying him, I would have seen him far enough before I had ever let your aunt invite him to dinner. Ay! you may mutter; but I say, no gentleman would ever have come into my house to seduce my niece's affections, without first informing me of his intentions, and asking my leave."

" Doctor Brown is a gentleman, Uncle Frazer, whatever you may think of him."

" So you think—so you think. But who cares for the opinion of a love-sick girl? He is a handsome, plausible young fellow, of good address. And I don't mean to deny his ability. But there is something about him I never did like, and now it's accounted for. And Sir Alexander——Well, well! your aunt will be disappointed in you, Margaret. But you were always a headstrong girl. Has this Jamie Brown ever told you who or what his parents were, or where he comes from? I don't ask about his forbears, for he does not look like a lad who has ever had ancestors; and you a Frazer of Lovatt! Fie, for shame, Margaret! Who is this Jamie Brown? "

" He is James Brown, Doctor of Medicine of the University of Edinburgh: a good, clever young man, whom I love with my whole heart," replied Margaret, reddening.

" Hoot! is that the way for a maiden to speak? Where does he come from? Who are his kinsfolk? Unless he can give a pretty good account of his family and prospects, I shall just bid him begone, Margaret; and that I tell you fairly."

" Uncle " (her eyes were filling with hot indignant tears), " I am of age; you know he is good and clever: else why have you had him so often to your house? I marry him, and not his kinsfolk. He is an orphan. I doubt if he has any relations that he keeps up with. He has no brothers nor sisters. I don't care where he comes from."

" What was his father? " asked Professor Frazer coldly.

" I don't know. Why should I go prying into every particular of his family, and asking who his father was, and what was the maiden name of his mother, and when his grandmother was married? "

" Yet I think I have heard Miss Margaret Frazer speak up pretty strongly in favour of a long line of unspotted ancestry."

" I had forgotten our own, I suppose, when I spoke so.

Simon, Lord Lovat, is a creditable great-uncle to the Frazers!
If all tales be true, he ought to have been hanged for a felon,
instead of beheaded like a loyal gentleman."

"Oh! if you're determined to foul your own nest, I have
done. Let James Brown come in; I will make him my bow,
and thank him for condescending to marry a Frazer."

"Uncle," said Margaret, now fairly crying, "don't let us
part in anger! We love each other in our hearts. You have
been good to me, and so has my aunt. But I have given my
word to Doctor Brown, and I must keep it. I should love him,
if he was the son of a ploughman. We don't expect to be rich;
but he has a few hundreds to start with, and I have my own
hundred a year "——

"Well, well, child, don't cry! You have settled it all for
yourself, it seems; so I wash my hands of it. I shake off all
responsibility. You will tell your aunt what arrangements
you make with Doctor Brown about your marriage; and I will
do what you wish in the matter. But don't send the young
man in to me to ask my consent! I neither give it nor withhold
it. It would have been different if it had been Sir Alexander."

"Oh! Uncle Frazer, don't speak so. See Doctor Brown, and
at any rate—for my sake—tell him you consent! Let me belong
to you that much! It seems so desolate at such a time to have
to dispose of myself, as if nobody owned or cared for me."

The door was thrown open, and Doctor James Brown was
announced. Margaret hastened away; and, before he was
aware, the Professor had given a sort of consent, without asking
a question of the happy young man; who hurried away to seek
his betrothed, leaving her uncle muttering to himself.

Both Doctor and Mrs. Frazer were so strongly opposed to
Margaret's engagement, in reality, that they could not help
showing it by manner and implication; although they had the
grace to keep silent. But Margaret felt even more keenly than
her lover that he was not welcome in the house. Her pleasure
in seeing him was destroyed by her sense of the coldness with
which he was received, and she willingly yielded to his desire
of a short engagement; which was contrary to their original
plan of waiting until he should be settled in practice in London,
and should see his way clear to such an income as would render
their marriage a prudent step. Doctor and Mrs. Frazer neither
objected nor approved. Margaret would rather have had the
most vehement opposition than this icy coldness. But it made
her turn with redoubled affection to her warm-hearted and

sympathising lover. Not that she had ever discussed her uncle and aunt's behaviour with him. As long as he was apparently unaware of it, she would not awaken him to a sense of it. Besides, they had stood to her so long in the relation of parents, that she felt she had no right to bring in a stranger to sit in judgment upon them.

So it was rather with a heavy heart that she arranged their future *ménage* with Doctor Brown, unable to profit by her aunt's experience and wisdom. But Margaret herself was a prudent and sensible girl. Although accustomed to a degree of comfort in her uncle's house that almost amounted to luxury, she could resolutely dispense with it, when occasion required. When Doctor Brown started for London, to seek and prepare their new home, she enjoined him not to make any but the most necessary preparations for her reception. She would herself superintend all that was wanting when she came. He had some old furniture, stored up in a warehouse, which had been his mother's. He proposed selling it, and buying new in its place. Margaret persuaded him not to do this, but to make it go as far as it could. The household of the newly-married couple was to consist of a Scotchwoman long connected with the Frazer family, who was to be the sole female servant, and of a man whom Doctor Brown picked up in London, soon after he had fixed on a house—a man named Crawford, who had lived for many years with a gentleman now gone abroad, who gave him the most excellent character, in reply to Doctor Brown's inquiries. This gentleman had employed Crawford in a number of ways; so that in fact he was a kind of Jack-of-all-trades; and Doctor Brown, in every letter to Margaret, had some new accomplishment of his servant's to relate. This he did with the more fulness and zest, because Margaret had slightly questioned the wisdom of starting in life with a manservant, but had yielded to Doctor Brown's arguments on the necessity of keeping up a respectable appearance, making a decent show, etc., to any one who might be inclined to consult him, but be daunted by the appearance of old Christie out of the kitchen, and unwilling to leave a message with one who spoke such unintelligible English. Crawford was so good a carpenter that he could put up shelves, adjust faulty hinges, mend locks, and even went the length of constructing a box of some old boards that had once formed a packing-case. Crawford, one day, when his master was too busy to go out for his dinner, improvised an omelette as good as any Doctor Brown had ever tasted in Paris, when

he was studying there.   In short, Crawford was a kind of
Admirable Crichton in his way, and Margaret was quite convinced that Doctor Brown was right in his decision that they
must have a manservant, even before she was respectfully
greeted by Crawford, as he opened the door to the newly-
married couple, when they came to their new home after their
short wedding tour.

Doctor Brown was rather afraid lest Margaret should think
the house bare and cheerless in its half-furnished state; for he
had obeyed her injunctions and bought as little furniture as
might be, in addition to the few things he had inherited from
his mother. His consulting-room (how grand it sounded!)
was completely arranged, ready for stray patients; and it was
well calculated to make a good impression on them. There
was a Turkey-carpet on the floor, that had been his mother's,
and was just sufficiently worn to give it the air of respectability
which handsome pieces of furniture have when they look as if
they had not just been purchased for the occasion, but are in
some degree hereditary. The same appearance pervaded the
room: the library-table (bought second-hand, it must be confessed), the bureau—that had been his mother's—the leather
chairs (as hereditary as the library-table), the shelves Crawford
had put up for Doctor Brown's medical books, a good engraving
on the walls, gave altogether so pleasant an aspect to the apartment that both Doctor and Mrs. Brown thought, for that
evening at any rate, that poverty was just as comfortable a thing
as riches. Crawford had ventured to take the liberty of placing
a few flowers about the room, as his humble way of welcoming
his mistress—late autumn-flowers, blending the idea of summer
with that of winter, suggested by the bright little fire in the
grate. Christie sent up delicious scones for tea; and Mrs. Frazer
had made up for her want of geniality, as well as she could, by a
store of marmalade and mutton hams. Doctor Brown could
not be easy in his comfort, until he had shown Margaret, almost
with a groan, how many rooms were as yet unfurnished—how
much remained to be done. But she laughed at his alarm lest
she should be disappointed in her new home; declared that she
should like nothing better than planning and contriving; that,
what with her own talent for upholstery and Crawford's for
joinery, the rooms would be furnished as if by magic, and no
bills—the usual consequences of comfort—be forthcoming.
But, with the morning and daylight, Doctor Brown's anxiety
returned. He saw and felt every crack in the ceiling, every

spot on the paper, not for himself, but for Margaret. He was constantly in his own mind, as it seemed, comparing the home he had brought her to with the one she had left. He seemed constantly afraid lest she had repented, or would repent having married him. This morbid restlessness was the only drawback to their great happiness; and, to do away with it, Margaret was led into expenses much beyond her original intention. She bought this article in preference to that, because her husband, if he went shopping with her, seemed so miserable if he suspected that she denied herself the slightest wish on the score of economy. She learnt to avoid taking him out with her, when she went to make her purchases; as it was a very simple thing to her to choose the least expensive thing, even though it were the ugliest, when she was by herself, but not a simple painless thing to harden her heart to his look of mortification, when she quietly said to the shopman that she could not afford this or that. On coming out of a shop after one of these occasions, he had said—

"Oh, Margaret, I ought not to have married you. You must forgive me—I have so loved you."

"Forgive you, James?" said she. "For making me so happy? What should make you think I care so much for rep in preference to moreen? Don't speak so again, please!"

"Oh, Margaret; but don't forget how I ask you to forgive me."

Crawford was everything that he had promised to be, and more than could be desired. He was Margaret's right hand in all her little household plans, in a way which irritated Christie not a little. This feud between Christie and Crawford was indeed the greatest discomfort in the household. Crawford was silently triumphant in his superior knowledge of London, in his favour upstairs, in his power of assisting his mistress, and in the consequent privilege of being frequently consulted. Christie was for ever regretting Scotland, and hinting at Margaret's neglect of one who had followed her fortunes into a strange country, to make a favourite of a stranger, and one who was none so good as he ought to be, as she would sometimes affirm. But, as she never brought any proof of her vague accusations, Margaret did not choose to question her, but set them down to a jealousy of her fellow-servant, which the mistress did all in her power to heal. On the whole, however, the four people forming this family lived together in tolerable harmony. Doctor Brown was more than satisfied with his house, his servants, his professional prospects, and most of all with his little energetic wife. Margaret, from time to time, was taken aback by certain moods of her husband's; but the tendency of these moods was not to weaken her affection, rather to call out a feeling of pity for what appeared to her morbid sufferings and suspicions—a pity ready to be turned into sympathy, as soon as she could discover any definite cause for his occasional depression of spirits. Christie did not pretend to like Crawford; but, as Margaret quietly declined to listen to her grumblings and discontent on this head, and as Crawford himself was almost painfully solicitous to gain the good opinion of the old Scotch woman, there was no rupture between them. On the whole, the popular, successful Doctor Brown was apparently the most anxious person in his family. There could be no great cause for this as regarded his money affairs. By one of those lucky accidents which sometimes lift a man up out of his struggles, and carry him on to smooth, unencumbered ground, he made a great step in his professional progress; and their income from this source was likely to be fully as much as Margaret and he had even anticipated in their most sanguine moments, with the likelihood, too, of steady increase, as the years went on.

I must explain myself more fully on this head.

Margaret herself had rather more than a hundred a year; sometimes, indeed, her dividends had amounted to a hundred and thirty or forty pounds; but on that she dared not rely. Doctor Brown had seventeen hundred remaining of the three thousand left him by his mother; and out of this he had to pay for some of the furniture, the bills for which had not been sent in at the time, in spite of all Margaret's entreaties that such might be the case. They came in about a week before the time when the events I am going to narrate took place. Of course they amounted to more than even the prudent Margaret had expected; and she was a little dispirited to find how much money it would take to liquidate them. But, curiously and contradictorily enough—as she had often noticed before—any real cause for anxiety or disappointment did not seem to affect her husband's cheerfulness. He laughed at her dismay over her accounts, jingled the proceeds of that day's work in his pockets, counted it out to her, and calculated the year's probable income from that day's gains. Margaret took the guineas, and carried them upstairs to her own *secrétaire* in silence; having learnt the difficult art of trying to swallow down her household cares in the presence of her husband. When she came back, she was cheerful, if grave. He had taken up the bills in her absence, and had been adding them together.

"Two hundred and thirty-six pounds," he said, putting the accounts away, to clear the table for tea, as Crawford brought in the things. "Why, I don't call that much. I believe I reckoned on their coming to a great deal more. I'll go into the City to-morrow, and sell out some shares, and set your little heart at ease. Now don't go and put a spoonful less tea in to-night to help to pay these bills. Earning is better than saving, and I am earning at a famous rate. Give me good tea, Maggie, for I have done a good day's work."

They were sitting in the doctor's consulting-room for the better economy of fire. To add to Margaret's discomfort, the chimney smoked this evening. She had held her tongue from any repining words; for she remembered the old proverb about a smoky chimney and a scolding wife; but she was more irritated by the puffs of smoke coming over her pretty white work than she cared to show; and it was in a sharper tone than usual that she spoke, in bidding Crawford take care and have the chimney swept. The next morning all had cleared brightly off. Her husband had convinced her that all their money matters were going on well; the fire burned briskly at breakfast time; and the unwonted sun shone in at the windows. Margaret was surprised, when Crawford told her that he had not been able to meet with a chimney-sweeper that morning; but that he had tried to arrange the coals in the grate, so that, for this one morning at least, his mistress should not be annoyed, and by the next he would take care to secure a sweep. Margaret thanked him, and acquiesced in all plans about giving a general cleaning to the room; the more readily, because she felt that she had spoken sharply the night before. She decided to go and pay all her bills, and make some distant calls on the next morning; and her husband promised to go into the City and provide her with the money.

This he did. He showed her the notes that evening, locked them up for the night in his bureau; and, lo, in the morning they were gone! They had breakfasted in the back parlour, or half-furnished dining-room. A charwoman was in the front room, cleaning after the sweeps. Doctor Brown went to his bureau, singing an old Scotch tune as he left the dining-room. It was so long before he came back, that Margaret went to look for him. He was sitting in the chair nearest to the bureau, leaning his head upon it, in an attitude of the deepest despondency. He did not seem to hear Margaret's step, as she made her way among rolled-up carpets and chairs piled on each other. She had to touch him on the shoulder before she could rouse him.

" James, James! " she said in alarm.

He looked up at her almost as if he did not know her.

" Oh, Margaret! " he said, and took hold of her hands, and hid his face in her neck.

" Dearest love, what is it? " she asked, thinking he was suddenly taken ill.

" Some one has been to my bureau since last night," he groaned, without either looking up or moving.

" And taken the money," said Margaret, in an instant understanding how it stood. It was a great blow; a great loss, far greater than the few extra pounds by which the bills had exceeded her calculations: yet it seemed as if she could bear it better. " Oh dear! " she said, " that is bad; but after all— Do you know," she said, trying to raise his face, so that she might look into it, and give him the encouragement of her honest loving eyes, " at first I thought you were deadly ill, and all sorts of dreadful possibilities rushed through my mind—it is such a relief to find that it is only money "——

" Only money! " he echoed sadly, avoiding her look, as if he could not bear to show her how much he felt it.

" And after all," she said with spirit, " it can't be gone far. Only last night it was here. The chimney-sweeps—we must send Crawford for the police directly. You did not take the numbers of the notes? " ringing the bell as she spoke.

" No; they were only to be in our possession one night," he said.

" No, to be sure not."

The charwoman now appeared at the door with her pail of hot water. Margaret looked into her face, as if to read guilt or innocence. She was a protégée of Christie's, who was not apt to accord her favour easily, or without good grounds; an honest, decent widow, with a large family to maintain by her labour—that was the character in which Margaret had engaged her; and she looked it. Grimy in her dress—because she could not spare the money or time to be clean—her skin looked healthy and cared for; she had a straightforward, business-like appearance about her, and seemed in no ways daunted nor surprised to see Doctor and Mrs. Brown standing in the middle of the room, in displeased perplexity and distress. She went about her business without taking any particular notice of them. Margaret's suspicions settled down yet more distinctly upon the chimney-sweeper; but he could not have gone far; the notes could hardly have got into circulation. Such a sum could not have been spent by such a man in so short a time; and the restoration of the money was her first, her only object. She had scarcely a thought for subsequent duties, such as prosecution of the offender, and the like consequences of crime. While her whole energies were bent on the speedy recovery of the money, and she was rapidly going over the necessary steps to be taken, her husband "sat all poured out into his chair," as the Germans say; no force in him to keep his limbs in any attitude requiring the slightest exertion; his face sunk, miserable, and with that foreshadowing of the lines of age which sudden distress is apt to call out on the youngest and smoothest faces.

"What can Crawford be about?" said Margaret, pulling the bell again with vehemence. "Oh, Crawford!" as the man at that instant appeared at the door.

"Is anything the matter?" he said, interrupting her, as if alarmed into an unusual discomposure by her violent ringing. "I had just gone round the corner with the letter master gave me last night for the post; and, when I came back Christie told me you had rung for me, ma'am. I beg your pardon, but I have hurried so," and, indeed, his breath did come quickly, and his face was full of penitent anxiety.

"Oh, Crawford! I am afraid the sweep has got into your master's bureau, and taken all the money he put there last night. It is gone, at any rate. Did you ever leave him in the room alone?"

"I can't say, ma'am; perhaps I did. Yes; I believe I did. I remember now—I had my work to do; and I thought the charwoman was come, and I went to my pantry; and some time after Christie came to me, complaining that Mrs. Roberts was so late; and then I knew that he must have been alone in the room. But, dear me, ma'am, who would have thought there had been so much wickedness in him?"

"How was it that he got into the bureau?" said Margaret, turning to her husband. "Was the lock broken?"

He roused himself up, like one who wakens from sleep.

"Yes! No! I suppose I had turned the key without locking it last night. The bureau was closed, not locked, when I went to it this morning, and the bolt was shot." He relapsed into inactive, thoughtful silence.

"At any rate, it is no use losing time in wondering now. Go, Crawford, as fast as you can, for a policeman. You know the name of the chimney-sweeper, of course," she added, as Crawford was preparing to leave the room.

"Indeed, ma'am, I'm very sorry, but I just agreed with the first who was passing along the street. If I could have known "——

But Margaret had turned away with an impatient gesture of despair. Crawford went, without another word, to seek a policeman.

In vain did his wife try and persuade Doctor Brown to taste any breakfast; a cup of tea was all he would try to swallow; and that was taken in hasty gulps, to clear his dry throat, as he heard Crawford's voice talking to the policeman whom he was ushering in.

The policeman heard all and said little. Then the inspector came. Doctor Brown seemed to leave all the talking to Crawford, who apparently liked nothing better. Margaret was infinitely distressed and dismayed by the effect the robbery seemed to have had on her husband's energies. The probable loss of such a sum was bad enough; but there was something so weak and poor in character in letting it affect him so strongly as to deaden all energy and destroy all hopeful spring, that, although Margaret did not dare to define her feeling, nor the cause of it, to herself, she had the fact before her perpetually, that, if she were to judge of her husband from this morning only, she must learn to rely on herself alone in all cases of emergency. The inspector repeatedly turned from Crawford to Doctor and Mrs. Brown for answers to his inquiries. It was Margaret who replied, with terse, short sentences, very different from Crawford's long, involved explanations.

At length the inspector asked to speak to her alone. She followed him into the room, past the affronted Crawford and her despondent husband. The inspector gave one sharp look at the charwoman, who was going on with her scouring with stolid indifference, turned her out, and then asked Margaret where Crawford came from—how long he had lived with them, and various other questions, all showing the direction his suspicions had taken. This shocked Margaret extremely; but she quickly answered every inquiry, and, at the end, watched the inspector's face closely, and waited for the avowal of the suspicion.

He led the way back to the other room without a word,

however. Crawford had left, and Doctor Brown was trying to read the morning's letters (which had just been delivered); but his hands shook so much that he could not see a line.

"Doctor Brown," said the inspector, "I have little doubt that your man-servant has committed this robbery. I judge so from his whole manner; and from his anxiety to tell the story, and his way of trying to throw suspicion on the chimney-sweeper, neither whose name nor whose dwelling he can give; at least he says not. Your wife tells us he has already been out of the house this morning, even before he went to summon a policeman; so there is little doubt that he has found means for concealing or disposing of the notes; and you say you do not know the numbers. However, that can probably be ascertained."

At this moment Christie knocked at the door, and, in a state of great agitation, demanded to speak to Margaret. She brought up an additional store of suspicious circumstances, none of them much in themselves, but all tending to criminate her fellow-servant. She had expected to find herself blamed for starting the idea of Crawford's guilt, and was rather surprised to find herself listened to with attention by the inspector. This led her to tell many other little things, all bearing against Crawford, which a dread of being thought jealous and quarrelsome had led her to conceal before from her master and mistress. At the end of her story the inspector said—

"There can be no doubt of the course to be taken. You, sir, must give your man-servant in charge. He will be taken before the sitting magistrate directly; and there is already evidence enough to make him be remanded for a week, during which time we may trace the notes, and complete the chain."

"Must I prosecute?" said Doctor Brown, almost lividly pale. "It is, I own, a serious loss of money to me; but there will be the further expenses of the prosecution—the loss of time—the "——

He stopped. He saw his wife's indignant eyes fixed upon him, and shrank from their look of unconscious reproach.

"Yes, inspector," he said; "I give him in charge. Do what you will. Do what is right. Of course I take the consequences. We take the consequences. Don't we, Margaret?" He spoke in a kind of wild, low voice, of which Margaret thought it best to take no notice.

"Tell us exactly what to do," she said very coldly and quietly, addressing herself to the policeman.

He gave her the necessary directions as to their attending at the police-office, and bringing Christie as a witness, and then went away to take measures for securing Crawford.

Margaret was surprised to find how little hurry or violence needed to be used in Crawford's arrest. She had expected to hear sounds of commotion in the house, if indeed Crawford himself had not taken the alarm and escaped. But, when she had suggested the latter apprehension to the inspector, he smiled, and told her that, when he had first heard of the charge from the policeman on the beat, he had stationed a detective officer within sight of the house, to watch all ingress or egress; so that Crawford's whereabouts would soon have been discovered, if he had attempted to escape.

Margaret's attention was now directed to her husband. He was making hurried preparations for setting off on his round of visits, and evidently did not wish to have any conversation with her on the subject of the morning's event. He promised to be back by eleven o'clock; before which time, the inspector assured them, their presence would not be needed. Once or twice, Doctor Brown said, as if to himself, " It is a miserable business." Indeed, Margaret felt it to be so; and, now that the necessity for immediate speech and action was over, she began to fancy that she must be very hard-hearted—very deficient in common feeling; inasmuch as she had not suffered like her husband, at the discovery that the servant—whom they had been learning to consider as a friend, and to look upon as having their interests so warmly at heart—was, in all probability, a treacherous thief. She remembered all his pretty marks of attention to her, from the day when he had welcomed her arrival at her new home by his humble present of flowers, until only the day before, when, seeing her fatigued, he had, unasked, made her a cup of coffee—coffee such as none but he could make. How often had he thought of warm dry clothes for her husband; how wakeful had he been at nights; how diligent in the mornings! It was no wonder that her husband felt this discovery of domestic treason acutely. It was she who was hard and selfish, thinking more of the recovery of the money than of the terrible disappointment in character, if the charge against Crawford were true.

At eleven o'clock her husband returned with a cab. Christie had thought the occasion of appearing at a police-office worthy of her Sunday clothes, and was as smart as her possessions could make her. But Margaret and her husband looked as pale and sorrow-stricken as if they had been the accused, and not the accusers.

Doctor Brown shrank from meeting Crawford's eye, as the one took his place in the witness-box, the other in the dock. Yet Crawford was trying—Margaret was sure of this—to catch his master's attention. Failing that, he looked at Margaret with an expression she could not fathom. Indeed, the whole character of his face was changed. Instead of the calm, smooth look of attentive obedience, he had assumed an insolent, threatening expression of defiance; smiling occasionally in a most unpleasant manner, as Doctor Brown spoke of the bureau and its contents. He was remanded for a week; but, the evidence as yet being far from conclusive, bail for his appearance was taken. This bail was offered by his brother, a respectable tradesman, well known in his neighbourhood, and to whom Crawford had sent on his arrest.

So Crawford was at large again, much to Christie's dismay; who took off her Sunday clothes, on her return home, with a heavy heart, hoping, rather than trusting, that they should not all be murdered in their beds before the week was out. It must be confessed, Margaret herself was not entirely free from fears of Crawford's vengeance; his eyes had looked so maliciously and vindictively at her and at her husband as they gave their evidence.

But his absence in the household gave Margaret enough to do to prevent her dwelling on foolish fears. His being away made a terrible blank in their daily comfort, which neither Margaret nor Christie—exert themselves as they would—could fill up; and it was the more necessary that all should go on smoothly, as Doctor Brown's nerves had received such a shock at the discovery of the guilt of his favourite, trusted servant, that Margaret was led at times to apprehend a serious illness. He would pace about the room at night, when he thought she was asleep, moaning to himself—and in the morning he would require the utmost persuasion to induce him to go out and see his patients. He was worse than ever, after consulting the lawyer whom he had employed to conduct the prosecution. There was, as Margaret was brought unwillingly to perceive, some mystery in the case; for he eagerly took his letters from the post, going to the door as soon as he heard the knock, and concealing their directions from her. As the week passed away, his nervous misery still increased.

One evening—the candles were not lighted—he was sitting

over the fire in a listless attitude, resting his head on his hand, and that supported on his knee—Margaret determined to try an experiment; to see if she could not probe, and find out the nature of, the sore that he hid with such constant care. She took a stool and sat down at his feet, taking his hand in hers.

"Listen, dearest James, to an old story I once heard. It may interest you. There were two orphans, boy and girl in their hearts, though they were a young man and young woman in years. They were not brother and sister, and by-and-by they fell in love; just in the same fond silly way you and I did, you remember. Well, the girl was amongst her own people; but the boy was far away from his—if indeed he had any alive. But the girl loved him so dearly for himself, that sometimes she thought she was glad that he had no one to care for him but just her alone. Her friends did not like him as much as she did; for, perhaps, they were wise, grave, cold people, and she, I dare say, was very foolish. And they did not like her marrying the boy; which was just stupidity in them, for they had not a word to say against him. But, about a week before the marriage-day was fixed, they thought they had found out something— my darling love, don't take away your hand—don't tremble so, only just listen! Her aunt came to her and said: 'Child, you must give up your lover: his father was tempted, and sinned; and, if he is now alive, he is a transported convict. The marriage cannot take place.' But the girl stood up and said: 'If he has known this great sorrow and shame, he needs my love all the more. I will not leave him, nor forsake him, but love him all the better. And I charge you, aunt, as you hope to receive a blessing for doing as you would be done by, that you tell no one!' I really think that girl awed her aunt, in some strange way, into secrecy. But, when she was left alone, she cried long and sadly to think what a shadow rested on the heart she loved so dearly; and she meant to strive to lighten his life, and to conceal for ever that she had heard of its burden; but now she thinks—Oh, my husband! how you must have suffered"—as he bent down his head on her shoulder and cried terrible man's tears.

"God be thanked!" he said at length. "You know all, and you do not shrink from me. Oh, what a miserable, deceitful coward I have been! Suffered! Yes—suffered enough to drive me mad; and, if I had but been brave, I might have been spared all this long twelve months of agony. But it is right

I should have been punished. And you knew it even before we were married, when you might have been drawn back!"

"I could not; you would not have broken off your engagement with me, would you, under the like circumstances, if our cases had been reversed?"

"I do not know. Perhaps I might; for I am not so brave, so good, so strong as you, my Margaret. How could I be? Let me tell you more. We wandered about, my mother and I, thankful that our name was such a common one, but shrinking from every allusion—in a way which no one can understand, who has not been conscious of an inward sore. Living in an assize town was torture; a commercial one was nearly as bad. My father was the son of a dignified clergyman, well known to his brethren: a cathedral town was to be avoided, because there the circumstance of the Dean of Saint Botolph's son having been transported was sure to be known. I had to be educated; therefore we had to live in a town; for my mother could not bear to part from me, and I was sent to a day-school. We were very poor for our station—no! we had no station; we were the wife and child of a convict—poor for my mother's early habits, I should have said. But, when I was about fourteen, my father died in his exile, leaving, as convicts in those days sometimes did, a large fortune. It all came to us. My mother shut herself up, and cried and prayed for a whole day. Then she called me in, and took me into her counsel. We solemnly pledged ourselves to give the money to some charity, as soon as I was legally of age. Till then the interest was laid by, every penny of it; though sometimes we were in sore distress for money, my education cost so much. But how could we tell in what way the money had been accumulated?" Here he dropped his voice. "Soon after I was one-and-twenty, the papers rang with admiration of the unknown munificent donor of certain sums. I loathed their praises. I shrank from all recollection of my father. I remembered him dimly, but always as angry and violent with my mother. My poor, gentle mother! Margaret, she loved my father; and, for her sake, I have tried, since her death, to feel kindly towards his memory. Soon after my mother's death, I came to know you, my jewel, my treasure!"

After a while, he began again. "But, oh, Margaret! even now you do not know the worst. After my mother's death, I found a bundle of law papers—of newspaper reports about my father's trial. Poor soul! why she had kept them, I cannot say. They were covered over with notes in her handwriting;

and, for that reason, I kept them. It was so touching to read her record of the days spent by her in her solitary innocence, while he was embroiling himself deeper and deeper in crime. I kept this bundle (as I thought so safely!) in a secret drawer of my bureau; but that wretch Crawford has got hold of it. I missed the papers that very morning. The loss of them was infinitely worse than the loss of the money; and now Crawford threatens to bring out the one terrible fact, in open court, if he can; and his lawyer may do it, I believe. At any rate, to have it blazoned out to the world—I who have spent my life in fearing this hour! But most of all for you, Margaret! Still—if only it could be avoided! Who will employ the son of Brown, the noted forger? I shall lose all my practice. Men will look askance at me as I enter their doors. They will drive me into crime. I sometimes fear that crime is hereditary! Oh, Margaret! what am I to do?"

"What can you do?" she asked.

"I can refuse to prosecute."

"Let Crawford go free, you knowing him to be guilty?"

"I know him to be guilty."

"Then, simply, you cannot do this thing. You let loose a criminal upon the public."

"But, if I do not, we shall come to shame and poverty. It is for you I mind it, not for myself. I ought never to have married."

"Listen to me. I don't care for poverty; and, as to shame, I should feel it twenty times more grievously, if you and I consented to screen the guilty, from any fear or for any selfish motives of our own. I don't pretend that I shall not feel it, when first the truth is known. But my shame will turn into pride, as I watch you live it down. You have been rendered morbid, dear husband, by having something all your life to conceal. Let the world know the truth, and say the worst. You will go forth a free, honest, honourable man, able to do your future work without fear."

"That scoundrel Crawford has sent for an answer to his impudent note," said Christie, putting in her head at the door.

"Stay! May *I* write it?" said Margaret.

She wrote:—

"Whatever you may do or say, there is but one course open to us. No threats can deter your master from doing his duty.

"MARGARET BROWN."

" There! " she said, passing it to her husband; " he will see that I know all; and I suspect he has reckoned something on your tenderness for me."

Margaret's note only enraged, it did not daunt, Crawford. Before a week was out, every one who cared knew that Doctor Brown, the rising young physician, was son of the notorious Brown, the forger. All the consequences took place which he had anticipated. Crawford had to suffer a severe sentence; and Doctor Brown and his wife had to leave their house and go to a smaller one; they had to pinch and to screw, aided in all most zealously by the faithful Christie. But Doctor Brown was lighter-hearted than he had ever been before in his conscious lifetime. His foot was now firmly planted on the ground, and every step he rose was a sure gain. People did say that Margaret had been seen, in those worst times, on her hands and knees cleaning her own doorstep. But I don't believe it, for Christie would never have let her do that. And, as far as my own evidence goes, I can only say that, the last time I was in London, I saw a brass-plate, with " Doctor James Brown " upon it, on the door of a handsome house in a handsome square. And as I looked, I saw a brougham drive up to the door, and a lady get out, and go into that house, who was certainly the Margaret Frazer of old days—graver; more portly; more stern, I had almost said. But, as I watched and thought, I saw her come to the dining-room window with a baby in her arms, and her whole face melted into a smile of infinite sweetness.

THE SEXTON'S HERO

THE afternoon sun shed down his glorious rays on the grassy churchyard, making the shadow cast by the old yew-tree under which we sat, seem deeper and deeper by contrast. The everlasting hum of myriads of summer insects made luxurious lullaby.

Of the view that lay beneath our gaze, I cannot speak adequately. The foreground was the grey-stone wall of the vicarage garden; rich in the colouring made by innumerable lichens, ferns, ivy of most tender green and most delicate tracery, and the vivid scarlet of the crane's-bill, which found a home in every nook and crevice—and at the summit of that old wall flaunted some unpruned tendrils of the vine, and long flower-laden branches of the climbing rose-tree, trained against the inner side. Beyond, lay meadow green and mountain grey, and the blue dazzle of Morecambe Bay, as it sparkled between us and the more distant view.

For a while we were silent, living in sight and murmuring sound. Then Jeremy took up our conversation where, suddenly feeling weariness, as we saw that deep green shadowy resting-place, we had ceased speaking a quarter of an hour before.

It is one of the luxuries of holiday-time that thoughts are not rudely shaken from us by outward violence of hurry and busy impatience, but fall maturely from our lips in the sunny leisure of our days. The stock may be bad, but the fruit is ripe.

" How would you then define a hero? " I asked.

There was a long pause, and I had almost forgotten my question in watching a cloud-shadow floating over the far-away hills, when Jeremy made answer—

" My idea of a hero is one who acts up to the highest idea of duty he has been able to form, no matter at what sacrifice. I think that by this definition, we may include all phases of character, even to the heroes of old, whose sole (and to us, low) idea of duty consisted in personal prowess."

" Then you would even admit the military heroes? " asked I.

" I would; with a certain kind of pity for the circumstances

which had given them no higher ideas of duty. Still, if they
sacrificed self to do what they sincerely believed to be right,
I do not think I could deny them the title of hero."

"A poor, unchristian heroism, whose manifestation consists
in injury to others!" I said.

We were both startled by a third voice.

"If I might make so bold, sir"—and then the speaker
stopped.

It was the Sexton, whom, when we first arrived, we had
noticed, as an accessory to the scene, but whom we had forgotten, as much as though he were as inanimate as one of the
moss-covered headstones.

"If I might be so bold," said he again, waiting leave to
speak. Jeremy bowed in deference to his white, uncovered
head. And, so encouraged, he went on.

"What that gentleman" (alluding to my last speech) "has
just now said, brings to my mind one who is dead and gone
this many a year ago. I, may be, have not rightly understood
your meaning, gentlemen, but as far as I could gather it, I
think you'd both have given in to thinking poor Gilbert Dawson
a hero. At any rate," said he, heaving a long, quivering sigh,
"I have reason to think him so."

"Will you take a seat, sir, and tell us about him?" said
Jeremy, standing up until the old man was seated. I confess
I felt impatient at the interruption.

"It will be forty-five year come Martinmas," said the Sexton,
sitting down on a grassy mound at our feet, "since I finished
my 'prenticeship, and settled down at Lindal. You can see
Lindal, sir, at evenings and mornings across the bay; a little
to the right of Grange; at least, I used to see it, many a time
and oft, afore my sight grew so dark: and I have spent many
a quarter of an hour a-gazing at it far away, and thinking of the
days I lived there, till the tears came so thick to my eyes, I
could gaze no longer. I shall never look upon it again, either
far-off or near; but you may see it, both ways, and a terrible
bonny spot it is. In my young days, when I went to settle
there, it was full of as wild a set of young fellows as ever were
clapped eyes on: all for fighting, poaching, quarrelling, and
such-like work. I were startled myself when I first found what
a set I were among, but soon I began to fall into their ways,
and I ended by being as rough a chap as any on 'em. I'd
been there a matter of two year, and were reckoned by most
the cock of the village, when Gilbert Dawson, as I was speaking

of, came to Lindal. He were about as strapping a chap as I was (I used to be six feet high, though now I'm so shrunk and doubled up), and, as we were like in the same trade (both used to prepare osiers and wood for the Liverpool coopers, who get a deal of stuff from the copses round the bay, sir), we were thrown together, and took mightily to each other. I put my best leg foremost to be equal with Gilbert, for I'd had some schooling, though since I'd been at Lindal I'd lost a good part of what I'd learnt; and I kept my rough ways out of sight for a time, I felt so ashamed of his getting to know them. But that did not last long. I began to think he fancied a girl I dearly loved, but who had always held off from me. Eh! but she was a pretty one in those days! There's none like her, now. I think I see her going along the road with her dancing tread, and shaking back her long yellow curls, to give me or any other young fellow a saucy word; no wonder Gilbert was taken with her, for all he was grave, and she so merry and light. But I began to think she liked him again; and then my blood was all afire. I got to hate him for everything he did. Aforetime I had stood by, admiring to see him, how he leapt, and what a quoiter and cricketer he was. And now I ground my teeth with hatred whene'er he did a thing which caught Letty's eye. I could read it in her look that she liked him, for all she held herself just as high with him as with all the rest. Lord God forgive me! how I hated that man."

He spoke as if the hatred were a thing of yesterday, so clear within his memory were shown the actions and feelings of his youth. And then he dropped his voice, and said—

"Well! I began to look out to pick a quarrel with him, for my blood was up to fight him. If I beat him (and I were a rare boxer in those days), I thought Letty would cool towards him. So one evening at quoits (I'm sure I don't know how or why, but large doings grow out of small words) I fell out with him, and challenged him to fight. I could see he were very wroth by his colour coming and going—and, as I said before, he were a fine active young fellow. But all at once he drew in, and said he would not fight. Such a yell as the Lindal lads, who were watching us, set up! I hear it yet. I could na' help but feel sorry for him, to be so scorned, and I thought he'd not rightly taken my meaning, and I'd give him another chance: so I said it again, and dared him, as plain as words could speak, to fight out the quarrel. He told me then, he had no quarrel against me; that he might have said something to put me up; he did not know that he had, but that if he had, he asked pardon; but that he would not fight no-how.

"I was so full of scorn at his cowardliness, that I was vexed I'd given him the second chance, and I joined in the yell that was set up, twice as bad as before. He stood it out, his teeth set, and looking very white, and when we were silent for want of breath, he said out loud, but in a hoarse voice, quite different from his own—

"'I cannot fight, because I think it is wrong to quarrel, and use violence.'

"Then he turned to go away; I were so beside myself with scorn and hate, that I called out—

"'Tell truth, lad, at least; if thou dare not fight, dunnot go and tell a lie about it. Mother's moppet is afraid of a black eye, pretty dear. It shannot be hurt, but it munnot tell lies.'

"Well, they laughed, but I could not laugh. It seemed such a thing for a stout young chap to be a coward and afraid!

"Before the sun had set, it was talked of all over Lindal, how I had challenged Gilbert to fight, and how he'd denied me; and the folks stood at their doors, and looked at him going up the hill to his home, as if he'd been a monkey or a foreigner— but no one wished him good e'en. Such a thing as refusing to fight had never been heard of afore at Lindal. Next day, how-ever, they had found voice. The men muttered the word 'coward' in his hearing, and kept aloof; the women tittered as he passed, and the little impudent lads and lasses shouted out, 'How long is it sin' thou turned Quaker?' 'Good-bye, Jonathan Broad-brim,' and such-like jests.

"That evening I met him, with Letty by his side, coming up from the shore. She was almost crying as I came upon them at the turn of the lane; and looking up in his face, as if begging him something. And so she was, she told me it after. For she did really like him, and could not abide to hear him scorned by every one for being a coward; and she, coy as she was, all but told him that very night that she loved him, and begged him not to disgrace himself, but fight me as I'd dared him to. When he still stuck to it he could not, for that it was wrong, she was so vexed and mad-like at the way she'd spoken, and the feelings she'd let out to coax him, that she said more stinging things about his being a coward than all the rest put together (according to what she told me, sir, afterwards), and ended by saying she'd never speak to him again, as long as she lived; she did once again, though—her blessing was the last human speech that reached his ear in his wild death-struggle.

"But much happened afore that time. From the day I met them walking, Letty turned towards me; I could see a part of it was to spite Gilbert, for she'd be twice as kind when he was near, or likely to hear of it; but by-and-by she got to like me for my own sake, and it was all settled for our marriage. Gilbert kept aloof from every one, and fell into a sad, careless way. His very gait was changed; his step used to be brisk and sounding, and now his foot lingered heavily on the ground. I used to try and daunt him with my eye, but he would always meet my look in a steady, quiet way, for all so much about him was altered; the lads would not play with him; and, as soon as he found he was to be slighted by them whenever he came to quoiting or cricket, he just left off coming.

"The old clerk was the only one he kept company with; or perhaps, rightly to speak, the only one who would keep company with him. They got so thick at last that old Jonas would say Gilbert had gospel on his side, and did no more than gospel told him to do; but we none of us gave much credit to what he said, more by token our vicar had a brother a colonel in the army; and, as we threeped it many a time to Jonas, would he set himself up to know the gospel better than the vicar? that would be putting the cart afore the horse, like the French radicals. And, if the vicar had thought quarrelling and fighting wicked, and again the Bible, would he have made so much work about all the victories, that were as plenty as blackberries at that time of day, and kept the little bell of Lindal church for ever ringing; or would he have thought so much of ' my brother the colonel,' as he was always talking on?

"After I was married to Letty I left off hating Gilbert. I even kind of pitied him—he was so scorned and slighted; and, for all he'd a bold look about him, as if he were not ashamed, he seemed pining and shrunk. It's a wearying thing to be kept at arm's length by one's kind; and so Gilbert found it, poor fellow. The little children took to him, though; they'd be round about him like a swarm of bees—them as was too young to know what a coward was, and only felt that he was ever ready to love and to help them, and was never loud or cross, however naughty they might be. After a while we had our little one, too; such a blessed darling she was, and dearly did we love her; Letty in especial, who seemed to get all the thought I used to think sometimes she wanted, after she had her baby to care for.

"All my kin lived on this side the bay, up above Kellet.
Jane (that's her that lies buried near yon white rose-tree) was
to be married, and nought would serve her but that Letty and
I must come to the wedding; for all my sisters loved Letty,
she had such winning ways with her. Letty did not like to
leave her baby, nor yet did I want her to take it; so, after a
talk, we fixed to leave it with Letty's mother for the afternoon.
I could see her heart ached a bit, for she'd never left it till then,
and she seemed to fear all manner of evil, even to the French
coming and taking it away. Well! we borrowed a shandry, and
harnessed my old grey mare, as I used in th' cart, and set off as
grand as King George across the sands about three o'clock, for
you see it were high-water about twelve, and we'd to go and
come back same tide, as Letty could not leave her baby for long.
It were a merry afternoon were that; last time I ever saw Letty
laugh heartily; and, for that matter, last time I ever laughed
downright hearty myself. The latest crossing-time fell about
nine o'clock, and we were late at starting. Clocks were wrong;
and we'd a piece of work chasing a pig father had given Letty
to take home; we bagged him at last, and he screeched and
screeched in the back part o' the shandry, and we laughed and
they laughed; and in the midst of all the merriment the sun set,
and that sobered us a bit, for then we knew what time it was.
I whipped the old mare, but she was a deal beener than she was
in the morning, and would neither go quick up nor down the
brows, and they're not a few 'twixt Kellet and the shore. On
the sands it were worse. They were very heavy, for the fresh
had come down after the rains we'd had. Lord! how I did whip
the poor mare, to make the most of the red light as yet lasted.
You, may be, don't know the sands, gentlemen. From Bolton
side, where we started from, it is better than six mile to Cart
Lane, and two channels to cross, let alone holes and quicksands.
At the second channel from us the guide waits, all during crossing
time from sunrise to sunset; but for the three hours on each
side high-water he's not there, in course. He stays after sunset
if he's forespoken, not else. So now you know where we were
that awful night. For we'd crossed the first channel about two
mile, and it were growing darker and darker above and around
us, all but one red line of light above the hills, when we came to
a hollow (for all the sands look so flat, there's many a hollow in
them where you lose all sight of the shore). We were longer than
we should ha' been in crossing the hollow, the sand was so quick;
and when we came up again, there, again the blackness, was the

white line of the rushing tide coming up the bay! It looked not
a mile from us; and when the wind blows up the bay it comes
swifter than a galloping horse. 'Lord help us!' said I; and then
I were sorry I'd spoken, to frighten Letty; but the words were
crushed out of my heart by the terror. I felt her shiver up by
my side, and clutch my coat. And as if the pig (as had screeched
himself hoarse some time ago) had found out the danger we were
all in, he took to squealing again, enough to bewilder any man.
I cursed him between my teeth for his noise; and yet it was
God's answer to my prayer, blind sinner as I was. Ay! you
may smile, sir, but God can work through many a scornful
thing, if need be.

" By this time the mare was all in a lather, and trembling and
panting, as if in mortal fright; for, though we were on the last
bank afore the second channel, the water was gathering up her
legs; and she so tired out! When we came close to the channel
she stood still, and not all my flogging could get her to stir;
she fairly groaned aloud, and shook in a terrible quaking way.
Till now Letty had not spoken: only held my coat tightly. I
heard her say something, and bent down my head.

" I think, John—I think—I shall never see baby again! "

" And then she sent up such a cry—so loud, and shrill, and
pitiful! It fairly maddened me. I pulled out my knife to spur
on the old mare, that it might end one way or the other, for the
water was stealing sullenly up to the very axle-tree, let alone
the white waves that knew no mercy in their steady advance.
That one quarter of an hour, sir, seemed as long as all my life
since. Thoughts and fancies, and dreams, and memory ran into
each other. The mist, the heavy mist, that was like a ghastly
curtain, shutting us in for death, seemed to bring with it the
scents of the flowers that grew around our own threshold; it
might be, for it was falling on them like blessed dew, though to
us it was a shroud. Letty told me at after, she heard her baby
crying for her, above the gurgling of the rising waters, as plain as
ever she heard anything; but the sea-birds were skirling, and the
pig shrieking; I never caught it; it was miles away, at any rate.

" Just as I'd gotten my knife out, another sound was close
upon us, blending with the gurgle of the near waters, and the
roar of the distant (not so distant though); we could hardly see,
but we thought we saw something black against the deep lead
colour of wave, and mist, and sky. It neared and neared: with
slow, steady motion, it came across the channel right to where
we were.

"Oh, God! it was Gilbert Dawson on his strong bay horse.

"Few words did we speak, and little time had we to say them in. I had no knowledge at that moment of past or future— only of one present thought—how to save Letty, and, if I could, myself. I only remembered afterwards that Gilbert said he had been guided by an animal's shriek of terror; I only heard when all was over, that he had been uneasy about our return, because of the depth of fresh, and had borrowed a pillion, and saddled his horse early in the evening, and ridden down to Cart Lane to watch for us. If all had gone well, we should ne'er have heard of it. As it was, old Jonas told it, the tears down-dropping from his withered cheeks.

"We fastened his horse to the shandry. We lifted Letty to the pillion. The waters rose every instant with sullen sound. They were all but in the shandry. Letty clung to the pillion handles, but drooped her head as if she had yet no hope of life. Swifter than thought (and yet he might have had time for thought and for temptation, sir—if he had ridden off with Letty, he would have been saved, not me), Gilbert was in the shandry by my side.

"'Quick!' said he, clear and firm. 'You must ride before her, and keep her up. The horse can swim. By God's mercy I will follow. I can cut the traces, and if the mare is not hampered with the shandry, she'll carry me safely through. At any rate, you are a husband and a father. No one cares for me.'

"Do not hate me, gentlemen. I often wish that night was a dream. It has haunted my sleep ever since like a dream, and yet it was no dream. I took his place on the saddle, and put Letty's arms around me, and felt her head rest on my shoulder. I trust in God I spoke some word of thanks; but I can't remember. I only recollect Letty raising her head, and calling out—

"'God bless you, Gilbert Dawson, for saving my baby from being an orphan this night.' And then she fell against me, as if unconscious.

"I bore her through; or, rather, the strong horse swam bravely through the gathering waves. We were dripping wet when we reached the banks in-shore; but we could have but one thought—where was Gilbert? Thick mists and heaving waters compassed us round. Where was he? We shouted. Letty, faint as she was, raised her voice and shouted clear and shrill. No answer came, the sea boomed on with ceaseless sullen beat. I rode to the guide's house. He was a-bed, and would not get up, though I offered him more than I was worth. Perhaps he knew it, the cursed old villain! At any rate, I'd have paid it if I'd toiled my life long. He said I might take his horn and welcome. I did, and blew such a blast through the still, black night, the echoes came back upon the heavy air; but no human voice or sound was heard—that wild blast could not awaken the dead!

"I took Letty home to her baby, over whom she wept the livelong night. I rode back to the shore about Cart Lane; and to and fro, with weary march, did I pace along the brink of the waters, now and then shouting out into the silence a vain cry for Gilbert. The waters went back and left no trace. Two days afterwards he was washed ashore near Flukeborough. The shandry and poor old mare were found half-buried in a heap of sand by Arnside Knot. As far as we could guess, he had dropped his knife while trying to cut the traces, and so had lost all chance of life. Any rate, the knife was found in a cleft of the shaft.

"His friends came over from Garstang to his funeral. I wanted to go chief mourner, but it was not my right, and I might not; though I've never done mourning him to this day. When his sister packed up his things, I begged hard for something that had been his. She would give me none of his clothes (she was a right-down saving woman), as she had boys of her own, who might grow up into them. But she threw me his Bible, as she said they'd gotten one already, and his were but a poor used-up thing. It was his, and so I cared for it. It were a black leather one, with pockets at the sides, old-fashioned-wise; and in one were a bunch of wild flowers, Letty said she could almost be sure were some she had once given him.

"There were many a text in the Gospel, marked broad with his carpenter's pencil, which more than bore him out in his refusal to fight. Of a surety, sir, there's call enough for bravery in the service of God, and to show love to man, without quarrelling and fighting.

"Thank you, gentlemen, for listening to me. Your words called up the thoughts of him, and my heart was full to speaking. But I must make up; I've to dig a grave for a little child, who is to be buried to-morrow morning, just when his playmates are trooping off to school."

"But tell us of Letty; is she yet alive?" asked Jeremy.

The old man shook his head, and struggled against a choking sigh. After a minute's pause he said—

"She died in less than two year at after that night. She was never like the same again. She would sit thinking—on Gilbert, I guessed; but I could not blame her. We had a boy, and we named it Gilbert Dawson Knipe: he that's stoker on the London railway. Our girl was carried off in teething; and Letty just quietly drooped, and died in less than a six week. They were buried here; so I came to be near them, and away from Lindal, a place I could never abide after Letty was gone."

He turned to his work; and we, having rested sufficiently, rose up, and came away

EVERYMAN'S LIBRARY: A Selected List

This List covers a selection of volumes available in Everyman's Library.

BIOGRAPHY

ESSAYS AND CRITICISM

FICTION

REFERENCE

RELIGION AND PHILOSOPHY

7

SCIENCE

TRAVEL AND TOPOGRAPHY

CHESTER COLLEGE LIBRARY